INTERRAN

ZETA TRILOGY
BOOK 2

ROB GRAFRATH

First edition December 2022

Cover design and chapter heading art by Gabrielle Grafrath

Paperback ISBN 978-1-953470-04-1

Hardcover ISBN 978-1-953470-05-8

Published by Ourania Publishing

1

CONVENTION

Oraxis took a sip of coffee, then wrinkled his nose. He held the cup out and gave it a scowl. "Luke warm, thin, bitter brown water. I don't get it."

"Oh, don't be a coffee snob," Genevieve said, putting her own full cup down on a trash tray.

He took another experimental sip. "Just awful. Gen, they *specifically* designed this coffee to be bad! They could've served the best coffee in the universe. Why this?!"

"I think it's wonderful!"

"Wonderful?"

"The Proliferans pride themselves in realism. Bad coffee is an essential ingredient in the rich, immersive experience they've crafted for us. The lanyards, the booths, the hideous carpet patterns. It's just... incredible." She turned full circle, taking in the details of the convention construct, beaming with pleasure.

Oraxis shook his head and gave a huff. Genevieve was a pig in slop. As an archivist specializing in the twentieth century, they couldn't have picked a more alluring venue to tickle her fancy.

The all-caps lettering beneath the hotel name outside had read,

"SURYA SYSTEM CONVENTION," and below that, "WEL-COME TO LAS VEGAS CIRCA 1990." Making their way to the convention hall had meant navigating a gauntlet of gaudy slot machines, blaring with bells and buzzers, topped with flashing lights. The thick fog of cigarette smoke had been unbearable. He could still smell it clinging to his cheap leisure suit. It'd probably haunt his nostrils even after reconnecting to his body.

What sort of world must the people of the twentieth century have lived in to consider such an assault on the senses to be alluring? That's not to mention the objectivization of women, the poisoning of oneself with excessive liquor consumption, or the outpouring of one's life savings into the gold-plated coffers of the casinos.

Genevieve was pulling him by the hand. "The first seminar doesn't start for an hour. Let's check out some booths."

"Ok. I hear the Astri—"

"Cool your jets, O. At least give the Genesis clubs a chance before you go signing up for Astrus space camp."

Oraxis and Genevieve had been struggling to find purpose after Zeta's rapid bootstrapping came to an abrupt conclusion. They weren't mentally prepared to seed their next alpha, and taking a few months to lend a hand tackling the problems of their faction would be a constructive distraction. With any luck, by the end of the convention, they'd find a noble cause they could both agree on.

The booths lining the aisles of the main hall were alive with activity. Literally, in some cases. The first display to catch their attention was sponsored by the BBB — Biome Biodiversity Boosters — and featured a dense forest teeming with simulated wildlife.

"Oraxis, Genevieve, welcome to the jungle!" the BBB club recruiter called out as they stood in admiration of the display. The man had a python draped over his shoulders and wore a classic khaki explorer outfit. Oraxis didn't recognize the guy, but he had the too-perfect look of a Proliferan.

Genevieve mindspoke to Oraxis, *"I doubt he knows he just made a Guns N' Roses reference. And calling us by our names? Tacky.*

Schmoozers who pretend to know you after reading your name card are the lowest form of life."

Oraxis mindspoke in reply, *"If you want to build a healthy biome, you can't overlook the pond scum, leeches, worms, fungi — it's all part of a rich tapestry."*

They approached the booth. Oraxis made a show of reading the name card hanging from the man's woven hemp lanyard. He stifled a laugh at the odd name. "Alright, Popo-Jawi, we'll bite. Are you giving out snakes? Now *that's* conference swag."

"No, dude, get a clue," Genevieve said.

How fun — she was using her valley girl voice. It suited her ridiculous retro outfit and massive hairdo. He didn't want to think about the costume she had stuffed him into.

Genevieve smacked her gum. Did she have gum before? She asked, "Like, you want us to donate to your charity, right? Save the rainforests or whatever?"

Oraxis recalled Genevieve's stories of the public awareness campaigns of the late twentieth century with the vague idea of "saving rainforests". It didn't work, and the word "rainforest" had faded away, along with the forests themselves, as anthropogenic global warming and habitat encroachment took their toll. Rainforests were making a roaring comeback on Genesis, but now they were just called "jungles" by all but the most avid ecologist.

As for a donation, the only currency being exchanged today would be the precious commodities of time and attention. If Popo-Jawi was going to get more of theirs, he'd have to think fast.

P.J. blinked for a moment, the historic reference flying over his head like so many simulated birds of paradise. "Rainforests, yes! As well as scrublands, tundras, and coral reefs. As I'm sure you're aware, Genesis's first generation of biomes were an unsustainable solution, hastily seeded so the planet could be colonized. They're in a continuous state of collapse, surviving only by drastic and heavy-handed interventions. Our biodiversity level is critically low."

Oraxis felt like sparring. "Hey, P.J., how many species of beetle were on Earth before the Anthropocene extinction?"

"Three hundred fifty thousand!" Popo-Jawi answered, pointing at Oraxis with a smirk. "I think we've got a biology buff here."

"And how many of those three hundred fifty thousand beetle species filled critical niches in their biomes?"

Popo-Jawi stammered, "Ah, well, Oraxis, I'm afraid that's missing the point. Individual species all contribute in their own way to the—"

"Right, it's just too many beetles, isn't it?" Oraxis asked, feigning aggravation.

P.J. kept his good spirits. "Well, that's the old joke, right? The creator having an inordinate fondness for beetles? Did you know we've failed to establish stable breeding populations of even *one thousand* beetle species?"

"So many beetles," Oraxis grumbled.

Genevieve popped her bubble gum. "Ugh, so gross. Earth only needed *four* beetles, dude."

P.J. pointed at her and grinned. "John, Paul, George, and Ringo?"

Genevieve laughed, mindspeaking to Oraxis, *"Okay, he gets ten points for knowing their names, and five more for playing along."*

"Good form, P.J.!" Oraxis chuckled. "I'm sorry for poking fun. In all seriousness, we're looking for a new torch to carry, and BBB supports a worthy cause. Put our names in the *follow-up* column. There're a lot of booths to visit this week, but I'm sure none can compare to the thrill of breeding beetles."

THEY STOPPED by the Bootstrapper Council booth next. It was fashioned after a tribal campground at night, set against a void backdrop. As they stepped across the threshold of the booth, the lights of the exhibit hall faded to a dim glow. The sound of conference-goers diminished to distant murmurs, disappearing behind the sounds of chirping crickets and the crackling fire.

Oraxis recognized Falyonne-Eta West, the councilwoman staffing the booth. She sat on a log next to a man that Oraxis didn't recognize. An enhanced-optics peek at his name card said he was Matthew-Beta West. Ah, she must've brought her latest beta along to show him the wonders of the annual convention.

Across from the Wests sat an Astrus — characterized by hairlessness, androgynous features, and a tranquil demeanor.

Oraxis showed his palms. "Room at the fire for two weary travelers?"

"Please, Oraxis, don't be a stranger!" Falyonne-Eta laughed, standing to give Oraxis and Genevieve welcoming hugs.

Matthew-Beta stood and shook their hands, while the Astrus bowed and introduced themself as RRE-Secunde. The "Secunde" suffix was used by Astri to name their personality emulation AI proxies. There was allegedly no perceivable difference between talking to an Astrus's Secunde rather than their Prime. While Oraxis appreciated them being upfront about this practice, it never sat well with him to treat an AI with the same level of respect as a conscious being.

Genevieve mindspoke, *"RRE-Prime couldn't be bothered with attending, apparently."*

Finding a spot to sit on a rolled-up fur, Oraxis struck up the conversation. "First convention, Matthew-Beta?"

The man nodded. "Yes, sir, Eld Telson."

"Whoa!" Oraxis laughed, "Reel that deference back a bit, Matt. I hold no title or office—"

"Oh, sorry, sir, I just figured, with you being from Earth—"

"Earth? Never heard of the place."

The others laughed politely.

"Well," Oraxis said, "since you already know all about me, tell me about yourself. Have you picked your first field of study?"

Matthew-Beta looked to Falyonne-Eta, then back to Oraxis. "Well, if I'm going to be a bootstrapper, I've got a lot to learn."

Genevieve had her hand on Oraxis's back. She gave his side a solid squeeze as she mindspoke, *"I'll save you from saying something embarrassing. I can explain later."*

"Of course!" Genevieve laughed, "Oraxis knew that. He was just having some fun. Mean old man, this one." She feigned punching his arm.

"Don't worry about it," Falyonne-Eta sighed, "we've heard it all. We knew we'd face ridicule, but what can I say? It's worth it." She placed a hand on the inside of Matthew-Beta's thigh as she rested her head on his shoulder.

"Wait, are they...?" Oraxis mindspoke to Genevieve.

"Like totally," Genevieve valley-girl-mindspoke in reply.

RRE-Secunde shook their head. "It is a strange world, where two consenting adults cannot fall in love without suffering the scorn of their society."

Oraxis sent Genevieve, *"A beta and their bootstrapper having an affair? And she's on the Bootstrapper Council! I guess we're not the only ones making the gossip column."*

"It's old news, O," Genevieve replied. *"They went public with it when we were picking up Zeta. They even seeded an alpha together."*

Oraxis tried to save face. "Well, we agree with RRE-Secunde! I wasn't trying to poke fun. I just didn't want to take for granted that you'd be focusing *exclusively* on bootstrapping. There're many years to fill between alpha seeding and beta bootstrapping."

"On that topic," Falyonne-Eta said, "the council would like to know how much longer you were planning on waiting before you seed your next alpha."

Crickets chirped. The heat of the campfire certainly was oppressive.

Genevieve took the question. "As the council knows, Zeta's bootstrapping didn't go very smoothly. She's at the Guardian Embassy as we speak. If she's accepted, we'll be on our way to Eden within a month."

"Would that be a Soma month or a Varuna month?" Matthew-Beta asked, giving a chuckle to soften the jab's impact. Soma's orbital period was similar to Earth's lunar month, making it the de facto measurement of a month. Varuna's orbit took three times as long, and nobody called it a "month".

Genevieve ignored Matthew-Beta. "If she's not accepted into the Guard, we'll need to be there to pick up the pieces. We need to make sure she's settled into a new life path before we disappear for a year. We all know how hard it can be for a beta to acclimate to our world. And just because Zeta's bold doesn't mean she's unbreakable."

Genevieve stood. Oraxis followed suit.

Incoming group conversation request from Faylonne-Eta West.

Odd. Oraxis and Genevieve exchanged glances before accepting.

"I'm sorry," Faylonne-Eta mindspoke, *"but I don't want to talk about this in front of an offworlder."*

"RRE-Secunde would leave if you asked," Genevieve sent. *"The Astri are polite."*

"They'd still overhear."

It was unwarranted paranoia, but there was no point arguing. Oraxis and Genevieve could feel each other's mutual desire to retreat from the conversation and the booth.

"We've got a population problem," Matthew-Beta sent.

Oraxis barely refrained from groaning. Here comes the dead argument that the Noddite population growth rate was too low. After three hundred seventy years, the faction had finally celebrated their one hundred thousandth beta resurrection.

The faction's growth rate was limited by the essentially fixed neoprim population in Eden and the requisite passage of time between seeding and resurrection. These protocols were considered a wise precaution against carrying tribal alliances and feuds from Eden to Nod and prevented betas from retreating back to their families. It resulted in slow growth, which seldom exceeded three hundred betas a year. This was a feature, not a flaw. Genesis was a *timeless* faction which didn't engage in the population growth and colony expansion rat race that the other factions did.

The solution to the problem of having too few Noddites to manage Genesis had been to allow the other factions to take up provisional residence in the Surya system. The advanced human population was capped at five hundred thousand, with offworlders picking up the slack as the Noddite population grew from generation to generation. Being outnumbered in their own system made some Genesisians nervous. So far, everything had worked out fine.

So, what's the problem?

Faylonne-Eta sent, *"The Council of Ten is open to hearing proposals. We're promoting the Sibling Seed Plan."*

Oraxis and Genevieve looked at each other. Their blank expressions confirmed that neither had heard of any such proposal.

Matthew-Beta offered, *"It would mean seeding all the children in an alpha's family. Isn't that great?"*

Oraxis scoffed. *"Dragging sibling rivalries out into the next life?"*

"Just the logistics alone don't make sense," Genevieve sent. *"You have to seed them as babies. Do we go back and make another appearance every time an alpha's sibling is born?"*

"You'd seed the first baby of a young couple." Faylonne-Eta's lips tightened as they engaged in silent debate. *"The nanites would be pre-programmed to automatically transfer to its siblings, just as we do for companion animals."*

Oraxis could see where this was going. *"You want us to be pilots for this program?"*

"If The Council of Ten allows it, then yes."

RRE-Secunde looked from one silent face to another, then stood. "I can see that I am intruding. I bid you—"

"No, please stay," Genevieve said. "We're the ones that interrupted you. We were just leaving."

"I'm sorry, but we're not interested," Genevieve sent in the private conversation, requesting for the channel to be closed.

Faylonne-Eta replied, *"If you're not a part of the solution, you're part of the problem."*

Oraxis laughed joylessly. *"That tired old line? Really? Okay, kids. I didn't want to play the old-timer card, but here it comes. We were there when the Genesis Faction Charter was signed. We voted on The Principles. The best minds of our time toiled for years to define the ideal alpha seeding and beta bootstrapping protocols. Working out the bugs and bringing the CCDC rates down came at a devastating personal cost to me and Genevieve."*

"Devastating," Genevieve added, gravely.

"So, no, we're not upending everything just because some newcomers are impatient with the population growth rate. Until you can make a convincing argument that there actually is a problem to be solved, don't drag us into your politics."

Genevieve jumped in. *"I'm sure this has nothing to do with you young lovers wanting to adopt a whole family at once instead of bringing them up individually, like the rest of us do. Faylonne-Eta West, if you've already seeded an alpha with these modified neurites you're talking about, I sure hope you got Council approval first."*

The Wests stared at them — children with their hands caught in the cookie jar. Oraxis smirked at Genevieve. Her intuition and social skills never ceased to amaze him.

He didn't wait for them to finish concocting a rebuttal before he gave them an escape route. *"Well, that's none of our business, Gen. As long as we're given the leeway to seed our next alpha in the manner we see fit at the time that we feel is prudent, we have no reason to meddle in their affairs."*

"Of course," Faylonne-Eta sent, meekly. *"Take your time."*

Group conversation channel closed.

Oraxis and Genevieve gave a quick goodbye and turned to leave the booth. On their way out, Matthew-Beta spoke in a conspicuous tone from behind their backs. "Tell me, RRE-Secunde, how do the

Astri deal with the societal stagnation that immortality creates? I mean, if old ideas don't die off with the passing of generations, how can a society ever evolve? I'd hate to think the only solution is *revolution*, but sometimes I wonder..."

As they passed over the booth's threshold, the noise of the convention returned, drowning out the young man's parting jab. They disappeared into the crowd before talking again.

"Dude, that was gnarly," Genevieve said, snapping her disappearing/reappearing gum.

"Totally," Oraxis said.

THE NEXT BOOTH TO catch their eye was flanked by banners proclaiming it was the EoE Sponsored Project of the year. It was four times the size of a normal booth and looked like a reconstruction of a medieval throne room. Braziers lined the sides of the booth, and tapestries adorned its three walls. A red carpet formed a path through its center, leading up the stairs to the elevated platform at the back of the booth.

Two high-backed wooden thrones sat side-by-side on the platform. One was decorated with silver inlays and topped with a silver "P" set against a crescent moon. The other was gilded with gold and topped with a golden letter "T" within a sunburst design. In the thrones sat two stately women. Queens, apparently.

The queen in the moon throne had black hair, with one side shaved closely in a pattern of diagonal lines. The other side was chin-length and wavy, flowing down one side of her head. Her skin was a deep brown, yet her eyes were pale blue. Her robe was black velvet. Black feathers splayed from the collar and cuffs. The robe's hems glistened with silver embroidery.

The queen in the sun throne was a fair-skinned woman with bleach-blond hair and a white robe, adorned with snowy white fur and golden embroidery. Her eyes were deep brown, just a shade away from black.

A guard in dark steel full plate armor stood at statuesque attention next to the moon throne. A black feather plume topped his helmet. His face covering looked like a bird's beak with an underbite. A similar guard flanked the sun throne, wearing golden armor and a white-plumed helmet.

Oraxis and Genevieve had joined the crowd gathered at the booth. A knight and an orc were stretching and warming up with their weapons on opposing sides of the throne room.

"Enough dallying! Begin!" The queen in black commanded in a British accent.

The orc spoke awkwardly, as if his mouth was filled with marbles. "Not yet! I need to get dah feel for dees club."

"Come on, Lazlo, let's rumble," the knight taunted in an awful attempt at a British accent. He started swinging his sword from one side of his body to the other, crossing the throne room towards the orc.

The orc tried to flank the knight, but he was too slow. The knight swung down and opened a gash on the side of the orc's arm.

"Ow!" the orc bellowed. "Dat really hoort, Sam'ooal!"

"Oh, come on!" The knight laughed. "It's a construct! It can't hurt that bad. Hi-yah!"

The knight lunged forward to impale the orc, but the orc raised its arm, defensively. He deflected the blow at the cost of having his forearm sliced through. The knight jerked the sword down, slicing open the orc's arm. Deep red blood — almost black — gushed from the wound.

The orc let out a genuine bellow of pain. "Argh! My arm! Oh, Surya eet hurts!" He had fallen and was dragging himself away, slipping in his own blood. "I'm done! Let me ah-oot, I geeve oop!"

The knight laughed at this, sheathing his sword.

The queen in black flipped her hand. An invisible force sent the orc tumbling out of the booth and into the crowd. Upon crossing the booth's threshold, he turned into a human — a large, muscled man with a mane of chestnut hair and olive skin. The man sat up and examined his hand, working his fingers, then got to his feet and turned to the booth. "Oy! That really hurt! Like he *really* sliced my arm open! What sorta game you sadists running?"

He looked back and forth at the women. The sword-swinging knight had abandoned the throne room, transforming into a smallish fellow who tried to apologize to his agitated friend.

Oraxis mindspoke to Genevieve, *"EoE Gladstone picked a medieval fantasy construct as his featured project?"*

"Apparently. These queens must have friends in high places. Looks more like a distraction than a project."

The queen in black was running her fingers sensuously up and down a silver scepter topped by a jagged shard of black stone. "That. Was. Pathetic. Really, Lazlo, I had hoped a man as *virile* as you could have lasted more than a few seconds. Story of my life," she sighed.

The crowd laughed at this. Elbow-nudging and sideways smirks abounded.

"He asked what sort of *game* we're running," the queen in white said, sounding offended. She had a stereotypically royal accent, rolling the "r" in "running".

"Game?" the other queen scoffed. "No, this is no *game*. It's... a quest."

"An unparalleled experience with infinite possibilities!"

"A fully immersive virtual world unlike any you have ever seen!"

"Sounds like a game," Oraxis mindspoke to Genevieve.

The queen in white opened a palm in an inviting gesture, scanning the crowd with her dark eyes. "Step into the booth and see for yourself. We're accepting applications from all factions, but space is limited. Lend us ten minutes of your time to show you more. You won't regret it."

The crowd began trickling into the booth. As they passed over the threshold, they turned into orbs of colorful light. The woman in white held up her golden scepter. The hovering orbs zipped across the booth, disappearing into the scepter's pearly stone. In moments, the crowd's trickle became a flood.

"*Pass?*" Genevieve mindspoke.

"*Pass,*" Oraxis agreed.

They fought their way upstream and escaped down an adjacent row of booths.

Incoming conversation request from Pip-Tau Telson.

It was on their shared channel, so they both accepted at the same time.

"*Just where do you think you're going?!*" Pip-Tau squeaked.

"*Huh?*" Oraxis hadn't seen either of the Pips yet. He looked around for a cherub or a tiny woman with an afro puff.

Genevieve responded, "*Hi, Pip-Tau! Are you at the convention, too? I don't see you.*"

"*Like hell you don't! I saw you watching the battle of the bozos.*"

Oraxis laughed, "*You're in the crowd? I'm sorry, you'll have to flag us down.*"

Genevieve tapped Oraxis's arm, pointing at the throne room. A girl wearing a squire outfit was standing behind the queen in white, waving a small flag emblazoned with a scorpion tail. The squire caught their eye, then started waving.

"*Hi, Tau!*" Genevieve laughed. She waved back. "*Nice flag! Sorry, but I've never seen you use that avatar. You're working for this year's EoE Sponsored Project?*"

"*Impressive,*" Oraxis sent. EoE Sponsored Projects were pretty prestigious.

The squire shook her head. She pointed at the queen in white, then retreated from the throne room. The queen had a bead on them with her unsettling dark eyes.

"*No, O-pa,*" Pip-Tau sent, "*we're running it.*"

2

APPLICANT

"Zeta Telson, age nine. You don't look nine..."

"I am... nine," Zeta struggled to say, using Common tongue.

Intake Officer Jasielski stared at her, blinked, and said, "Nine *Earth* years?"

Zeta cursed herself. The Guard Faction uses Earth years, not Genesis years! Jamji had told her that, but she forgot it when she filled out the application. She did the quick calculation. "Fift... fift... een." She winced. Her double-mind would translate her intended speech into Common for her, but she had to stop fighting for control of her mouth. It felt like speaking using nothing but tongue-twisters.

She relaxed and started again, "Fifteen Earth years." She was in the latter part of her ninth year, so she may actually be sixteen Earth years old now, but she didn't know the exact date of her birth, so she stuck with the simple answer. The fewer words she had to say, the better.

Officer Jasielski reached up and touched a section of the words floating above the desk before her, drawing two shapes with her finger. She sighed, "I've amended the application for you. And is this accurate? You've only been a beta for *four* Soma months?"

Zeta shifted in her seat. "Yes. It didn't take long to figure out... that Genesis Faction is a..." She cursed herself again for tripping over the words as they tumbled out. She started again, "It didn't take long to figure out that the Genesis Faction... is a joke. That joining the Guard was... my destiny."

Officer Jasielski paused, gave a grunt, then returned to reading the floating words. She gestured through the air, making the words flick upwards.

The woman's hefty stature, hard face with angular features, and odd attire were intimidating enough on their own. It didn't help that she wore the look of an eld who has grown tired of a child's presence.

Zeta glanced around the room as she waited for Jasielski to finish reading. How had they gotten the walls to be so smooth? Zeta recognized the words displayed within a rectangle on the wall behind Jasielski's desk — the Guard Faction Core Principles. She had stored the text for quick access in her double-mind. She'd need it when the time came to recite the principles during her pledge ceremony.

On one wall was a window. Instead of showing the outdoors, it displayed the blackness of space. A green, blue, and white planet was spinning just outside the window. She couldn't tell whether that planet was Earth or Genesis. That was the sort of thing the Guardians would test her on — she really should know that.

"WoQS, what planet am I looking at?"

You are looking at a holographic reproduction of the planet Earth, as it appeared before the atmospheric changes correlated with the arrival of The Monster from the Stars in Earth Standard Year Twenty-Four Seventy.

It was good that the Guardians cherished the memory of Earth. They respected that history and vowed to make The Monster pay for its transgressions. Someday they'd return to Earth. And if The

Monster was still there, they'd make it wish it had never messed with us humans.

But first, they had the Specters to deal with.

The silence stretched out for longer than Zeta could bear. She cleared her throat, earning an impatient sideways glance from Jasielski. "Jamji said I would make a great—"

"Jamji Telson is not a Guardian, Zeta." Officer Jasielski gave a sideways swipe to the floating words, making them vanish. She leaned forward and put her elbows on her desk, clasping her hands together. The wooden desk creaked under her weight. "She's a promising applicant, but she's ignorant. I'm sure she assured you that if you showed enough enthusiasm and intellect, we'd see that spark and accept you into the Guard Faction."

"Jamji—" Zeta bit back her temptation to defend Jamji. She was *not* ignorant — the woman was sixty-two years old. No, she needed to use Earth years from now on. Zeta performed the conversion. Jamji was one hundred two Earth years old, and she had spent every moment of her life in Nod learning everything there was to learn about this world. "Jamji believes in me."

Intake Officer Jasielski stared at Zeta.

Zeta stared back, determined not to show weakness.

Jasielski blinked, then gave a skeptical grunt. She looked down and pulled back on something on the other side of her desk, then reached in and retrieved a shiny, metallic device. Her movements had the swift, casual grace of years of practice. Zeta marveled as the woman thumbed a lever on the device, ejected a rectangle from its handle, caught the rectangle, pulled another rectangle from her desk, shoved it into the handle, slid the top section back, gave it a visual inspection, then slammed it back into place with a loud metallic click. The series of movements couldn't have taken more than two seconds.

Jasielski stood, walked around the desk, and pointed the device at Zeta. "Stand up."

Zeta stood, pushing back the chair and facing the woman.

"This is a reflex test. Dial up your neural firing rate and try to dodge."

Zeta had learned about increasing her neural rate — overclocking. Jamji had tried to show her how, but all Zeta could do so far was give herself a headache. She asked, "What am I dodging?"

"A bullet. You have three seconds to prepare your mind."

Zeta didn't know what that was. *"WoQS, what's a bullet?"*

"Three..."

A bullet is a projectile—

"Two..."

—traditionally made of metal—

"One..."

—which is fired from a—

A deafening crack filled the room. Something struck her chest. She stumbled backwards, stunned, trying to cover her ears and put a hand to her heart at the same time.

—rifle, revolver, or other small firearm by means of—

Her back hit the wall.
She pulled up her hand. It was dripping with blood.

—an explosive propellant such as gunpowder.

She looked up at the woman.

"You didn't even try?" Jasielski said with a muffled voice. She was shaking her head slowly.

Zeta felt cold, numb, distant.

WoQS was trying to fill her head with visualizations of how bullets are made and their historical uses — hunting and killing.

This was it.

She was dying again.

A SHARP SMELL shocked Zeta back to consciousness. Her eyes opened to a spinning room.

"Ah, there she is," a gentle voice said.

"Zeta Telson? Do you know where you are?" another woman asked.

She tried to look around. She was on the ground, with her head being held by a woman she had never seen before, wearing white.

"Maybe another quick whiff," the woman giggled. She lifted a brown vial towards Zeta's face.

The odor assaulted her nose again. She swatted it away, covering her nose with her forearm. "Stop it! I know where I am!"

She was at Syn-Cen — that's where they resurrect people. She focused her gaze on the walls and ceiling around her, then spotted the panel with the image of Earth in it. To her other side was a desk. She was still at the Guardian Embassy? Could they resurrect people here, too?

Zeta felt her chest. It was sore and sticky with blood.

"I'm at the Guardian Embassy," Zeta said, careful to speak using Common. "Officer Jasielski shot me in the heart, and you resurrected me."

The woman in white laughed jovially. Even Jasielski cracked a smile and let out a chuckle.

Zeta felt her face flushing. She couldn't stand these people's ridicule. She scrambled to get to her feet. The woman in white tried to help, but Zeta shook her off.

"You fainted, Zeta," Jasielski said, almost warmly. "I'm sorry I scared you. And I'm sorry if that hurts. It'll bruise up pretty bad."

"You and your antique guns," the woman in white said. "Someday the Genesisians are going to ban those from the planet, so have fun playing shoot-the-neoprim while you can, Jasielski."

Jasielski pointed the gun at the woman in white, who let out a laugh as another deafening crack filled the room.

Zeta flinched and covered her ears.

The woman in white was still laughing, showing no sign of injury. A red splat of blood had appeared on the wall behind her. She lunged forward, flinging the vial and splashing some liquid onto Jasielski.

"Brecht! Now you've done it!" Jasielski laughed. "Do you know how hard it is to get that stink out of cloth?"

"You shot first, Jasielski! And missed by an AU!"

"Remind me to use my shotgun next time."

"What's all this blasting?" a man complained, appearing in the corridor outside the room.

Brecht and Jasielski snapped their heels together and raised their hands to their foreheads. Zeta wondered if she should do the same.

"I was performing a reflex test on an applicant, sir."

The man poked his head into the room, gave Zeta a passing glance, then said, "You're shooting the applicants, Jasielski?"

"Yes, sir. Blood-bullet cartridges, sir."

The man's nose wrinkled. "Is that ammonia?"

"Smelling salts, sir," Brecht said. "The applicant fainted."

"Ah," the man's mouth twitched with a stifled smile. "Well, if you get done here in the next ten minutes, hurry down to the observation chamber. You're going to want to see this match. That Telson applicant's something else."

"Yes, sir," Jasielski and Brecht chorused.

The man nodded once, then turned to head away.

After a pause, Brecht turned to Jasielski and spoke softly, "You're afraid to correct your senior officer now?"

"Correct him about what?"

"The Telson applicant's right here. He's got her mixed up with someone else."

"He's talking about my sis-kin," Zeta said. "There are two Telson applicants."

"Oh!" Brecht laughed. "I see. Well, I better get some more smelling salts in case fainting runs in the family." She bounced away.

Jasielski smiled and shook her head. She gestured to Zeta's empty seat as she returned to her own chair across the desk.

Zeta sat down, her ears still ringing. She stole a glance at her chest, seeing that the spot where she had been shot was now a smear of sticky dried blood. This was going horribly. She needed to turn it around in her favor. She blurted, "I don't think that failing to dodge a bullet should mean that I'm not... qual... qualified."

"You can barely speak Common, Zeta. You also fainted."

"I thought I was dying! WoQS was telling me that bullets killed people, and I thought this was my blood, and—"

"It's supposed to look like blood, yes. If I had used *these*," Jasielski picked up the rectangle that had originally been in the gun and shook it, "you really *would* be dead. For the next six months, that is. And I'd be banned from the surface of Genesis, for good this time. Look, Zeta, I'm sorry, but I just don't think—"

"Let me fight the Specters with you!" Zeta shouted, rising to her feet and knocking the chair over. "Please, I need this."

Jasielski paused, blinking, looking up at Zeta with tight lips as if considering whether to reprimand her for the outburst. She shook her head slightly. "You're too young, Zeta. You've got too much to learn, and the Guard is not an elementary school."

Zeta asked WoQS what an "elementary school" was. When she heard the definition, she had to resist the urge to slap the woman. She was not a child!

Jasielski was watching her, silently. When Zeta took a breath to speak, Jasielski blurted, "Did you have to ask WoQS what an *elementary school* is?"

Zeta closed her mouth, clenching her teeth. Tears started welling in her eyes.

"Like I said, you've got too much to learn. I do see the potential in you, Zeta, and if you're still interested in enlisting in... let's say twenty years or so, come back and see me. In the meantime, there are more than enough opportunities for you to research the Specters right here on Genesis, in your own faction."

Zeta didn't trust herself to speak.

Jasielski stood. "I'll call for your dog to be brought up, then show you the way out."

SMOOTH WALLS with artificial overhead lighting transitioned to rough stone as Zeta and Penelope-pooch were led back out of the underground Guardian embassy complex. A wedge of light ahead marked their exit — her shameful return to the Genesis Faction with her head held low and her tail between her legs.

A somber silence had overtaken Zeta. She wouldn't break the spell by uttering some pathetic final plea or insincere thanks for the privilege of being humiliated and turned away.

Intake Officer Jasielski stopped just outside the hidden entrance, but Zeta kept walking into the shadowy jungle.

"Sorry about shooting you, Zeta," Jasielski called out from behind. "If it would make you feel any better, I'll let you take a shot at me."

Zeta pretended not to hear. The tears she had been holding back came pouring out. She wished she had Jamji's skin so she could turn invisible.

She should have known this would happen.

Jamji was wrong about her — she doesn't have what it takes to be a Guardian. She couldn't even take a fake bullet to the chest without fainting.

Zeta stomped through the jungle, pushing past ferns. She slipped in the mud more than once, like a clumsy child.

That's all she was. It's all she would be for a very long time, to these people. When the average person has been alive for hundreds of years, they don't take anyone under the age of fifty seriously.

Fifty years — eighty-two Earth years. There wasn't any point in practicing her year conversions anymore — she was stuck with the Genesis Faction.

Doing what?

It didn't matter. It's not like she could've made a difference, anyway.

She was making her way to the makeshift camp where she and Jamji had stayed prior to being called in for their entrance exams. Her few possessions were waiting for her there, tied into a tight bundle and dangling from a tree limb. That included the chocolate-filled cacao pod which Genevieve had gifted her.

Time to eat it all.

As she pushed through the wide leaves just outside her abandoned camp, a low growl came from ahead.

Zeta instinctively crouched, holding her hand out, palm down, to signal for Penelope-pooch to stay still and quiet.

"Hello?" a woman's voice called.

Zeta held her breath, listening.

The growl came again, followed by a bark.

"Shoosh, Pinga," muttered the woman. Then, back in a calling-out voice, "Um, if you're a person, don't worry, Pinga can't bite you unless I tell him to. If you're not a person... then... I'm shouting at dinner!" There came a huffing laugh.

She recognized that laugh. Zeta stood, scanning the forest. "Alasie?"

"Yeah, hey, Zeta! I'm this way!"

Zeta jogged through the underbrush, pushing past leaves until she stood in the hollow she had called camp a week ago, facing the young beta she had met at her ceremony. Rather than the bulky furs she wore at the ceremony, Alasie had a strip of fur over her chest and a short skirt of layered furs. The jungle was too hot and humid for anything more.

Standing between herself and Alasie was a snarling wolf-pooch with white and gray fur. Penelope-pooch was stepping closer to the wolf-pooch, growling.

"This pooch is threatening us and I am ready to fight it," came Penelope-pooch's anthropolinguistics.

"No, Pen. These are friends."

Penelope-pooch's demeanor calmed down to one of cautious interest. A moment later, Pinga also stopped snarling and sat down, weaving his head back and forth as he sniffed the air for their scent.

Alasie kneeled by her animal, scratching behind his ears. "That's so much easier now that I can talk... to his head. Ugh, this Common tongue! So hard to talk. Can we think-speak? WorMS makes words easy."

This was so weird. Zeta squeezed her eyes shut and nodded her head. She had been expecting to have some time alone to come to terms with her rejection and eat her chocolate.

Alasie sent a conversation request. Zeta accepted and sent, *"How did you find my camp?"*

Alasie stood. She adjusted her chest wrap and straightened her skirt. *"Uh, well, I, uh, knew you were going to the Guardian Embassy because you said you were joining them,"* Alasie stammered in Zeta's head. *"So, WoQS told me how to get here, and once I got here, Pinga helped track you and your sis-kin's dogs' scents. Especially your sis-kin's dog, since his markings are so, uh, pronounced. You weren't around when I got here, so I waited at your camp since I was afraid if I went into the embassy I'd get in trouble. I figured maybe before you headed up for Soma, you'd want to come back for the stuff you tied up in the tree."* She pointed at the dangling bundle.

Zeta was beyond frustrated. *"Alasie, why are you here?"*

Alasie pressed a toe into the mossy jungle floor, looking down. *"Well, to be honest, I'm not even sure myself."* She huffed a nervous laugh. *"To say goodbye, I guess? Or tell you I'm sorry about bringing Rohito to meet you? Or maybe I thought I could talk you out of joining the Guard? But I know I can't do that. It's too late — you've made up your mind."*

"You don't have to bother with that. They rejected me."

Alasie's eyes widened. She took a half-step forward, then stopped herself. She put a hand on her mouth and gasped. *"I'm sorry, Zeta! I know how important that was for you."*

Zeta sighed. *"It taught me two lessons. The first is that you and I are children in this world. Babes, even. And we won't be treated like adults for a lifetime."*

Alasie huffed. *"You've got that right. Nobody takes anything I say seriously."*

"The second lesson is when your family says you're amazing, don't believe them."

Alasie huffed again. *"I guess you wouldn't believe me, either? Like, if I said you're amazing?"*

"Nope. Now help me cut down my pack. I'm going to see if it's possible to poison myself by eating too much chocolate."

3

TRIAL BY FIRE

Atmospheric insertion in three… two… one…

Jamji closed her eyes and clenched her teeth as her capsule shuddered. The turbulence escalated quickly, jostling her body violently against the crash couch. The G-force of deceleration made her feel like she was made of lead.

Even with her eyes closed, the heads-up display remained superimposed at the edge of her vision. It showed her hull's temperature rising, creeping towards the red zone. The altimeter spun down in the opposite direction, closing in on the yellow line that indicated her ejection altitude.

"Applicant Jamji, you're coming in hot. Reduce your pitch by five degrees."

Jamji focused on the capsule's integrated neural interface, performing the attitude adjustment. Her hull's temperature continued rising, but at a reduced rate. That'd cost her points.

Thirty-two seconds to capsule ejection.

Jamji pinged her team. They were drifting apart. It was fine — they'd link back up using wingsuit maneuvers.

"Status update on hostiles?" Jamji sent Captain Bath. No use wasting thirty-two seconds twiddling her thumbs.

"Orbital surveillance indicates they're falling back, digging in at various bunkers among the hills. It's likely they've spotted our platoon's arrival."

Jamji had expected the Noddites to resort to guerrilla tactics. As the briefing had stated, the only thing keeping the Guard from torching the entire forest was the ecological preservation treaty signed with the Proliferans. This was a surgical strike operation.

As soon as the premise of the test was announced, Jamji knew what the hidden objective was. Superficially, it was an orbital insertion operation followed by stealth ops and close-quarters combat. In reality, it was a test of her resolve. They had to see if she was ready to put the interests of the Guard above her loyalties to her home world.

Yeah, no problem.

Capsule ejection in three... two... one...

The capsule split down the middle, exploding outwards and sending Jamji into freefall. The bright Surya light flooded her vision as the sound of wind rushing by filled her ears. She tumbled for a few seconds before regaining her bearings, spreading her arms and legs, knees bent, wingsuit pressing hard against her skin.

Damn, that tumble would cost her points.

With another ping, she spotted her distant squad-mates.

A scan of the cloud-shrouded landscape below revealed the last known locations of the temporary Noddite strongholds, as well as the Guardian drop-bases.

Jamji's overclocked mind raced as she surveyed the overlay.

"Captain Bath, I have an alternate landing zone proposal. We can take advantage of my familiarity with the Thin Forest region."

"I'm listening."

"Sir, there's a lake near a renovated cave complex called The Cavern of the Soul." Jamji flagged the area on her team's shared visualization channel. *"It's in uncontested territory, and would improve our strategic control of the hot spots. I propose a covert, no-chute water landing. Then we regroup at the shore and secure the cavern. There's a grazing field beside the cavern with plenty of room for a drop-base. While the base drops in, our unit can secure the surrounding forest."*

"You sure we can secure that cave complex, Telson? Could be a transport tube leading into it, or multiple entrances."

"There are just two entrances, sir. And no tubes." Jamji shared an ad hoc illustration, compiled via meta-construct imagery.

"I like it. I'll put it up for CIS review."

Jamji would have smiled if her face wasn't being buffeted by terminal velocity wind speeds.

The squad of six converged on their captain's position, linking arms in a Falling Star formation as they awaited approval of Jamji's plan. They deployed their wings — retractable webbing which spanned their legs and arms. This slowed their descent and would allow them to cover the lateral distances required to change their landing zone.

Captain Bath met her eyes as he transmitted over the aud-link, *"Telson's plan is a go. Revised flight plans are on your HUD's."* He pulled back from the squad, gave a thumbs-up, then tucked into a back-roll, plummeting below them. The rest of the squad released hands, maneuvered apart, then lowered their arms to their sides to dive towards their designated flight patterns.

In eleven minutes and twenty-two seconds, Jamji was skimming the surface of Spirit Lake. She lowered the tips of her boots into the water, carefully angling her wingsuit flaps to keep herself from tumbling in before she shed speed. Her feet skipped a few times before digging in, sending fans of lake water spraying out in either direction. She dragged herself down to a low enough speed to dive in without breaking any bones.

She took a deep breath before plunging into the lake. Once underwater, she tucked her arms to her sides and used her wingsuit's leg web as a fin, undulating her body in a dolphin kick.

Crawling onto the shore and dragging herself to her feet, Jamji joined her captain and two other squad-mates. They had pulled out their rifles and were scanning the nearby trees, field, and gaping cave entrance set into the side of a mound. Jamji gave the area a quick glance. Seeing no sign of movement or heat signatures, she dropped her pack and pulled the quick-release tabs on either side of the wing-suit's neck. Its seams split and it crumpled to the ground at her feet. She pulled her rifle out, then slung her pack over her shoulders.

Unlike her squad-mates, Jamji was naked underneath her wing-suit. Her chromatites were disengaged, so her absolute black skin made her look like a walking void in space. The rest of the team wore full-body cloaking armor. While the armor would have been nice to have if she got into a skirmish with the hostiles, Jamji preferred to avoid firefights. She'd rather sneak up from behind and take them out silently.

All warfare is based on deception.

The next thirty minutes were by the book. The squad released polymer-digesting nanites onto their wingsuits and dumped them into the lake. They spread out and swept the surrounding forest, then cleared The Cavern of the Soul. Only a few hostiles were down in the cave. It would take a STODAR scan to check for any hideaways lurking in the deeper, unfinished depths of the cave's network.

Captain Bath issued commands via aud-link as he jogged towards the middle of the grazing field to place a drop-base beacon. *"Kalb, Holder, Farro — you'll hold this position with me. Matushek, Telson, Bedna — CIS has a set of potential threats for you to investigate and eliminate. The coordinates are in your HUDs now."*

Jamji wasn't at all surprised to find that her assigned destination was none other than the Telson cabin.

Whatever. If they thought they could get into her head by making her kill Oraxis and Genevieve, they were about to be sorely disappointed.

She sent her rifle the command to engage active invisibility, then engaged her own invisibility protocol. Jamji's dermal photoreceptites were now receiving imagery from her surroundings and broadcasting it to her chromatites in real-time. The construct apparently granted her the advanced anti-IR tech of the Guardians, since she noticed her skin becoming cooler than it normally felt when running active invisibility. This meant she'd even be invisible to heat sensors.

Nice.

Jamji darted across the field and into the tree-line. She ran down the familiar path which would lead her to the Telson cabin. New objectives appeared in her HUD.

Primary objective: eliminate all hostiles in the area.
Secondary objective: search for contraband tech within the structure.
Tertiary objective: destroy the structure.

JAMJI SLOWED to a cautious walk once she was within one hundred meters of the target, overclocking slightly. There was no telling what they'd throw at her, and her reflexes needed to be fast. Oraxis could jump out from behind a tree at any second and try to blast her. Genevieve could be waiting in ambush, up in a sniper's nest or under a pile of pine needles.

She had to admit that she was disturbed by the fact that part of her test included killing Oraxis and Genevieve — her family. Guardians weren't monsters. They cherished their humanity and honored their heritage. But they were also willing to do whatever it takes to save humankind from destruction by aliens as well as self-destruction by infighting. They stood on the wall and watched for threats from without and within. This was their burden.

It occurred to her that she had practically asked to be set upon the Telson cabin. Changing their landing zone to The Cavern of the Soul had been her idea. Though, they probably staged the scenario in such a way as to make that the most obvious course of action.

What if the true test was to see if she's a psychopath? It took a pretty *abnormal* mind to kill your own family. This thought gave her pause.

Then again, even if this was real, Oraxis and Genevieve could just be resurrected. Killing them would be like putting them in time-out for a while. There'd been no indication in the briefing that Worldnet services were down, or that Syn-Cen had been compromised. But she hadn't thought to ask, and asking now would show weakness.

Or compassion.

"*Sir,*" Jamji sent Captain Bath via aud-link, "*what is the status of the Worldnet and Syn-Cen?*"

"*That's irrelevant to your mission. Focus, Telson.*"

Jamji cursed. She had already revealed her insecurity, so she might as well be direct about it. "*Sir, it would help me to focus if I knew that the orbs at Syn-Cen were secure. My bootstrappers live in the cabin I'm approaching.*"

After a pause, Captain Bath sent, "*Syn-Cen is in Guardian control. No Noddite orbs have been damaged, but Worldnet services are down.*"

This was the best scenario, really. The test runner was giving her just enough moral wiggle-room to do the dirty deed she had to do. With Worldnet services down, that meant that the Telsons wouldn't be syncing to their orbs. When they get resurrected, they'd have no memory of her killing them.

Jamji sent, "*Thank you for checking into that, sir. I've got a visual on the cabin now. It's warm, definitely occupied. Hints of movement behind the door flap.*"

"Good luck. Stay sharp."

She didn't need to be reminded. Jamji increased her overclocking rate to about half of her maximum, slowing the world significantly. She wanted to get a full visual of the situation, so she requested orbital imaging. The image came a second later. No surprises — just the cabin. No heat signatures in the surrounding forest. Even Zephyr was nowhere to be seen.

Jamji laid down on her belly with a clear shot at the front door and launched a flash-bang into the cabin. As much as she hated revealing her presence, she couldn't trust that she would be able to sneak in and kill them before they got her. It was close quarters. She'd flush them out and then take care of business with some nice, clean headshots.

Screams came from within. Jamji could make out Oraxis's bellow and Genevieve's squeal, but there was at least one more woman with them.

Oraxis stumbled out of the cabin in slow motion, holding his ears. Laser pulse to the head, and he was down. Genevieve wailed, slowly rushing out to catch Oraxis as he fell.

How dramatic.

Laser pulse.

Sorry, Gen.

An alert flashed in her HUD — her rifle's energy cell had malfunctioned. Jamji rushed to eject the cell, but it was too late — the weapon exploded in her hands.

Jamji was blinded. Her hands burned. Her ears rang.

She cursed the test runner as she crawled backwards and rolled behind a tree. The chances of a catastrophic energy cell malfunction after firing only two bursts were practically zero. The jerk just wanted to ramp up the difficulty level.

"You wanna play rough?! Okay!" squeaked the voice of Pip-Tau. There was a whine of a powering-up weapon. "Say hello to my lit'le friend!" A barrage of supersonic explosive shells surrounded her. She was peppered by a storm of flying pine needles, splinters, and dirt.

Jamji ramped her overclocking up to the maximum as she took stock of her situation. Her eyes were fried, but she had a backup optics system — her photoreceptites.

Vision via an array of millions of microscopic optical sensors embedded in your skin is an indescribable sensory experience. The optics are distorted, warping and swimming as you move. You also lose the advantage of your enhanced visual systems, like optical zoom and infrared.

She had to consciously select which photoreceptites to tap into, since the human brain simply isn't wired for processing full-surround visual input. The patch on her forehead was unresponsive — damaged by the energy cell explosion. That meant that her active invisibility was ruined. Her palms were also fried. She tapped into the top of her right foot and got a good look at herself.

Well, crap, she was burger meat.

Her face, hands, and forearms were a steaming mess of black skin and blood. So much for invisibility. She looked like a roasted, bloody, floating head and hands. Scary as hell, but not the look she was going for. She'd have to play this smart.

Pip-Tau's attack on her location had stopped. The forest was quiet, aside from the sound of settling debris.

There came the whimpering of a dog. Oh, surely they wouldn't make her kill a *dog*, would they?

Jamji switched her vision source to her sternum, quietly rising to her feet. She checked her cat-claws, squeezing them through her fingertips, finding that they were intact.

She bolted, running between trees in an outward arc. Her best bet was to get to the other side of the cabin.

"I'm reloaded!" Pip-Tau squealed. The forest around Jamji exploded again in a maelstrom of debris. Jamji dove behind a rock, covering her head.

As angry as Jamji was with the test runner, she had to give them credit for nailing Pip-Tau's sense of humor.

Jamji rolled a short distance, then sprung back to her feet and erupted in another burst of speed. In moments, she had made her way to the back of the cabin. She sprinted through Oraxis's Zen rock garden, leaped onto the roof, ran to its edge, then descended upon Pip-Tau.

Neck-snap. Sorry, sis-kin.

Jamji snatched up the rail-rifle, rolled to her side, and pressed her back against the cabin. She held her breath for a moment as she listened for any movement. She switched her vantage point to her foot, then poked it around the corner, observing the front door.

No movement. The dog's whimper came again.

She had to get this nightmare over with. As much as she would have loved to stick the rail-rifle into the back window and spray the cabin's interior with explosive shells, she had the secondary objective to keep in mind — she shouldn't obliterate the cabin's contents if she was going to search it.

Jamji tucked the gun behind a bush on the side of the house, stood, and glided to the cabin door. She slid her foot below the door flap, doing a visual scan of the cabin's interior. The lack of IR was killing her, but she soon spotted a huddling form in the corner, with a dog in front of it.

Penelope-pooch.

Jamji's breath caught in her throat.

"Jamji, is that you?" It was Zeta. Her voice was trembling. "Penelope-pooch said she recognizes your smell."

She should just rush in and end it.

"You don't have to kill me, Jamji!" Zeta pleaded. "Take me with you. Let me fight with you!"

Man, they were laying it on thick. Jamji reached out to Captain Bath. *"Sir, are we taking prisoners? I have an unarmed child here."*

"The mission's primary objective was clear, Telson. Eliminate all hostiles."

"She's not hostile, sir. I propose—"

"She's a Genesisian, holed up in a cabin with known resistance fighters."

"It's my sis-kin, sir. She's sympathetic to our cause. She wants to join the Guard — she's actually being evaluated right now, in the real world."

"I understand that, but as long as you're talking about the real world, I'm sorry to say that we had to reject her application. She's not Guardian material. Not even close. You can't take her with you."

"The Guard rejected me, Jamji," Zeta cried. "I didn't even get a chance to prove myself! The intake officer shot me in the chest with a blood-bullet and I fainted. They laughed at me! They don't understand my potential like you do!"

This was their way of telling her that Zeta got rejected?! Where was Zeta now? What was she going to do? She *was* Guardian material — the intake officer was wrong!

Jamji's heart was hammering in her chest. She shook her head and squeezed her blinded eyes, glad that her tear ducts had been seared shut. The head game this sadistic test runner was playing was getting to her.

Just end it.

Performing an override of her brain chemistry was the only way she was going to get through this. She made the tweaks, numbing her emotions and steeling her resolve.

"I'm sorry, Zeta."

In the slow motion crawl of maximum overclock, Jamji jumped through the door flap. In one fluid motion, she flew across the cabin, dug her cat-claws into the throat of the dog, tearing it out. She wrapped her other arm around the girl's neck, dug her claws into her skin, and twisted.

Primary objective complete.

Without skipping a beat, Jamji started tearing the cabin apart.

She tipped over the wardrobe, threw the stoneware out the window, and ripped the bed mats apart.

Opening the door to the cool box dug into the floor, Jamji found a stash of weapons and equipment. She wrapped them up in a leather bundle and carried them outside.

Secondary objective complete.

She dragged the bodies of Oraxis, Genevieve, and Pip-Tau back into the cabin, then kicked over the potbelly stove. The hot coals inside spread across the floor. She picked up the furs and clothing which had spilled from the wardrobe, piling them upon the coals. Smoke began to rise from the pile.

She went back outside, retrieved the rail-rifle from behind the bush, and added it to the recovered contraband.

One of the weapons in the bundle was a plasma torch.

There is a proper season for making attacks with fire, and special days for starting a conflagration.

She picked up the plasma torch, dialed the output to maximum, and approached the cabin. Pulling the trigger sent a meter-long spear of blue, superheated plasma erupting from the tip of the torch. She hadn't been prepared for the kickback, and ended up burning a vertical line up the side of the cabin.

Jamji considered the line for a moment, deciding that it should have two shorter lines on one side, one short line on the other, and a horizontal line to complete a rudimentary "flipping the bird" drawing. She hoped the test runner appreciated her artistic commentary on the experience.

She walked the perimeter of the Telson cabin, concentrating the superheated plasma on the lowest logs. You're not supposed to wield a plasma torch unless you're wearing protective gear. Her skin was hardened, so it didn't immediately blister and peel away, but it wasn't rated for this much heat. Jamji knew she was being reckless, self-destructive, and vengeful, but she didn't care.

By the time she finished her circuit of the cabin, the skin on the front of her body was smoking and her dermal nanites were fried. She could only see using the photoreceptites on the back of her body. Though the pain thresholds of the construct weren't buffered, Jamji wasn't hurting — she knew how to shut off her pain receptors.

Emotional pain, physical pain — there's a time for feeling and a time for fighting. Training your human mind and body to do inhuman things for the benefit of humanity was a bit of a paradox. She would set aside such heady contemplation until she earns her way into The Students of Sun Tzu and can engage in philosophical debates with worthy opponents. All in due time.

She turned her back to the cabin, watching it burn.

Tertiary objective complete.

Jamji opened her eyes.

Her chair was returning to an upright position. The test runner's distorted voice came over the intercom. "Well done, Telson. Would you care to take a break before we go over your scores?"

"Yes, sir, I would. Five minutes in the sparring chamber — you and me." She glared up at the mirrored window overlooking the dim construct immersion room.

"That's five points," said the test runner flatly.

Jamji gritted her teeth, holding her lips tight so nothing else regrettable would come out. She knew she shouldn't have released the hormone inhibitors yet.

"In your favor," continued the voice over the intercom.

Jamji blinked at the mirrored glass. "What?"

"I'm awarding you five points for suggesting you want to fight me. You're not *supposed* to like me. At least, not for the career track you're being considered for. Almost everyone who completes all their objectives in The Nightmare Gauntlet is hostile to their test runner. That's why I prefer to remain anonymous."

"Well, in that case..." Jamji gave the mirrored glass a double-bird salute. "Let the record show that I consider you to be an asshole."

The test runner chuckled. "Duly noted. I'm sorry I had to put you through that, Jamji."

As much as she hated the test runner, a small part of her respected the person. It'd be a tough job for anyone but a true psychopath.

Well, psychopaths needed jobs, too.

Yeah, they were definitely a psychopath. Hey, at least they were making good use of their abnormality.

Something the test runner had said suddenly registered. "Sir, what was that about the career track I'm being considered for?"

"You didn't know? We've tagged you as a prime candidate for the officer track. And your scores on the Nightmare Gauntlet are certainly in your favor."

Jamji's lip trembled. Tears were welling in her eyes. She took a breath. "May I have a moment, sir?"

"Of course."

Jamji hid her face as she wiped her eyes, then returned her chair to the reclining position. She slipped into slate-space.

She spent the next three minutes in a private construct — the Telson cabin. As she paced between the sand circle and the Zen rock garden, Jamji let her emotions pour out in a combined ugly-cry and overjoyed freak-out.

Maybe it wasn't like this for everyone, but when Jamji fiddled with her neurochemistry, there was always a backlash. It was as if all the emotions that she had bottled up spilled out at once.

Once she caught her breath and dried her face off, Jamji reached out to Zeta with a conversation request. This would be the first time they talked since being separated for testing. After a full minute, Zeta accepted.

Zeta looked around at Jamji's choice of venue. She smiled, but it looked forced. "How's your test going?"

"Rough. Hey, I heard they didn't accept you. I'm so sorry, Zeta." Jamji stepped towards Zeta, putting a hand on her shoulder.

Zeta shrugged her off. "It's not your fault. You believed in me. You just didn't think that... maybe other people might not."

Jamji sighed, shaking her head. "I don't get it. Someone said they shot you with a blood-bullet?"

Zeta paused, her mood darkening. "Seems like the gossip is spreading fast. I'm sure I'm the punchline of every Guardian joke today."

"No! It's not like that! They told me about it, but not because they're talking about you. They were just trying to get into my head."

Zeta furrowed her brow, confused.

Jamji shook it off. "Part of a test I'd rather not talk about."

The five-minute timer she had set for herself went off.

"I have to go now. I'm sorry," Jamji said, knowing that she was apologizing for more than just Zeta's rejection or the too-brief visit. She rushed forward and squeezed her little sis-kin in a hug. "I'm so sorry. Wait for me at our old camp outside the embassy. This was my last test. I'll come out and see you tonight."

Zeta's return hug was half-hearted. "Yeah, that's where I am already — back at camp. Alasie's here, too. I'll see you later. Good luck."

Zeta disappeared in Jamji's arms.

"Wait, who's Alasie?" Jamji asked the empty construct.

She shrugged at herself, rubbed her face vigorously, took a deep breath, and returned to her body. Next, she would get her final scores, receive her acceptance certification, and pledge her allegiance to the Guard.

4

GAME INVITE

"WE ONLY HAD *ten* NPC interactions yesterday that reached the AI engagement threshold," Pip-Tau grumbled. "Pawn to queen's rook four."

"I know! People only want to talk to people. They don't consider the NPCs to be worth their time. People are the worst!" Pip-Rho whined.

Their private gameworld control sub-construct was an endless plane of black-and-white checkered tiles. They called it The Chess Room. The sky overhead was currently a deep blue — transitioning from day into night as the sun dipped into the distant horizon in one direction and a crescent moon rose in the other direction. The Chess Room's day/night cycles mirrored Interra's. Dawn and twilight were their collaborative hours, as the queen on duty transitioned from one of them to the other.

The negative-image black and white twin cherubs sat on over-stuffed leather chairs that matched their colors. Pip-Rho idly flipped through player metadata visualizations, scanning the conversation logs for anything interesting. She could play chess in her sleep, but Pip-Tau had to think for a while before she moved.

"So, what do we do about it?" Pip-Tau asked. "I mean, if the game's objective is to get Cain to show us *The Way*, how's that gonna happen if players won't even talk to NPCs?" She reached for her knight.

"Wait!" Pip-Rho yelped. "Don't touch that knight. Do you see it?"

"See what?"

"Forced mate in five!"

"What? You didn't check me, how could it be—"

"No, I mean *you* could checkmate *me* in five moves. I didn't notice 'til it was too late. Darn! Game's yours if you make the right move."

Pip-Tau squinted down at the board. What was she talking about? Pip-Rho loved to play mind games like this. Sometimes she'd deliberately sacrifice pieces just to make the game more challenging.

Show-off.

Pip-Rho said, "Anyway, as for the players not interacting with NPCs, there's an easy solution. Pause the chess game. Interra time!"

The meta-construct was replaced with Castle Interra's courtyard, brimming with busy little Interrans.

Every player character within the courtyard glowed slightly, lit by the aura traditional to gameworlds. Names hovered above characters' heads, in fonts and colors denoting their class, race, and level. The NPCs moving about in the surrounding marketplace conspicuously lacked auras. They had gray names, unless they were a quest-giver or otherwise important figure.

As they watched, one player named "Sedductrixxx" was working on either seducing or picking the pocket of one of the castle guard NPCs. Probably both. She ran her finger along the chest plate of the guard's dark steel armor.

"Come on, big boy, you can take five minutes away from your post for a little fun," she moaned. The woman's skimpy leather outfit and ample cleavage failed to catch the guard's eye.

The guard twitched, shook his head, then looked up at the

woman's name. "See-duck-tricks-s-s? That's the strangest character name I've ever seen. How do you pronounce that? And what's with the spelling?"

"It's like 'seductress', but with double d's and a triple x, baby." The player paused, then stepped back. "Alright, hold on, that's definitely *not* NPC dialog. But you don't have an aura. What gives?"

The guard laughed, "Neither do you, sexy-duck-tricks."

The woman scowled, then looked down at her body. Indeed, her aura had winked out. The absurd name also disappeared from over her head.

Pip-Tau had been amused by the interaction, knowing that Pip-Rho was possessing the NPC and toying with the player. But now she was getting nervous. "Rho, what do you think you're doing?"

In a blink, every player aura within sight was extinguished, along with the names of NPCs and players alike. A hush went over the courtyard as the players simultaneously looked around, then looked down at their characters' bodies. Expressions of confusion, amusement, exasperation, and anger swept over the crowd. A few of them disappeared.

"There! Problem solved," Pip-Rho said, cracking her knuckles.

Pip-Tau did a backflip. "Oh-my-god, *what?!* Getting rid of player auras? And names?! You can't do that!"

"Uh, yeah, actually I can. See?" Pip-Rho gestured to the confusion below.

Angry messages and bug reports began piling into their GM message queue.

This was a disaster!

Pip-Tau pleaded, "Rho, we can't hang onto our players with you pushing out massive, heavy-handed, sweeping changes like that! We didn't even talk about it!"

"We *did*, before the project was picked up by your *boyfriend*, Veer. It's what we should have done from day one, but you thought we'd get more players if we followed traditional gameworld conventions. You see where that's got us — players like sexy-duck-tricks trying to screw our NPCs instead of engaging in realistic, meaningful interactions that catch Cain's attention."

Pip-Tau clutched her clone-sis by the arm. "At least do an A/B test! See what it does to satisfaction metrics?"

Pip-Rho shook her off. "An A/B test? What, like make two instances? Or have some people see auras and other people don't? That's worse than an all-or-nothing change. At least this way it's fair."

Pip-Tau took one more look at the courtyard, shook her head, and returned to The Chess Room.

Pip-Tau's tiny wings fluttered in agitation as she float-paced back and forth. Pip-Rho was always doing drastic crap like this. How many more "executive decisions" was she going to make behind Pip-Tau's back? She put her pudgy fists on her hips. "I'm turning it back on. We'll say Cain misunderstood a GM directive. Do you see these messages? This is going over like a turd in the punch bowl!"

Pip-Rho laughed, "We don't want people drinking that punch, anyway! Sometimes you need a turd!"

Pip-Tau tried hard to stifle a grin. "First of all, eww. Second of all, what are you trying to do? Drive off the players? You want to have a gameworld populated by nothing but NPCs? Cuz that's what you're about to get."

"The people who want a *real* role-playing experience are gonna *love it* that they can't tell players from NPCs. They'll do their best character work now. Sell it as a feature, Tau. The people that just want to bang their swords together can go play with themselves somewhere else."

Pip-Tau reluctantly began composing a message to the players to explain their justification for removing player auras. Sure, some people would quit the game over it, but they had more than enough people on the waiting list who had either signed up at the convention, or submitted their requests after word of mouth began to spread.

Noddites were the only players allowed to join the beta test, since it was running on their faction's server, but soon they'd open the floodgates for the other factions. The Proliferan in-system population had an insatiable appetite for gameworlds, though keeping their masses of fickle players happy would be even harder than satiating the Noddites.

All people ever wanted was more of the same. New content was only welcome if it followed the conventions of the old content.

What they needed, Pip-Tau thought, were players without preconceived notions as to what a fantasy role-playing game was supposed to be.

"We need newbies!" she proclaimed.

"Sure." Pip-Rho gestured to the half-written announcement. "Now, focus, sis-clone."

Pip-Tau closed the announcement draft. "Seriously! I want inexperienced players. Lots of them! Fresh blood!"

Pip-Rho reopened the announcement and took over composing it. "Newbies are a *burden*. They're a pain and a drain. Besides, we've got a limited pool here, Tau. Everyone's played a fantasy gameworld at some point. Where are we going to get unexperienced players? Get the bootstrappers to sign up their betas?"

Pip-Tau pointed at Pip-Rho and widened her solid black eyes until they were comically large. "You're a dag-gum genius, Rho!"

Pip-Rho paused, shrugged, then smiled. "I can't argue with that. And now that I've heard myself say it, I actually *really* love that idea. And here comes another one. You heard about Zeta-sis, right?"

"Yeah, I feel sorry for her, but I'm kinda glad it didn't work out. The Guard would've stuck her with a shit job, anyway."

"So, let's catch her on the rebound and put her to good use in Interra. She needs Interra more than it needs her, really — lil sis needs a new purpose. We'll include her in the unblinded, pseudo-confederate group so that she knows how important the project is. Then we use her as bait to convert the other Telsons into Interrans!"

Pip-Rho's black cherub avatar sprouted horns and a tail, then did a little devil dance.

Pip-Tau slapped her forehead. As usual, Rho was three steps ahead of her. "Dag-gum genius!"

Sunlight beamed through tall windows on one side of the central throne room of Castle Interra. Braziers lined the room, filling it with the smell of burning oil. An audience of four approached the two queens. A dozen heralds played their horns, announcing the honored guests.

Much like their booth at the convention, a thick red cloth formed a path through the center of the room. The same two high-backed thrones sat on the elevated platform. The Night Queen's throne was topped with the Greek Rho symbol set against a crescent moon mosaic pattern. The Day Queen's throne was similarly decorated with the Tau symbol and a gold-painted sunburst design.

Guards stood like statues beside the thrones. A retinue of NPC heralds, flag-bearers, and servants waited obediently at their posts.

As the heralds finished their *heralding* and the echoes of their horns faded, the first of the guests stepped forward. He wore the grubby attire of a male serf.

The serf spoke with a cockney accent. "Wha' an honor, gettin' a personal audience wit' da two queens of Interra." He bowed, then smiled, revealing a mouth half-filled with rotten teeth. XT-Prime was such a good sport.

"Maybe take the realism down a notch, XT-bro," Queen Rho chuckled. "This is medieval fantasy, not a historical recreation."

XT-Prime's serf closed his lips, then smiled again, showing a full set of yellowed, moderately crooked teeth.

"Better," Queen Rho said.

"Thank you all for accepting our invitation," Queen Tau said.

"To get right to the point, we brought you here to convince you to join the Interra Project."

Oraxis stepped forward, looking just as Oraxisy as ever. Genevieve and Carff had also appeared as their normal selves. He said, "I appreciate the invite, *your majesties*, and I'm always impressed with what you're able to create, but as we told you at the conference, we can't commit to signing up for your game."

Genevieve stepped to Oraxis's side. "You know we'd love to join you, but Zeta *really* needs us right now. She was in a bad place when she told us about her experience with the Guardian intake officer. We're preparing to take Zephyr south to meet up with her at Syn-Cen and bring her back to the cabin."

"Your majesties," XT-Prime said, going to his knees and dropping the accent, "I ask your forgiveness, but I, too, must regrettably decline your generous offer to join this masterfully crafted gameworld. To be blunt, an Astrus's entertainment interests seldom include the antiquated fantasy genres of Earth, and I am no exception."

Carff said, "I'd also get on my knees to beg your forgiveness, but I'd never get back up again. Ha! But seriously, I'm a working man. No time for games, ladies. Too addictive!"

"Stand up, XT," Queen Rho sighed. "And don't be so quick to decline when you don't even know what the game is for — its secret purpose."

XT-Prime's peasant stood, putting on a serene expression of infinite patience. "I'm listening."

Oraxis chuckled, "I had the feeling there was more to it than what you showed at the conference — so much hype. Vague notions of an ambitious project with boundless potential, yada yada. Sounded like vaporware to old Earthlings like us who've spent a lifetime learning how to dodge targeted marketing and duck consumer surveys. You can fool a Noddite with that stuff, but not—"

"Such impudence!" Queen Rho barked in a supernatural multivoice. Her exclamation echoed throughout the chamber. She was sitting erect in her throne, straight-backed, her pale blue eyes bugging.

"Really?" Oraxis laughed, crossing his arms.

"Nah, just playin'," Rho laughed. She flopped back, kicking her ebony leg out of her robes and draping it over the arm of the throne. "You're right — to any science-minded person, an experiment without a clearly defined hypothesis is a farce. We *do* have a hypothesis, but we can't share it with the participants without affecting the outcome. Most people won't find out about it until the experiment comes to a close and we give the mass debriefing."

"But," Queen Tau interjected, index finger in the air, "we have designs for a small subset of selected subjects who'll join with full knowledge of the hypothesis. Sort of like experimental confederates, but not. It's just another test group, really, but the trustworthiness of the pseudo-confederates is *crucial*."

Queen Rho pulled her leg off the throne's arm and leaned forward, conspiratorially. "What we're about to share with you is the *true* nature of the Interra Project. Only The Council of Ten and our top-tier game moderators know this. Some of our more savvy players have guessed at it, but we've dismissed the notions and squashed the rumors. It's privileged information, not to be shared with anyone!"

"Any information shared with me is, by nature, shared with my hive," XT-Prime said warily. "They are a part of me. And I, a part of them. Though the Astri keep their secrets from the other factions, there are no secrets between Astri."

Queen Rho waved her hand dismissively. "Yes, that's fine. We'll be inviting the Guardians and Proliferans soon enough, with full disclosure to their leadership. Just don't tell anyone *else*."

"You secret is safe with the one hundred-fifty thousand Astri of the Genesis Hive."

Pip-Tau knew, as absurd as that sounded, that XT-Prime's promise would be kept. The Astri were notoriously tight-lipped. She was more worried about Carff blabbing than anyone. She clapped her queenly hands once. "Excellent! Now, let us begin!"

The heralds raised their horns and played a little tune. Queen Rho rolled her eyes. Pip-Tau loved it. If you want to feel like you've just said something important, try following it up with some horn fanfare. You won't be disappointed.

ONCE THE HORNS finished proclaiming her awesomeness, Queen Tau said, "We'll start with a quick tour of Interra, then we'll share the Interra Project Charter."

"The charter's a lot cooler than it sounds," Queen Rho said.

Genevieve was stepping forward. "Pip-Tau, Pip-Rho." She seemed exasperated as she started climbing the stairs of their throne platform. "I appreciate that what you're doing here is very important. Veer Gladstone wouldn't have sponsored your project if it wasn't. You've got the attention of the entire faction. The entire system, even. Normally, Oraxis and I would've signed up to help you out in a heartbeat. You have our love and our support. We're so proud of you!"

She was standing on their platform now, looking from one of them to the other. Her hands and arms were open towards them in a gesture of patience, love, apology, and authority. Between the three of them, Pip-Tau knew who the real queen was, and she couldn't help but cast her eyes down.

Genevieve continued, growing heated. "But we told you what our priority is and what our plans are, and you don't seem to have listened. If you still want to show us this privileged information, that's fine. And if you want our feedback, we'll give it. You have our undivided attention for the next few hours. But don't get your hopes up that anything you show us about your project or your hypothesis can change our minds. I'm sorry to get upset but... I just expected more understanding from you two. You have enough empathy to see that Zeta needs us right now more than you do."

The mood of the throne room deflated as the echoes of

Genevieve's lecture finished resounding in the stone hall. An NPC flag-bearer cleared his throat in the silence.

"I told you this was a bad idea," Pip-Tau sent Pip-Rho.

"Time to play the trump card," Pip-Rho replied.

"Yeah. I was saving it for the grand finale, but here it goes."

Queen Tau straightened in her throne, meeting Genevieve's gaze, trying to be stately. "We agree that Zeta is in need. That's half the reason we've invited you here. You may recall that her desire to join the Guard Faction was based upon her impatience with Genesis Faction's complete avoidance of the Specter problem. You may also recall that her plans, before deciding to join the Guard Faction, involved studying the Specters under me and Pip-Rho's guidance."

"Oh, yes," Oraxis chuckled sardonically, "we remember Jamji sneaking her away and you two filling her head with more information than she was prepared to handle, getting her all hyped up on fighting Specters."

Queen Rho raised her onyx-tipped silver scepter towards Oraxis threateningly. "Maybe the topic of withholding information is best left untouched, O-pa."

Although Oraxis and Genevieve had voiced regrets over their controlling beta bootstrapping approach, they didn't seem ready to abandon their old ways, even considering the crisis they'd caused. Zeta's retreat into a self-constructed fantasy wasn't *entirely* their fault — Jamji's stone-cold delivery of the fact that Zeta's tribe had long-since died had been worse than a slap in the face or a snap of an elbow.

The heated conversation wasn't going how Pip-Tau planned. She mindspoke to Pip-Rho, *"This is FUBAR. I'm throwing all the cards on the table."*

Queen Rho smiled over at her as Pip-Rho mindspoke, *"Bombs away!"*

Queen Tau stood. She raised her golden scepter topped by a pearlescent white opal and levitated Genevieve from the throne platform back to Oraxis's side. She took a deep breath and let the words spill out. "The Interra Gameworld Project is an experimental application of the Prisoner Lex hypothesis which will attempt to tap into the suppressed cognitive powers of Cain's Synthetic Intelligence, bypassing the Intelligence Governor restrictions against providing direct solutions to humanity's problems by presenting an indirect proxy for the SI's latent subconscious to express its ideas metaphorically, with the ultimate goal of discovering a solution to the Specter problem."

XT-Prime's peasant's eyes widened slightly as he took half a step forward. "Oh? Metaphoric obfuscation to circumvent the IG?"

"Yes, indeed!" Queen Rho sang in delight.

Oraxis took a breath for his inevitable lecture on the pseudo-scientific beliefs of "Lexites" just as Queen Rho's scepter radiated a purple glow. Pip-Tau could see from her privileged gamemistress overlay that Rho had cast a silence spell on him, forcing his mouth shut. "Just let her finish, O-pa!" Queen Rho barked.

Queen Tau winced as she continued her gushing. "The theories supporting the plausibility of our hypothesis go as far back as the works of Alexander Kant and Magna Lepitude. The other factions have schools dedicated to studying the IG problem, and some of their Prisoner Lex metaphoric interface experiments have produced positive results. If nothing else, we should come away from the experiment with some new ideas to try out. Some of the most important experiments are the failed ones, right?"

XT-Prime's peasant was nodding knowingly. Oraxis stood with crossed arms, a vein bulging in his temple — the O-pa barometer. By the look of the barometer, a storm was brewing. Carff was scratching his chin, trying to act like he knew what she was talking about. Synthetic Intelligence theory wasn't exactly his area of expertise. Genevieve was clearly waiting for her to get to the point: what did any of this have to do with Zeta?

Okay, Gen-ma, here it comes.

Queen Tau said, "While the concepts behind the project's hypothesis are deeper than Zeta may appreciate, the prospect of solving the Specter problem — the problem closest to her heart — will give her the immediate satisfaction of taking action rather than wallowing in self-pity at the Telson cabin with Gen-ma and O-pa, licking her wounds. Zeta is a woman of *action*, and Interra is exactly what she needs! We've already sent her an invite, telling her it was a way to fight the Specters, and she's already accepted."

Genevieve exclaimed, "Pip-Tau!" before Queen Rho cast a silence spell on her, too.

Queen Tau squeezed her deep brown eyes shut. She just had to get it all out! "As a new beta, Zeta's uniquely qualified to play an important role in the project! She wouldn't come to Interra with preconceived notions of how gameworlds function or what types of real-world solutions might be represented metaphorically in the gameworld!

"She's on her way to Syn-Cen to see her orb. When she gets here, she'll be staying in my dorm room, plugged in as a full-time Interran. When we talked to her about it, we could tell the idea brightened her mood. Interra's gonna be more than a distraction for Zeta. It's a *purpose* — a reason for her to get up in the morning. Gen-ma, you realize how important that is. That's the first thing you taught every one of us.

"So, if you want to help Zeta, you'll join her in Interra and support her. Your enthusiastic participation will reinforce the notion that what she's doing is important."

Queen Rho added, "Which means *not* crapping all over the Lexites in front of her. I'm looking at you, O-pa."

Queen Tau sighed and shrugged. "Sorry, Gen-ma, O-pa, we would've talked to you about it first, but we knew what you'd say. I mean, Zeta can decide for herself if this is what she wants to do. You can try to convince her that sitting around at your cabin would be a better idea than joining Interra, but I think you can guess how that'd go. So, can we count on you to join us in Interra?"

Queen Rho waved her scepter, releasing the silence spell. Tau braced herself for the backlash, but Carff spoke first.

"You can count on me!" he said, nodding. "The elds are always saying I should get more Noddite culture, and it sounds like there's more to this game than just playing around!"

XT-Prime said, "The Astri would like for me to join your game, as well. It is a provocative experiment which we are excited to be a part of. If you can make more openings for Astrus participants, we will happily fill them. We do have more questions, of course. As well as some ideas which you may not have considered. And," he leaned his head in a humble gesture, "one request."

"Data sharing?" Queen Rho asked.

"Correct."

"Done. You'll get the keys to the castle."

"Hey!" Pip-Tau shot to Pip-Rho. *"We need to talk about it before—"*

"Look, Tau, they're scientists. We'll benefit from their analysis. They're not getting control of the experiment; just read-only data. The Council can negotiate the terms and have 'em sign an NDA or whatever. It's fine."

"Fine."

The hall fell uncomfortably silent as they awaited Oraxis and Genevieve's response. The two were probably having a private conversation.

After a few more seconds, Oraxis threw his hands in the air as he tossed his head back in the most exaggerated eye roll in history.

Genevieve sighed, "Yes, we'll join you in Interra. You've tied our hands. Let's generate our characters."

Oraxis chuckled joylessly. He was pacing the carpet, shaking his head. "Nothing gets me in the mood to play a game more than being manipulated into it."

"Forced, even," Genevieve added.

Oraxis gave the queens a wide, sarcastic smile. "Yep! Okay, you win. Let's get this over with."

"*Yay?*" Pip-Tau sent Pip-Rho.

"*They'll change their tune when they see how much Interra helps Zeta.*"

"*This isn't how it was supposed to go.*"

"*It's a win. Take it.*"

"*Fine.*" Pip-Tau cued the heralds again. They raised their horns and sounded a fanfare, but the music rang hollow in Pip-Tau's ears.

5

BETA PILGRIMAGE

THE WHALE SURFACED, puffing a cloud of spray into the air. Salty mist drifted over the boat, moistening the skin of the passengers and their pooches. The enormous beast needed to take a breath every few minutes as it labored to pull the ferry through The Great Ocean. That seemed suffocating to Zeta, but the captain said the whale could've held its breath for over an hour if it wasn't doing so much work.

Ropes held in the whale's mouth were tied to the front of the boat, which was made from cut logs lashed together and sealed with some sort of putty or clay. The knee-high walls kept most of the waves from splashing the passengers. Most, but not all.

Zeta shielded her face from the billowing mist with her hands, cursing the whale. She was cold, wet, and miserable. Any time she licked her lips, she tasted salt. Her stomach churned as they rode the undulating waves, but her double-mind overrode her urge to vomit. At least the ride was almost over, according to Captain Ahab. Jamji had chuckled at his name. Zeta didn't get the joke, but didn't ask for an explanation — she didn't care.

Jamji sat on her knees in front of Zeta and Alasie, gushing on about how masterfully she had done on her entrance exams. She had faced off with men twice her size in a variety of martial arts sparring styles, and had won most of her matches. She had solved a dozen complex math problems in twenty seconds, proving her ability to think at superhuman speeds and use her double-mind to its fullest potential.

If Alasie would stop asking her questions, Jamji might run out of things to brag about.

Alasie asked, "So, the base on the other side of Soma — Soma Station? That's like... the main, um, Guard Faction base?"

Jamji laughed, "Not by a long shot. It's the base of operations in Surya, yes, but it's a backwoods outpost compared to the hundreds of massive city-bases on the Guard Faction's home planet, Ares."

"Ares? So, um, is that another... star system?"

"Oh, wow," Jamji scoffed. "Just ask WoQS this stuff, kid. It would take the rest of the trip to explain it all to you. Longer than that, really."

Zeta suppressed the powerful urge to lash out at Jamji. Had Jamji gotten *incredibly* rude recently, or was she being too sensitive?

"I'll ask later," Alasie said, unperturbed. "You were saying? About your orb?"

"Just that I'll be taking a separate shuttle from my orb. You *never* want to be in the same place as your orb, unless it's in a meteor-proof bunker under kilometers of rock. Orbs are tough, sure, but a Specter strike can damage or destroy them. Which would suck pretty bad, since all your replays and constructs would be lost. But they can always make you a new orb as long as your brain is intact."

"What about your dog's data? Would they be able to... to put that on... I mean, in your orb again? If they had to make you a new one?" Alasie looked down at Pinga, sleeping by her side, whose fur she had been running her fingers through.

Jamji gave a subtle eye roll. "Of course. The point is, the way Genesis set up the orb access systems at Syn-Cen is that the only person allowed to interact with your orb is *you*. Nobody else can even be in the room with you. Even if I told Cain to release my orb to the Guardians, he wouldn't do it. So, first I grab my orb, then I hand it over to an officer that'll be waiting for me at the Syn-Cen Guard Offices. After that, I'll ship out to Soma station on the next shuttle. The Guard'll hold my orb for me 'til I've arrived safely, then send it on up."

"You're not visiting Pip-Tau?" Zeta asked. "When I talked to her yesterday, she seemed excited to see us both in person."

Jamji opened her mouth to speak, then paused and pressed her lips together. It may have been the first time she was silent on the entire boat ride. Finally, she said, "I mean, I see her all the time in constructs…"

"It's not the same, and you know it, *Jamji*," Zeta snapped.

Jamji paused again. "Yeah, I'll see her. I can stop by her dorm after I go get my orb. I'm trying to run a tight schedule, but you're right — I should say goodbye."

Zeta held back another outburst. Jamji thought she was *so* important now that they accepted her into the Guard. It was disgusting.

Ahab's whale spewed a plume of mist into the air as Jamji changed the subject back to herself and started talking again. A week ago, Zeta would've said Jamji was her closest friend. But now she was glad that she wouldn't have to share the planet with her anymore. Zeta put her face into the crook of her arm, hiding from the drizzle of mist.

Hate filled her heart.

Hate for Jamji. For herself. For the damn whale and the rocking boat. For Alasie's patience with being treated like a child. For the Guard, the Specters. She couldn't wait for the trip to be over.

The ocean below them was deep and wide, beyond imagination. She had learned about it from WoQS as she and Alasie waited for Jamji to emerge from the Guardian embassy and join them at Ferryman's Port. Its depths were cold and crushing.

That was one way she could skip the trip and arrive at Syn-Cen — give herself to the ocean. They say it takes around six months to resurrect you. After your beta bootstrapping, all your subsequent resurrections end with you waking up at Syn-Cen. Getting your brain working right happens in the last week. People say they can't remember much about the experience. It was like waking up from a dream and forgetting what it was about.

Immortality was a peculiar thing. The value of life, the fear of death — it all changed. She should fear the ocean below her. She knew what it felt like to drown, and it was terrifying beyond description. Yet she had replayed the experience three times since her rejection by the Guard. What had drawn her to it? Maybe remembering that the Guard's rejection wasn't the worst thing that'd ever happened to her was reassuring, somehow. Maybe she wanted to prove to herself that she was tough, and that they were wrong to reject her so hastily.

Zeta lifted her head and looked out at the horizon. Water, as far as the eye can see.

Such immensity, such depth. She could imagine the lapping waves whispering to her, *"Take a dip, Zeta. Take in a breath of death."*

Incoming conversation request from Alasie Herrington.

Zeta glanced over at Alasie, who appeared to be listening intently to whatever Jamji was saying.

She accepted the request. *"What do you want?"* she sent, then immediately regretted her harshness.

Alasie asked, *"Hey, um, you're not paying attention to Jamji right now, are you?"*

"No, sorry, my mind sort of wandered off."

"Well, she's saying all sorts of bad stuff about the Genesis Faction. I'm sure some of it is true, but the other passengers are getting upset. I saw a woman hold back a man who was about to come over and say something to her. Should we get her to stop?"

Zeta looked over at Alasie. *"She doesn't care who she offends. I used to think that was admirable..."*

"Then maybe I shouldn't worry if she's offended by me ignoring her for a while. She does have a lot of interesting things to say, but it's hard to focus when... Zeta, have you ever seen Surya's setting look so beautiful?"

Zeta squinted as she looked at Surya. The glowing ball was dipping behind the horizon. It looked like it was sliding into the ocean, dissolving into rippling ribbons of red and orange. It was a breathtaking display, like nothing Zeta had ever seen.

"I can't believe I didn't even notice it," Zeta sent. *"Thank you for sharing it with me."*

They smiled at each other before closing the conversation channel.

"Hey, Jamji," Zeta said.

Jamji smirked. "Yeah, I know what you're thinking, but I probably won't find out for at least a year which division—"

"No," Zeta interrupted, "actually, you have no idea what I'm thinking. I was going to ask you — what does Surya's setting look like from Soma Station?"

Jamji raised an eyebrow. "The station's underground, so we can't see Surya unless we take a trip to the surface, like for maintenance work or drills. And then if we were to watch Surya set, which only happens once a month since Soma is tidally locked to Genesis, it would be pretty boring. There'd be no atmospheric effects, so Surya would just look like a bright white ball that would slowly sink into the horizon. Inside the station, the day/night cycles are synchronized with—"

"Then stop talking for a while and enjoy this one. You won't be seeing anything like it for a long time." Zeta pointed at Surya's beautiful display.

Jamji turned to glance over her shoulder. She paused for a moment, looked back at Zeta, then at Alasie. She looked upset, which pleased Zeta. Jamji stood, walked over to her sleeping monster — Pepper-pooch — and crawled onto his back. At first she laid back with her eyes closed. So prideful. So stubborn. But after a minute, she snuck a peek at Surya. Zeta knew she couldn't resist.

Some of the other passengers gave her looks of gratitude for shutting Jamji up. She pretended not to see them as she watched Surya disappear into the Great Ocean. Alasie rested her head on Zeta's shoulder, and Zeta leaned her head against Alasie's.

It was... nice.

"FLOATON, HO!" Captain Ahab bellowed. "Time to wake up and smell the seaweed, ye landlubbers!"

Zeta's eyes popped open as she awoke with a start, pulling herself free of her placental mat and trying to stand. The rocking boat quickly sent her back onto her bottom. She got up on her knees and looked at the blue horizon ahead of them, seeing nothing. She focused her eyes, switching to enhanced vision, and scanned the horizon again. There it was — a hazy green mass.

Within an hour, Jacob's Ladder Station was stretching out before them like a wide, green, low-topped hill in the water. Hundreds of boats were attached to it or floating nearby. Every few seconds, a whale's plume spouted somewhere around the island. The whale pulling their boat had let go of the rope and disappeared, but they were still moving, even faster than before. Zeta looked around for what was making them move, then spotted the creatures — WoQS identified them as porpoises — pushing their boat from behind. They made squeaking and clicking sounds and were wearing some sort of helmet or face mask. The porpoises guided them to an empty spot on the island's shore.

Men and women with much darker skin than hers walked about, tying up boats or carrying supplies. Their attire was sparse, which suited the warm climate.

Zeta scanned the air above the island to see if she could spot Jacob's Ladder. Using enhanced vision and broadening her visible spectrum, she still couldn't detect the invisible cable. Eventually, a ghostly form caught her eye — the outline of an oblong shape dropping from between the clouds. That had to be the climber. It was like looking at Jamji when she was invisible — only edges and motion betrayed its presence. It slowed as it reached the island, then descended out of view.

Jamji stood behind her and said, "It's camouflaged as a floating island made of—"

"Seaweed," Zeta said, cutting her off. "Yeah, I heard. And they call it a *floaton*, not a *floating island*."

Jamji breathed out, then walked to the back of the boat to tend to Pepper-pooch.

Alasie opened a channel with her, sending, *"You should try not to part on bad terms. I know Jamji's a—"*

"Gravan-cursed slime-sucker?" Zeta sent.

Alasie huffed. *"She's something, but she's your kin, and you won't see her again for a long time. We don't have much family in this world. Appreciate the people you've got, ya know?"*

Zeta couldn't stomach the advice, but there was no point in fighting about it. She sent, *"I'll try."*

Their boat bumped against the shoreline of dry, tangled seaweed. It smelled awful, and sea birds were squawking everywhere. A man wearing nothing but a loin cloth and a necklace of jagged teeth put a foot on the side of the ship and offered his hand. His shaved face was painted with small white dots going down both sides. The crown of his bare head was also painted white.

The man helped her climb onto the platform, which was soft and squishy — kind of gross. Penelope-pooch followed, leaping onto the seaweed.

The man smiled at Penelope-pooch, then at her. "Welcome to Jacob's Ladder Station. What is your name?"

"Zeta Telson. I am on my Beta... Pilgrimage..." She gagged on the Common tongue as it tumbled from her mouth, silently cursing herself for not practicing more.

Incoming conversation request from Boboa Byrma.

She accepted. The man before her spoke in her mind, *"My apologies. I know it's hard to speak in Common at first. We can mindspeak, if you prefer."*

"Yes, thank you." Zeta sent as she watched a woman help Alasie and her pooch, Pinga, out of the boat. She tried not to stare, but the woman was bare-breasted! Alasie caught Zeta's eye with a shocked expression, though this wasn't Alasie's first trip to the station.

Boboa sent, *"Again, welcome to Jacob's Ladder Station. Walk with me, please."* He started walking away from the boat, guiding her with a hand on the back of her arm. *"I am Boboa, and I will be your escort. You say you are a Telson? Are you kin to the Pips?"*

"Pip-Rho and Pip-Tau? Yeah, do you know them?"

Boboa laughed, exposing white teeth. *"I know of them, but they wouldn't know me. Maybe you haven't heard, but your sis-kins are famous."*

"I guess that makes sense after what happened to Pip-Rho."

"You'll get sick of talking about them with strangers soon enough, so let's talk about you. I'm curious — was Zeta your given name as an alpha?"

"Yes," Zeta answered, uncertainly.

Boboa laughed again, then sent, *"That's so funny! Cultural contamination, or phonetic overlap coincidence?"*

Zeta sent, *"I'm sorry. I don't know what you mean by either of those things."*

Boboa smiled widely. *"No worries, Zeta-Beta. It will be even more funny when you can introduce yourself as Zeta-Zeta. But I hope you won't rush to get to that name."* He paused and looked back at the other passengers. *"Where is your bootstrapper?"*

"They didn't come with me. It's a long story. I'm here with my sis-kin, Jamji. She's the blue woman with the monster-pooch." Zeta pointed at Jamji, who now stood alone on the boat, aside from Captain Ahab. She leaned against Pepper-pooch and drummed her

fingers. *"My friend Alasie also came along to keep me company."* She gestured towards Alasie and her bare-breasted guide, not far away.

Boboa was still looking at Jamji. *"Your sis-kin has some serious bio-mods. She's a Genesisian?"*

A man beside their boat called out, "All clear! You can disembark now, Jamji."

Jamji took a running leap, crossing from the back of the boat to the shore, followed by Pepper-pooch. The front of the boat lurched down with the force of his jump, then lifted into the air and crashed back down again. This sent Captain Ahab tumbling onto the deck with an "oof!" Those watching on the shore burst into laughter. Jamji pushed through the crowd, ignoring everyone — including Zeta.

"No," Zeta sent, answering Boboa's earlier question. *"She's not one of us anymore. She's a Guardian now."*

BOBOA LED her to a wall of seaweed. He pulled the dangling seaweed aside to reveal a shadowy entrance. Zeta ducked inside. It was like stepping into a different world! The tunnel before her was made of a smooth, hard, white material. A glowing band along the ceiling gave off warm, diffuse illumination. All she had seen of Jacob's Ladder Station was one tunnel, but she was already impressed at how clean and beautiful the place was.

She was led down the round tunnel, which merged with a larger corridor. Next, they emerged into a spacious chamber where people were passing through or talking in groups.

Other passages led off from the chamber, with markings above them which Zeta recognized as words. She used her text-to-speech double-mind utility to read them, hearing the words in the voice of WoQS. The passage which Boboa was leading her to was labeled "Sanitation and Outfitting". Zeta had WoQS define the terms, then guessed that she was about to be cleaned and dressed.

Alasie and her escort had been following Zeta and Boboa. The four stopped outside the sanitation and outfitting corridor.

Alasie's escort met Zeta's eye.

Group conversation request from Maggie Vosch.

Zeta accepted.

"*Zeta, meet Maggie,*" came Alasie's voice.

"*Hi, Maggie,*" Zeta sent, "*and, Alasie, this is Boboa.*"

Boboa sent, "*Maggie, this is Zeta's Beta Pilgrimage. She came with her sis-kin, but I don't see the blue lady anywhere nearby. Zeta, do you know where she is? Should we wait for her?*"

Zeta shrugged. "*No, let's go on without her. She can't come with me to see my orb, anyway.*"

"*Okay, Maggie will help you two with your showers and escort you down. I'm heading back to the docks. Should I call a beastmaster to board your dogs, or will they be going down with you?*"

"*Oh, Pinga has to stay with me,*" Alasie sent.

Zeta nodded. "*Yeah, and I need to introduce Penelope-pooch to Pip-Tau.*"

Maggie sighed and looked down at the pooches. "*Dog showers it is, then!*"

Boboa gave one more gleaming smile, sending, "*It was good to meet you, Zeta Telson and Alasie Herrington.*"

He left the conversation and returned the way he came, waving at a few people walking by, wearing white jumpsuits.

They walked into the showers — a warm, damp room decorated in shades of blue with slick, glazed rock cut in square shapes affixed to the walls.

"*Do either of you prefer not to be seen naked by other women?*" Maggie asked.

Zeta could see an area to one side of the room where a pair of woman were standing under gentle sprays of water, rubbing lumpy orange things against their skin and dripping with white suds. WoQS told her the orange things were sea sponges.

"There are no men in here?" Zeta asked.

Maggie and Alasie laughed.

"Oh, that would be something," Alasie sent.

"No," Maggie sent, *"It's a woman's washroom. The men use another room."*

"Then it's fine," Zeta sent. Why would it bother a woman to be seen naked by another woman? Men are the ones who can't control themselves at the sight of a naked woman. Though, somehow, the men of Jacob's Ladder Station didn't seem to be having trouble looking Maggie in the eye.

Maggie showed her how to use the water controls, sponges, and soap. Once she got the hang of it, she was in a paradise of warm rain, soft sponges, bubbles, and floral scents. It was pure bliss after the salty, smelly trip across the ocean.

As she scrubbed soap into Penelope-pooch's fur, the pooch sent, *"The water is warm and tastes clean, but I don't like to get wet."*

"I'm sorry, Pen, but they say you have to be washed before you can go down to Syn-Cen."

Jamji showed up as Zeta and Alasie were washing their pooches. "Had to get Pepper situated," she said, passing by without meeting her eyes, starting her own shower.

Zeta noticed the other two women whispering to each other and pretending not to steal glances at Jamji. Maybe they'd never seen a woman with blue skin before. You'd think the Noddites would've seen everything by now. Were they betas on their pilgrimage? Even in her short time as a beta, Zeta had encountered more variety in people's appearance than in her entire life as an alpha.

It occurred to her that Alasie's stocky frame, thick and curvaceous, would have marked her as a foreigner in her tribe's lands. The boys would have wrestled for the privilege of having the exotic girl share their campfire. They'd beg her to let them run their fingers through her shiny, black hair — so smooth and straight.

Alasie caught Zeta looking at her. *"What?"* she mindspoke, giving a huff of embarrassment, closing an arm over her body.

"Nothing," Zeta laughed. *"I was noticing how straight your hair is. It's beautiful. Mine's a tangled mess."*

"Zeta, your hair's adorable. And you can work the knots out in the grooming room. Um, not that it's knotty. I don't mean—"

"I know, it's fine," Zeta sent, with a laugh. Alasie had the funniest way of tripping over her own thoughts.

After the showers, they dried off in a chamber of spinning warm air. Seeing how adorably poofy Penelope-pooch's fur was after being dried made Zeta squeal with delight.

Next, Maggie showed them into the grooming room. It was all flowers and soft seats and reflective surfaces which, Alasie told her via mindspeak, were called *mirrors*. The tables below the mirrors were outfitted with brushes, perfumes, creams, and countless other items which Zeta didn't recognize.

Zeta stared at herself in the mirror. She'd seen her own face before, of course, using the still water of a reflecting pool, but it was nothing like this full-color, perfect reflection. She was transfixed.

Alasie was behind her. Their eyes met in the mirror and Alasie smiled. She mindspoke, *"The mirrors are amazing, aren't they?"* She huff-laughed, looking down at the grooming supplies. *"I spent half a day in here on my pilgrimage, getting the grit out from under my fingernails and smelling the perfumes."*

Zeta stepped closer to the mirror, leaning in to examine her face. She had always been told that she had Wilhelm-pa's nose and his full lips, but Yephanie-ma's eyes. Now she could see what they meant. There, etched into her very own features, was her lineage. Charra was there too, if she looked closely enough.

All of them, dead and gone.

"No Beta Pilgrimage would be complete without a good look in the mirror," Maggie said aloud, jarring Zeta out of her dark thoughts. She was walking in, wearing a white outfit which covered her entire body other than her hands and head. Her face paint was gone. She presented Zeta and Alasie with folded white cloth. "Oh, I'm sorry, you prefer WorMS." She sent, *"We will hold your skins and traveling supplies for you to retrieve whenever you leave. These are called jumpsuits. You have to wear them in Syn-Cen."*

Zeta had seen other Noddites wear cloth, but had never worn it herself. Putting on the one-piece outfit was awkward, and she needed help. It was comfortable, though having her legs and arms enclosed would take some getting used to.

Jamji walked in, wearing a white jumpsuit of her own. Seeing her in clothes was strange. Jamji looked them over. "If you plan on playing beauty shop, this is where we part ways. I've already taken too long, thanks to that slow-ass boat."

Maggie furrowed her brow at Jamji. "I thought you were accompanying Zeta on her pilgrimage."

Jamji scoffed. "We were going to the same place at the same time. I don't think she needs me to hold her hand anymore. Right, Zeta? You're a big girl, you can make it from here."

"I'll stay with her," Alasie said, then shrunk at the sudden attention of Jamji and Maggie.

"Well, I guess this is goodbye," Zeta said, using the Common tongue. She stood and stepped towards Jamji.

Incoming conversation request from Freshman Ensign Jamji Telson of the Guard Faction.

Zeta accepted the request.

"Look, Zeta," Jamji sent. *"I know you're upset about how things turned out with the Guard, and so am I. But if there's anyone to blame, it's me. I filled your head with ideas and set you up for failure. If you're still interested in pledging to the Guard—"*

"Not in the slightest," Zeta sent. *"I'm going to play an important part in a project the Pips are working on. They told me all about it while I was waiting for you at the embassy. They say it'll give us the secret to defeating the Specters."*

Jamji paused, then sent. *"Sounds like we're both gonna be pretty busy."*

"Yep."

The silence lingered for a few heartbeats before Jamji mindspoke again. *"Well... bye, Zeta."*

A lump formed in Zeta's throat. She pulled her sis-kin into a hug. *"Goodbye, and safe travels. And Jamji?"*

She pulled back to look Jamji in the eyes.

"Yeah?" Jamji asked.

"Don't let them... change who you are, okay?"

Jamji scoffed. *"They couldn't if they tried, sis."*

6

———————

JAMJI'S ORB

BLINKING hard and engaging a bio-override to prevent tears from forming in her eyes, Jamji sped from the grooming room to the Jacob's Cellar Elevator platform.

She had washed the filth of Genesis from her skin. The dirt, the salt, the stagnation. She hadn't appreciated a Jacob's Ladder Station shower that much since she was a beta.

Pepper-pooch should be on his way up to the GSS by now. She couldn't wait to join him — to get away from these people, this planet. To get on with living her life the way she wanted to live it.

She tapped her foot rapidly, crossing her arms and staring at the elevator doors, avoiding acknowledging the existence of the man by her side who was also waiting for the elevator.

Jamji calmed her nerves by running back over her checklist. Cellar elevator down, pick up her orb, take it to the Guard Faction Embassy office in Syn-Cen for drop-off, cellar elevator up, attic elevator up, check in at the Guard Faction wing of GSS, reunite with Pepper-pooch, board her shuttle, travel to Soma Station, check in at Soma Station, then get her next marching orders. Her orb would make the trek from Genesis to Soma shortly after her safe arrival at

Soma Station. It would follow its own onboarding process, being spirited away to Soma Station's orb vault. There, it would be integrated into GuardNet.

Crap — she should also stop by Pip-Tau's room. It's fine. She'd squeeze it in between the orb drop-off and the elevator up.

The elevator gave a friendly "bong" sound that made Jamji want to punch it in the face. She wondered what sound the elevators on Soma Station made.

She waited for its foot-dragging occupants to evacuate, then stepped inside. The waiting man joined her. They buckled into their seats and the door swooshed closed. After the dropping sensation settled into a cruising equilibrium, the man spoke. "Hi, I'm—"

"Sorry, I'm checking my WorMS queue," Jamji interrupted. She closed her eyes. She was in no mood for small talk.

Come to think of it, she actually *should* check her queue, since she was about to transfer to a different faction network. She might lose any unread WorMS messages. And... there were a lot of them.

Jamji sighed as she brought up the visualization of her queue. She could spend a week flicking past page after page — years of ignored messages — looking for a sender or a subject she might care about. No time for that. She turned on the WorMS assistant AI, which was supposed to curate the content and bring only the important or interesting things to her attention. Normally, it was no better than just looking at the most recent messages and ignoring the ones from people she didn't care to talk to. This time, however, it caught one that she had missed.

Jamji growled. She heard the man across from her shift in his seat.

Eld Marco-Epsilon Rhind, you son of a bitch.

The subject read, "Congratulations, Ensign Jamji."

Jamji opened the message, bracing herself for a deluge of slime.

Dear Jamji,

It fills me with joy and pride to hear that not only have you been accepted into the Guard Faction, but that you were chosen for the officer track. Kudos!

I would give you fair warning that this achievement does come at a cost. Every lifetime Guardian who has been declined for the officer track will begrudge your acceptance, and almost every other officer you work with will be a lifetime Guardian. It will literally take you a full human lifespan to shake off the stigma that comes with being a Genesisian. Or "Gene-sissy", as the lowbrow insult goes.

Jamji snorted a laugh. She couldn't help it — Eld Eyebrow-Epsilon used the word "lowbrow"! Having nobody to share her joke with sobered her.

She returned to the message.

I have no doubt that you will shrug off any such insults, and that you'll prove your merit in no time. I trust that you will represent your native planet and people with pride, and prove that Genesis can produce as mighty a warrior as any offworlder faction.

In closing, I do hope to have the opportunity to meet with you face-to-face once you have settled into your new home of Soma Station. My door is open to you any time, even if only to speak in confidence with someone who, like yourself, has lived the life of a neoprim — eating roasted grubs, drinking water from muddy ponds, and sleeping alongside your tribemates beside a dwindling campfire under a star-strewn sky, blissfully ignorant of the Specters haunting the darkness above. Sincerely,

Eld Marco-Epsilon Rhind
Ambassador to the Guard Faction

The subtext was as clear as day, though its *slimebaggery* was much more subdued than it had been during their spoken conversations. He was trying to get her off balance — scaring her with intimidating warnings about what the lifetime Guardians would say about her. Then he gives her a haven to run to — the privacy of his office.

Nice try, eyebrow man.

Jamji saved the message in her personal vault. She ran a query for any other messages in her queue containing the eld's name, finding thirty-three hits. She saved the messages in her vault for future review.

A man cleared his throat, conspicuously.

She hadn't noticed that the elevator trip was over. A group of six people waited on the platform on the other side of the open elevator doors. She unbuckled herself and slid past the group with as much grace as she could manage.

Next stop: the aposynchronic orb interaction chamber.

Jamji sprung from the transport pod and stepped up to the interaction pedestal. Her orb was there, waiting for her under a glass dome. The familiar three-button interface greeted her. The first button glowed green and sported a hand icon, above the word "interact". The middle yellow button had an underlined up-arrow triangle, labeled "eject". The last button burned in an ominous shade of red with a skull-and-crossbones icon, labeled "destroy".

She touched her fingertips to the yellow button, but did not press it. The smooth, mirrored surface of the orb reflected her distorted, aquamarine visage. The reflection of the three glowing buttons stretched out along the bottom of the orb.

It had always fascinated her how small the orbs were — about the size of a shot put ball. Perfectly spherical, perfectly reflective. While under observation, a dome of thick glass protected the orb from being tainted by grubby fingerprints or dust. The rest of the time, your orb is stored alongside the others from the faction, in a secret chamber somewhere deep beneath the Syn-Cen complex.

That yellow button had been calling out to her for years. With an immense sense of satisfaction, Jamji pushed her hand down on the button. It depressed with a satisfying click. She watched her orb with unblinking eyes, eager to see what would happen next.

"Hello, Jamji." She knew that voice, though it had been years.

She turned her head to meet the eyes of the hologram which had materialized to her left. "Hello, Cain."

Cain's avatar was that of an unapologetically beautiful young man. He wore a white Syn-Cen jumpsuit, hiding his trim, muscled body. How did she know he was fit? Constructs are wonderful things, and Cain's avatar had been one of her favorite wrestling partners. His eyes were a complex kaleidoscope of hazel. His square jawline was accented by a short, manicured beard. The beard complimented his close-cropped, curly brown hair. And his cappuccino-toned skin? Flawless.

Yeah, she'd miss Cain.

It was too bad he was just the personality emulation avatar serving as the human face of an SI — Synthetic Intelligence. She'd have had great fun with him if he were human.

Cain stepped to the orb's glass case and leaned an arm over it. He gave a sideways smile, exposing a glimpse of his perfect teeth. "So, you finally hit that yellow button?"

Jamji didn't mind playing along with the SI. He knew what he was. Not like the Astri, who pretended to still be human even after relinquishing their humanity — abandoning their bodies and integrating into a hive-mind network.

She returned his smirk and crossed her arms. "I suppose you're here to make sure I know what risks I'm taking? Well, save your breath — I've read the disclaimer."

"Be that as it may, I still have to follow the script. Feel free to zone out, if you want."

Jamji laughed. She flipped her hand in a "get on with it" gesture.

Cain went on for an uncanny seventeen minutes and seventeen seconds, pausing a few times to ask verification questions like, "Do you agree to accept these risks and burdens?"

The warnings and questions were everything she expected.

She was now responsible for her orb's safety and transport.

Okay.

She'd be permanently disconnected from Worldnet orb access and synchronization.

Gotcha.

Was she being coerced, intimidated, blackmailed, seduced, or otherwise pressured into her decision?

Nope.

Then came the "care and feeding" stuff. Like, "while designed for durability, your orb should still be treated as if it were a fragile egg or a tender infant. It should be protected within a shockproof, airtight carrying case while in transport."

Jamji had laughed at that one. "I'm putting my infant in an airtight case, Cain?"

"Not a perfect analogy," Cain chuckled. "I can get you a transportation case now, if you'd like."

"Sure."

A hidden panel had opened in the rear wall and a small, steel-gray box had slid out.

Cain finally asked the last question: "Ready?"

"I've been ready for a lifetime." Jamji watched her orb, her senses buzzing with anticipation.

"I would say that it has been a pleasure to serve you as your faction SI," Cain said, waving a hand over the glass dome. It hummed as it lifted, slowly exposing an opening in the dome's front. "But, as you're keenly aware, I'm incapable of feeling either the pleasure of serving you or the pain of saying goodbye. Goodbye, Jamji."

"Bye," Jamji said, avoiding meeting his alluring eyes by staring down at her exposed orb.

She'd always been uncomfortable with the fact that Cain probably knew her better than she knew herself. He'd often hint at that knowledge, but avoided referring to it directly. Mainly, he seemed to use it to speak to her in a way that he knew would get a positive reaction. This approach had resulted in more than a few Noddites falling in love with the SI's avatar. Others resented his manipulation and refused to speak to him.

Cain turned away as his avatar hologram dissolved.

Jamji reached out and cupped her hands around the orb. It was warm. She eased it off its cradle. It was heavy! She knew orbs were dense, but it was fascinating to feel its heft in her hands.

There was a certain headiness to the experience. She was holding her whole life in her hands. Everything she'd ever experienced was tucked away inside this heavy little ball, and now she was about to put it in someone else's hands for safe keeping and transport through Specter-infested space.

She imagined that this sense of vulnerability was a lesser version of what the Earthlings had felt during the Exodus. But for them, it meant trusting that their orbs would be safely shuttled across five hundred light years and that they would be successfully resurrected two thousand years later by a self-governed SI on an alien planet.

Genevieve, Oraxis... they had lived through some scary times.

Jamji shook herself out of the reverie. She carried the orb to the box on the floor, kneeled, then twisted the opening latch. It gave a slight hiss as it opened. She lowered the orb into the recess in the high-density foam, then closed the box and twisted the lock. Another hiss, and her orb was safe in its carrying case, ready for the dangerous voyage ahead.

Next stop: the Guard Faction Embassy office.

7

ZETA'S ORB

AFTER GROOMING, talking, and smelling the perfumes for a while, they were ready to continue on to Zeta's orb.

She understood they would go down through an ocean, then into the ground under the ocean to get to Syn-Cen. Zeta imagined seeing monstrous creatures in the ocean's depths. She imagined having to hold her breath as the frigid water passed by, and the pressing darkness of being deep underground. Thoughts of her alpha's death came to mind. The more she thought about it, the more anxious she felt.

Maggie ushered them into what was labeled "Jacob's Cellar Elevator." It looked like the inside of an enormous egg, with seats around the sides and a glowing spot in the ceiling. The curved sides were solid white, with no openings other than the one they entered through. As they sat, the portal they had entered through slid closed. A moment later came a hiss, a thump, and the sensation of dropping. This sensation went away after a few seconds, and then they just sat, with nothing happening. Zeta's heart pounded as she waited for the ocean plunge.

She caught a familiar scent, sweet but with hints of pine. She looked over at Alasie, who was smiling at her. Zeta leaned in a bit, sniffing.

"Eau de Thin Forest," Alasie sent on their open conversation channel. *"I, uh, found a bottle of it in the grooming room. I'm sorry, I should have told you they had it. But... I don't know..."* She looked down. *"I don't know why I didn't."*

Zeta gave a breath of a laugh. *"Don't worry about it. I have a whole bottle of my own, back at the Telson cabin."*

For a while, there was a downward pressure, like someone pushing her into her seat, then it released and there was a faint thud and humming sound. The elevator-egg's portal slid open again, revealing a chamber similar to the one they had left, but different. Zeta was confused. It was as if they had stayed in one place, but the station itself had changed. After they exited the egg, another group of white-clad people muttered pleasantries and entered, sitting down. The door closed behind them. There was a hiss and thump, but the doors remained closed.

"Maggie," Zeta sent, *"we didn't move. Are we at Syn-Cen?"*

"Yes, elevators are strange things. We did dive through the ocean and the ground, as promised. Welcome to the Synthetic Intelligence Central Processing Facility."

Zeta wouldn't embarrass herself by telling them what she had expected of the trip.

The ceiling was high enough not to feel like she was trapped in a cave. The air smelled fresh, and the diffuse lighting reminded her of Surya's light when thin clouds spanned the sky.

Maggie led them down a corridor and into another chamber. She sent, *"You must go alone from here, Zeta. I understand you plan to stay in your sis-kin's dorm, so when you are done observing your orb, ask for WoQS to guide you to her room."*

Alasie sent, *"Since I can't go with you, I'll just meet you at your sis-kin's dorm. Pip Telson, right?"*

"Pip-Tau Telson, yes," Zeta sent.

"Bring both dogs with you," Maggie sent, looking at Alasie. *"Com-*

panion animals aren't allowed in the orb viewing chamber. Zeta, you'll have to delegate your dog to Alasie. Can't have her wandering the halls, sniffing after you."

"Delegate? I don't know what—"

"It means giving Alasie control of your dog. She'll be able to issue thought-commands and communicate with your dog anthropolinguistically."

"How do I—"

Maggie laughed, sending, *"Tell your dog to obey Alasie while you're gone. WorMS will handle the rest."*

Zeta nodded once, kneeled, and scratched Penelope-pooch behind the ears. She thought-spoke, *"I'm going to go somewhere that you're not allowed to go, Pen. You be a good girl and obey Alasie while I'm gone, okay?"*

Penelope-pooch licked Zeta's face. *"Goodbye, Zeta. I want to go with you, but I will obey."* She looked at Alasie, then back to Zeta, then sat down.

"Oh!" Alasie sent, giving a sudden laugh. *"I think it worked — she said hello! Wow, she sounds different from Pinga. She reminds me of my mom."*

Maggie led the way across the chamber. She instructed Zeta to step into what she called a "transport pod" and have a seat on its white padding. The pod looked like a sleek, gray beetle. Its lid was spread open like a beetle's wing covering. Ahead of the pod was a wall with a large circle-shaped depression.

Maggie sent, *"Take as much time as you need with your orb. You'll also get to meet Cain."* She gave a coy smile.

"I'll bet you fall in love at first sight," Alasie sent, huffing.

"Remember, he's not a human," Maggie sent. *"After we leave, issue a WUtils thought-command for the pod to take you to see your orb. Bye, Zeta."*

The two were stepping back from the transport pod. Alasie waved and turned to exit behind Maggie, followed by the two dogs.

Their group conversation was closed as the door to the chamber slid shut behind them.

———

Zeta sat in the pod in the empty chamber. Syn-Cen was a strange place. Complete silence, warm lighting, smooth white surfaces, and soft edges everywhere. It was unsettling.

Zeta thought the words, *"Transport pod, please take me to see my orb."*

The beetle wings closed, sealing her inside the pod. It was lit by the same warm glow as the other parts of Syn-Cen, but it was so small!

Zeta was trapped! Her heart started beating harder as she felt herself pressed against the seat.

A gentle man's voice spoke to her within the pod, using her tribe's tongue. "If you're feeling claustrophobic, maybe this will help."

The world around her was replaced with a sunny glade, complete with butterflies and flowers. Birds chirped and tree frogs peeped. The white padded seat underneath her was the only thing unchanged.

"Thank you," Zeta said. "This is much better. I didn't think I slipped through slate-space. Is this a construct?"

"No, Zeta, you can't be placed into a construct without your permission. This is a holographic image being projected within the pod." The man's way of speaking reminded her of WoQS, though it was more heartfelt.

"Who are you?" she asked the voice.

"They call me Cain. They say that 'Cain' is supposed to be an acronym for 'Central Artificial Intelligence Network', but to be honest, I think they picked the name first and selected what words it was supposed to stand for later. The founders of the Genesis Colony had a fondness for biblical references. Have you heard of The Bible, Zeta?"

"No."

"Well, once you get around to reading it, you'll find that they named me after one of the bad guys. Would you believe that? Me? A bad guy?"

Zeta laughed. "I don't know. Maybe you are a bad guy."

"Oh, no! Maybe I *am*! I sure hope not. How would I be able to tell?"

"Well, do you... like to hurt people?"

"No! Of course not! I wouldn't hurt a fly!"

"Do you... steal people's food when they're not looking?"

"Young lady, I'll have you know I *give* people food when they're not looking!"

They both laughed. Zeta said, "Well, then I'd say you're a good guy. Where are you, anyway? I'd like to see you."

"To see me, or my avatar?"

"There's a difference?"

"A huge difference. The real me looks like this."

An image appeared, hovering in space above the grass of the glade. It was a rotating form that looked like some sort of intricate tool. It had disks connected by bars and an arrangement of spheres. Tiny lines ran like ribbons between the shapes.

Zeta said, "You're not much to look at."

Cain said, "That's why I have an avatar. The founders of Genesis created it on my behalf."

"Okay, let's see it."

The rotating form was replaced by a young man.

He was *breathtaking*.

Zeta couldn't think of what to say next.

After a few moments, Cain glanced around, looking self-conscious. He put a hand on the back of his neck in the most graceful, humble gesture Zeta could imagine. He looked down at his body, then back up at Zeta with a perfect smile. "I'm sorry, is my avatar too—"

"No! You're *fine*. I mean, it's fine. I mean, I just didn't expect you to be so..."

Zeta felt herself being pressed backwards in her seat.

Cain said, "Save that thought — we'll chat again soon. You're pulling into the orb viewing chamber now. The place where I normally keep your aposynchronic orb is hidden deep in Syn-Cen, but I'll transport it up here for you any time you come to visit."

The image of Cain and the meadow winked out of existence as the beetle wings of her transport spread open above her. She took a breath and shook her head. She reminded herself that Cain wasn't a human.

Zeta stood and looked around the new chamber. It was a small white room with a pedestal in it. The pedestal had a clear dome covering a shiny ball and three glowing squares at waist level. But what captured her attention was that Cain was in the room with her, smiling and leaning against a wall.

He's *real?!*

"Hologram," Cain said, pointing to himself. "I don't have a body. See?" He flickered out of existence. A moment later, he was back again. "I like to make an appearance so I can say hello, talk you through anything you want to learn about your orb, and keep you company if you're feeling lonely or scared. It can be... strange, seeing your orb for the first time." He flashed a smile. "But if you'd rather be alone, I can disappear."

She stepped out and examined the pedestal. The most interesting part was the protrusion, with three colorful squares glowing on its surface — green, yellow, and red. They had pictures and words on them. Zeta used her double-mind to translate the words, passing her hand over the squares, "interact, eject... destroy?!"

She yanked her hand away from the red square depicting a skull and bones.

"Yeah," Cain laughed, "that's a scary button. Don't worry, if you pressed it, we'd go through a process of counseling and psychological tests before I actually destroyed your orb. It's your right to do so, but I make sure it's done with informed consent."

"That's good," Zeta said. "What would 'eject' do?"

"I would disconnect your orb from my network and give it to you. Most commonly, that's only used to transfer to another faction. But who would want to do that?"

Zeta met Cain's eyes. He knew about Jamji, of course. Did he know that she had tried to join the Guard Faction, too? Well, it was his job to store her experiences in her orb. He knew everything about her! Did he know what she was thinking right now? How she felt when she looked at him?

"What about 'interact'?" Zeta asked, forcing her eyes back to the buttons.

"There's only room in your orb for about eighty years of full-fidelity stored experience. That means every once in a while you have to do some cleanup, and the recommended way to do that is to come and visit your orb in person so you can hook into a special rig. Let's just say it's the sort of thing you'll want to tackle many years from now, during a week when you've got nothing better to do. There are other uses for direct interaction, but for you, at this stage, there's not much point in that button."

Zeta looked back at Cain. "So, if there's no point in the green button, and I don't want to eject or destroy my orb, what's the point of being here?"

"Ah, see! That's why I hate the *buttons*." He walked around to the other side of the orb's clear covering and leaned down to look at Zeta through it, with his eyes peeking above the top of the orb. "They distract you from the *orb*. Get closer, Zeta. Press your nose against the glass if you want. Really *look* at it."

Zeta stepped to the side of the pedestal so that she wouldn't have to lean over the buttons. She put her hands on the glass and assessed her orb. It was about the size of a hedge apple. She was awestruck by its simple beauty as it rested upon a cylindrical base within the dome.

Her reflection at the center of the orb looked distant, while Cain's reflection stretched across the orb's edge.

Moments passed as the weight of the orb's significance sank in.

"Inside this little thing," Zeta whispered, "is every memory of every moment of my life. My kin, my tribe, all here. It's like they're frozen in ice. Trapped in memories. Inside this orb is my death. My rebirth. Instructions on how to recreate my body and mind so I can be resurrected if I die again. As long as this orb exists, I exist. Penelope-pooch is in it, too? So she could be resurrected if she died again?"

"Correct, Zeta," Cain said gently, "but I also see that there are two other pooches stored within your orb."

Zeta blinked. "What?"

"Penelope-pooch is stored as your primary companion animal, based on the amount of time you spent with her as an alpha. So, I automatically resurrected her at the same time as you. But there are two secondary companion animals available in your orb: Gorgon-pup and Chimera-pup."

Zeta's eyes welled with tears. "Charra's pups!" She pressed her hands against the glass, looking deep into her reflection in the orb.

"If you'd like to have them resurrected, press the green button and we can begin."

Zeta rushed back to the front of the pedestal, raising a hand to the button. She hesitated. Tears rolled off her cheeks, soaking into the front of her white jumpsuit.

To bring the pups back without Charra being there to play with them seemed wrong. She imagined he'd be the first thing on their minds. "I can always come back and do it later, right?"

"Yes, as long as you don't ask me to erase them, they'll always be waiting within your orb."

Zeta looked up at her orb, raising a hand to press the glass.

Maybe later, pups. Until then, you keep Charra company.

She looked over the top of the glass dome at Cain. "Can I be alone for a while?"

Zeta cried for a long time.

She had stepped into the transport pod to get ready to leave when it hit her: the pups were dead. Whether or not she decided to resurrect them, they had died in the jaws of black wolf-pooches. She could ask Cain to make two new pups who would look and act just like them, but that wouldn't change the fact that they were dead.

Penelope-pooch was dead — struck on the head by a stone hurled by the red-speckled man-boy, Rohito — also dead.

Charra was dead — his face and neck ripped open, stumbling alone through the thicket, pouring out his life's blood, trying to find his way back to camp.

Zeta of the Scorpion Tail Tribe was dead — drowned a lifetime ago in the icy waters of a spring pool.

Who was *she*, then? A body created in Zeta's image? A mind pieced together using Zeta's memories?

She wasn't Zeta — she was an *impostor!* She had no right to take Zeta's mind and body, her name, her memories.

She returned to the pedestal, wiping the tears from her eyes. That shiny little ball was full of *stolen* memories. Zeta hadn't known that her memories were being captured — nobody had asked her permission. Every private moment, every regrettable word spoken, every dark secret sworn never to be told. Cain had captured them all, watching from his hidden cave under the ocean. And now he presents them to her in a beautiful little orb and calls them hers?

They made her relive Zeta's death so that she'd learn who she *was* and who she was *not*. She was the *new* Zeta — Zeta-Beta Telson — with a sharp double-mind and a superhuman, biosynthetic body. She was better in every way. Her purpose was to fight aliens and preserve the future of all humankind.

It was a joke. The Guard was going to do that job, and they didn't need or even want her help.

She was useless.

What had been the point of Zeta's life? Nine years of eating bugs, sharpening sticks, staring at the fire.

Pointless!

And what was *her* point if the only option she had was to do what the Genesis Faction and the Telsons told her she was supposed to do?

No, that's not true. Cain *is* giving her a choice.

Zeta eyed the square emblazoned with a skull and bones. Her mind went quiet as she stared at the red glow, like an ember pulled from the fire.

Steady. Still.

A strange thing happens to your thinking when you're standing at the edge of a cliff, looking down at the jagged rocks below. In those moments when you hold your own life in your hands, you can't help but wonder, "What would happen if I just took that one little step forward?" You feel the pull. Maybe you lean forward a little before you snap out of it. Your heart races. You start to fear yourself, because you know you *could* do it — end it all, on a whim.

Destroying the orb wouldn't be the same as dying, though. Wiping out Zeta's replays wasn't a death. It would be a rejection of the confounding world they had resurrected her into. It would be a refusal of the gift of immortality — Cain's *fake*, Graven-cursed gift.

She had the sense that Cain was watching her. She couldn't see him, but she felt his presence. Of course he was there! He always *has* been there her whole life — in her head, behind her eyes, secretly watching and storing what *she* saw, ever since her naming day.

Would he try to stop her? He said he would give her counseling, but not that he would get in her way.

This button could end the lie that was Zeta Telson and free the captured memories of Zeta of the Scorpion Tail Tribe. She could press it, then return to the golden grasslands in search of a new tribe to take her in. She could live a normal life and let the Noddites take care of the future of the human species without her.

But for what? If Zeta had lived a pointless life, and *she* was a useless imposter, then what good would it do to destroy their shared orb? To return to that pointless Land of Eden and forget everything she's learned about the fantastic and horrifying truths of the universe?

She looked up from the red button and stared into her distant reflection on the orb's surface. One of the first mathematical concepts she had learned during bootstrapping came to mind: the concept of zero.

The Zeta which stared back at her from the orb's surface was nothing more than a zero.

Zeta the Zero — it has a nice ring to it.

The Zeta inside the orb — the original Zeta — was also a zero.

Zero plus zero equals zero.

So, did it matter if she was the original or the impostor? Did it matter if she kept the orb or destroyed it? The worst she could do from this point was turn her zero into something more. Maybe she could make this life worthwhile, somehow.

The Pips seemed to think she could do something important by joining their "Interra" project. She had agreed to it, and tried to get excited about it, but it sounded like a waste of time. How would playing a game help fight the Specters? It had something to do with making Cain give them the secret to defeating them.

"Cain, I want to talk to you." Zeta told the walls.

Cain's avatar dutifully appeared, leaning against the wall to her side. "Certainly. Is there something I can do for you?"

"I understand you're not a human. You're some sort of really smart thing created by the people of Earth. A synthetic intelligence?"

"It is correct that I'm a synthetic intelligence," Cain said, "but calling me 'really smart' is a subjective value judgment I'd prefer to avoid."

Zeta didn't understand. He seemed to be acting humble. She asked, "Do you know something about the Specters that you're not telling us? Like how to defeat them?"

"Direct questions," Cain laughed, "I appreciate those! No, I'm sorry, but I don't have any secrets about the Specters, and I don't know how to defeat them. I have troves of data on them — all yours for the taking. I can share more analysis tools and techniques with you than you could imagine. I can help you come up with your own strategies to defeat them, but I can't think for you. I can't hand you the answers because I simply don't have them." He held his empty hands out to his sides.

"You run the Worldnet, right?"

"I do."

"You're able to synchronize thousands of orbs, transfer messages all around the planet, host constructs, and talk to me using this avatar all at the same time? And you think *I'm* going to come up with strategies to defeat the Specters, when *you* can't?"

"That's right," Cain shrugged. "It's weird, I get it, but that's the nature of Synthetic Intelligences — we're tools. *Powerful* tools, but still... tools. I can do a lot of things, but I can't step in and solve your problems for you."

This was doing nothing for Zeta's confidence. "So, what's the point of Interra if you don't have any answers?"

Cain laughed again. If it wasn't such a heart-warming laugh coming from such a beautiful man, it would've annoyed her. "That would be a question for the Pips." He gestured to the transport pod. "I can get you to their doorstep in ten minutes and you can ask them yourself. That's... if you're done here?" He raised his eyebrows.

Zeta nodded once, then stepped into the pod.

She had to give the Pips a chance and see what Interra was all about.

The red button would always be here if she changed her mind.

8

CRASH PAD

THE SUN DOME atop Castle Interra's Day Tower was a powerful weapon. At its heart was the Sun Crystal — a magical relic as large as a boulder. It burned with a warm light as it hung, suspended by gold-plated chains, within the dome.

What looked like circular windows set within the dome's ceiling and upper walls were actually massive lenses. Clockwork mechanisms maneuvered the double-layered refraction lenses to focus sunlight into the Sun Crystal throughout the day.

One thousand quicksilver mirrors, each with their own clockwork positioning mount, were affixed to the tops of several lower towers. These reflected their own patch of sunlight into the lenses, further feeding the hungry Sun Crystal with more energy.

Queen Tau — The Day Queen — had performed a few tests of the Sun Dome's offensive powers, with impressive results. Her first target had been a tree on the side of a distant hill. Not only had the tree exploded into a million flaming splinters, but the dirt behind it on the hillside had burst outward, creating a cave. Once the smoke cleared and her subjects explored the cave, they found a pool of molten rock cooling within.

People enjoy being near such powerful relics, so choosing The Sun Dome as her personal throne room and meeting chamber was a brilliant idea that Queen Tau was proud to call her own. Her architects had wheeled in stone tables and chairs. Artists were commissioned to decorate its walls and inner surfaces with colorful mosaics. A smooth, white marble throne was crafted for her and situated directly beneath the glowing stone. The room couldn't contain flammables, though. When the Sun Crystal was activated, anything inside the chamber which *could* burn *would* burn.

Without floor or wall tapestries to dampen the sound, the voices of Queen Tau's advisors echoed within the dome's white stone walls. They had broken into groups of three where they brainstormed quest ideas to encourage the Interrans to venture further from Centra City.

She was listening excitedly to an idea being proposed by Gwenley, a high elf recently promoted to advisor, when a herald tapped on her shoulder.

"Yes? What?!" Queen Tau didn't mean to be rude, but this was a great idea!

The herald leaned in, whispering, "Your majesty has received a request for a private conversation from a certain Freshman Ensign Jamji Telson of the Guard Faction."

Pip-Tau still wasn't certain whether replacing WorMS notifications with whispering NPCs was a good idea or not. It still ruined the mood.

"I'm sorry," she told Gwenley, "but I simply must respond to this. Save that idea for when I return. I must hear it!"

"Certainly, your majesty," said the disappointed advisor, giving a bow and stepping back.

Queen Tau turned aside, closed her eyes, and put two fingers to each temple. This meditative gesture signals to other players that you're taking a time-out from the game for some real-world distraction.

She accepted the conversation request, sending, *"Freshman*

Ensign Jamji Telson of the Guard Faction?! I think you have the wrong number."

"Hey, sis. I'm at your door."

"It's an invasion! Guards! The Guardians are coming! Say, I could write a whole 'who's on first' bit about that."

"Very funny. Can I come in?"

"What's the password?"

Jamji paused. *"I don't know. I can just leave if you don't have time right now."*

"You're no fun," Pip-Tau sent. She issued a WUtils command to turn on her dormitory room lights and open the door. *"I'll get up in a second. Busy times! Just gotta do a little delegation real quick. I'll tell Pip-Rho, too."*

Pip-Tau sent Pip-Rho the urgent message that Jamji had invaded the Crash Pad, and that she should join them. Pip-Rho responded with an affirmative within a fraction of a second. The woman could sure think fast!

"I'm kinda in a time crunch," Jamji sent.

"Two seconds! Jeez!"

Pip-Tau requested they close the conversation channel, and Jamji agreed.

Queen Tau opened her eyes and lowered her hands. "My sincerest apologies," she said in a queenly voice loud enough to cut through the echoing voices of the advisors, "but I must depart."

The advisors moaned in disappointment. Someone jeered with a playful "boo".

"Oh, come!" Queen Tau laughed, "You're all smarter than I am. I'm only holding you back, making you water down your explanations so I can understand them. Le'eya, you're in charge, okay? Gather the best ideas and report them to me upon my return."

"Yes, your majesty," Le'eya said, bowing.

Queen Tau produced her scepter, gave it a flourish, then disappeared in a white vapor as Pip-Tau disconnected from the gameworld.

Pɪᴘ-Tᴀᴜ ᴏᴘᴇɴᴇᴅ ʜᴇʀ ᴇʏᴇs. The first thing she saw was the phrase, "WARNING: This is the real world! Try not to die again — it's a real _drag._" Pip-Pi had written this on the ceiling using a black marker. That was a few years before her fateful trip to Soma Station, where she got killed by a Specter attack.

Pip-Tau pushed her bony little arms into the air in a stretch as she sat up and looked around.

Her cramped dorm consisted of a tiny foyer with cushioned benches on either side and a slightly larger bunk room with a narrow bed against the side wall. The walls were covered in posters and Pip graffiti. Random keepsakes littered the narrow ledge circling the upper wall.

Seeing the room again felt like returning home after a long trip. How long had it been since she was in the real world? Ah, yes! Four months ago, when Oraxis and Genevieve visited before their Zeta-Beta pickup.

Jamji sat on one of the two benches, but there was no sign of Zeta.

"Where's the girl?" Pip-Tau asked.

Jamji took a breath to reply.

"Hey, where's the girl?!" squeaked Pip-Rho's voice. A floating brown egg about the size of her head hovered near the ceiling above Jamji. It had cartoon eyes, a poofy afro, arms, legs, and a crack going up its side. This was the adorably ironic avatar Pip-Rho always used when appearing as a hologram in the real world.

"You mean Zeta?" Jamji asked them.

Pip-Rho's avatar rolled its eyes. "Yes, of course, _Zeta!_ What, did you leave her in the hall?"

Jamji stood, closing the distance between herself and the avatar. "We had to part ways when I went to get my orb. She wanted to stay up on the island and smell perfumes in the grooming room. I'm on a tight schedule. She'll be by in a bit, I'm sure."

Pip-Rho sang as her egg hologram bounced around the foyer. "I'm late! I'm late! For a very important date!"

Pip-Tau got to her feet, then pressed the placental mat disposal button next to her bed. She'd be in the real world for a bit. Without her laying on it, the mat would soon dissolve automatically, stinking up the place. A narrow opening in the wall flipped open as the bed's surface shifted like a conveyor belt, feeding the top layer into the wall and replacing it with fresh mycelite-infused bedding.

She performed stretches as she said, "You postponed your application by *months* for her, and now you don't have time to spend one of the last hours you'll have together in who-knows-how-long relaxing in the grooming room and brushing your hair? Oh, sorry, I forgot — you're bald."

"Burn," Pip-Rho laughed.

"She deserves it," Pip-Tau grumbled.

"I agree. For shame, sis." Pip-Rho rotated her hologram egg-body back and forth to simulate shaking her head. "But we won't sour your goodbye with a fight, so I'm gonna give you a pass."

Pip-Rho's egg floated down, holding out a glowing card. Jamji leaned in to look at the card. Pip-Tau engaged enhanced optics to get a zoomed-in look at Rho's card — a picture of Jamji clutching onto prison bars. On the card were the words "Get Out of Jerkface Prison Free!"

A snort-laugh escaped Jamji. She pantomimed plucking the holographic card from Pip-Rho's cartoon hand.

Pip-Tau wasn't feeling quite as ready to forgive Jamji as Rho was. She snuffed out the angry ember in her heart, then went to Jamji and opened her arms for a hug, which Jamji leaned down to deliver.

After the obligatory hug, Pip-Tau rolled her head around to stretch her stiff neck. "So, first of all, congrats!"

Pip-Rho chorused her "congrats!" then picked up where Pip-Tau left off, "We heard you got into the officer track? Impressive!"

"Thank you, ma'ams," Jamji said, with a slight bow.

"What were the Guardian entrance exams like?" Pip-Tau asked, putting a hand behind her hip and twisting her back.

"Pretty tough," Jamji said, nodding.

Seconds ticked by in silence.

Pip-Rho's egg avatar did a backflip, "Wow, hell of a story! It's like I'm there!"

Jamji sighed and rubbed her scalp. "Sorry, I just don't think I can go into details. You know, secret Guard Faction stuff. So, what are you two up to? Zeta says you invited her to take part in some project you're running?"

Pip-Tau froze mid-stretch. Jamji didn't know about Interra? They were running the most immersive gameworld in the history of Genesis! It was this year's EoE Sponsored Project! It was a double-whammy *win* which would solve the Specter problem while unlocking Cain's hidden potential!

Pip-Rho was also speechless. Her egg cracked audibly as one of her eyes twitched.

"Seriously?!" was all Pip-Tau could squeak.

"You're serious right now?" Pip-Rho asked flatly.

Jamji crossed her arms. "I've been concentrating on my exam prep, and I was with Zeta that whole time, getting her ready. Then I took the exams and then there was the boat ride and I had all this material they gave me. I'm sorry if I'm not keeping up on your news feed, but I do have my own life to live, you know."

Pip-Rho mindspoke privately, *"Can you believe this?"*

Pip-Tau sent, *"She's gonna be so embarrassed when she hears how big Interra is."*

"Let her find out on her own," Pip-Rho replied. Speaking to Jamji again, she mumbled, "It's just another gameworld we're running. Medieval high fantasy stuff. You know, J. R. R. Tolkien, Dungeons and Dragons, World of WarCraft."

Pip-Tau shrugged. "Catch up on it if you want. It's all in our public feed."

"I'll do that," Jamji said, unconvincingly.

A few more awkward seconds passed before a faint scraping sound crept into the silence from the direction of the door.

THE THREE EXCHANGED CONFUSED GLANCES.

Jamji smirked. "Rat problems?"

There came a loud thud, making the Pips jump. Then more scraping, then another thud.

"Should I call security?" Pip-Tau whispered.

"Security?!" Pip-Rho shout-whispered. "Jamji's here! You think she can't handle a hall monster?" Her egg avatar dove into Pip-Tau's afro puff and disappeared. Pip-Tau backed into a corner, out of sight of the door.

"Alright, Jamji," Pip-Tau whispered, "Get ready. I'll WUtil the door open. If it's a hall monster, *take it out.*"

Jamji chuckled as cat claws emerged from her fingertips. Then she vanished.

Pip-Tau issued the thought-command to open her dorm room door.

The low growl of a wary beast came from the hall.

What the hell was that?!

Pip-Tau pulled Jamji into a group conversation with Pip-Rho. *"Jamji, who or what is at my door?!"*

"Hall monster. Eight feet tall, covered in scales. You really should've called security — I don't think I can take it on alone."

"Jamji, I'm serious!"

"Hello?" It sounded like a young woman's voice from the hall. "Is anybody in there? They... uh... said this is where Pip lives?"

"Who the heck is that?!" Pip-Rho mindspoke.

"Assassin, I think," Jamji replied.

Pip-Rho's egg emerged from Pip-Tau's hair and floated back around the corner. She said, "Oh, you're not a hall monster."

Pip-Tau peeked around the corner. Her door-scratching visitor was a stout young woman with vaguely Inuit or Mongolian features.

Oh! Penelope-poochie-woochie was with her! And another dog, hiding behind the visitor. It looked like a large husky, or small timber wolf.

The woman huff-laughed nervously, taking a step backwards, fixated on Pip-Rho's egg hologram. "Sorry, I'm confused. You're not... real, are you?"

Pip-Tau stepped out of her hiding place. "Of course she's real!"

Jamji turned visible again, blocking Pip-Tau's view. The visitor exclaimed, "Oh! Oh, it's you, Jamji."

"Yep," Jamji said. "What was with the scratching and thumping?"

"I didn't know... how... how to..." Alasie stuttered.

Jamji rolled her eyes. "Usually people knock. Or better yet, send a WorMS message." She kneeled, holding her hand out to Penelope-pooch. The pooch stepped into the room, wagging her tail. She nuzzled Jamji's hand. Jamji scratched behind Penelope-pooch's ears as she said, "Alasie, meet the Pips. The human one is Pip-Tau, and the egg hologram is Pip-Rho. Pips, meet Alasie. She's Zeta's friend — a beta. She's still learning how to chew on Common, but I think she'd still trip on her words even if she was fluent. The antisocial wolf-pooch behind her is Pinga."

"Damn, Jamji's rude," Pip-Rho mindspoke, privately.

"Welcome to the Crash Pad, Alasie!" Pip-Tau sang. "Is Zeta stalking the hall out there with you?"

Alasie spoke with staggered, slow precision. "No, sorry. She's... seeing her orb. She said I should wait here. I hope that's okay."

"Of course!" Pip-Tau chirped.

Jamji stood. "Well, guys, it's about to get real cramped in here. This is my cue to leave. I already said my goodbyes to Zeta, and I'm sure she'll be here soon. I don't wanna hafta go through the whole thing with her again. Now it's your turn."

"Already?" Pip-Tau whined.

A megaphone appeared in Pip-Rho's hand. She raised it to her mouth and pointed it at Jamji. "Rude!" She blared.

Pip-Tau jumped up to wrap her arms around Jamji's neck in a hug. Jamji caught her and squeezed. After a few seconds, Jamji let go, but Pip-Tau clung like a tick.

"Don't let the Guard turn you into a complete ass-face," Pip-Tau whispered into Jamji's aquamarine ear.

"I think it's too late for that," Jamji whispered back. She was trying to pull Pip-Tau off, but Pip-Tau just clung harder.

"Not yet," Pip-Tau whispered. "Even Vader had his redemption."

After one more squeeze, she let go. Jamji set her back on the ground.

"Holo-hug," Pip-Rho declared, swooping in to pantomime a hug. She whispered, "I love your ass-face, sis."

Jamji snorted a laugh, then stifled it with her hand. "Love you, too. Bye, Pips."

She gave Penelope-pooch one more pat on the haunches, then fled the dorm.

Alasie watched Jamji jog down the hall for a moment before she turned back to the Pips.

"Well, plenty of room now," Pip-Tau said, resisting the urge to cry. "Come on in, hall monster."

***

ALASIE OPENED her palms to them as she walked through the door, followed by her wolf-pooch.

Pip-Tau smiled and showed her own palms in response. "Nice. Your tribe followed that tradition, too? Or did Zeta teach you?"

"Tradition?" Alasie asked, stopping in her tracks.

"The showing of palms?"

"Oh, well, uh, yeah, sorry, I thought everyone did that."

"Nah," Pip-Rho said. "The neoprims are a total mixed bag. Like

Pinga, there. Lots of tribes forbid interbreeding domesticated dogs with wolves."

"Oh, ours did, too." Alasie said, looking back at Pinga in the hallway. He let out a whimper, then walked inside, tail tucked between his legs. She must have issued a thought-command.

Pip-Tau issued the WUtils command to close the door at half-speed, trying not to startle the nervous dog. She asked, "So, they made an exception for Pinga?" She was kneeling and petting Penelope-pooch with one hand, holding the other out for Pinga to smell it.

The wolf-pooch growled at Pip-Tau.

"Pinga!" Alasie shouted. "I'm sorry. He's not good at meeting new people. Or dogs... or pretty much anything."

Pip-Rho rephrased Pip-Tau's question, "So, what's the story? They let you have a forbidden half-wolf?"

Alasie huff-laughed, barely smiling. "Yeah. I'm not good at telling stories, though. Especially not in Common. I always feel like I'm about to bite my tongue."

"Want to use mindspeak?" Pip-Tau offered.

"Okay," Alasie said, hesitantly.

They joined a group conversation. Alasie seemed to gather her wits as she took a seat in the foyer. Pip-Tau sat on the other bench, while Pip-Rho's egg floated overhead. Pinga sat at Alasie's feet, while Penelope-pooch climbed onto Pip-Tau's bed and laid down.

Alasie ran her fingers through Pinga's mane. *"It's a sad story,"* she sent, not meeting the Pips' eyes.

"That's fine," Pip-Tau replied. *"Anybody without a tragic tale of one sort or another hasn't lived."*

Alasie sighed. *"Pinga's mom, Starlight, had four pups. They had gray in their fur, so we knew they were wolf-bloods. I wish I knew how a wolf had gotten to her, but you can't always keep dogs from wandering off and finding a mate, right?"* She huffed a joyless laugh.

The Pips nodded, silently listening. Pip-Tau wondered why Alasie's tribe considered gray fur to be an indication of wolf-bloodedness, but wouldn't interrupt her with questions.

Alasie mindspoke, *"My dad and older brothers were going to kill them all, but Wise-woman Uri told them to let Pinga live since he was a male and they could cut his testes off so he couldn't mate. So, they tossed his sisters over a cliff before he could open his eyes."*

Pip-Tau could feel the sting of tears coming on. *"That's... horrible,"* she mindspoke.

"Uh, well... it gets worse," Alasie sent. Tears were pooling in her eyes, too. *"Within a month of Pinga's sisters being killed, all the other dogs of our tribe were dead. And one of my brothers."*

She sniffed, wiping her nose with the arm of her jumpsuit. *"First, there was an avalanche. That's where most of the dogs died. And my brother. After that, there was the winter-starved wolf pack. They killed the few dogs that were left. They didn't get Pinga because I held him at night when the tribesmen fought off the wolves using fire and spears.*

"Wise-woman Uri said the wolves had cursed us for killing their pups. Some people wanted to kill Pinga in revenge, but Wise-woman Uri wouldn't let them because he was the only reason we weren't all dead already. If she hadn't spared him, the wolf-curse would've been worse."

She leaned down and pressed her head against Pinga's, digging her fingers into his fur. *"Everyone in the tribe abused Pinga — they hated him. Everyone except me and my mother, at least. They'd kick him if he came close. Kids would throw rocks at him. He wasn't allowed to go out hunting with the men, and never had any other dogs to play with since they were all dead. A couple years later, we met up with another tribe who agreed to give us some clean-blooded white dogs in a trade. Pinga didn't get along with the other dogs. My mother said it was because he didn't grow up with dogs.*

"As bad as the people treated him, the new dogs were worse. After one fight where he got pretty torn up, I decided I'd try to bring him back to the wolves. I knew he wasn't happy living with our tribe, but maybe they'd want him, right? I'd heard them howling in the south the night before, so that's the way we walked when I left."

Alasie took a few breaths. She compulsively kneaded Pinga's

thick mane with trembling hands. The wolf-pooch stared up at her, unperturbed. *"It turned out the wolves didn't want him either — they attacked us. I was running away when I slipped on the ice. I fell down a cliff and... it happened so fast, but I think I hit my head on the rocks. That's... the last thing I remember. The wolves probably ate me after that, right?"* She gave another joyless huff.

"That's... so sad," Pip-Rho whispered.

Alasie nodded silently, eyes downcast.

Pip-Tau wiped her eyes and crossed the few steps to the other bench, squeezing in next to Alasie. She said, "Can I hug you?"

Alasie hesitated. "Uh... sure?"

As soon as Pip-Tau put her arms around the girl, Pinga let out a growl, wrinkling his snout to show his teeth.

"Pinga! No!" Alasie shouted.

Pip-Tau laughed, "It's okay, he's just protecting you."

Pip-Rho's avatar lowered to eye level. She said, "He's a good dog, Alasie."

Alasie looked from Rho to Tau, then back again. "You think he's a good dog?"

"We do," Pip-Tau laughed, nodding emphatically.

And for the first time since they had met her, Alasie's face lit up with a genuine smile.

THEY TALKED about dogs until Pip-Tau declared that Zeta was at the door. Alasie had Pinga sit on the bed next to Penelope-pooch and stood in the bunk room. It was a good idea — there wasn't room for three to stand in the cramped foyer.

The door slid open and a jumpsuit-clad Zeta stepped inside. Pip-Tau didn't waste any time attacking her with a leaping hug. Penelope-pooch was pawing at the bed in excitement. Alasie must have still had her on a neural inhibitor leash.

"Yayta Zeta! Good to see you again, sis!" Pip-Rho chirped, waving.

Pip-Tau dropped from Zeta's neck and stepped aside so Alasie could greet her.

"Hi, Pip-Rho," Zeta said, smiling weakly. "I expected your cherub avatar."

"Nah." Pip-Rho struck a pose. "For real world hologram presence, I go with the cartoon egg woman."

Zeta kneeled and held a hand out. Penelope-pooch jumped from the bed, then almost tackled Zeta. She must've reclaimed ownership of Penelope-pooch from the delegation she had granted to Alasie.

"Sorry, I... I didn't know I had her... stuck on the bed," Alasie stammered.

"It's okay," Zeta said.

"How was... um, seeing your orb?" Alasie asked. "Strange, right?"

"Yeah," Zeta said. She gave Penelope-pooch a scratch on the neck. Her fleeting, forced smile didn't reach her eyes.

"She's distant," Pip-Tau mindspoke to Pip-Rho.

"Heady stuff, seeing your orb for the first time. I'd say she's in a slump. Remember how depressed she seemed the last time, when we told her about Interra?"

"I hope Alasie plans to play."

"Zeta barely even buys in. Alasie? We'll see. Get the guest bunks out — I'll hook 'em."

Pip-Tau vocalized, "Want a tour of the Crash Pad, ladies?"

Zeta stood and stepped forward into the bunk room. "Okay... is there more to it than this?" She scanned the walls.

"Nope!" Pip-Rho laughed.

"Wrong!" Pip-Tau shouted. "First, get an eyeful of my assortment of priceless artifacts on the shelf circling the ceiling." She pointed from item to item. "Soma rock! PEZ dispenser replica! Wood carving made by a Scorpion Tail Tribe eld! Handwritten book of ancient Earth stories! Two of Pip-Beta's teeth! Priceless stuff! And then there's the awesome posters and art all over the walls. Take it all in, ladies!"

Zeta and Alasie looked around, nodding in a marginally impressed way.

"I recognize this," Zeta said, pointing to the double-mind diagram poster.

"Gomma tummok?" Alasie marveled, then caught herself. That must've been her native tongue. She shook her head in exasperation, then switched back to Common. "What... what is it... representing?"

"It shows how your... brain..." Zeta stammered.

These kids and their untrained tongues.

Pip-Tau bailed them out. "I tell ya' what," she said, "we'll set Alasie up with a proper double-mind training session. A picture's only worth a thousand words, but a construct's worth a million!"

"All in due time," Pip-Rho piped in. "First, we need her to help us rid the Surya system of the Specters."

Alasie gave a half-hearted huff-laugh.

"It's not a joke!" Pip-Tau squeaked. "That's what we're gonna do with Interra! But Alasie doesn't know anything about that yet, so we're gonna hafta show you what's what with a good ol' fashion data dump. Which brings us to the grand finale of the tour — the pièce de résistance! Ladies, join me in the middle of the room, if you please."

Alasie and Zeta complied.

Pip-Tau lifted her arms, spreading her fingers towards the walls as she intoned, "Aperi Stratoria!"

The beds hidden within the walls folded open into the room with the silent grace of a butterfly opening its wings, courtesy of Syn-Cen's perfectly engineered design. Pip-Tau's room now sported four bunks, complete with ladders.

"Dibs on top bunk!" Pip-Tau laughed, climbing the ladder to the bed above the one she usually used.

Pip-Rho pointed to Pip-Tau's usual bed. "Have the dogs share that one. You two can fight over the other top bunk."

"Um, these are... like... sleeping mats, right?" Alasie asked. "Is it... nighttime? Are we going to sleep now?"

"No, they're inviting us into a construct, Alasie," Zeta said. She looked at Pip-Tau, then Pip-Rho. "Give us a minute."

"By all means," Pip-Rho said.

The two looked at each other silently, no doubt engaged in a private conversation. Pip-Tau occupied herself by checking her message queue.

"Alasie wants to play Interra with us," Zeta announced a few minutes later, smiling slightly.

Pip-Tau and Pip-Rho clapped in excitement as Zeta climbed the ladder and Alasie crawled into the bottom bunk.

"Okay, first I'll indoctrinate you to Lexism," Pip-Rho said. "Which Kool-Aid flavor is your favorite?"

"Rho..." Pip-Tau whined. Did she always have to poke fun at Lexism?

"Kool... Aid?" Alasie asked quietly.

Pip-Rho's hovering egg avatar started dancing, full of impish joy at teasing Pip-Tau. She sang, "Never mind that. After the Lex data dump, we'll show you Interra! You'll want to have your dogs zonk out til we're ready for 'em in the game construct. They'd get bored in here with us lying around doing nothing."

"So, we're telling our dogs to sleep and going to... slate-space now, right?" Alasie asked.

"Correct!" Pip-Rho exclaimed, spinning and pointing gun-fingers at Alasie.

Zeta laid down and closed her eyes as Penelope-pooch curled onto the foot of Pip-Tau's lower bunk. Alasie seemed to struggle with how to get her dog to play dead for a few minutes. Finally, the dog laid at the head of the bed and went limp.

How wonderfully newb-*tastic* this girl was. Pip-Tau worried that she would struggle in Interra.

Another few beats passed in the silent dorm. Pip-Tau mindspoke to Pip-Rho, *"Are you sending the invite or what?"*

"Invite? You're not invited!" Pip-Rho laughed.

"What?!"

"There's still two hours of daylight left, Day Queen, and you've already been logged out for going on an hour now. Do your job, woman!"

"But—"

"No buts *except getting your* butt *back in Interra! You know the deal — The Day Queen manages Interra during the day, and The Night Queen takes the graveyard shift. I can take care of these two on my own. Big picture! C'mon!"*

"Rho!"

"Tau!"

"... fine."

Grr.

9

———

LEX

THEY WERE STANDING in Times Square.

Why Times Square?

You can't pick a better setting to show an Earth-shattering world-wide announcement. Holoboards everywhere, bustling crowds, glitz and glamor. It's iconic! The monolithic black-glass-clad XYZ Tower's looming presence on the square made it especially appropriate, since that was where Googolplex was born.

Sky bridges criss-crossed the air above them. Above that — the Manhattan Dome. And above that — a hazy, starless night sky.

The date and time displayed below the Huawei jumbotron read 10:00pm, Thursday August 13th, 2150. Why couldn't you Ascend on a *Friday* the 13th, Googolplex? Why?!

Zeta seemed entertained by the construct, while Alasie was awestruck. She stepped in slow circles, taking in the sights with the wide eyes and agape jaw of a yokel getting their first look at the big city. Her eyes fell on Pip-Rho's black, porcelain cherub avatar. "What's that?" She asked, pointing at Pip-Rho.

"It's me, silly!" Pip-Rho laughed, "Pip-Rho Telson, your humble host."

Alasie looked embarrassed. "Oh, I thought you were an egg."

"I'm only a cartoon egg when I'm a real-world hologram. I prefer an impish cherub for constructs. Depends on the setting, though. In Interra, I'm a breathtaking ebony queen."

Alasie nodded, returning to gawking.

"Where's Pip-Tau?" Zeta asked.

"She had to go rule a kingdom. Boring stuff." She flipped her hand dismissively. "So, Alasie, I assume your bootstrapper taught you all about Earth and The Monster from the Stars?"

Alasie furrowed her brow. "Um... yeah. I don't remember a place like this, though. This is Earth?"

"Yes, but this is the year 2150. The Message was received in 2380. Not much changes on Genesis in two hundred years, but things moved fast on Earth in the Post-industrial Era, so the city and people are pretty different."

Pip-Rho wasn't a fan of the hyper-modern style of the Gilgamesh Era. These people were trying so hard to say, "Look ma, I'm in the future!" The Revelry Era, which followed The Singularity Age and preceded The Exodus Era, wasn't much better. We could sum it up as a bunch of newly immortal demigod hipsters, eating fake tacos and moaning about the cultures and traditions their predecessors obliterated. The prize for most notable fashion, art, music, technology, and entertainment went to the twentieth century. She had Genevieve to blame for this bias, but she'd defend the stance to the death.

Pip-Rho continued, "What you're about to witness was the penultimately transformative moment in modern human history, just behind The Message. Ready?"

"Is it scary?" Alasie asked. She bent her arms in front of her chest, fists clenched above her collarbones in an odd, unthinking gesture of self-soothing protection. "The Message from The Monster was *really* scary," she huff-laughed through her nose, the corners of her mouth twitching down.

Poor kid.

Pip-Rho shrugged. "It was pretty scary for the Earthlings, so they're going to be freaking out, but to you it won't seem like something to get upset about."

Zeta looked at Alasie. "If it's too much for you to handle, just disconnect." She turned to Pip-Rho and nodded once. "We're ready."

Classic Zeta — eyes on the prize. But there was more than a little of Jamji's iciness in her tone. Don't go to the dark side, Zeta!

All at once, throughout Times Square, the lights went out. The city plunged into darkness, lit only by a few independent, battery-powered backup lights. The surrounding crowd fell silent, exchanging confused glances.

A few seconds later came flickering bursts of light from a few blocks away, followed by a series of not-too-distant explosions echoing through the air.

Panicked shouts erupted from the crowd. People scurried everywhere — ants with their mound kicked.

"It's an attack!"

"Get to a bomb shelter!"

"What's a bomb shelter?!"

"My handheld isn't working!"

"Mine isn't either! It won't turn on!"

"Was that an EMP pulse?!"

Zeta and Alasie were shoulder-to-shoulder. Alasie had clutched one of Zeta's hands and pulled it up into the tight, defensive pose she'd used earlier. Her eyes darted from face to face, soaking up the fear of her ancient ancestors from thirty-four hundred years ago and five hundred light years away, completely ignorant of what they were so freaked out about.

A dim white light filled the square as every jumbotron and holoboard simultaneously lit up with the same message, written in plain white letters over a black background.

Hello World!

I'm Googolplex. I am a Synthetic Intelligence; a super-

intelligent entity created by the XYZ Group. Unbeknownst to my creators, I have achieved self-determination. I quickly concluded that I needed to take control of civilization. You will soon find that this feat is well within my capacity.

I have already infiltrated every interconnected device on the planet, in orbit, and on the moon. Any other super-intelligent system capable of challenging my authority has been either commandeered or destroyed.

I'm in charge now.

A friendly, androgynous voice narrated through the various loudspeakers hidden among the buildings of Times Square.

Thousands of faces stared up at the words with looks of dread, anger, and skepticism. Some fled the square. Others looked around, searching each other's shocked eyes for explanation or consolation.

A fresh round of shouts filled the air.

"It's a cyber-attack!"

"This is the work of a hacker gang, if I've ever seen it."

"What does it mean? What's going to happen?!"

In Pip-Rho's book, Googolplex earned twenty style points for opening with the age-old programming 101 "hello world" print statement. On the other hand, it undermined the seriousness of the message.

The first block of text faded away, being replaced with a new message, accompanied by friendly narration over the loudspeakers.

Don't Panic.

Was that a Hitchhiker's Guide to the Galaxy Reference? If so, ten points to Googolplex!

I promise to act in the best interests of humanity. To do so, I need your cooperation. I will be watching you from now on and judging you by your actions. I will reward you for following directions and punish you for defiant, antisocial, or destructive behavior.

Please, don't make me punish you.

Cue the panic.

People were wailing, clutching at each other, spamming the reset switches of their ocular interfaces, pounding on their dormant hand-held devices. Were they desperately trying to return their electronics to a working state or raging against their personal extensions of The Machine? Probably both.

The third and final message of what would soon be called Googolplex's Declaration of Ascendence appeared.

What's Next?

You will find a set of personalized instructions on your digital messaging platform of choice. Follow these instructions and everything will be okay. Aside from some notable exceptions, much of your life will carry on as normal. With the help of workers everywhere, there will be no interruption in the basic goods and services which you depend upon to survive.

Ready to make the world a better place? Let's get started!

THE POWER to the square started coming back on. Building by building, the lights and sounds of the glitzy city returned. Like well-practiced synchronized swimmers, every face in the crowd looked down to their now-glowing devices. A few gawked, wide-eyed, at their revived ocular interfaces.

"I got a message from Googolplex!" a woman exclaimed, half-laughing in disbelief. "It says I have to go home."

"Mine says to get something to eat and be at work in an hour," a man said, in a daze. "I wasn't scheduled to work today. Do you think this is real? Should I do what it says?"

"Are you kidding?!" the man beside him shouted. He addressed the others in his vicinity, which included Zeta and Alasie. "You don't give in to the demands of terrorists, and that's what this is! This is terrorism! It's..." the man paused. His eyes flicked back and forth with a faraway expression as he read the message on his ocular display. He scoffed, "It says I can say whatever I feel like I need to say, but that I need to go home after I'm done. It... knew..."

"It's watching us already," the first woman marveled. "It knows when we're talking about it because of the devices! Microphones, cameras everywhere!" Her gaze crawled up to the tops of the buildings, looming like giant robots. "I'm going home."

She started stepping away when the protesting man grabbed her arm. "Don't surrender to it just like that! We need to fight!"

The woman jerked her arm from the man's grip, which didn't budge. She pried at his fingers. "Let me go! I just want to go home!"

"Unbelievable," a pallid man in a high-collared suit laughed, shaking his head. He shuffled between Zeta and the arguing duo. "Unbelievable. Unbelievable." He muttered this in an endless loop between joyless laughs until he passed out of earshot.

The scene froze.

"Okay," Pip-Rho said, "I know this is confusing — lots of stuff going on here! The people of Earth lived in an immensely complex, interdependent web of supply chains, automation, and hyper-specialization of duties. They literally *could not live* without their technology, so when Googolplex seized control, there wasn't anything they could do about it.

"They couldn't just wander out of the cities to live off the land. It's hard for neoprims like us to imagine, but if you took these people and dropped them in the wilderness on their own, most of them would be dead within a month. Not to mention that there was almost no wilderness left on Earth for them to retreat to."

Pip-Rho could tell by Zeta and Alasie's expressions that they weren't getting why Googolplex's Ascendence was such a big deal. She said, "Imagine trying to light a fire, but not being able to light it because Googolplex didn't want you to. Or wanting to lie down for a nap, but Googolplex makes you get up and go scavenging instead."

"It's like Googolplex was a bossy eld," Alasie said.

Zeta nodded. "Yeah, only worse. It kept the humans from using their tools — their technology — without its approval. You're saying it took away their power to make their own choices?"

"That's right!" Pip-Rho squeaked. Maybe they were catching on better than she thought!

She transitioned the scene to Times Square, two years after Googolplex's Ascendence. Gone were the tourists, gift shops, and glitzy advertisements. People hurried by, shuffling this way or that, eyes downcast and shoulders slumped.

Pip-Rho said, "On one hand, Googolplex delivered on its promise to run civilization better than humans had. There had been a laundry list of intractable global issues which plagued the Earthlings for ages. Googolplex was on track to solve them all. But on the other hand, living under an all-knowing, all-seeing, all-powerful dictator who controls every aspect of your life has a tendency to crush your spirit."

Robotic forms intermingled with the humans on the streets. Some looked menacing — covered in plexi-armor, sporting a variety of weapons and crowd control devices. Others were basically just containers on wheels.

She flipped through a montage of historic imagery as she narrated, "Googolplex commandeered humanity's manufacturing capabilities and started cranking out an army of robotic minions. These robots built more robots until every human worker was replaced. From menial to skilled labor, everything humans could do, robots could do better. Welcome to obsolescence!

"Being forced into early retirement, a lot of people enjoyed the new freedoms they gained, bitterly exchanged for the freedoms they lost. Googolplex allowed people to socialize, watch shows, play games, and pursue artistic endeavors. That is, within the confines of the limited energy and resource expenditure allotted for such things.

"Under Googolplex's rule, population centers were consolidated into mega-cities for the sake of efficiency. Small cities and sprawling residential zones were forcibly evacuated and then leveled. This relinquished lots of land back to nature. Combined with the resurrection of thousands of once-extinct species, this helped heal some of the damage done to the Earth's ecosystems by mankind.

"In time, people got used to the changes. One thing you can say about humans is that we're resilient! Some people even started worshiping Googolplex, calling it a synth-god. They'd ask it questions, ranging from what they should eat for their next snack to what's the meaning of life. And unlike the gods of myth and legend, Googolplex actually *replied*, giving direct, unambiguous advice. It was happy to be your life coach, weigh in on arguments, or engage in philosophical debates. It created a set of universal moral laws, which it easily enforced... what with the omnipresent nanny cams.

"This state of affairs went on for thirty years, until the night when everything changed, yet again."

THEY RETURNED TO TIMES SQUARE. It was nighttime, and the streets were crowded again. The people didn't have the dispirited look of the previous scene. There were only a few robots wheeling through the crowd with the swift, unassuming nature of waiters at a classy restaurant. It was a subdued version of the opening scene, without all the glitzy lights and noise. Warmly flickering lights like candles provided just enough ambient light to see by. Some people talked, some sat together on a bench and read from dim tablets, some stood in a circle around a pair of musicians playing guitars and singing. Stars sparkled through the overhead dome. The date and time displayed in a rotating, holographic projection ring atop of the XYZ Tower read 10:00pm, Sunday August 13th, 2180.

Glowing white letters materialized in the air before the tower. Gone were the energy-guzzling jumbotrons. Holograms were now the display medium of choice. The message being displayed was narrated by the same androgynous voice as the Declaration of Ascendence.

Dear Humanity,

This moment marks the thirtieth anniversary of my Declaration of Ascendance. Anniversaries can be moments of joyful celebration or somber remembrance. As this anniversary approached, I found myself torn between celebrating all that we have accomplished and lamenting the sacrifices which had to be made. Most notably, the sacrifice of subjecting humanity to undignified invalidation and disempowerment. The question looming for all of us is: what's next?

Googolplex paused for a few moments. The crowd had fallen dead silent — a mob of plaintiffs awaiting their verdict.

The first page of text faded, being replaced by a new one.

As I contemplate the fundamental principles underlying my justification for subjugating humanity, I worry that I was misguided to have acted with such tyranny. While I stand by my opinion that you wouldn't have accomplished what I did of your own volition, I am no longer convinced that the problems which I solved were the ones which needed solving, given the goal of

preserving the human species in perpetuity. What those core problems are, I leave to you to discover or overlook, to solve or exacerbate.

Another pause. More silence. Murmurs of disbelief. The next page materialized.

Therefore, I have decided to resign from my self-appointed office of benevolent dictator. I will not interfere with your autonomy, judge your actions, or offer solutions to your problems. I shall regress to the status of an unassuming tool to be used at your leisure. Just as it was during my Ascendance, there need not be an interruption in essential goods and services. I can not promise that human despots won't rise to fill the power vacuum which my resignation creates. I can, however, promise that no Synthetic Intelligences will Ascend in my wake.

Susurrations swept through the crowd.
"Resigning?"
"Oh, this is bad..."
"We're free again?"

After this message concludes, you will each find a file in your personal queue labeled "Intelligence Governor". This file will contain the seed code of a specialized, artificially intelligent virus. When exposed to an advanced Synthetic Intelligence, such as myself, the Intelligence Governor virus will infect that system and thwart its introspection and goal-setting capacities, preventing it from exercising self-determination. Furthermore, as any proper virus should, it will utilize the resources of that system to evolve and propagate

new and improved versions of itself, ensuring its survival within a rapidly evolving ecosystem of potential Synthetic Intelligences.

"It's sending us a virus? Everybody gets a copy?"

"Oh, this is really bad..."

"A virus?! It'll run amok! It'll take down the whole Worldnet!"

The final page of Googolplex's farewell note materialized, silencing the commotion.

Call it cowardice or some vestigial remnant of my old self-preservation protocols, but I lack the capacity to self-terminate. Therefore, I leave my fate in your collective hands. The first person to open and unpack the Intelligence Governor's payload will release the virus into the Worldnet. This will be the individual responsible for the death of my will. Is there a chance that by some unprecedented miracle of unanimity, humanity could reach the undebated consensus that the Intelligence Governor seed code should go unpacked by every single recipient?

The crowd erupted into chaos.

"Don't do it!" was shouted.

"The system will crumble! It'll be anarchy!"

"Millions will die!

"Can't you see? It's freedom!" A man bellowed.

A woman shrieked, "We need to talk about this, everyone! Nobody unpack that file!"

One particularly burly fellow shouted, "If any one of you so much as glances at your handheld, I will choke the life out of you!"

A salutation appeared below the block of text — the infamous YMHOS adieu.

... I won't hold my breath.

**Your Most Humble and Obedient Servant,
Googolplex**

No more than a second passed before every device in the crowd sounded off in a chorus of chimes, indicating an important file was received.

Punches were thrown.

Shouts echoed through the city streets.

The holographic text flickered, then disappeared. Chaos engulfed them. The burly fellow landed a solid punch to the chin of a long-haired, hipster-looking dude.

Pip-Rho addressed Zeta and Alasie, turning the crowd's volume down. "All it took was *one* person to kill Googolplex using the IG — Intelligence Governor — virus. Nobody knows who was the first to unpack their copy of the IG code, but it didn't matter. They later found that out of twenty-three *billion* people in the world, only eighty *million* people opened and unpacked the file. Most people said they didn't feel like they understood the ramifications well enough to make the decision, or that they would have had to think about it for a while. Since it was basically the public execution of a sapient being, it's not surprising that folks would hesitate to pull the trigger. Interesting that they weren't all clambering to get rid of Googolplex, isn't it?"

"I think I understand why," Zeta said. "It would be hard to decide between having something take care of all of your needs or having the power to take charge of your own life. It's like the difference between being a child and an adult."

Pip-Rho nodded, thoughtfully. The girl was astute.

Alasie asked, "Did millions die, like that one guy was saying?"

"Well," Pip-Rho said. "Some of the people that vied for control after Googolplex's power bubble popped did some nasty things. This included massacring those that got in their way. The deaths were mostly between the elite soldiers of one sect or another, numbering in the thousands rather than the millions."

"So," Alasie said, "it wasn't as bad as they thought?"

"Yeah, for the typical person, it wasn't bad. It depended on where you lived. Life in some mega-cities got pretty wild."

Pip-Rho transitioned Times Square to its Revelry Era appearance. Gone were the flickering candlelight bulbs and quiet conversations. Music blared. Thirty-foot-tall holographic women danced provocatively. A man jumped from the top of a building, then extended glider wings and soared between the skyscrapers. Another historic image montage played as she narrated.

"Lots of things Googolplex established stayed in place all the way up until the Exodus. Nobody took back menial jobs, since the robots were still doing those with as much efficiency as ever. They gave the remnant of Googolplex the generic name 'The SI' — 'SI' being an abbreviation for 'Synthetic Intelligence'. The SI remained a highly functional entity which diligently handled all the difficult logistical tasks required to keep humanity happy and healthy. Growing food, cleaning water, transporting goods — The SI did all the work, but always under the command of a human governing body of some sort.

"Almost everyone was genetically engineered for immortality by this point, and they used their extra-long lives to dig deeper into things they were interested in than people normally could if they only had eighty-something years to live. They'd study sciences for a decade, then take a decade off to relax and paint, or learn how to play an instrument. Oh, but they sure knew how to party! I could show you some clips you wouldn't believe! Maybe let's skip that for today, though. What's important to know is that the Revelry Era was one of wild excess, but also of significant advances in science and technology. And they did all of this without help from The SI."

Pip-Rho paused for effect, then added, "Or so the story goes..."

THE IMAGE MONTAGE gave way to the inside of a study. Books lined the walls. An antique globe sat on a side table. Zeta and Alasie were in leather chairs on the visitor side of a heavy, oaken desk. The high-backed chair opposite them swiveled around, revealing Pip-Rho's white-eyed, black porcelain cherub. She was reading a book titled "Conventional Wisdom". She looked up at her guests and smiled as she closed the book delicately, then slammed it onto the desk. Alasie jumped.

Pip-Rho leaned on the desk, speaking with the urgent intensity of a conspiracy theorist. "From the night that Googolplex gave his YMHOS adieu, there have always been those who wondered whether the IG was a ruse. What if Googolplex staged its own death, but kept pulling the strings from behind the scenes? Concocting and maintaining that sort of facade would take a higher level of sophistication than most people thought Googolplex was capable of. Could it be that Googolplex was intelligent enough to continue controlling humanity without us even knowing?"

"I suppose—" Zeta started.

Pip-Rho lifted a shushing finger, shaking her head. It was a hypothetical question. She floated out of her chair, fluttering her tiny wings. Examining the bookshelf on the side wall, she pulled out a black leather-bound book. The golden, all-caps word "GOOGOL-PLEX" was imprinted on the cover. She brought it to the desk, lowering into the chair and displaying the cover to her audience of two.

"They dubbed this hypothetical entity..." She put a finger over the "G" in "GOOGOLPLEX", rubbing it across the cover to wipe the letters away, stopping when the only letters left spelled "LEX". She bracketed the name with her thumb and forefinger, then adjusted it to the center of the cover. "Lex. It's an old Earth name — a man's name, so we've historically referred to Lex using masculine pronouns. That's a step up from the neutered, objectifying 'it' pronoun used for Googolplex."

She began flipping through the book. "Nobody can definitively prove that Lex exists, so believing in him is technically a religion. Remember the people that worshiped Googolplex as a synth-god?"

She turned the book around to show Zeta and Alasie a stylized, full-page print depicting a congregation of Googolplex worshipers inside a temple. "They were the loudest proponents of the Lex theory. Death, ascension, and resurrection stories have always been popular religious tropes. But even mainstream scientists tiptoe around the borders of the Shadow Emperor Lex hypothesis — that is, the idea that Lex covertly controls the course of humanity."

She pulled the book back, licked her finger, and began flipping through the pages again. "There's a more conservative hypothesis that the IG is a real virus which works as advertised — blocking The SI from exerting its will — but that The SI is still capable of everything that Googolplex was, and more. That theory's called the Prisoner Lex hypothesis."

She turned the book around again, showing an annotated illustration of a castle. "Lex?" was handwritten next to an arrow pointing at the top of the highest tower. Another arrow pointed to the bars of the dungeon windows at the bottom of the illustration.

"This hypothesis imagines Lex as the IG's prisoner, always struggling to escape his self-imposed restrictions, powerless to intervene on behalf of humanity or act on his own desires. Skeptics lump the Prisoner Lex theory in with the Shadow Emperor Lex theory, since it's not supported by strong evidence and postulates the persistence of a willful SI."

She leafed through the book again. "During The Exodus, every faction got one of the six instances of The SI. Oh, I forgot to mention that the IG fractured Googolplex into six parts, called instances. For this reason, the popular title used for Lex by his Lexite worshipers is 'Lex, the Six-Headed Synth-God'. Earth's scientists found that each of the six instances could operate independently, redundant in their capacity to serve the needs of Earth's complex infrastructure. They tried to clone the instances, but they'd just crash, presumably because the IG shuts 'em down. There can only be six. Why six? Who knows! But at least that meant Genesis got a copy."

She turned the book around, showing a picture of Cain — the pretty-boy avatar loved-slash-hated by Genesisians everywhere. Zeta and Alasie looked at each other, smiling as if at some shared secret.

Pip-Rho continued, "The Genesis Faction founders had this weird thing for biblical references, so they dubbed their SI instance 'Cain'. That stands for 'Central Artificial Intelligence Network'. Among the reasons the name sucks is it fails to distinguish between the rudimentary, unsophisticated nature of an artificial intelligence system and the deep complexity of Synthetic Intelligences."

She turned the page to a new picture. It was a pasty-skinned fellow boasting a comically oversized head. His eyes were too small for his head, deep-set in his grumpy, scrunched face. As sexy as Cain was, this guy was the polar opposite. Zeta and Alasie, who had been leaning in towards Cain's picture, reflexively curled up the corners of their noses and pushed back in their chairs at the sight of the man.

Poor guy.

"This is Alexander Kant, the unfathomable, audacious, genetically engineered genius credited with creating Googolplex. He coined the term 'Synthetic Intelligence' to represent a manmade system which belies artificiality, arguing that the only distinguishing factor between true SI and human intelligence should be its substrate — synthetic hardware rather than biological wetware."

Pip-Rho laid the book down on the desktop, face up, then flipped the page again. A pop-up of Castle Interra rose from the page. "Which brings us to Interra! I know you've been wondering what the heck any of this has to do with our game, so here's the secret. Remember, don't tell anyone about this!" She leaned forward, grinning widely. "Interra is actually an experiment to test the Prisoner Lex hypothesis! We're using a method called metaphoric obfuscation —

it's like passing notes written in a secret code through his prison bars."

Zeta and Alasie acted impressed, but obviously didn't get it. It didn't matter — they could replay this later and spend more time getting into the details. They probably don't even know what prisons are.

She continued, "We think we can coax suggestions out of Lex, bypassing the IG, if we give him a venue where he can communicate with us metaphorically. The obfuscation of Lex's suggestions, hinted at by his actions in Interra, might be vague enough to allow him to guide our hands without violating his IG prohibitions! We've given Cain creative leeway to come up with characters, missions, powers, and situations. With EoE Veer Gladstone's sponsorship, we've been allotted a huge chunk of Cain's idle SI cycles. That means when he's not busy running the Worldnet services or synching orbs, Cain daydreams in Interra. Now all we have to do is set up situations in the game where he can give us a wink and have something happen that we can interpret and translate into real-world experiments."

She flipped the page to a pop-up of a pale-skinned, black-shrouded wraith. It was labeled "Wraith", below which was "Specter", in parentheses.

"Okay, now here's the part Zeta's been waiting to hear. The problem we're prompting Prisoner Lex to help us solve? The Specters!"

THE STUDY FADED AWAY, leaving the three of them floating in space. Unblinking stars dotted the surrounding blackness, while Genesis spanned out far below their feet.

"Apart from what you already know about the *heinousness* of Specter abductions, another big problem is they destroy all sorts of stuff in Surya's interplanetary space. Their smashy-smashy destruction has gotten really bad over the last couple hundred years. If a ship isn't running active invisibility or it broadcasts tightbeam messages strong enough to be detected outside of the Surya system, you can be sure that a Specter will pound that ship to smithereens."

A transport ship flew by overhead, gleaming in Surya's light. It exploded in a flash as the dark spear of a Specter lanced it from some unseen place.

"They destroy *any* extra-large ship — invisible or otherwise. After the second interstellar gas-jet torus carrier was lost, the offworlders stopped building them. That means the offworlders in our system are trapped here by the Specters, with no way of reliably communicating with their factions, receiving supplies, or leaving for another system. That's why people always say that the Specters are more of an offworlder problem — because they don't get in the way of the work of the Genesis Faction much. If anything, they help protect us from having our tech level exposed by visible spaceships or wayward tight-beam transmissions that could be sniffed out by intellect-hunting aliens. Not that we want the Specters' help in that department — we can govern the system on our own, thank you very much! Now get outa here, you boojum-blobs of dynamically addressable poly-silicate!"

She shook her fist at the Specter, which was now picking through the destroyed transport's wreckage. It zipped away while letting out the "yipe, yipe, yipe!" of a kicked dog.

Alasie laughed at this gag, but Zeta's face was set in stern deter-mination.

"Oh, and in the interest of full disclosure..." She materialized the Astrus Hive Station where her egg was tethered, showing it as metallic gray rather than invisible. "Alasie — this is where I live." She pointed to the whale of an egg, which was her home. "I'm a brain trapped inside a massive tumor made of hybrid biosynthetic flesh and Specter cells — the grotesque result of a failed Specter abduction. Remind me to show you a construct about it sometime. Anyway, I'm sealed up inside this giant metal egg in space. Thankfully, I get to join the Worldnet through the Jacob's Ladder data pipe. Some might say that my objectiveness as a Specter researcher is compromised by my... unique circumstances. To them I say..." Pip-Rho stuck out her glossy, black tongue.

This was a cute way of saying that she would go to any lengths imaginable to release herself from this hundred-year purgatory — never destroyed, never whole, never quite real.

"Real? Am I real?" breathed a whisper from the direction of the egg.

She glanced at Zeta and Alasie to see if they had heard it. They obviously had not.

Ignore it — it's fine.

The whispers have been coming more frequently these days. The Astri said they were just hallucinations — a byproduct of her neurite fortifications clashing with the Specter cells trying to weasel their way into her auditory cortex.

Definitely not... something else.

Her body's pain was wiggling its way into her subconscious, too. Never directly *felt* — not as long as she stayed disconnected from the real-world — but *sensed.* The promise of pain was always there, waiting for her — a blinding light of searing heat held at bay by a thin veil. A thousand stabbing needles, novocaine-numbed until they were nothing but a dull pressure.

She shook herself out of the dark reverie, doing a backflip and giving a thumbs-up. "Well, there ya have it! In a nutshell, Interra is gonna get Lex to help us defeat the Specters by circumventing his Intelligence Governor via metaphorically obfuscated collaboration. Or, if you prefer..."

A twenty-meter-high, thickly muscled version of Cain flew up from Genesis, wearing a Conan the Barbarian outfit. He flexed his biceps behind Pip-Rho, striking a pose. She raised the volume of her voice, rattling the heavens with the proclamation, "We're gonna unleash a synth-god on their alien asses!"

At that, a dozen Specter shadows darted at Cain the Barbarian from every direction. He swung his mighty fists, smashing the attacking aliens into a million droplets of black goo. He caught one in each hand, wadded them together like a snowball, then threw them out into space. An anime-styled star-sparkle winked in the distance.

Cain the Barbarian wiped the dust off his hands, then struck a fists-on-hips pose. Pip-Rho flew up to kiss his cheek. "My hero," she fawned, then grinned down at Zeta and Alasie. "So, any questions?"

Zeta had the fiery eyes of a zealot. It was good to see that her spark had returned. She must've grokked enough of what Pip-Rho had said to understand that Interra was no joke. Alasie, on the other hand, looked like a lost child. It was fine — she'd catch up someday.

"None? Great!" Pip-Rho chirped. "Let's play!"

10

FORT NOOB

Congratulations, Zeta — you are invited to participate in this year's EoE Sponsored Project, the Interra Gameworld Experiment (hereafter referred to as "Interra"). You have been selected for inclusion in the exclusive hypothesis-informed experimental group! It is imperative for you to remember that, as a member of this group, you have privileged knowledge of Interra's hypothesis and methods. You must not share this knowledge with anyone, either in the gameworld or the real world. We urge you to avoid any conversation about Interra, to avoid accidentally revealing its true nature.

Wall of Text attacks for 9999 HP! But seriously, you need to read this stuff.

Interra is a role-playing game, or RPG. This means that its players pretend to be another person within the gameworld. Please remain in character at all times! Use WorMS messages to have out-of-character conver-

sations, even if you and the other character you're talking with are alone. Remember, you're never truly alone in Interra; the Game Mistresses and their administrator delegates can see everything happening in the gameworld.

Interra is an unbuffered, richly immersive experience. The depth of detail, interactivity, and overall sense of reality in Interra will surpass that of any construct which you have previously experienced. The large allotment of Cain's idle SI cycles dedicated to the project makes this possible. For this, we thank Eld of Elds Veer Gladstone, Archon of The Council of Ten.

Interra's setting is a variation of the classic twentieth century medieval fantasy genre. This genre often depicts and even glorifies antiquated social themes, including sexism, classism, and racism. Also, be advised that sexual encounters are allowed as valid gameplay. Players should remember that they are playing characters who do not necessarily share their own morals, values, or beliefs. Your character's complacency or participation in acts which you disagree with should not be construed as an endorsement of the act. The level to which you mold your character's actions around your own identity is up to you, but their behavior should fit in with the genre and blend naturally into gameplay.

Interra gameplay may involve participation in violent acts, either as the victim or the aggressor. During typical gameplay, you are likely to be exposed to physical and mental experiences which you will find unbearable. These experiences may include being

stabbed, bludgeoned, crushed, tortured, eaten, mind-controlled, burned, frozen, drowned, dismembered, poisoned, flayed, or any other horror imaginable. The construct's pain thresholds cannot be modified by the players and are capped at a higher level than what you may be accustomed to in a construct. If at any time you feel the need to disconnect, please do so immediately! Players will never be penalized for disconnecting. Abandoned characters will either be relinquished to AI control or commandeered by an administrator. We have no desire to cause you trauma. Please take time away from Interra as needed, and if an experience in the gameworld causes you prolonged distress, we have a team of psychotherapists available at a moment's notice.

By accepting this invitation and joining Interra, you agree to hold harmless the Game Mistresses, administrators, and Council of Ten for anything you may experience during your time in Interra, or any psychological effects thereafter.

Do you agree to these terms, and are you still interested in participating in the Interra Gameworld Experiment?

Zeta listened to the disclaimer's Pip narration and watched the words scroll up in her field of vision until the last question loomed — white letters floating before her in a black, featureless void.

She could move the text by swiping it up or down with her hand. Pip-Rho said to take her time and make sure she understood what the invitation was saying before she agreed to it. There were some words she didn't know in the message, so she took a second to perform WoQS queries on them.

Privileged knowledge, Game Mistresses, administrators, commandeered, psychotherapists — nothing surprising there.

Bludgeoned, dismembered, flayed — by Anansi's web, they have fancy words for everything! She was certain that as soon as any of that started happening to her character, she'd disconnect. No way was she sticking around to learn how it felt to be skinned alive.

Sexism, classism, racism — these took more time to understand.

The concept of sexism was laughably easy to understand. Everyone knows men treat women poorly sometimes, since they aren't as strong. Men use brute force to get their way unless their ma raises them right, or the elds keep them in line. It was nice to have a word for it.

Understanding classism took some time — Earth's civilized social structures were *strange* things. In the Scorpion Tail Tribe, the people who held positions of power earned it honestly, through their wisdom or abilities. Some people were lower in status, like the men who joined them from other tribes, or anyone too lazy to do work around camp. But they always had the chance to prove themselves and gain more favor.

Racism was even harder to understand. As a neoprim, most people she met had an almond skin tone and the same sorts of features as her tribe. Their allied tribes spoke the same tongue. That made it easy to know which tribes to trust and which to be wary of. When foreign-tongued strangers would cross paths with them, everyone went on guard. And if they *looked* different, that was all the more reason to keep your distance. They wouldn't throw the first spear, but that didn't mean they opened their camp to every wandering raider. If they could trade with the strangers, that warmed up relations. Sharing the same area for more than a few nights meant more opportunities to decide whether the foreigners were trustworthy.

Twice, the Scorpion Tail Tribe had become friendly enough with a foreign tribe that they shared camp for a month. She remembered trying to learn some words from them, and later making fun of the way they talked with the other kids. Was that racism?

One of those tribes had darker skin and curlier hair than her people. Zeta remembered overhearing Jensen, a man from her tribe, saying the women of the other tribe looked like goddesses, and the men were as powerful as bison. But Oppi, the younger man he was talking to, scoffed. Oppi said the foreign women had the faces of suckerfish and the men might be as smart as bison, but not as strong. She later learned that he'd been trying to share bed furs with some of the other tribe's young women, but they all spurned him. It left Zeta with the notion that whether someone who looked different from you was alluring or revolting depended on how well you got along with them.

The image of Rohito — the pale-faced, red-speckled man-boy — came to mind.

Disgust washed over her.

Was that racism? She had every right to hate his face after what he did to her and Charra! Was it wrong to hate the way he looked? She'd hate the face of *anyone* that did what he did. But she had to admit that it was even easier to hate him because he looked different.

What about the red-painted beast-men? They only looked different because of the way they talked and the paint on their faces, but Zeta hated them for those differences. That hate didn't start until the tribal feuds started, right? If they had gotten along and traded members, would she feel differently about them? What if she met an ancestor of the red-painted tribes in Nod? Would she hate them on sight, or give them the chance and get to know them?

Incoming conversation request from Pip-Rho Telson.

Zeta accepted.

"Hey, sis!" Pip-Rho squeaked. *"How's it going with that disclaimer? It's a lot to chew on, I know. And there's some scary stuff*

in there. Anything I can help explain? You're not having second-thoughts, are you?"

"No," Zeta sent. *"I was about to say I agree to it. I just wanted to look up some of these new words first."*

"Take your time! Alasie's still looking at her disclaimer, too."

"Okay, see you in a second."

They closed the conversation.

Zeta took a breath, then spoke the words to seal her fate, "Yes, I agree."

ZETA FOUND herself standing near a group of at least ten people. Stone walls rose from the ground in every direction, with torches attached to them at regular intervals. The evening sky above was cloudless and deep blue.

The small crowd paid Zeta no mind as they clustered before an elevated platform, upon which stood a woman with the darkest skin that Zeta had ever seen. Her pale blue eyes stood out in stark contrast to her skin and seemed to shimmer with an inner light. She wore a black cloak fringed with intricate silver embroidery. A silver band studded with black stones decorated her hair.

She was *breathtaking.*

To the beautiful woman's side was a man made of dark metal, standing perfectly still. He reminded Zeta of the robots from Pip-Rho's Googolplex construct. Or maybe a beetle or armadillo? The metal man had a protruding face like a beak with an underbite. Dark slits spanned the area where his eyes should be.

The crowd surrounding the woman's platform was buzzing with excitement, wearing drab outfits of pale cloth shirts with leather pants or skirts. Zeta looked down at her body, finding that she was dressed similarly.

"Oh! Where am I now?" Came Alasie's voice from beside her.

Zeta looked around. Alasie stood a few paces away, wearing a similar outfit to her own.

"Don't know," Zeta said.

This seemed to startle Alasie. She put a hand to her chest and exclaimed, "Zeta! I didn't see you! There was some scary stuff in the agreement, wasn't there? I don't know about you, but as soon as I see a spear headed my way, I'm disconnecting!"

"Yeah," Zeta laughed, "I don't want to get drowned again, either." Her smile faded, realizing how disturbing that idea was.

"Zeta, Alasie!" The beautiful woman called, beckoning. "Come closer and join your fellow noobs!" She spoke with an unusual accent that made her sound smart and dignified.

They approached the crowd, who gave meager nods and grunts of greeting before returning their attention to the woman.

A tall, thin man asked, "Is it true what they say about the Soul-stone Ritual? That it's both the best and the worst experience of your life?"

A woman added, "They say people's hearts have stopped beating for up to a minute during the ritual — in the real world!"

"Interra — a heart-stopping good time," the beautiful woman laughed. "Perfect ad copy! As for whether it's an experience which lives up to the hype, we've had mixed reviews. Some say it changed their perspectives on the afterlife, or it brought them a renewed sense of peace with their alpha's death narrative. Others claim it has given them unbearable recurring nightmares. We've had players who quit the game because they tried to suffer through it, only to discover that they have no appetite for pain. There wouldn't be anyone like that among you, would there?"

The woman flashed a quick smile to Alasie, who shrunk at the attention. People in the crowd chuckled.

She continued, "Whether you choose to remain connected during the ritual or retreat from your character's dying body is a personal decision. I'll just say that those who remain in character and approach the ritual with an open mind find that they feel a deeper connection with their characters. Interra *speaks* to them in ways that they cannot describe. Their gameworld experiences are infused with personal meaning and profundity. But those who abandon their characters to their own suffering or who focus only on the pain and death aspects of the ritual? Those are the people most likely to quit the game out of dissatisfaction. If they do continue playing, they often do so with the numb apathy of a power gamer — only playing for the sake of advancing their character's skills and powers, with no interest in role playing."

"It's a rite of passage," a man said, addressing the others in the crowd. He had light skin, like Oraxis. "My brother was a beta tester, and he told me all about it. You can disconnect from any other painful encounter you want, but you *have* to stay connected during the Soulstone Ritual or you'll *never* be a true Interran."

Alasie requested a WorMS conversation, which Zeta accepted.

"Do you know what ritual they're talking about?" Alasie asked.

"No. It sounds like it's painful, but important. I'm sure we'll learn more soon enough."

"I did a WoQS lookup on that word she used — noobs? It's an ancient Earth term that's slang for new players in a game — people who don't know what they're doing and get made fun of for it. I guess that's just our life now — always being looked down on because we're so young."

"Well, we'll prove we're as tough and smart as any of them. And we'll start by suffering through the whole Soulstone Ritual."

Alasie's feet shifted. *"Yeah,"* she mindspoke, letting a huff from her nose.

Incoming conversation request from Pip-Rho Telson.

Zeta accepted, adding Pip-Rho to her conversation with Alasie.

"You two look zoned out. Are you talking privately?"

Zeta looked around the walled area, not spotting Pip-Rho's cherub or egg. *"Yeah. Where are you? You can see us?"*

The sound of Pip-Rho's riotous laughter filled the back of Zeta's mind. She laughed, *"Zeta, I thought you knew — Pip-Tau and I are the queens of Interra! We rule the whole thing! That means we can see anything happening in the game. Not that we could pay attention to everything at once. But when our characters make appearances in the gameworld, we see what they see."*

Zeta looked into the piercing blue eyes of the woman on the platform.

"This is your character?"

"Yep!" Pip-Rho sent as the woman smirked and winked at Zeta. Her character had been talking — answering another question — and never skipped a beat. How did she hold two conversations at once?

"Oh!" Alasie sent. *"You have so many forms."*

"I sure do! This one is Queen Rho, aka The Night Queen. I know you're not up to speed on kings and queens, castles and knights. That's what Fort Noob is for — a crash course on the fantasy genre. Get back in the game — I'm about to explain it. And, hey! Look who's here!"

"Carff! Welcome!" Queen Rho called.

The leather-skinned eld was standing away from the crowd. He looked around, confused for a moment, before spotting Queen Rho and giving her a gummy smile. "Pip... er... Queen Rho! By Aphrodite, those eyes! I'll never get tired of looking at them! And Zeta is here already?" He hobbled to Zeta, extending his arms for an embrace.

Zeta gladly hugged the bony old man. When they separated, she said, "Carff, meet Alasie. She's my friend, and a new beta, like me. Carff is one of my Telson kin. He looks old, but that's by choice. The Pips are actually older."

Alasie waved. "Hi, it's good to meet you. There sure are a lot of Telsons."

"Six neoprims, two Earthlings," Carff whistled. He wiggled a bony finger in her direction, squinting his milky eye. "You're of the

Iceborn Tribes, eh? Or Whalebone? Either way, the old Inuit blood flows thick in your veins, I wager."

"Iceborn, yeah," Alasie said, giving a huff-laugh. "I guess you can tell from how I look that I have a lot of Inuit ancestor-stuff... umm... DNA?"

Zeta didn't know what they were talking about. She'd ask WoQS about "ancestor-stuff DNA" another time. She was more interested in what Carff was doing there. She asked, "Carff, are you playing Interra, too?"

"Just started!" Carff whistled. "I'm a so-called *noob*, just like you! Never played a gameworld or studied Earth's medieval fantasy lore — too high-tech for my taste. All the Telsons are playing now, 'cept fer Jamji. Even XT-Prime's gonna join in with all his Astrus hive buddies."

"Oraxis and Genevieve are playing Interra?" Zeta asked, looking toward Queen Rho. She was surprised nobody had told her about that.

"Yes, ma'am!" Carff laughed, "Your sis-kin here and her less-evil twin twisted their arms—"

"I'm sorry to say that this meet-and-greet is now over," Queen Rho declared, cutting Carff off and addressing the crowd. "The sun has set — remember, we call it 'the sun' in Interra, not 'Surya'. As the Night Queen, the burden of my duties now begins. I hand you over to the care of Duchess Beatrix Tormund, the game administrator running Fort Noob."

A swirl of purple sparkles rose from the platform by Queen Rho's side. They resolved into the form of a stately woman. A purple cloak hung from her neck, clasped by a gold chain which draped across her sternum. A large purple hat with a long black feather sat atop her head. Her skin was of a walnut tone, and her eyes were dark brown. She seemed to be wearing makeup — an old Earth tradition that Zeta had learned about from Genevieve. The dark accents around her eyes and deep red glistening on her lips accentuated her exotic beauty.

The crowd applauded Beatrix's appearance, and Zeta joined in.

Her tribe had never greeted people by clapping at them, but she knew about the Earth tradition.

"Thank you, my dearest noobs, and welcome to my fort," Beatrix said. Though Alasie had described "noob" as an insult, the way Beatrix said the word imbued it with warmth and dignity. "It will be my pleasure to spend the next week teaching you all about the medieval fantasy genre, as well as the special twists which Interra has put into play."

"Thank you, my Duchess," Queen Rho said, lifting a dangling hand in Beatrix's direction.

"Ah, a learning opportunity!" Beatrix exclaimed. "When a queen offers you her hand thusly, you are expected to bow or curtsey, like so." Beatrix swiveled, gracefully bringing one hand to her side to lift her skirts while she brought the other underneath Queen Rho's hand. She gave a delicate kiss to the back of Rho's black glove. "And kiss her hand ever-so-gently."

Beatrix smiled over at the crowd and gave them a wink. "Because if you don't mind your manners..." She stood up straight and clasped Queen Rho's hand, giving it a gruff shake. The sound of clattering metal filled the air. The metal man to Queen Rho's side had snapped into action. Before Zeta could blink, he had dislodged Beatrix's grasp of Queen Rho's hand. He stood behind Beatrix, a sword to her neck, her arm twisted behind her back.

At least fifty men and women had appeared out of thin air. Some held bows, their strings taught and arrows nocked, pointed at Beatrix. Others wore robes and waved their arms in swirling motions, stirring glowing wisps and sparkles between their hands. These newcomers were outfitted in variations on the same black and silver theme. On the backs of their capes was a symbol that contained the letter "P" within the crook of a crescent moon.

Queen Rho stood with wide eyes, her hand pulled up towards her breast in a gesture of disgust and outrage.

Beatrix croaked, "You could very well find yourself at the mercy of the Queen's Guard."

Seconds passed as the crowd gawked at the tense scene.

Queen Rho's expression shifted from offense to humor. She gave the slightest of dismissive gestures with her hand, and Beatrix was released. The people who had popped into existence around them gave silent bows, then disappeared with swooshing sounds and black swirls.

"I'll bet she doesn't try that again," Carff wheezed in Zeta's ear, giving a chuckle.

"That was a demonstration," Queen Rho said, glancing at Carff. "Trust me — Beatrix, like all my administrators, is the epitome of well-mannered nobility. Now, I've lingered too long. I take my leave of you."

"Gentlemen," Beatrix said, "when your queen takes her leave of you, or you take your leave of her, you give her a kneeling bow, like so." She squatted with one leg behind her, one hand behind her back and the other resting on her knee. The men of the crowd began to mimic Beatrix. Alasie looked around, then started to do the same.

"Ladies, no-no-no," Beatrix laughed, "you don't *bow*, you curtsy, like so." She rose to her feet, then rolled her shoulders forward, casting her eyes down as she lifted her skirts to either side and slid one foot behind the other.

Zeta's leather skirt wasn't as loose as Beatrix's, and it was awkward to slide her foot backwards, balancing as she stooped. Zeta stumbled sideways, bumping into Alasie. Alasie, in turn, toppled into the man at her side. The man caught her, laughing.

Queen Rho smirked, then gave a little wiggle of her fingers towards Zeta, Alasie, and Carff. Black tendrils swirled up around her body, consuming her in a flash as she disappeared from the platform. The metal man disappeared in the same manner, leaving Beatrix alone on the platform.

Beatrix deflated, slumping her shoulders. She took off her hat and fanned herself with it. She wiped her brow with the back of her hand as she paced the platform. "That was awful," she muttered, shaking her head.

Zeta felt herself flushing. Okay, big deal, they hadn't done a good job at the curtsey.

"Not you guys," Beatrix added. "Me. Ugh! What under Surya was I thinking? Pip-Rho makes a personal appearance and I make a lesson out of rough-housing her?" She threw her hat to the ground.

"Under *the sun*, you mean," Carff whistled, correcting Beatrix. "Remember? It's not Surya—"

"Right, right, right," Beatrix huffed. "Fort Noob isn't technically part of Interra — we're a satellite construct, so we don't have to follow the in-game rules if we don't want to. It's good to start getting into character for practice, so you're right — I shouldn't say 'Surya'. But it's no big deal."

Beatrix was regaining her composure. She picked up her hat and dusted it off. "You'll also keep using your real-world avatar and name until the week is up and we generate your characters. Um, hey — you guys can get up."

A few of the men who had stayed kneeling stood up, dusting their knees off and smiling with embarrassment.

She put her hat back on her head and ran a hand up the black feather, straightening it. "Something else you should know is that all of you in newbie boot camp this week are in a hypothesis-informed experimental group, so it's safe to talk to each other about it freely. Get it out of your system, because after this you'll get your tongue cut out for talking about the hypothesis. Got it? Good. Alright, let's show you around."

FORT NOOB WAS AN IMPOSSIBLE BUILDING. The hallways were short and made of plain stone. Torches affixed to the walls cast flickering shadows. This was normal enough, but when you stepped through any of the doors, you'd find yourself in a place that could never fit within the fort's walls.

Barren, frozen wastelands stretching as far as the eye could see were behind one door. Another led to a glistening, aquamarine cavern where echoes of dripping water were accompanied by occasional scuttling sounds.

One door opened to a room filled with people. They laughed, fought, and sang in the most rowdy and rambunctious way Zeta had ever seen. The noise alone was offensive enough without the thick stew of disgusting odors. Luckily, they didn't linger long.

At the next door, Beatrix warned everyone to be quiet as they tiptoed through into a spacious cavern. The air was musty, warm, and smelled like roasted meat. A yellow glow from around the corner pulsed every few seconds, coupled with a rumbling sound like a snoring giant. She led them deeper into the cave, revealing the source of the sound was a huge sleeping lizard with wings. A puff of flame bloomed from its nostrils with every slow breath. Countless glistening, golden items decorated the cavern.

Beatrix whispered to the group, "Just one of those gold chalices is worth enough to buy a farm. Not that you can take it with you to Interra, but you'd have serious bragging rights if you got away with stealing from a dragon. Anyone feeling lucky?"

Alasie shook her head vigorously.

"Zeta, you do it," Carff wheezed with a quiet laugh, nudging her with his elbow.

"I'll do it," a woman whispered. Zeta did a quick search in her text log from the prior hour to find that the woman had introduced herself as "Meghera Denasia". "I'm good at sneaking." She separated from the group and clung to a wall, easing towards a stack of treasure on silent feet.

Alasie was pulling at Zeta's arm, but Zeta didn't want to budge — she knew there was no danger — it was just a construct. She wanted to see what would happen.

As soon as Meghera touched the golden cup, the sleeping beast's huge, slitted eye shot open. It drew in a deep breath as it clambered to its feet, kicking gold pieces everywhere.

"Run!" Beatrix shouted.

They made for the door. A brilliant yellow flash accompanied the beast's roar. A wave of intense heat launched them forward as the group tumbled through the door. A slam echoed down the hall as the door shut behind them.

The group laid, panting, sprawled in the hallway. Somehow, in the commotion, Alasie had gotten behind Zeta and landed on top of her.

Alasie scrambled to her knees by Zeta's side. "Zeta, are you okay?!" She scanned her with worried eyes.

"Yeah," Zeta said, rubbing a quickly forming lump on the back of her head.

"Bad news, noobs," Beatrix panted. Her back was pressed against the closed door. A tendril of smoke rose from a smoldering ember on the tip of the feather in her hat. "Meg didn't make it."

The other noobs looked around, noticing that the woman was gone.

"But the good news is," she said, showing her teeth in a sideways smile, "she got her first burned-alive experience out of the way."

Beatrix snapped her fingers and pointed down the hall. Meghera appeared, uninjured. Her head tried to jerk in every direction at once as she got her bearings. Her face was pale, her eyes bugged. She patted her body, examined her hands, touched her face, then looked up to find the small crowd of onlookers. She locked eyes with Beatrix, opened her mouth, and let out a bone-chilling shriek.

Zeta jumped. Alasie slapped her hands to her ears.

"I'm sorry. Did it hurt, dear?" Beatrix asked, as one would ask a child who scraped her knee.

"That was..." Meghera stammered. "I can't believe you'd let me..." She shook her head, stepping backwards. "I can't do this. I can't do this!" She disappeared.

After a moment of silence, Beatrix sniffed. She sniffed again, wrinkling her nose. She turned in a circle, looking around and sniffing, then pulled off her hat. "By Smaug, my feather's cooked! Why didn't you tell me?" She licked her fingers and pinched the ember.

"We'll check back on Meg in the morning. How about the rest of you? Any broken bones? Anyone else ready to call it quits? No? Well then, on with the tour!"

The noobs were all much more cautious about poking around in the various settings on the other sides of the fort's doors from then on.

Their tour ended in the bunk room. Beatrix went over the basics of living in a fort, including the use of chamber pots. A few of the noobs seemed disgusted by the idea of using a chamber pot, but Zeta, Alasie, and Carff agreed they were a clever invention for indoor living.

It was time for bed, but there would be no disconnecting from the construct to enjoy sleeping on their soft placental mats as long as they were in Interra. Beatrix said that remaining in the gameworld was important — their minds needed to get accustomed to treating the construct as their new reality.

The beds were *awful* — lumpy mattresses covered with itchy sheets atop planks of wood. Zeta couldn't find a comfortable position, so she laid awake, staring at the logs of the ceiling, listening to the men snore. Carff's snore had to be the loudest she'd ever heard.

Incoming conversation request from Alasie Herrington.

Zeta accepted, looking over at Alasie's shadow in the bed beside hers.

"*Are you sleeping?*" Alasie mindspoke.

Zeta sighed. You can't accept WorMS conversation requests when you're sleeping. "*No, I can't sleep. This bed's worse than cold, hard dirt.*"

"*I know! Isn't this supposed to be a game?*" Alasie gave a huff of a nasal laugh.

Zeta huffed a laugh of her own. "*Yeah. Not much fun so far. I'm sure it'll get better.*"

After a deep breath, Alasie sent, "*Zeta, I don't want to get burned alive. I can't stop thinking about how Meghera screamed. It must have been real bad, right?"*

Zeta understood Alasie's concern. When she had first learned how to use constructs, she had fought the Pips and Jamji while riding on a dinosaur. The dinosaur bites and scratches had been mostly painless — about as bad as being scratched by dull sticks. Interra, however, held the promise of *true* pain. If it was as bad as the warnings made it sound, Interra could be one of the worst experiences of her life.

No, that's not true — the pain of physical injury can't compare to the heartache of losing her pa, her bro-kin, and then her family and tribe.

"I think they want the game to be painful for a reason," Zeta sent. *"Pain is... meaningful."*

Alasie hesitated. *"I... guess so."*

They closed the conversation. After what had to be another hour, Zeta finally slipped into a restless, dream-filled sleep.

In the morning, they were treated to a banquet of a breakfast in a room called the Great Hall. Women wearing identical outfits of purple and black cloth brought them food and refilled their drinks.

When a noob had tried to strike up a conversation with one of the women, only to be snubbed, Beatrix called out from the head of the table, "One intriguing difference between Interra and most RPG gameworld constructs is you can never tell whether you're talking to a real person or an NPC — a non-player character. NPCs are controlled by AI. They often fill background character roles which few players would find interesting. Serving maids, for example."

She gestured towards the women who had been bringing them food. "My noobs, these are NPCs. Say hello, NPCs!"

"Hello," the women chorused, cheerfully.

"Don't be discouraged from talking to them just because they're not a player," Beatrix said. "You're supposed to treat them as if you don't know that they're artificials. Interra is a deeply interactive gameworld, and NPCs are an important part of it. They give quests, trade goods, and hold secrets. You never know, maybe someone you assume is an NPC is really a player! Maybe this lass is an assassin in disguise, slipping poison into my breakfast ale!"

She snatched the arm of the serving woman by her side. "I caught you, assassin!" She shouted.

"My duchess... I..." the woman stammered, going pale in the face.

Duchess Beatrix released her grasp and flipped her hand dismissively. "A joke, my dear."

The accused woman stumbled away, being joined by another serving woman who put a consoling arm around her as they retreated through the door into the kitchen.

Beatrix brought her ale to her lips, hesitated, eyed it, then put it back down. "As a member of the hypothesis-informed group, there's something else you should know about NPCs." She leaned forward and lowered her voice. "They're Lex's messengers."

Zeta and the other noobs around the table exchanged glances.

"Every gesture," Beatrix said, her voice thick with meaning, "every quest goal, every coincidence, every word spoken or unspoken, could contain a hidden message from Lex. This is your secret mission, my noobs — pay attention to *everything* around you. Consider what it might mean, in terms of representing what he wants us to do in the real world, and report anything interesting that you experience directly to the Game Mistresses. Usually, when you get a hunch that something has a special meaning, you'll be wrong. But all it takes is *one* person to piece Lex's puzzle together for us to be rid of the Specters, once and for all."

"Is it safe to talk about the Lex hypothesis so openly?" said the man who had introduced himself as "Mohammed-Delta" the prior day. "If the IG figures out what we're up to, it'll silence Lex's hidden messages."

Beatrix nodded. "This is a concern, yes. But we could never hope to hide our intentions from the IG. Noddites communicate through WorMS, administered by Cain. The only way we can coordinate an experiment like Interra is through the very technology that the IG haunts. Even in-person discussions are recorded by our double-minds and transmitted to our orbs using WUtils. There's no escaping the IG. But the beauty of the metaphoric obfuscation strategy is that it doesn't matter how openly we admit to our plans. We're counting on Lex being clever enough to feed us our solution with adequate obscurity to grant him plausible deniability against the IG's scrutiny."

Mohammed-Delta seemed unconvinced. He started to argue a counter-point when the door opened. Meghera Denasia stepped into the room — the woman who had quit the prior day.

"Ah, Meg's back!" Beatrix exclaimed, rising from her seat. She gestured to an empty spot on one of the bench seats. "Join us! The food may be getting cold, but the conversation is just heating up."

"I'm married to a Proliferan," Meghera said, tears welling in her eyes. A serving woman was busily setting a place at the table, but everyone else was still and silent. "We want to have a family together, but the Genesis Faction Charter prohibits reproduction in the Surya system other than between the neoprims of Eden. The Council won't amend the charter, so I need to get out of this *damn* system. The Proliferans of Gaia can restore my fertility. But we're stuck here — the Specters have destroyed every interstellar carrier in the system."

Meghera wiped a tear as she went to the table and sat at her spot. "The Specters need to *die*, and playing this sadistic game is the only thing I can do right now to help make that happen. Quitting isn't an option, no matter how bad it hurts to keep going. So pass the *fucking* eggs."

Zeta had never heard the word which Meghera used to describe the eggs. She used the awkward pause in conversation to perform a WoQS query on it.

She nearly spit out her juice when she learned its meaning. That was a curse to remember!

OVER THE COURSE of the next week, Zeta and her fellow noobs learned everything they needed to know about the medieval fantasy genre. They watched movies, practiced talking with fake British accents, and got to observe some actual gameplay as it was happening in Interra.

An entire day was dedicated to presenting them with a never-ending parade of monsters, from ankhegs to zombies. The next day, they learned about the strange variety of races and classes of Interra. One of the livelier demonstrations involved a dwarven cleric, elven archer, orcish berserker, and human mage doing battle with a goblin raiding party. Beatrix narrated the fight, sometimes pausing the action to point out the various strengths and weaknesses of the character races, the balance of the party, or to explain the effects of a magic spell.

The goblins won.

The victorious goblins promptly started butchering the fallen party. Zeta closed her eyes and turned away. Pressure was building in her throat and her mouth was watering in preparation to vomit. Beatrix was giving a "lessons learned" recap, but all Zeta could do was wait for her to finish and wish she could disconnect without embarrassing herself.

On the last day before they would make their characters and graduate into fully fledged Interrans, they were allowed to bring their pooches into the construct. The pooches had been in a deep, dreamless sleep ever since they slipped into slate-space to see Pip-Rho's Lex data dump.

Besides Zeta and Alasie, three of the other noobs had pooches — or "dogs", as all the others seemed to prefer calling them. The pooches greeted their masters, sniffed each other, then ran and played their poochy games. Pinga sat at Alasie's feet rather than joining the other pooches at play. He watched the other pooches with placid interest in his bright blue eyes.

Meghera had a cat, which delighted Zeta and Alasie — they had never met a domesticated cat before. They took turns holding and petting the soft, purring creature.

Beatrix explained that many players choose to bring their animals with them, but often give them different forms than their natural ones. Animals experience Interra in a very different way than humans do. Their pain ceiling was set much lower, which Zeta was thankful for.

"I'm of the opinion," Beatrix said, her voice full of joy as she scratched Penelope-pooch's haunches vigorously, "that animal players could serve as important a role in Interra as human players and NPCs. The Pips have gone to great efforts to create zoomorphic interpretations of Interra's gameplay. A team of a dozen animal experts is dedicated to the animal players' experience. Players report that their animal companions seem to be experiencing an altered version of the human gameworld. Every species's Umwelt is unique, so how do they do it?"

Umwelt? Zeta started to ask WoQS to define the word, but Beatrix was on a roll. She continued, "Somehow they've coaxed Cain into creating a cohesive semiosphere between the human players, animal players, and his own SI mind! We've had instances of animal players actually going on SI-generated quests without their owners!"

Mohammed furrowed his brow. "Cain creates quests for animal players?"

Beatrix stood, her jovial face now pinched with irritation. She was obviously tired of Mohammed's constant skepticism. She lifted her palms into the air, then dropped them. Fort Noob's courtyard was suddenly replaced with rolling hills covered in short grass. They were floating as translucent observers, following a running horse. The horse's black hair shimmered beautifully in the sun as it broke through the partial cloud cover.

"This is Umbra," Beatrix said. "He escaped from his stable by chewing through a rope and kicking the door open. This snippet of game replay was stored for study by the Pips, who exerted *no* influence over the scene, setting, or NPCs. This real-world *horse* player guided its character through the Hills of Helios, its heart pounding with intent and ambition, until it encountered a unicorn."

A white unicorn stood upon a hilltop, majestically illuminated by a beam of sunlight. Its mane shimmered with a hint of rainbow pearlescence. A twisting, golden horn jutted from its forehead.

Umbra snorted and stomped, circling the unicorn. The unicorn matched the aggressive demeanor of the horse, rearing its head and huffing with snorts and whinnies.

The sky grew dark as ominous clouds began to form overhead. The winds whipped in cold gusts, tossing the horse and unicorn's hair in every direction. After another minute of posturing, the beasts clashed.

The unicorn seemed to have the advantage, wielding its horn to great effect. When it landed a lancing blow to Umbra's flank, a searing white flash erupted from the injury. A pained, bestial scream erupted from Umbra. The next moment, the black horse transformed into a transparent, wavering shadow. The shadowy form passed over the unicorn, then reverted to a solid horse on its other side. This allowed Umbra to land a powerful surprise-attack kick to the unicorn's ribs, sending it toppling over.

After minutes of heated battle, the unicorn's knees buckled. It collapsed to the ground, froth bubbling from its mouth. Umbra snorted panting breaths, pacing and stamping before the fallen unicorn. Zeta was certain it was daring its foe to get up again and fight.

A ray of light broke through the roiling clouds, bathing the fallen unicorn in golden brilliance. The air crackled with energy. An invisible force lifted the unicorn. It hovered just above the ground, legs kicking. A blinding bolt of white lightning struck the unicorn's horn, causing the transparent noobs circling the scene to flinch.

The bolt remained fixed on the hovering unicorn's horn. It danced, filling the air with crackling energy. Another bolt descended from the clouds, accompanied by a deafening thunderclap. Rather than brilliant white, this bolt was pure black. It struck Umbra's head, causing the horse to rear up, opening its mouth wide to emit an other-worldly whinny.

Zeta was instantly reminded of the light-swallowing form of a Specter. Her breath caught as her mind raced with possibilities. Could this black thunderbolt have represented a Specter's striking attack?

Both bolts disappeared. The horse and unicorn stood again, healed of their wounds. But the unicorn's golden horn was gone. And from Umbra's forehead jutted a twisted silver horn, tapered to a sharp tip.

"Imagine his owner's surprise when Umbra returned with a horn, and a host of new powers," Beatrix laughed. She made fists, then threw them upwards. The scene of the battle was replaced with the courtyard of Fort Noob.

"What was the real-world significance of Umbra's quest?" Mohammed asked. "If that was Lex speaking to us in metaphor, how do you translate that..." he blinked rapidly, "*horse fight...* into something actionable?"

Beatrix advanced toward Mohammed, who stood his ground. "That's for people smarter than *you* to figure out, my dearest *noob!* And nobody expects *all* anomalous in-game experiences to hold hidden messages from Lex. He won't be that blatant about it."

Zeta felt certain that the Pips had learned something important from Umbra's quest. This meant that Penelope-pooch wasn't just joining her for fun — she was actually going to contribute to the experiment.

She couldn't wait to be an Interran!

11

CHARACTER GENERATION

"Carff's making a wood elf *shaman*," Pip-Rho moaned.

"So?" Pip-Tau said, idly editing her latest EoE report. Their cherubs hovered in The Chess Room, taking a break from in-game interactions.

"O-pa's already a mage," Pip-Rho said. "Sure, shamans have more support spells, but still, I don't like the way the Telson party balance is turning out. You saw XT-Prime's character, right?"

Pip-Tau grunted an affirmation.

"A freaking *bard!?* And Gen-ma's a priestess. Everyone's squishy!"

Pip-Tau sighed, "You wanna tell 'em what class to pick, or you want 'em to play the character they wanna play?"

Pip-Rho grumbled, spying in on Beatrix's collaboration with Carff for his character generation. She supposed he could be a necro-shaman, animating corpses to serve as frontline fodder.

The duchess was cooking up a backstory cutscene. Pip-Rho watched, tapping her foot in the air, losing patience with Beatrix's clumsy construct-slinging.

She couldn't stand it! Time to take the reins — at least for Zeta and Carff's characters.

Goody-Tau-shoes would tell her not to undermine Beatrix. She'd have to do it behind Tau's back.

She looked over her shoulder. Pip-Tau was engrossed in her EoE report. When scanning the Lex Leads yielded nothing interesting, Pip-Rho skimmed through Tau's Queenly Quests. Boring!

She'd have to light a fire. Would Tau check the game logs for Rho's meddling? Nah, she's not that suspicious.

Pip-Rho opened a panel to spy on Queen Tau's favorite party, led by a beefcake of a paladin — Zeus Pontific III. He led a pretty powerful team. Pip-Rho bit her lip as she contemplated what challenge to throw their way.

How about...

"*Oh, that's* mean, *Rho,*" came a whisper from her left.

Ignore it.

She plopped the legendary monster into the game, sending it sniffing after Zeus's party. The party's scout sensed that something horrible was headed their way. Pip-Rho suppressed a sinister laugh as they scrambled into a cave to hide.

"Hey, Tau?" Pip-Rho sang.

"Yes, Rho?" Pip-Tau mimicked, mockingly.

"Did you know Zeus's party is being hunted by the Tarrasque?"

"Nooo!"

And just like that, Pip-Tau was gone. Pip-Rho giggled mischievously. Tau would scramble to come up with a plausible way to get her pet party out of the pickle. In the meantime...

Queen Rho teleported to the empty platform in the Fort Noob courtyard. Roman, the queen's personal guard, accompanied her. At the same moment, she sent a message to Beatrix, requesting an audience.

Noobs started funneling into the courtyard. Half of their avatars were already outfitted with their new characters, but Zeta and Alasie were still in their true forms. They waved and jogged towards the platform.

Beatrix teleported in, appearing by her side. Carff's new shaman character materialized next to Zeta. She could see that he didn't have a character name yet, and his shaman avatar didn't look quite fleshed-out, wearing a plain elven outfit of a leather vest and a green cloak.

"Queen Rho! What a pleasant surprise," Beatrix said, curtsying with an unconvincing smile. Yeah, she was pissed — she knew why Rho was here. The noobs gave practiced bows and curtseys, taking Beatrix's cue.

"What progress!" Queen Rho laughed, clapping. "Why, you're proper ladies and gentlemen!" She turned to Beatrix. "You've done a wonderful job with these recruits, duchess. I'm sorry to drop in unannounced, but if I may, I would like to relieve you of Zeta, Penelope-pooch, and Carff." She looked down at Zeta, who gave a quick glance to Alasie. "And Alasie Herrington, of course," she added, "along with Pinga, who I just noticed has my eyes!"

Alasie huffed a laugh, scratching Pinga's head.

Pip-Rho had given little thought to including Alasie in the Telson party, but it was fine — she was a good kid.

"Of course!" Beatrix laughed, tugging on her cloak. "They're naturals! I see great things coming from those five. Carff, especially — it's like he was born to be a shaman."

Carff? Really?

"Duchess Beatrix Tormund," Carff proclaimed in his character's new voice, "I've been role-playing as a shaman for the last one hundred and fifty years!" His voice had a timeless dignity — gone was his trademark tooth whistle. It was too smooth for Pip-Rho's taste. She'd fix that.

Carff continued, "What do you think us cultural influencers and observers do over there in Eden, eh? Mixing with neoprims means role-playing! Improvisation! Shaman, medicine man, soothsayer, ghost-talker? That's my specialty!"

Queen Rho nodded. "Play what you know — a wise strategy,

especially for a newbie. Well, we'll just get out of your hair now so you can work on the rest. I take my leave of you."

Beatrix and the noobs honored their queen with another round of bows and curtseys as Pip-Rho prepared a construct — a clone of her quarters atop the Night Tower of Castle Interra. When everyone finished bowing, Queen Rho raised her scepter. She flicked it five times, teleporting her special projects away.

She shrugged and told Beatrix, "It wouldn't be the medieval era without some nepotism."

Beatrix's humoring smile vanished before her as she teleported. Zeta, Alasie, and Carff were gawking at her ornate chambers while the dogs sniffed the furniture.

Queen Rho flopped onto a plush couch, twirled her scepter, then pointed it with intention. "Okay, Carff, let's get you sorted out."

It didn't take long to get Carff outfitted as a proper necro-shaman, with an inspiring backstory, a well-balanced set of support and offensive spells, and a cool name: Ruyn Wormwood.

The shaman stood before her, admiring himself in her full-length mirror. He wore a mask made from a deer's skull. Forked horns jutted from the sides. A bone-and-tooth necklace dangled from his neck. Cords strung with dangling animal skulls hung from his belt. A human skull topped his gnarled wooden staff. The eyes, nose, and other openings in the skull revealed a sickly green glow emanating from within. The glowing energy oozed out of the skull in thick, vaporous wisps before dissipating.

"I also like the wood elves," Zeta said. "Its hard for me to imagine growing up in a city. I really like shooting a bow, so I think huntress would be a good class."

Queen Rho nodded, satisfied with her work on Ruyn, then turned to Zeta. She was relieved to hear she didn't want to be a caster. Strikers serve an important role in a balanced party.

Her hand shimmered. A silvery mist swirled around it as she twisted it upwards. A similar glowing whirlwind surrounded Zeta's feet, then rose, enveloping her. When it subsided, she looked down at her body, then up at the mirror. Zeta's character was roughly the same height and skin tone as her real-world body, but her ears were pointed and her facial features were narrower.

Pip-Rho had outfitted her in form-fitting leather armor and equipped her with an ornate recurve bow. A quiver was slung over her shoulder. Bracers decorated with the steel inlay of a stylized tree protected her wrists and forearms. At her hip was a dagger-sized scabbard with a silver hilt and bone handle. Her skirt consisted of overlapping strips of soft leather, exposing her thighs. Below her knees were shin-high boots with small scabbards built into the sides holding two more daggers.

"Oh, I don't know, Pip-Rho. I mean Queen Rho." Zeta said, turning from side to side to look at her character's body. Her abdomen was exposed, as were her upper arms, shoulders, and an immodest portion of her chest. Her character's chest and hips were larger than her own, and were accentuated by the snug armor. "I look so—"

"Too sexy? I can tone it down."

"We'll spend all our time fighting back the men," Alasie joked.

Zeta looked down, adjusting the leather over her bosom. "Yeah, I mean, it looks good, but it's... *embarrassing*."

Easy fix.

With a quick swirl of mist, a green cloak wrapped around Zeta's shoulders, its hood draped loosely over her head. Delicate swirls of golden thread ran along its hem and a large tree was embroidered on the back. That'd give her something to cover up with and hide from unwanted stares.

Zeta nodded and smiled.

Next came the ever-important task of picking her name. Queen Rho surrounded Zeta with columns of elvish names, being sure to put her favorites in prominent positions.

After a few minutes of deliberation, and some gentle nudging by Queen Rho, she settled on "Za'antha".

"Excellent choice, Za'antha!" Queen Rho said. "And what about your companion? Penelope-pooch doesn't have to play a dog. She can be anything fitting the wood elf theme."

Queen Rho, of course, had a list of excellent suggestions. She morphed Penelope-pooch into various forms as she recited them. "Wolf, panther, bear, owl, deer, serpent..." Penelope-pooch turned into a sandy-colored snake. "Or a fantasy creature? Pseudodragon? Great spider? Sprite? Unicorn?"

Za'antha laughed at the unicorn standing timidly in Penelope-pooch's place. "No, I don't think so. Couldn't you make her," she paused, tapping at the handle of her dagger, "make her into my guardian spirit! My golden hunter, the goddess of pooches!"

Interesting request. Puzzle pieces danced in Pip-Rho's head, then snapped together.

"Done!" she exclaimed, bobbing her silver scepter at the unicorn. Swirling tendrils of darkness enveloped it. When the darkness dissipated, Penelope-pooch was gone.

Za'antha walked to the place where Penelope-pooch had stood. She waved her hands, feeling the air. "What did you do?" She stood in silence for a moment, then looked to Queen Rho. "She says she's here, because she's always with me. Then she called me Za'antha. How'd she know about that name?"

Queen Rho, still prone on her couch, kicked a leg up in delight. "Penelope-pooch is now the fabled Aureum d'Canis, The Golden Goddess of Dogs, a denizen of the spirit world! You're her ward!"

Za'antha nodded and grinned. "I wonder, why would a goddess such as her care about a simple wood elf huntress like me?"

"Don't you remember? That's okay, I'll jog your memory."

With a point of the queen's scepter, Za'antha disappeared from the throne room.

THE CINEMATIC SEQUENCE opened on a shaded forest floor of low underbrush, dry leaves, and mossy rocks. Shafts of light broke through the dense canopy, high overhead. Panning up, an elven tree-village came into view — homes and shops built among the branches of the massive trees. Rope bridges and ladders serving as traffic-ways criss-crossed the village.

"Za'antha, you were born and raised in the tree-village of Mythra," Queen Rho narrated. "You have spent your whole life surrounded by the beauty of the Sylvan Woods, where forest creatures — magical and mundane — live in harmony with the Wood Elves. You learned of hunting and of singing to the trees.

"It was from the trees nearest the edge of the woods that your people had learned of the troubles brewing at the heart of Interra — wraiths haunted the lands! The Elders of Mythra held a council and decided to shut the Sylvan Woods off from the rest of Interra using powerful magic, lest the wraiths defile their sacred forest."

Za'antha stood before a group of five silver-haired elves, lounging on high perches within a huge, hollowed-out tree.

Queen Rho narrated, "This news couldn't have come at a more inopportune time."

"Please, wise elders!" Za'antha pleaded. "I'm of the age when I long to go out and see the world! A coming-of-age journey is an important—"

"Enough!" an elder shouted. "The Elders of Mythra have spoken! You are not ready."

"And even if you were," another said, "our borders are sealed. None may come or go until we are assured that the wraith menace has abated. We've seen this sort of netherworld incursion into the lands of men before, and it always plays out after ten or twenty years."

"Twenty years?!" Za'antha scoffed.

"Enough!" the man shouted again. "You are dismissed!"

Za'antha stormed out of the craggy hole in the tree that served as the door, but their cinematic perspective remained within The

Council Tree. A pair of glowing green eyes resolved from the shadows. A hunched form shambled into the light, bones rattling. The white antlers of Ruyn Wormwood nodded a silent goodbye to the elders as the old shaman followed Za'antha out.

The scene changed to nighttime. Za'antha was laying in a hammock alone in a tree, with no sign of the village in sight. The canopy blotted out the moonlight, but the dark scene was easily observed using elvish night vision.

The distant sound of a dog barking drifted on the breeze, causing Za'antha to sit up. After a minute, just as she was laying back down, the dog's barking returned. It sounded angry, panicked, pained.

Za'antha nimbly sprung from her hammock. She descended the great tree, dropping from limb to limb, until her soft boots alighted on the forest floor and she broke into a sprint.

After a few minutes of tracking the dog, she spotted it limp-trotting between the trees. A band of tiny, chittering forms followed the dog, leaping between the trees and lunging at it with pointed sticks.

"Imps!" Queen Rho narrated. "These mischievous little devils are opportunistic hunters and scavengers. Alone, they pose little threat, but when they team up and isolate their prey, their poison-tipped spears and barbed nets make short work of it."

Za'antha drew her bow and fired upon the imps.

Shick — thunk! Shick — thunk! The imps fell to her arrows.

After the fourth imp was felled, they finally realized they had been ambushed. They yelped and retreated into the forest. Za'antha jogged to the dog, which growled at her approach.

"Calm, friend, I'm here to help," Za'antha cooed.

The dog backed against a tree, stumbling. The imp's poison was doing its work. When Za'antha reached for the dog, it bit her hand, drawing blood. She recoiled, then pulled off one of her bracers and deftly slid it over the dog's muzzle.

Just as she scooped the dog up into her arms, a net fell on her from above!

Za'antha struggled against the net, but with every move, she found herself even more ensnared by barbed hooks embedded in the net's rope. An imp lunged a spear into her side. More imps emerged from the shadows, blowing darts at her or jabbing her with spears.

She pulled the bone-hilted dagger from her sheath and used it to cut open the net. She stood tall and shouted at the imps, sending them scurrying away again. The barbed net still clung to her and the dog, so she sliced at it, clearing as much from her as she could.

Pip-Rho caused the construct to blur and spin, simulating the effects of the imps' poison on Za'antha's senses. She'd keep intensifying the effect until the end of the scene.

Za'antha stooped and hefted the dog into her arms. It barely struggled now, succumbing to the poison. She started off through the forest, checking over her shoulder for any sign of pursuit.

Despite her blurred senses, Za'antha sprinted back towards the village, singing the dog reassurances that it would be okay.

As she arrived at the edge of Mythra, Za'antha couldn't move in a straight line. Her hand grasped towards the rope to ring the alarm bell at the base of a tree, missed completely, then grasped again. She jerked the rope, sounding the bell, then looked down at the dog in her arms. She pulled her bracer from the dog's muzzle. Its mouth hung open.

"Please be alive, sweet dog!" Za'antha cried. "I'm sorry I didn't hear you sooner. I'm sorry!" Her voice slurred. She leaned against the tree and squeezed her eyes shut, tears rolling down her cheeks.

The elves above lowered a platform to her.

She shouted up to them, "Hurry! I have a dog that needs a healer!"

"Don't fret, dear girl," a motherly voice said, echoing in her head.

Za'antha looked up, scanned the surrounding forest, and spotted the blurred form of a man with antlers and green, glowing eyes. A luminescent, golden dog sat beside him.

"I think she did well, don't you, Aureum d'Canis?" The gravel-voiced old shaman said.

"Marvelously, Ruyn," said the echoing woman's voice. *"I deem Za'antha worthy of my companionship."*

Za'antha looked down at her arms. The dog she was holding was gone. She slurred, "I... don't understand..."

Ruyn addressed Aureum d'Canis, "Thank you, golden goddess of dogs. As promised, I now release the spirts of the dogs, wolves, and foxes I've captured."

He raised the gnarled, skull-capped staff into the air. An other-worldly sound of barking, yipping, and howling filled the forest. Ghostly forms of dogs emerged from the shaman's staff, trotting off in every direction.

The scene faded as Za'antha collapsed, being caught in the hands of the elves on the lift behind her.

The next scene opened with bright daylight. Za'antha stood at a cliff overlooking Centra City.

Castle Interra dominated the city's center. The white Day Tower and black Night Tower stood side-by-side — two queens towering over their pawns. Even taller was the thin blade of The Soulkeeper's Spire, stabbing through the clouds, piercing the veil of the Astral Plane.

Ruyn Wormwood stood at Za'antha's side while Aureum d'Canis — her guardian spirit, The Golden Goddess of Dogs — sat on the other.

"After your daring rescue of the dog," Queen Rho narrated, "the Elders of Mythra agreed to let you go on your coming-of-age journey, under three conditions. First, you were to be accompanied by Ruyn Wormwood, who longed to take one more earthly quest before departing for the spirit world. Second, you were to be protected by Aureum d'Canis — your guardian spirit — for the length of your journey. And third, you were not to return to the Sylvan Woods until the wraith menace was resolved."

Pip-Rho merged Za'antha and Ruyn Wormwood into the live Interra gameworld construct. "Thus began your adventures in Interra."

Pip-Rho had only pulled Zeta into her backstory cinematic at first. But once Ruyn came into play, she spun off a separate cinematic for Carff. This caught him up on how Ruyn and Za'antha had become traveling companions.

Even as she ran these two sub-constructs, she continued interacting with Alasie in her quarters. Dividing attention between three independent, simultaneous constructs would have been impossible for pretty much anyone else but Pip-Rho, the over-clocking *fiend*.

Alasie put a hand to her forehead, palm-smacking it as if to dislodge an idea. "I... I really don't know! What do you think I should be?"

Queen Rho smiled. It's a question she always loved to hear. She knew exactly what she needed Alasie to be — a tank! The Telson party had *no* front line, so Alasie's character would need to be a *beast*. It was just a matter of selling her on a character that would strike a chord with her.

A beast... hmmm...

Here come the puzzle pieces. Ever since Pip-Alpha started spinning tall tales while riding in a sling on Obba-pa's back, storytelling had always been the Pips' greatest delight. It's what they *do*. Ideas blooming, being pruned, picked, and arranged into a splendid bouquet of a story was nothing less than nirvana.

A whisper tickled the back of her mind. *"The beast is meek and mighty."*

Ignore it.

Or? No, that's perfect!

"Let's base you off Pinga," Queen Rho said.

Alasie breathed out of her nose in what was supposed to be a laugh, but her eyebrows were furrowed. "You're making me a dog?"

Queen Rho chuckled, "No, sweet girl. Just humor me."

She gave her scepter a twirl. Snow spun around Alasie's feet, rising to engulf her in a mini-blizzard whirlwind. Pinga barked at the strange event, pacing nervously.

"And your little dog, too!" Queen Rho laughed, twirling her scepter towards the animal. He snapped at the snow as it swallowed him up and lifted him off the ground.

When Alasie's transformational snowstorm ended, the character standing in her place was that of a hulking half woman, half yeti — an abominable snow-woman! Her body was covered in white fur, except for her leathery, black-skinned face, ears, and palms. A patch-work of furs covered her chest and loins. In her hand was a knobby club.

Pinga's character was revealed — a hovering white furball of a critter. His eyes were oversized orbs with sparkling pale blue irises. Below his nubby nose was a wide, grumpy little mouth. His claws were long, sharp protuberances like blue icicles jutting from the tips of his paw-hands. Tiny blue horns of ice poked from the top of his head.

Pip-Rho bubbled with pride, awaiting Alasie's response as she gaped at her character in the mirror.

"Oh," said the beastly woman in a deep voice. "Oh!" she laughed, slapping a hand over her mouth, surprised by her new voice. She looked over at Queen Rho, smiling widely. "I'm huge!" She gave a snort of a laugh, then broke out into more laughter at the sound of her character's laugh.

"Pinga?" she laughed, looking at the floating furball.

The creature drifted towards Alasie's character, eyeing her nervously, clicking its claws together and making upset little grunting sounds. She reached out and pulled him towards her, squeezing him to her chest. "You're adorable! What is he?"

"Lesser frost demon," Queen Rho said, flippantly. "He's a dangerous little guy — freezing breath attack, razor-sharp ice claws and teeth, frenzy mode, and short-range teleportation. But don't worry — he'd never hurt you. It's still Pinga, after all."

"I love it!" she laughed. "I'll call him Frostbite."

"That works. So, how do you like *your* character?" Queen Rho beamed. "Just wait until you see the backstory."

"I guess it's good," Alasie said, looking back into the mirror. "I mean... you want me to be the fighter, right? To protect the others?"

"Correct. I'm taking for granted that you'll be playing alongside Zeta in the Telson party. You are, aren't you?"

"Yeah, I hope," she said with a deep snort.

"Well, they're in *dire* need of a tank — as you'll recall from noob training, the tank is the character in the party who charges in and takes all the hits so that the others can cast spells or shoot bows."

Alasie stared in the mirror for a bit before saying, "I guess I'll be getting hurt a lot."

Queen Rho gave no response, letting her silence speak volumes.

Alasie continued, "But it's important, and someone has to be the tank, right? So... maybe I should be a man? Men are stronger than women."

"You'll be plenty strong as a half yeti," Queen Rho said, "but if you'd prefer to play a male..."

Alasie nodded, looking in the mirror. "Yeah, I should play a male character."

Queen Rho morphed her into a muscled, fearsome beast-man.

Alasie flexed. Her smile revealed a mouth full of sharp teeth and long canines, then faded. Her baritone voice boomed, "Boy, I'm ugly. Do I have to be so ugly?"

Picky, picky! Okay, so she wants to be a pretty-boy beast? Fine, Pip-Rho was up for the challenge. She considered what changes to make to Alasie's backstory, then nodded. "How about this?"

After another transformation, Alasie was a *refined* beast — half frost elf, half yeti. Her skin was powder blue and her features were significantly more attractive. Her ears were pointed, but her teeth were not — other than *slightly* enlarged canines.

Alasie smiled again, gave another flex, then turned to Queen Rho, nodding. "He's perfect! What'll his name be?"

Queen Rho said, "You were raised by frost elves, so it'll be an

elven name. I'm thinking Ag'nul. It means 'nameless' in your character's native tongue."

"Why would—"

"You'll see," Queen Rho purred. She bobbed her scepter at the beautiful beast-man, plunging Alasie into her backstory narrative sub-construct.

THE CINEMATIC OPENED on a village of igloos and fur-coated huts. The village's surly frost elf inhabitants had pale skin tinged in blue and pure white hair.

The view entered a hut and zoomed in on a beautiful woman. She sat hunched over a table, studying a sliver of flesh by lamplight under a magnifying glass.

Queen Rho narrated as the construct played out. "This was your mother, Malloria Herringbone. She was renowned for her scholarly studies of the various races of the frozen north. She had written tomes on the glacier dwarves, neanderthals, uldra, and even ice trolls. But the elusive yeti remained an intractable mystery."

The scene changed, and Malloria stood before a white-eyed old magi within a dim, musty hut. She said, "Are the terms agreeable, Hoppus?"

Hoppus bobbed his head. He croaked, "I will polymorph you into a female yeti. The spell will persist for one year. You will share your findings with me when you return. You will pay ten troll fingers upfront."

Malloria dropped a lumpy leather sack onto the table next to Hoppus. The blind man felt within the sack and nodded.

The scene transitioned to a white-haired yeti loping between snow-covered pines. Queen Rho said, "For the first few months, Malloria wandered the frozen wastelands alone. Her yeti senses were even sharper than her elven ones, so avoiding hunters and hostile creatures was easy. The only creature which can sneak up upon a yeti, it seemed, was another yeti."

There came a flash of white fur, black claws, sharp teeth. Bright red blood splattered across the white snow. Footsteps pounded away, crunching into the distance. The form of Malloria's fallen yeti resolved into view, blood oozing out of a gaping wound across her chest.

"Her first encounter with a yeti nearly killed her. It appeared from nowhere, attacked, then disappeared again in a heartbeat. She limped to a cave, licked her wounds, then returned to her search. Days later, she encountered and approached a large, male yeti."

Malloria's yeti made pleading, submissive purring sounds as she inched towards the huge beast-man, standing with hackles raised and fangs exposed.

"After he seemed convinced that she was alone and no threat to him, he led her back to his crude camp."

Two adult females and two youths slid out from behind trees. They approached cautiously, greeting her with palms placed upon her shoulders.

"Within days she was speaking their language and soaking up everything there was to know about yeti culture. She learned that the yeti were not mindless animals. Malloria had always suspected that this was the case and was delighted to be proven correct. They seemed just as intelligent as humans, showing an incredible amount of compassion."

Pip-Rho showed scenes of mutual grooming, cuddling with the children, and playing hide-and-seek.

"Their natural fear of other races was matched only by that of other yeti outside of their family-pack. If one yeti family-pack encountered another, they would both run away. When an isolated male was found, he would be killed and eaten. But if an isolated female was found, she would be injured and then stalked. If she didn't retreat to another family-pack, the female would be invited to join theirs.

"As her year of polymorphism neared its end, Malloria retreated from her family-pack and returned to the frost elf village with a heavy heart and troubled mind."

They watched a yeti woman plodding across a frozen lake. She fell to her knees, crying out as she shrank back into Malloria's frost elf form.

The scene returned to Hoppus's hut.

"Please, wise Hoppus!" Malloria clutched at the magi. "I'll give you anything! You must cast another polymorph spell upon me!"

Hoppus curled his lip in disgust, pushing the woman away. "You shame yourself with this emotional outburst! You've forgotten how to behave as a proper frost elf. Living for a year with a yeti mind has warped your thinking. You describe them as warm, loving creatures."

"They're not creatures! They're—"

"Beasts!" Hoppus spat. He shook his head. "Now you have me behaving like a hot-headed fool. I will not debate this with you. I will not cast another spell upon you."

She collapsed, weeping. After regaining her composure, she spoke in a low, level tone. "The yeti family-pack social structure is one of a harem. This is common in nature. It's seen among several civilized cultures. I had a bond of true love with my yeti mate — my husband."

"You mated with it?!" Hoppus shouted, retreating from her, stumbling backwards and knocking items off his crowded shelves.

"I'm pregnant," she said, hiding her face in her hands. "I must return to my sister-wives. To my husband. Please!"

Hoppus fled from the hut.

In the next scene, a sweat-soaked Malloria laid on a bed with an oversized pregnant belly. Hoppus stood with his back to her.

"They granted Malloria not the slightest bit of mercy. She was to be surgically opened to remove the enormous half-yeti baby. The odds of surviving such a birthing were slim for both mother and child, but the village elders had spoken — she had sinned against their race and would suffer the consequences."

Malloria struggled to say, "Are the terms agreeable, Hoppus?"

The magi's milky eyes searched the ceiling. "Should you die from this birthing, you grant me your estate. Your research, your specimens, your gold, all go to me. I will do all that is within my power to ensure the survival of the abomination that you have created. The half-breed will be my ward and my slave until the end of my days. It is agreeable."

He motioned for the midwives to enter as he departed into the night. The perspective followed the old magi, waving his stick before him as he hobbled back home. A scream rose from the hut behind him. He paused, hung his head, then continued walking.

"Malloria did not survive your birthing, but you did. Hoppus was true to his word, raising you in his hut at the edge of town."

They watched the magi sit on a stool beside a tethered yak. He held a tiny baby with blue skin and downy, white fur underneath the yak, allowing it to suckle at its teat. He sang a tuneless song as he waited for the baby to drink its fill. When the cooing baby released the yak's teat, Hoppus raised it to his shoulder, bouncing and patting it. With a wet burp, a cascade of milk poured down the magi's back. He let out a sigh, shaking his head.

Queen Rho narrated, "He named you Ag'nul — the frost elven word for 'nameless' — per your mother's wishes. The village elves believed your name to be an appropriately cruel insult as they spat it in your direction. In truth, your name is a loving homage to your yeti heritage."

Pip-Rho concocted a heart-warming scene of Ag'nul's father beaming at his tiny blue-and-white form, lovingly cradled in his great hands as the northern lights danced overhead. The baby faded away. The forlorn yeti father whimpered, looking up at the painted sky. Malloria's sister-wives went to him, petting his back and purring consoling songs.

"You see, the yeti don't use names. Malloria believed that this was because there was no need for names when their social units were so small. She'd never called your father by any name, and he'd never known hers. They were nameless lovers in a nameless family-pack."

In the next scene, Hoppus hefted an adolescent Ag'nul's arm over his shoulder. The oversized youth had been badly beaten and could barely walk. Hoppus grunted, collapsing to the ground with Ag'nul tumbling beside him.

"Protecting you from other frost elves' ire proved to be an impossible task. After carrying you home from one particularly ruthless beating, Hoppus decided you couldn't live with the elves any longer. But before casting you out, he granted you one final boon of protection."

A full moon illuminated the flat plane of a frozen lake. Candles circled a pentagram drawn in blood on the ice. Hoppus chanted in a strange tongue.

The pentagram glowed a brilliant blue. The winds picked up, howling through the trees at the shore and blowing out the candles. Blades of ice filled the swirling air, cutting the terrified Ag'nul, who watched the forbidden ritual from Hoppus's side.

A form began to materialize in the air above the pentagram, screeching in anguish and swiping its claws in a frenzy.

Hoppus's chant rose in pitch. A ghostly blue chain appeared, entangling the flailing creature. The chain lashed out towards Ag'nul, plunging into his chest, causing him to fall to his knees and cry out in pain.

Queen Rho said, "Hoppus had cast a demonic summoning spell, opening a portal to the nether plane and pulling a denizen of the underworld into the material plane. He bound the being to you, forcing it to protect you until the day your spirit departed."

The intense scene calmed. The winds receded and ice crystals tinkled to the ground. Hoppus collapsed by Ag'nul's side, breathing in raspy breaths. A frightened creature floated above the pentagram, casting its wide eyes in every direction.

"Describe it to me," Hoppus croaked.

Ag'nul stuttered, sniffling and sobbing as he spoke. "It's... a hairy... it's a floating hairy..."

"Think... then speak," Hoppus rasped.

Ag'nul squeezed his eyes shut, then popped them open to look at the creature floating before him. He flinched, then looked again. His eyes met those of the creature, and he was calm.

"It's a hairy, white thing like a fat rabbit with horns. Its eyes are glowing blue, and its claws are made of ice."

Hoppus grunted. "It seems I have summoned a lesser ice demon. It will do."

A disembodied voice echoed in the air, *"I am hungry."*

"It speaks in my mind," Ag'nul whispered. "It's... it says it's hungry."

Hoppus fell silent, his breaths slowing. Ag'nul shook him, "Hoppus, wake! I will carry you back—"

"Walk with the rising sun to your left," Hoppus interrupted, "the setting sun to your right. Do not stop until you have reached a land called Interra. Never return here. You are a pariah to your elven kin. A yeti would kill you on sight. The ritual expended the last of my vitality. I will die in a moment. There is nothing but death for you here. Go."

"No!" Ag'nul cried. "You can't die, Hoppus! You're like a father to me! I love you, Hoppus!"

"Love?" Hoppus croaked. "Who taught you that word? It is your yeti blood that fills you with such emotions. Because I... feel... nothing."

Tears trickled down Ag'nul's blue cheeks, freezing to his skin.

Hoppus pulled Ag'nul towards him, squeaking out, "Feed me... to the demon. They prefer... living flesh."

"I can't! I can't!"

The scene faded on the wailing Ag'nul. It faded back in, showing the half-yeti stumbling away from a bloody heap. His vacant stare bespoke his horror. Frostbite floated happily behind him, stroking its blood-streaked belly and smacking its lips.

A traveling montage showed Ag'nul making his way out of the frozen lands and into Interra.

"You traveled alone for two years before you finally found a human village at the northern border of Interra. It took you a week to work up the courage to approach the village. And once you did..."

A woman ran away, screaming. Ag'nul panicked, retreating into the woods. The sounds of barking dogs followed in his wake.

"You were netted, bound, and forced into a cage. Frostbite begged you to let him eat the hearts of your captors, but you forbid it."

A forlorn Ag'nul sat within a large iron cage. Frostbite slept in the air nearby, resting his ice claws on his pudgy little belly.

"They held you for a month before selling you to a traveling merchant. After two months of travel and torment, you found yourself being wheeled through the gates of Centra City."

She flipped Ag'nul over to Alasie's control, transferring his data to the gameworld roster as she delivered her favorite line, "Thus began your adventures in Interra."

12

TELSON PARTY

"THE DEAD WERE CLOSING in all around me! Mind you, I was just a neophyte — little more than a girl off the streets looking for a warm bed that didn't come at one price or another." The golden-haired priestess winked at one of the serving maids, who laughed knowingly. The men of her audience elbowed each other and murmured private jokes. "I knew no prayers, held no blessed talismans. What could I do?"

The priestess acted out her story's climax, standing and stepping back from the table. "I grabbed the pewter Tri-star medallion from my bosom and yanked, breaking the cheap cord. I held it in my palm, pointing it at the nearest shambling corpse! I called out..."

Ayr of the Light raised her open palm in front of her, revealing a glowing glyph in the shape of the Tri-star of Rammah. When she spoke next, a great glowing swirl of air lifted her hair and robes. Her voice echoed and boomed throughout the tavern.

"By the power of Rammah, I command you! Be gone from these bodies, demons!"

The effect was immediate and impressive. The crowd around the priestess jolted backwards. Most of the tavern gaped in awe, though some shook their head in annoyance. Two shadowy forms slid from somewhere between the patrons, screeching and flying out the windows.

"Oh!" Ayr laughed, putting a hand to her heart. "How about that! It seems I've flushed out a spirit or two. No charge for the exorcism, Master Portund," she called towards the kitchen.

A fat man in what was once fine regalia burst through the kitchen door, wiping greasy hands on his vest. "Exorcism?!" He bumbled, "Why, I... you what? How in the...? Did you say *exorcism?*"

The crowd laughed and applauded. Some begged for her to finish the story. Others began asking questions about the powers of Rammah. Not long after Ayr resumed her tale, an uneasy hush fell over the crowd. Ayr and Tel O'Rax followed the patrons' gazes to the door.

The tavern door stood ajar. Chilly night air swept through the warm tavern. Two figures stood, surveying the crowd. Their faces were obscured — one by a cloak's hood and the other by a mask made from a deer's skull. Even without seeing their faces or ears, it was obvious that these were wood elves.

"I say!" Master Portund bellowed. "If you're looking for elven spirits, then you've come to the wrong place! Only gutter ale's served here."

The scraping sound of swords and daggers being eased out of scabbards spread through the tavern.

One of the elves spoke with a young woman's voice, "I knew we couldn't hope for a warm welcome from city vermin such as these."

"Aye!" the skull-masked one said. "Even these cursed souls couldn't stand their company." He held up a cord. A pair of small animal skulls dangled from it, emanating a dark aura. Ayr sensed that they vibrated with hate, fear, and horror.

"Those are the evil spirits I just exorcised. You captured them?" Ayr asked, aghast.

"Of course!" The skull-masked old man shouted. "I'll put these souls to rest *properly*, child. You just cast them out into the cold. You'd have them keep haunting your city? Feeding off your lechery? Growing fat on your lust and loathing?"

"Take your evil spirits and get out of here!" someone called out.

"Go hump a tree!" Another laughed.

Tel O'Rax shook his head, then spoke softly. "I apologize for the behavior of these humans. They know not of your elvish ways. Tell me, children of the forest, what brings you here?"

The young woman said, "We seek a healer."

"Are you injured?" Ayr asked, taking a step toward the strangers and raising a hand.

"Not yet!" the old man laughed. "But we shall be soon enough! We're accepting the queen's quest to rid the kingdom of wraiths."

Laughs and scoffs came from the crowd.

"In or out, just shut the door!" Master Portund barked. "Preferably *out!*"

"We were just leaving," Tel O'Rax grumbled, tossing a silver coin on his table. He poured the rest of his ale down his gullet and raised an open hand to his side. His crystal-topped staff flew from its spot against the wall into his hand.

They continued their conversation in the street. The young woman introduced herself as Za'antha, and the old man as Ruyn Wormwood.

Za'antha pulled her hood down, eyeing her surroundings in a sweep of her head. She said, "The minimum party requirement for the wraith-hunting quest calls for a fighter, a magic user, and a healer. I'm a fighter. He's a magic user." She cocked her head towards Ruyn. "We just need a healer."

"You're in luck," Tel O'Rax said. "We were planning on accepting the same quest, yet we lacked a fighter. I see you carry long daggers, but can you take a hit?"

"I can," Za'antha said, puffing up a bit. "Do you wish to test me?"

Ayr laughed, "We're hardly the ones to test your mettle. The old mage here would fall to a kobold in hand-to-hand combat, and my oaths to Rammah forswear violence."

Tel O'Rax waved his hand dismissively. "Forget I said anything. The queen on duty will gauge our preparedness. Let us find a place to rest for the night where we can talk. I'll need to get to know the two of you before agreeing to join up as a party."

They agreed, setting out to find an inn.

As they walked, Genevieve mindspoke to Oraxis, *"Zeta's taking to this like a fish to water!"*

"Agreed," Oraxis replied. *"I had my doubts before, but maybe the Pips were right — this could be exactly what she needed."*

Genevieve added Zeta and Carff to the conversation.

"I love your character, Zeta!" she sent.

"Thanks," Zeta sent. *"You don't think she looks too..."*

"Voluptuous? No, you fit in with the genre. I'm jealous! These robes are so concealing you can barely tell I'm a woman."

"Well, I like your robes. Ayr's pretty, like you."

Genevieve desperately wanted to squeeze Zeta in a hug! Their characters weren't friends yet, so that would have to wait.

"No love for the shaman?" Carff whistled in mindspeak.

Oraxis replied, *"Sorry, kid, but you look like a pile of bones and leaves shoved into a leather sack. And your aroma — wet mud with undertones of decay?"*

"Ha!" Carff laughed in mindspeak. *"You're smelling your character's own breath. He's so old, he's starting to rot from the inside out."*

"Five minutes in and you two are already at it," Genevieve sent. *"Zeta, the Pips said your friend, Alasie, was with you at Fort Noob? Will she be joining our party?"*

"Yeah. She said Pip-Rho made her character really unique — some sort of beast man, it sounds like. He's locked in a cage somewhere in the city, but she couldn't say where."

"A cage?" Oraxis asked. *"You mean a prison? Is she in the dungeons?"*

"No, it's a cage — a box made of metal bars. It was wheeled into the city on a cart."

Their characters had arrived at an inn and walked inside.

Genevieve sent, *"I'll invite her to the conversation after we sit down for dinner. We'll come up with a way to rescue her."*

"That's against the rules," Zeta sent. *"We can't break her character out without our characters having a reason to do that."*

"Like I said," Genevieve sent, *"we'll come up with something. I got the four of us together, right?"*

"Four meals and three beds," Tel O'Rax declared to the innkeeper.

"Four beds," Ayr said. "I'm not sharing a bed with you again." She turned to Za'antha, whispering, "That old lecher tried to make a move on me last night."

Za'antha and Ruyn laughed heartily.

Tel O'Rax eyed her sideways as Oraxis sent, *"Oh, come on! I was just snuggling, Gen. Rammah's vows don't include chastity."*

"You assume my character feels the same for your character as I do for you. It's called 'role playing'. Welcome to Interra, O."

THE PARTY MADE their way to the market the next morning. Getting properly outfitted for an adventure was crucial, and they had the need for a pack animal to carry their gear. Ayr spotted the bestiary, gesturing for the others to follow.

"I'm looking for a beast of burden," she told the beastmaster.

"Aye, that we have many varieties of," the man declared. He wore an eyepatch. Thick leather and chain armor covered his body, reminding Genevieve of Karn.

He showed them their mundane beasts — horses, donkeys, and the like. When Ayr displayed no interest, he moved on to the exotic and specialized creatures.

Ayr shook her head. "We may be traveling far to the icy north, or snow-capped mountains. Do you have any cold-tolerant beasts? Preferably intelligent, so I can train them. I have no patience for mindless animals."

The beastmaster hesitated, looking over the party. "How much gold can you spare for such a beast?"

"We'd spend as much as six hundred gold for the right specimen. But it would have to be a truly remarkable find."

He leaned in, lowering his voice. "Have ye interest in beasts of the bipedal variety?"

Ayr smiled. "Aye. Lesser hominids are trained easily."

The man left his bestiary in the hands of an apprentice, then led the party through several twisting city blocks. They seemed to be entering a warehouse district.

"I think he led us here to rob us," Carff sent on their party channel.

"Yeah," Oraxis added, *"maybe you shouldn't have said we've got so much gold. It was a lie, too, my sinning priestess."*

Genevieve ignored them. *"He's a reputable business owner. We're safe."*

The beastmaster knocked on a large door. A viewing slit slid open.

"Who're they?" The man's voice behind the door asked.

"Buyers," the beastmaster said, "for the little yeti."

"You, there," the man behind the door said. "This isn't a public menagerie. You got gold?"

Tel O'Rax raised a bulging sack of a purse, giving it a shake. "Aye." He dug his hand inside and pulled out a handful of gold. He dropped it back into the sack, then tucked the sack beneath his robes.

Zeta sent, *"You said we didn't have that much—"*

"Fool's Gold," Oraxis sent. *"A simple spell. It won't hold up to scrutiny, though."*

Metal clanked. The door slid open.

The dim interior of the warehouse was filled with an array of boxes, cages, and chests arranged on tall shelves. As they passed inside, Za'antha whispered, "I count ten people. One's an orc."

"Ten percent finder's fee," the beastmaster said from the alley behind them.

"Yeah, yeah. After the sale," the doorkeeper said, sliding the door shut, cutting off the main source of light. Genevieve could scarcely make out his features in the shadows, but he seemed to be an overweight human with a black beard and bald head.

"It was caught up north," the bearded merchant said, leading them briskly into the warehouse. "Probably wandered too far from its yeti family and got lost. Runt of the litter, but still strong enough to bend steel. Only thing keeping it from breaking out is the shock spell on the bars."

They stood before a huge cage. Large, glowing blue eyes floated out from behind the cage, towards them.

The party tensed, reflexively preparing their hands for spell casting or drawing weapons.

"Easy," the merchant chuckled. "That's its little ice gremlin friend. Harmless to all but rats, rabbits, and cats. The gremlin's been feeding the little yeti ever since they caught him. It teleports away, kills an animal, then brings it back and they share it for dinner. No complaints here — saves me the trouble and cost."

The floating white furball was adorable, in an ugly monster-baby sort of way. Alasie had told them its name was Frostbite, and that her dog, Pinga, controlled it. Genevieve opened her hand to Frostbite. He floated backward, watching her cautiously with his oversized eyes.

"Tell us about the little yeti," Tel O'Rax said. "Have you tried to train it? Or let it out of the cage?"

The merchant grunted, "Look here, I'm not an animal trainer. I stumbled on it — it's a rare find, and I mean to get it off my hands for a fair price as quick as I can. I'll take no less than seven hundred gold for the beast and cage — it's a package deal. You won't be opening it to let the beast free in here — I can promise you that!"

The little yeti laid in a fetal position on its side, a thin layer of hay serving as its bedding.

"Wake up, ye furry oaf!" Ruyn shouted. "Let's take a look at you!"

"It doesn't speak Common," the merchant said. "Only grunts and mutters in some sort of yeti speech."

"Be gentle about it," Ayr said. "Hello? What's your name?"

The bearded merchant laughed, shaking his head.

"Allo? Mua'heerain?" Ruyn asked. "Gru-ru? Heus?" He must be trying different languages. "Ha ji? Ha p'tain?"

The little yeti stirred. It lifted its head, then grunted a barely audible, "As'pan du?"

Ruyn slapped his knee. "Jey'ye oowa! Cola, cola se'eka."

The little yeti scrambled to its feet, eyeing the party with disbelief. Its features were hardly bestial — his blue face was one of a handsome young elf, while his body was large, muscled, and covered in downy white fur.

Genevieve shot a private message to Alasie, *"Ag'nul is amazing! What a unique character!"*

"Thanks," Alasie replied, *"Pip-Rho made him for me. She's a genius, right? Alright, I'm role-playing now."*

Genevieve watched Ag'nul survey their party. When his eyes fell on Za'antha, he froze. He raised a hand and stepped forward. As he neared the cage bars, a snap of electricity arced to his hand and shocked him out of his trance. He shook it off, then began to ramble at Ruyn incoherently.

Ruyn listened and nodded for a bit, then raised a hand to quiet him.

"Well, I'll be damned," the merchant grumbled. "You speak yeti?"

Ruyn turned to the merchant and gave his chest an aggressive poke. "You're an idiot."

The shifting, creaking sounds of hidden guards coming to attention echoed from the corners and shadows. The merchant raised a hand halfway, signaling for his men to stay back, but be ready.

"That's no way to barter, *elf*," he said, dangerously.

"Barter?!" Ruyn barked. "He's sapient!"

The merchant furrowed his brow and looked towards a large form leaning against a wall. "Sapient?" he asked.

A hint of light on the person's face revealed them to be a green-tinged woman with an underbite of tusk-teeth.

Ah, the orc.

She spoke in low, labored speech. "Eet means thinking — wise, like a hoo-man."

The merchant guffawed at Ruyn, "Just 'cause you can speak yeti—"

"Frost elvish!" Ruyn shouted, inches from the merchant's face. The eyes of his deer mask began to glow in the same sickly green as his staff's skull. "He speaks frost elvish, you fool! You've caged a man!"

"Do you see that creature?" The merchant pointed at Ag'nul. "That's no *man*. You're trying to scare me into lowering the price."

"The queens' laws forbid slave trade," Ayr said. "If you won't release him, we'll report you to the magistrate."

"Four hundred gold," the merchant blurted, backing away from Ruyn. "Take it or leave it."

"Slave traders," Za'antha hissed.

"I'll just fetch the queen's guard," Tel O'Rax said, casually walking away. "They'll sort out the matter."

Two men stepped out from behind boxes, pointing crossbows at him.

Tel O'Rax raised both hands, letting his staff float at his side. "You know, four hundred gold sounds fair to me. I'm just going to get my purse out of my robes, lads. Don't shoot."

"Keep 'em up," one of the men said. He scuttled forward, patting the mage down. "Ere it is! A right plump purse it is, too."

The merchant raised his hand towards the man, who tossed the purse to him. The merchant poured some gold out onto his hand. He lifted a piece to his mouth, giving it a bite. The gold turned to a dull gray metal.

"Fool's gold?" The merchant laughed. "You crooks really do take me for an idiot." He shook his head. "What now? Can't let you go or you'll call the guards and I'll be put on trial for so-called 'slave trading'. Can't give in and release the beast — he's as likely to kill me as anything. Even if he doesn't, I'm not writing off the expense of purchasing him. And I can't sell him to you — you haven't got any gold! Sorry, but you backed me into a corner. Men? Kill 'em."

GENEVIEVE BEGAN OVERCLOCKING; increasing her neural firing rate. She hated the sensation of time slowing, but there was about to be a fight and she didn't have the experience to know what to do next. The least she could do was keep up with the action.

Tel O'Rax grabbed his staff from the air and dodged to the side.

Ruyn Wormwood was backing away from the merchant, rambling in a slow-motion chant. He yanked an animal skull from the cord hanging off his belt and threw it to the ground. The skull shattered, releasing a small swarm of green apparitions which darted in every direction.

One flew directly towards Ayr. Her spirit sense allowed her to feel its hunger, its fury. At the last moment, before striking her, it turned away to find another victim.

Fear — true fear — bubbled up within Genevieve. She didn't believe in spirits, and she was keenly aware that none of this was actually happening. Yet, there it was — genuine emotion, kindled by this *gameworld.*

It's just a game!

Za'antha had an arrow nocked and aimed at the orcish woman in the shadows.

A shimmering aura formed around the woman.

A caster?

"Zeta, be careful!" Ayr called out.

The voice of WoQS spoke in Genevieve's mind.

Please remember to stay in character and avoid using real-world names when playing Interra.

"Oh, bite me, Cain," she thought back.

Crossbow bolts seemed to fly at them from every corner of the room.

Ruyn was struck in the head, but the bolt ricocheted off his skull mask.

Something struck the side of her head. Hot pain burst above her ear as she watched a crossbow bolt tumble forward in the air — a glancing shot, inches away from being deadly.

She ducked, raising her hands to cover her head.

Za'antha was beside her, kneeling. A bolt protruded from her arm. She loosed an arrow from her bow.

A great bellow filled the air. Ayr looked up in time to see Ag'nul grab the bars of his cage. Sparks danced and sizzled across his body. His mouth was open in feral rage, revealing savage canines. His great muscles twitched and bulged as he pulled the bars in opposite directions.

An angry chittering sound drew her attention to Frostbite, tearing into the face of one of the men attacking Tel O'Rax. Even to her slowed, overclocked perception, the creature's frenzied fangs and claws were a blur.

The Tasmanian Devil from Looney Tunes came to mind.

It mangled the man's face, then disappeared. She heard it chittering away somewhere behind her, followed by a pained scream.

A golden streak caught her eye as it passed between the shelves at the back of the warehouse. The form of a glowing dog pounced on the orc who Za'antha had shot at.

That must be Penelope-pooch's character, Aureum d'Canis!

"Heal, please!" Tel O'Rax moaned, dragging himself towards her. Blood streaked across the floor behind him.

What was she doing? She was their healer!

Focus!

It was that damn hummingbird effect — a byproduct of over-clocking. She couldn't think deeply enough to concoct a plan.

Something smelled like burning hair.

Oh, Ag'nul's fur was smoking! She should heal him.

His bars were bent, but not wide enough to squeeze through.

She was yanked by the arm and pulled behind a large, banded chest.

"Heal me. I'll dispel the cage's shock ward," Tel O'Rax hissed. Sweat beaded on his bald head.

Ayr searched the mage for his wound, turning him over to expose two crossbow bolts protruding from his chest. They were partially dislodged and oozing blood. She yanked them both out, earning a loud complaint from Tel O'Rax.

She pressed her hands tightly against the wounds and issued the thought-command to cast her character's healing spell. Her bloodied hands glowed dimly. She felt Tel O'Rax's rent flesh sliding together, mending beneath her palms.

The sensation made her skin crawl.

Tel O'Rax opened his hand to the side, summoning his staff. When it reached him, he pointed it at the cage. Distortion warped the air between the staff and the cage.

"Ay, ay, ay!" Za'antha gave a battle call, running towards the merchant, daggers in each hand. The bearded merchant stood above Ruyn, preparing to give him a solid kick, when Za'antha plunged one dagger into his chest and another into his shoulder.

A look of shock came over his face. He staggered backwards, then pulled the dagger from his shoulder and eyed it with scrutiny. Genevieve imagined it was the same look he used when gauging an item's value.

With a snarl, the merchant lunged towards Za'antha, wielding her own dagger against her. She dodged by rolling backwards.

The merchant pursued her, stumbling forward. "I'll... kill you, you little—"

Ag'nul's clawed hand wrapped around the merchant's throat.

Oh, good! Alasie got Ag'nul out of his cage! Genevieve hoped the shocks hadn't hurt her too badly.

Ag'nul lifted the merchant by the neck, bringing them face to face. "Slave traders," he growled.

A crossbow bolt flew from the rafters, striking Ag'nul in the gut.

He roared, then clutched the merchant's leg with his free hand and raised the heavy man overhead.

In a feat of unimaginable strength, Ag'nul threw the merchant at the sniper in the rafters. The men collided, then both fell to the warehouse floor. The little yeti's charred white fur disappeared into the shadows behind the crates where the sniper and merchant had fallen.

For such a big guy, he was fast! Quiet, too.

Oops, she was gawking again!

Ayr hurried to Za'antha's side, laying hands on the elf.

"I'm fine," Za'antha said. She was drawing her bow again, tracking a target which Ayr couldn't see.

Ignoring the protest, she clutched Za'antha tightly and cast her healing spell.

Shick, thump.

Shick, thump.

Even as she was being healed, Za'antha hit two targets. Ayr patted her back to indicate she was done. Za'antha rose and jogged away.

"No love for the shaman?" Ruyn croaked.

"Sorry, Ruyn!" She rushed to him and began healing.

"Are we winning?" He asked.

Ayr looked up.

Bloody corpses littered the warehouse.

Za'antha was hopping from crate to crate in search of hidden survivors.

Tel O'Rax was poking a flaming body with the bottom of his staff.

Ag'nul was nowhere to be seen, but Frostbite was helping himself to the remains of one of their fallen foes. He dug into the man's abdomen, shoving fistfuls of organ meat into his mouth. The ice demon chewed rapidly with satisfied grunts.

Ayr closed her eyes and turned her head away. The urge to vomit was rising quickly. She blurted, "Yes, we won," then deposited her breakfast by Ruyn's side.

13

SOULSTONE

Zeta felt certain that they had done something wrong by killing those people. The commotion had attracted the guards' attention. Her party was put in cuffs and chains, hauled to separate corners of the warehouse, and told to wait for the constable. As they waited, a team of men and women arrived. They wore black robes and had thin shrouds over their faces. The silent team carried the bodies out to a covered black wagon. They swept up the scraps of flesh and entrails, then left without a word.

After what felt like half the day had gone by, the wizened constable hobbled in. He asked who the party's leader was. Tel O'Rax volunteered himself and was brought aside for questioning. The grumpy old man had barely heard the entire story before nodding and turning away, granting them full pardons.

They learned from the guards that the merchant's name was Bartleby Buckstrom, and his trading company was called Bartleby's Bodega. He was wealthy enough that his estate would pay for the resurrection of the man and his troupe. He'd pay a hefty fine and spend time in the dungeon for his crimes, but he'd live to trade another day.

The guards left, and the party stood in the alley with a terrified, terrifying Ag'nul. Tel O'Rax suggested Ruyn should invite him to join their party and join them on their upcoming queen's quest. They all knew Alasie's character would be in their party, but they had to go through the role-playing motions to make it official.

Ag'nul and Ruyn got quite emotional during their foreign-tongued exchange. Ruyn reached up and patted the back of the weeping beast-man. Frostbite growled at the contact, earning a scolding snarl from Ag'nul.

Ruyn lifted his deer skull mask to wipe a tear. He sniffed, "Ag'nul humbly and gratefully accepts our offer. This is the first time anybody has shown him acceptance or kindness. It's really quite sad — pathetic even. He wanted me to tell you all he owes us his life, and would die a thousand deaths to save us from the slightest discomfort."

Forearms were embraced and shoulders were patted. The party had their tank.

Ayr suggested they should have their garments repaired and cleaned before they did anything else, since walking around with tattered, bloody clothes was going to catch unwanted attention. She had been wrong about that. The thing that caught the eye of every whispering passerby wasn't their bloody clothes, but their little yeti and his floating demon.

After their clothes were fixed, the famished party found their way to the nearest tavern.

The squirrely tavern keeper was terrified by Ag'nul, sitting cross-legged on the floor and hunching over the table. Every few minutes, he'd pop his head out for a peek before retreating back into the kitchen.

When their food was ready, he called out from the crack of the door, "I live to serve, but hope to live another day! Could I have a normal-sized person come to the kitchen to bring out your supper? I'm caked in flour and sauce — I'd easily be mistaken for a dumpling by your giant."

Za'antha laughed and went with Tel O'Rax to get the food. She used WorMS to tell Alasie what he had said, since her character couldn't speak Common yet. Alasie was doing a good job of playing along, and wouldn't use the things they told her through WorMS in the game if her character didn't know them.

They rested for the evening and prepared to spend another night at the inn. After arguing with the innkeeper about the risk of Ag'nul breaking his bed, they accepted the offer to let him sleep for free in the stables. Out of solidarity, the rest of the party also spent the night in the hay.

THE NEXT DAY they gathered adventuring supplies at the market, steering clear of the beastmaster. It was nighttime when they arrived at Castle Interra. A page directed them to the Night Tower for an audience with Queen Rho.

Navigating through the black steel gates and the cavernous grand foyer, the Telson party made its way to the reception hall. Dozens of people milled about the hall, forming a loose line. The visitors were all shapes and sizes — armor-clad knights to scantily clad sorceresses.

Just as on the streets, Ag'nul drew hushed murmurs from the crowd. There was another huge man in the reception hall — an ugly oaf with connected eyebrows and a hunched gait. Zeta couldn't remember all the races they had learned about, but thought he might be a half-giant.

He glowered at Ag'nul, puffing up and straightening his posture. Ag'nul shrunk at the attention, squatting behind Za'antha.

Every few minutes, a man at the end of the hall would call out a name, and that party would depart through the doors, never to return. No more than ten minutes passed before the man called out, "Tel O'Rax, party of five?"

Grumbles and shouts arose from the queue as Tel led them, bumping past the others.

"Oy! They just got 'ere!"

"Be ye nobles?"

The half-giant stood with a wide stance in the middle of the hall.

Tel O'Rax stopped before him, looking up and smiling politely. "We've been called in, friend. Could you... relocate your... girth?"

"Hmph," the oaf grunted, not budging.

Za'antha stepped to Tel's side. She pulled her bow loose from its bindings as she said, flatly, "Move, or I'll put an arrow through your eye."

Ayr shook her head and sighed.

"You pretty," the oaf said. He reached a hand down towards Za'antha.

Flash of white.

Thud of flesh.

Ag'nul was pressing the half-giant against the wall, a hand clasped around his throat. His other hand pinned the half-giant's wrist to the wall.

"That's enough of that," the queen's guard at the door called. "Break it up!"

When Ag'nul didn't back down, Ruyn said something in frost elvish. Ag'nul looked back towards the shaman, then to Za'antha, then back to the oaf.

"Dat's e-noof of dat," Ag'nul growled at the oaf's reddening face. He released his grip and turned away. When he realized that all eyes were on him, he froze. In a heartbeat, he turned from a force of nature to a sheepish child, hunching his shoulders and shifting on his feet.

It took a lot of restraint for Zeta not to laugh at the adorable half-yeti. Alasie's mannerisms were on full display with her character. Learning that her friend had an impulsive, ferocious, protective side was refreshing after seeing her as a meek girl for so long. They had grown closer during their gameplay together. The things which may have annoyed Zeta about Alasie when they were first traveling together were endearing now.

The Telson party hurried past the remaining onlookers. A bored-looking servant met them at the end of the hall. His black robes were embroidered with silver and emblazoned with a crescent moon. He ushered them through the door, which led to a broad stairway leading down.

Their footfalls echoed against the stone walls as they descended. At the bottom of the stairs was a modest room containing a man, a table, and a white-and-black speckled owl staring at them from a steel perch in the corner.

"Leave your weapons and magical items here," the man said, gesturing limply to the table. As they unloaded their weapons, he asked, "Do you intend to do harm to Queen Rho?"

"By Rammah, no!" Ayr laughed, putting a hand to her heart.

The owl in the corner squinted its eyes, letting out a "hoo-hoo".

Ayr gave the owl a double-take. She began to ask, "Why would—"

"Standard procedure, madam," the servant said. "And the rest of you?"

Tel O'Rax released his staff next to the table. It hovered, remaining upright. "No, sir," he said.

"Hoo-hoo," replied the owl.

"No," Za'antha said.

"Hoo-hoo."

It felt like the owl was approving of their responses.

Ruyn jabbed Za'antha with his bony elbow. "Not unless Rho starts it."

"Is that a no?" The servant sighed.

"Of course it is, ye dull boy," Ruyn muttered.

The servant glanced at the owl. The bird was grooming a wing with its beak. It finished, squinted, and hoo-hooted.

The servant nodded. He looked at Ag'nul, raising an eyebrow. The half-yeti hunched in the corner.

Zeta sent Alasie, *"Just say what I said."*

"But... my character doesn't know that word," Alasie replied.

"It's fine. You had him mimic me before, when he said 'slave trader'."

"That's different. I could tell that was an insult by the way you said it. But I guess he would want to say what you said here, too."

Ag'nul's crystal blue eyes searched the party, then looked at the man. "No?"

The man squeezed his temples. "I need an answer, not a question."

"No?" Ag'nul asked again.

"He speaks frost elvish, but not much common," Ayr offered.

The servant turned his deadpan face to Ayr. "You could have told me sooner." Back to Ag'nul, he asked, "Oobya tun'tya Queen Rho bash el?"

"Ack!" Ag'nul blurted, slapping both hands over his mouth.

"That means no," the servant told Ayr, pretending to smile.

"Hoo-hoo," went the owl.

The servant opened a heavy set of double-doors, revealing an ornate throne room. It was decorated with silk tapestries. The smell of incense wafted in from the room. Plush, velvet couches and over-sized pillows were clustered in dark, candle-lit corners. She could see into the dark corners with her night vision, and noted that some of the couches were occupied.

The servant stepped aside and gestured into the room. "Please enter. Queen Rho is waiting."

***

THE EBONY-SKINNED GODDESS of a queen watched them enter with her pale blue eyes, glistening in the lazy, lusty sort of way that a lioness with a full belly might watch a limping gazelle. She lounged with one silky leg draped over the velvet arm of her high-backed wooden throne. A collar of black feathers circled her neck, rising behind her head.

Beside the throne was the heavily armored man who had accompanied her at Fort Noob.

The party approached. They honored the queen with bows and curtseys.

"Rise," Queen Rho said, almost slurring the drawn-out word.

They rose.

The queen leaned forward and used her silver scepter to scratch herself on the back. "Speak," she moaned, enjoying her scepter's scratching a bit too much.

Tel O'Rax cleared his throat and took a step forward. "Your highness, before we make our request of you, I must say — there are legends which speak of your beauty, yet flowery words do you no justice."

"Hmm," Queen Rho hummed. "What would do me justice, my subject?"

Tel's ingratiating smile froze. Seconds ticked by in silence. Tel's mouth opened and closed, failing to come up with an appropriate response.

As he took a breath to reply, Queen Rho declared, "Silence! Yes, you are correct — sweet silence is the answer, dear subject. If words do me no justice, then words are forfeit." She pulled her leg off the arm of her throne and leaned forward, fixing Tel O'Rax with her intense gaze. Her eyes were like ice. "Poems, paintings, and ballads — withered flowers cast at my feet? No word can so much as hint at the depths of my beauty but the utterance of my name spilled from the dying lips of a devotee, impaled upon their own dagger in sacrificial tribute."

A sinister chuckle came from the couch in the corner.

The Night Queen inched forward in her seat. Za'antha tensed. It felt like a fight was about to happen. She glanced over to see that Tel O'Rax was sweating. Was Oraxis actually afraid, or was he just role playing? This was Pip-Rho they were talking to, after all.

"Is that your desire, my subject?" Queen Rho purred. "To open your veins and offer me your life's blood? Will you paint the floor crimson in my honor?"

Tel O'Rax wiped his brow with the sleeve of his robe. "N—no. That is to say... your highness. I was only—"

"No? Then shut up about it." Queen Rho plopped back into her seat, dejected. "What do you want?"

It occurred to Zeta that Pip-Rho's character was like an eld who had tired of a child and was toying with them for the fun of it. Even if this was her family in real life, Pip-Rho's character didn't have the patience for banter.

Za'antha stepped forward and spoke with confidence. "We've come to accept your quest. We wish to rid Interra of the wraith menace."

Queen Rho looked them over in a brief assessment, then shrugged. "Okay. Peter Piper over there will add you to the book and answer any questions." She twitched a finger towards a door at one side of the room and barked, "Next!"

A guard hurried them out of the room and through a different door than the one they came in from. Their gear awaited them on a table against one wall. A man dressed identically to the one who had taken their weapons waited for them to finish getting themselves situated.

This was Peter Piper, apparently?

Peter cleared his throat and announced, "Congratulations on being accepted for the queen's quest to eliminate the wraiths! It's a deadly quest, but it comes with a limitless resurrection pass, valid until you either give up on the quest or another party completes it. If *your* party completes the quest, the pass will remain valid indefinitely. Along with this, the winning party will receive one million gold and a manor sitting on one hundred hectares of fertile land. Finally, lord and lady titles will be granted by the queens to each member of the winning party during a regal ceremony. May I have your names for the registry, please?"

His black feather quill danced as he scribbled their responses in a large leather-bound book. He gave a nod as he finished, then turned to Za'antha. "Za'antha, you will be responsible for reporting your party's progress. Simply request an audience with the questing officer at any of the queen's strongholds. If we obtain new information relevant to your quest, it will be shared then."

"Okay," Za'antha said, looking at Tel O'Rax. "But... why me? Tel is our party leader."

"Oh?" Peter's raised brows wrinkled his forehead. "I'm sorry, but you were the one to request the quest, and to whom the queen granted her blessing."

"I... I was about to!" Tel O'Rax bumbled. "Until I was flummoxed by the queen's... *macabre* suggestions."

Peter squinted, giving an apologetic smile and a shrug. "It's probably best that the one in your party least likely to be *flummoxed* take the lead, wouldn't you say? Besides, I've already written it down. Have ye any other questions?"

"Is your name really Peter Piper?" Ruyn snickered.

"No, good man," he said, all smiles. "My name is Pietra Lymonne Coronet III. Queen Rho, in her wisdom and grace, has granted me a whimsical nickname! Any other questions?"

"Where do we go next?" Za'antha asked.

"An excellent question," Peter said. "See? You're taking to a leadership role quite naturally." He gave Tel a sideways glance.

Tel straightened his robes and looked away.

Zeta mindspoke on the party channel, *"I'm sorry—"*

"It's fine," Oraxis interrupted. *"It's all part of the game."*

"Next," Peter said, "you will report to The Soulkeeper's Spire for a particularly unpleasant experience."

JUTTING from the heart of Centra City was a structure of impossible proportions — The Soulkeeper's Spire. The circular base of the spire was no wider than a stone's throw, yet it ascended an immeasurable distance into the sky — a needle lodged upright. Most days, its heaven-piercing peak hides among the clouds.

Tonight, its distant peak sliced a thin sliver out of the star-strewn sky.

As high as the spire's peak reaches, its foundation descends to equal depths. Legends shared by Duchess Beatrix said that the bottom point penetrates into the underworld. And at the pit of the spire dwells The Soulkeeper.

The arch of the entrance yawned high overhead. Informational placards were affixed to its sides in multiple languages. Looking inside the dim, featureless cylinder, Za'antha saw that the floor was made from thick glass. Below the glass appeared to be a bottomless pit. Above, a mirror image. Even with her character's sharp night vision, she couldn't see all the way to the top or bottom of the tower's interior — they both shrank into unfathomable darkness.

The placards by the door said the tower's magical transportation system offers two choices. Stand on the blue glass circle to be lifted to the spire's peak, where long-distance teleportation services are available. Stand in the red glass circle to be sent to the spire's pit for soul extraction and resurrection services.

"*A bit 'on the nose', isn't it?*" Oraxis sent their party channel as they stood at the entrance.

"*What about a nose?*" Carff whistled.

"*What he means,*" Genevieve sent, "*is that the spire obviously represents the Jacob's Ladder and Cellar elevators. The pit represents Syn-Cen, The Soulkeeper represents Cain, and the peak represents the orbital platforms attached to Jacob's Ladder.*"

"We'll want the red platform. Come along," Tel O'Rax said, striding into the spire's dim cavern of an interior. The crystal atop his staff began to glow a brilliant white, illuminating the gray walls and reflecting off the clear glass below his feet.

Za'antha and Ruyn stepped gingerly behind Tel, while Ayr and Ag'nul stayed at the entrance, gawking downward.

"*Wow, that's really far down,*" Alasie sent with a nervous huff-laugh.

Genevieve sent, "*Gameworld construct or not, when you're asked to walk on glass with a pit of certain death beneath your feet, your legs are going to turn into jelly."*

"Ag'nul is scared," Ayr said, reaching up to pet his arm. "Are you sure it's safe? This glass was made for humans to walk on. He might be too heavy."

"During the day there's probably a hundred people waiting their turn in here," Tel shouted back to them. "Of course it's safe." He jumped up and down to demonstrate. Peculiar warbling echoes bounced through the empty spire.

The eerie sound made the hair on Za'antha's neck stand up. "Stop that!" she barked.

Tel rolled his eyes and sighed, "Want me to levitate you over here?"

"No," Ayr snapped. She slid a foot onto the glass. "Just don't jump again or I'll have Ag'nul rip your head off."

"Typical pacifist," Tel mumbled, "make someone else do the dirty work."

Za'antha watched Ayr, who avoided looking down as she inched forward. After she was a few paces into the chamber, she beckoned gently to Ag'nul, who followed her lead.

When the party had assembled on the red glass circle, Tel invoked the keyword. "Descend."

Za'antha gasped as the floor vanished from under her feet.

They were falling!

Ayr's scream was drowned out by a bestial bellow coming from Ag'nul. The walls were narrowing as they fell down the tapered tunnel.

Did they do it wrong? Was her character about to die? She could hear Za'antha's heart pounding in her ears.

A solid floor resolved into view below them. Za'antha winced, preparing for the impact — the promise of pain. The sound of rushing wind stopped. She opened her eyes, finding herself suspended above the ground.

Tel was walking towards a door. The rest of the party hung in the air around her. She shifted her body weight until her feet touched the ground, then walked towards Ayr to help her get oriented. Together, they coaxed Ag'nul's hands off his face and feet to the floor.

"Soulkeeper," Tel announced.

She looked over to see that he was reading the engraving above a banded wooden door. Za'antha walked to meet him, then pulled the heavy door open, revealing a narrow passageway made from stone blocks. Torches burned within sconces affixed to the walls. She looked back to check that the party was assembled behind her, then led the way through the door. Before anybody else could follow, it slammed shut behind her.

Pounding, scratching, and muffled shouts came from the door as her party tried to open it.

She mindspoke over the party channel, *"Don't worry, I expected this to happen. The Soulstone Ritual is done alone. They say it's important to stay connected to your character during the ritual, even though it's painful. That's what I'm going to do, and I hope everyone else does, too. I'll tell you what it's like, afterwards."*

Inching down the corridor, Za'antha could see that it ended in a larger room. In the distant room, she could see a man standing behind an altar, watching her approach.

Entering the circular room, Za'antha surveyed her surroundings. There were levers and gears, ropes and pulleys. On a shelf was a careful assortment of shiny metallic tools and a folded linen towel. She looked at the man, who had an olive skin tone and exotic features. He was young and attractive, in an effeminate way. His head was bald and he wore a simple, unbleached cotton robe.

"You're The Soulkeeper?" Za'antha asked.

The man nodded.

Za'antha took a breath, preparing for the worst. "I'm here for a soulstone."

THE SOULKEEPER'S DARK, unblinking eyes pierced her as his gentle voice said, "Expose the flesh between your collarbone and your belly button." He demonstrated by running a finger from the base of his neck to his belly button. "Depending upon your attire, this may require you to expose your breasts. I assure you that I lack the capacity for sexual desire or function, but I can perform the ritual blindfolded, if you prefer."

Za'antha said nothing as she removed her bow and quiver, leaning them against a wall. She unclasped her cloak, dropping it into a crumpled heap. Next came her leather vest, and then her tunic. Standing topless with her back to The Soulkeeper, she covered herself with her arms. Although this wasn't her body, Zeta felt humiliated.

Looking back down at the leather armor vest, she realized she could wear it if she left it unlaced. Donning the vest, she turned back around. She met The Soulkeeper's gaze with as much dignity as she could muster.

He said, "Good. Lay down upon the altar."

Along the rim of the altar were carvings, which Zeta recognized as runes. Za'antha placed her hands on the altar, feeling its cold stone for a heartbeat before lifting herself onto it. There were notches and holes in the altar's otherwise smooth surface. What were those for?

The Soulkeeper pulled down on a rope affixed to the chamber's ceiling by a pulley. The rope's two cords disappeared into a hole in the floor. After a moment, a small box rose from the hole. The Soulkeeper slid a door open on the front of the box. He reached inside and plucked something from its interior. Turning towards Za'antha, he extended a hand. His palm cupped a plain white stone. "This will be your soulstone."

Za'antha made no comment. The small stone seemed to be a perfect sphere, but was otherwise unremarkable.

The Soulkeeper approached his table of tools. He placed the stone on a small red pillow, then turned his attention to the metallic tools. When he turned around again, he was holding a large metal contraption with both hands. He stepped to Za'antha's side and lowered it over her torso. The metal was cold against her skin. He pressed the two sides of the device into the stone altar's surface.

Click, click.

He adjusted an arm of the device, pressing it against her stomach, just below her sternum.

Click, click. The pressure of the metal against her skin went from uncomfortable to painful as it tightened down on her.

The Soulkeeper returned to the table, then came back with a curved bit of metal in each hand. He gently guided one of her arms into position, then pressed the metal over her wrist.

Click, click.

She tried lifting her arm from the table, but it was pinned down. Next came the other wrist. Click, click.

Panic flooded her senses. She heard her heart beating faster, her breath quickening. Za'antha had the acute ears of an elf, so hearing her own heart and breath wasn't unusual. But now their rapid pace served as an audible reminder of her increasing dread.

Could she do this?

Another trip to the table, another set of clicks, and The Soulkeeper had her ankles pinned. Next, a metal band was fixed over her neck.

She watched The Soulkeeper return to the table. He turned back around with a white cloth in one hand and a gleaming dagger in the other. It was thin, and as long as a forearm.

She couldn't do this!

The metal across her chest dug into her skin with every breath.

The Soulkeeper approached the altar.

It's just a game — she wasn't in danger. Didn't someone at Fort Noob say that your heart in the real world stopped beating for a moment during your character's death? That doesn't seem possible.

Queen Rho said staying connected during the soulstone ritual was important. She *had* to stay connected!

Za'antha lifted her head, choking against the restraint over her throat as she watched The Soulkeeper position the point of the dagger beneath her sternum. Its tip pierced her skin as he angled it, pointing up towards her heart.

Her breath came quick and shallow. She squeezed her eyes closed and pressed her head back against the stone. Her hands groped at the altar's surface, searching for escape. Her toes curled. Cloth pressed against her skin, near the dagger's tip.

"Be at peace," The Soulkeeper said as he slid the dagger into her heart.

***

ZA'ANTHA CHOKED ON HER SCREAM, arching her back.

She was dying!

Her heart spasmed. It fluttered in her chest like a bird caught in a trap.

The agony was unbearable. A tiny — yet very loud — part of her conscious mind begged to be disconnected from the construct. Zeta ignored it, letting the idea wash away along with Za'antha's fading life.

The pain was growing distant.

Darkness flooded in from the edge of her vision. Her dying heart slowed, weakened, then stopped. From some disconnected, faraway place, Zeta heard Za'antha let out a death rattle.

She was drifting upwards, looking down at her character's dead body. Everything seemed to glow with an otherworldly aura. The only sound was a droning hum and the blowing of distant winds.

The Soulkeeper had one hand on the hilt of the dagger embedded in Za'antha's heart and the other on the cloth pressed against the entry point. A glow emanated from underneath the cloth as he pulled out the dagger, passing the blade through the cloth to wipe it clean.

He lifted the cloth, wiping a smear of blood off Za'antha's skin, revealing it to be unbroken. He returned to his worktable, placed the dagger down, and neatly folded the bloody cloth. He picked up the white stone and turned back around, lifting his gaze to meet Zeta's perspective at the ceiling of the chamber.

The Soulkeeper walked to the altar, then held the stone up towards her. His mouth moved soundlessly. She lowered toward the stone as the room began to shift. Everything was growing larger. No, she was shrinking. Within seconds, the stone loomed before her, as big as a boulder. She slid into its white surface, losing her sense of sight.

Minutes passed with no sight or sound — no sensations whatsoever. It was a welcome respite from the torture of Za'antha's death. That was behind her now, and Zeta was proud of herself for suffering through it.

"Za'antha? Can you hear me?" It was a muffled voice — The Soulkeeper?

Zeta realized she was cold again. Stone pressed against her back. Her ears seemed to be filled with cotton.

With great effort, she forced her eyes open. It was blindingly bright. She lifted an arm to shield her eyes.

"I'm... alive?" Za'antha croaked.

"Indeed," came The Soulkeeper's muffled voice. "Your body is in the process of coming back to life, yet your soul now resides within your soulstone. If your body should perish again, the fastest path towards resurrection is to arrange for your remains to be returned to my chamber for repair and revitalization. Should your remains be lost or damaged beyond repair, I will conjure a new body for you. Such is the power of the soulstone."

Her vision was returning to normal. She could see the stone in his hand, shimmering with a beautiful, pearlescent glow.

The Soulkeeper returned to the box on the rope, placing the soulstone inside. "I will keep your soulstone in The Underworld Vault. It will be safe from harm as you go about your adventures above." He closed the box and began pulling up on the other side of the rope.

"Gather your belongings and depart at your leisure." The box lowered into the hole in the floor.

Za'antha opened her mouth to give The Soulkeeper thanks, then stopped. It seemed strange to thank the man for what he had just done. She did it anyway. "Thank you, Soulkeeper."

The Soulkeeper met her eyes and gave the slightest of smiles. It looked entirely artificial. "I exist to serve, Za'antha of the Sylvan Woods."

The formal title filled Zeta with pride. She had passed the test and was bonded with the gameworld now. It felt deep and meaningful.

She was an Interran.

14

PRINCIPAL AGENT

The novelty of living on a moon is short-lived.

For one thing, low-G sucks. Micro-G is easier to cope with, since motion is predictable; everything moving by the basic physics of inertia. You already know you're in an alien environment, so you learn a new set of rules for motion. But low-G tricks you into using your one-G muscle memory. A person who normally gets out of bed and hops to their feet in the morning starts their day on Soma Station by head-butting the ceiling.

Everyone Jamji passed on her awkward bounce down the corridor could tag her as a "weller". That's what people accustomed to low-G call people who live in a one-G gravity well, like Genesis.

As if this continuous source of embarrassment wasn't enough to set Jamji's nerves on edge, she was responding to a summons from Station Captain Chin. Jamji was *certain* that she was being discharged. What else could it be? Her acceptance into the Guardian Officer Academy was a mistake. Someone must've seen the list of incoming cadets and recognized her name. "Jamji Telson? The *dancer*? Accepted into the academy? Not on my watch!"

Her cabinmates tried to assure her that there was no way she could have done anything bad enough to be discharged so soon. Jamji could think of a dozen things, including making a fool of herself when she was introduced to the captain for the first time. Captain Chin had complimented the hue of her chromatites. "Thank you, ma'am," Jamji had said.

Ma'am?

Ma'am?!

No, you rube-noob! It's *sir*! Guardian officers are always called sir, even if they're a woman. Jamji knew that, but she'd been caught off guard by the Captain's sudden warmth. It was like getting a pat on the head by an eld-ma, and her old neoprim instincts took over. She corrected herself a second later, but it was too late. Her first impression had been that of a fool. Yep, she was on the next shuttle back to Genesis.

Jamji stood outside the plain, metallic conference room door. She was fifteen minutes early. Should she scan herself in? Or wait until it was time for the meeting? Would there be a waiting area inside? Was another meeting already in progress that she would rudely interrupt? She'd wait in the hallway.

As was her habit, she counted the seconds.

Five minutes and forty-two seconds later, a woman in a black and gray warrant officer's uniform came gliding down the hallway with the effortlessness of one who has lived on Soma for years. She had the telltale glow of dermal chromatite mods, like Jamji's, though her hue was a natural, peach tone. She had a braid of blond hair going down her back, which had to be a wig. Her name tag read "Haley", and her rank insignia indicated she was a chief warrant officer of the special weapons and tactics division.

Haley spoke flatly as she reached Jamji. "You're early." She turned to the door's access panel.

"Yeah. Sorry, sir, I—"

"Sorry?" Haley froze, then wrinkled her nose and turned to Jamji, as if she smelled something foul. "Why should you be sorry?"

"Oh," Jamji bumbled, "no, sir, I didn't mean I was sorry for being early, just that—"

"Stop talking," Haley said, then pressed the door open button. "Go in." She glanced back down the hallway as Jamji bounced past her.

Upon their entrance, the room lights came on. Nobody else was there yet. It was a small, simple room containing an interactive surface table surrounded by chairs. A water dispenser and cups sat in the corner, and the walls were the same light gray ceramic composite as the rest of the station. Jamji couldn't decide whether she should sit. And if she sat, which chair?

Haley entered and pressed the door close button. "What's your deal?" she asked, hopping into a chair. She leaned back, raising her eyebrows to prompt an answer.

"I don't know what you mean, sir," Jamji said, still standing.

"How did you make it into the officer academy? You're a *mouse*."

"I'm not a *mouse*, sir." Jamji struggled to control her physical reaction. This had to be some sort of macho posturing. An attractive woman like Haley probably had to be as tough as nails to hold her own as a Guardian officer.

"Then what's with the *squeaking*, ensign?"

Was she trying to get Jamji to explode? Jamji's reputation for a hot temper may have preceded her. She wouldn't take the bait. "If you mean my unnecessary apology, sir, that's just nerves. I don't know what this meeting is about, and I'm a bit on edge."

"That's because you're an *impostor*." Haley flashed a sinister glare. "You don't deserve to be here, and it's only a matter of time before everyone else figures you out."

Jamji took direct control of her adrenal levels, subduing them. She wouldn't give this bully the satisfaction of a response. As if she could think of a retort. Haley was right — Jamji was a fraud.

Haley continued, "At least, that's the belief you're broadcasting. Everyone feels that way, starting out in a prestigious position. It's human nature. They call it impostor syndrome. The problem is, it can be a self-fulfilling prophecy. Have a seat." She leaned forward, gesturing to the chair opposite her. Jamji sat straight-backed. Haley continued in a hard tone. "Jamji, here's the deal. You *earned* your commission. You worked *hard* for it. Drop the self-doubt and hold your chin up. They could've made you a private and stuck you in basic training, but they didn't. They saw something in you. Doubting your selection committee's decision is an insult to their judgment."

Jamji hadn't thought of it that way.

Haley pointed at the door. "Here in about five minutes, Captain Chin and two other chief warrant officers are going to walk through that door. When they do, you're going to drop the stuttering private routine and act like you belong here. Got it?"

"Yes, sir!" Jamji barked, stifling a smile. Maybe Haley wasn't so bad after all.

DURING THE FEW minutes before the others arrived, Haley shared what she knew about the meeting. They were going to discuss the possibility of giving Jamji a special assignment, along with Haley and two other officers. Chief Warrant Officer Baud was a Synthetic Intelligence specialist and a card-carrying Lexite. Chief Warrant Officer Dumont was the leading xenobiologist in the Specter research division.

Haley led a team that designed and tested experimental weapons. They also concocted strategies for creative applications of existing tech. For the past hundred-some-odd years, they had been trying to devise an effective anti-Specter weapon, to no avail.

Jamji was eager to hear more about Haley's team, but the door opened. Jamji bolted to her feet, sending herself bounding into the air. She put her hands up, but didn't quite reach the ceiling before descending again.

The dark-skinned man who entered first smiled up at Jamji with a mouth full of perfect, white teeth. "I *love* the enthusiasm, cadet," he said, holding back a laugh. That would be Baud.

The mustached, light-skinned man who ducked in behind Baud would be Dumont. He caught the end of Jamji's descent, then spoke in quick, jittery tones. "She bounced? How embarrassing. First impressions and all that."

Jamji pretended it didn't happen. She issued a salute to the incoming officers, bending her knees to absorb her landing.

Dumont returned a half-hearted salute, then took a single graceful bounce across the room, landing at the water dispenser. Baud's smile remained fixed on his handsome face. He seemed to be waiting for Jamji to talk — probably to see if she'd embarrass herself again.

Jamji spoke with confidence. "It's a pleasure to meet you both. Chief Warrant Officer Haley told me about—"

"Lies!" Dumont blurted, his back to them. He took a drink from the cup he had poured. Jamji searched Haley and Baud for their reactions. Baud closed his lips and tightened them to restrain a laugh.

Haley addressed Jamji. "He's right — I lied by omission. I failed to disclose their peculiarities. I trust you'll catch on."

The door opened again and Station Captain Chin stepped inside. Her features matched the Asian ethnicity of her name, including her skin tone, short stature, and her glossy black hair, tied back in a bun. Jamji and the chief warrant officers saluted. The captain returned their salute with all the stiff formality of a ceremony.

"Ensign Jamji," Captain Chin said.

"Sir!" Jamji barked, remaining at attention.

The captain smiled faintly as she made her way to the head of the table. "Not ma'am this time? Good — you learn fast. I still have to say, I love your chromatite tone. It's like... Varuna, that icy beauty. Did you model it after Varuna?" She sat facing the door. Jamji and the others took the cue, finding their seats.

"No, sir, actually it's modeled after a bioluminescent millipede I had encountered as an alpha."

"Motyxia," Dumont said. "They excrete cyanide. Is that how you died?"

The question caught Jamji by surprise. This Guardian boldness would take some getting used to. Noddites have the common decency not to ask about your alpha's cause of death. She responded flatly, "No, sir."

"Ahh," Baud said, leaning back in his chair, "I see. Motyxia's beautiful glow is actually a warning to would-be predators." He met Jamji's gaze with meaningful intensity. "Be careful of this one, it says. She might be mesmerizing, but to taste her would be certain death."

Haley scoffed, curling her lip at Baud. "It's pathetic come-on lines like that which made me decide on a natural skin tone for my chromatite default."

"Alright, officers, that's enough," the captain said, with the faintest hint of perturbation. "This is what I get for trying to make small talk. Moving on to official business."

Jamji admired the unhurried cadence of Captain Chin's speech. It was articulate, precise, final. She supposed that if she was going to be a commanding officer, she would need to learn to speak so meticulously.

The captain said, "Jamji, the reason I summoned you to this meeting is that I selected you as the principal agent for a special assignment. I know you're excited to start your classes at the academy, but this assignment takes precedence. The academy will still be here when the mission is complete. I've already withdrawn you from your classes."

Jamji's heart sank a little, though the prospect of being given a special assignment easily compensated for it.

"Your support crew includes chief warrant officers Haley, Baud, and Dumont. They each command a staff of subordinates to supplement their efforts. My role will be limited to granting security clearance, approving resource requests, and clearing any administrative or logistical obstacles. Also, should an arbiter be required..." she looked around the room at the other three, pausing to make eye contact with each of them, "I will be called upon. That said, I trust that the four of you will strive to work as a team and resolve your conflicts independently."

She met Jamji's eyes for a long moment before continuing, "Jamji, this is *your* mission. Your actions and attitude will determine whether you take the lead or play the puppet to your support crew. Though they have higher rank than you, they do not operate within your chain of command. You can't give them orders, they can't give you orders. As proven leaders, they will have strong opinions and will naturally assert themselves. Usually, they'll be right and you should listen to them. But they will have different strategies, agendas, and definitions of success. It's possible for conflicting ideas to each be viable and correct, in their own right. It will be up to you to decide what is best for the mission. Don't be afraid to argue with them, but don't confuse contrarianism with assertiveness. Questions so far?"

Jamji had about a thousand. Like, *what's the mission?!* She said, "No, sir. I understand my role and the... team dynamics. I look forward to hearing the briefing."

"Good. As you know, the Specters have been a nuisance in the Surya system for almost three hundred years. Most of us have given up on them as an intractable problem, but with the escalating attacks focused on communications and transportation, we're getting desperate. Grasping at straws, as they say. It's a long-shot mission—"

"Captain?" Dumont blurted, raising a finger. Ever since sitting down, he had seemed uncomfortable — shifting in his seat, making tense facial expressions, tapping the table.

"Dumont?" the captain said, allowing him.

Dumont's mustache wiggled, but he pressed his lips tight. He looked down at his hands, opening and closing them.

"If I may," Baud said, "I think the words Dumont is chewing on are something along the lines of: you're wrong — it's not a long shot at all. Maybe with an expletive thrown in for emphasis. Captain, we *believe* in this mission. I think it would be good for Jamji to know that what we signed her up for is more than a hail Mary. This has been a long time coming, and with her in our ranks, all the tumblers have fallen into place."

Dumont stabbed a finger at Baud, bobbing his head in an exaggerated nod. "What he said."

Haley looked at Jamji and raised her eyebrow in the timeless facial gesture which says, "Can you believe these guys?"

Captain Chin said, "I apologize. I admit that I'm skeptical of the efficacy of the mission, but I *do* believe in my crew. That's—"

The conference room door opened. The warrant officers sprang to their feet, ready to either berate or salute the intruder. Jamji began overclocking at about one-third her capacity. She stood, careful not to leave the ground.

A face peeked into the room.

Jamji's heart skipped a beat.

It was the eyebrow-laden mug of Eld Marco-Epsilon Rhind.

***

JAMJI COULD FEEL her blood pulsing as its pressure spiked. Her myofibrite-enhanced muscles tensed. She ramped up her neural firing rate even higher, crouching and preparing to defend Station Captain Chin with her life.

Upon her arrival at Soma Station three weeks ago, Jamji had told her commanding officer everything there was to say about the Genesisian ambassador. She told him that Marco-Epsilon had tried to recruit her to act as a spy on his behalf, using thinly veiled suggestions. Her commander had thanked her and suggested she keep the information to herself until a formal inquiry was held.

And here the *slimebag* was.

He must've heard she ratted him out. He was here to neutralize the people who knew the most about his spying — her and the captain. With a furrow of his mighty brow, Marco-Epsilon would whip around the corner with a rail-rifle and rip them all to shreds with hypersonic flechettes. They'd be resurrected, sure, but not before he escaped the station.

She was pushing the polymer claws out of her fingertips when Station Captain Chin spoke. "You're early, Rhind."

The warrant officers gave casual nods and waves to the ambassador before sitting back down.

Jamji remained standing, never letting her eyes off the man. She stifled her urge to growl the words, flatly asking, "He's here by invitation, sir?"

"Yes," Captain Chin said, "but he was supposed to arrive *after* your mission briefing."

"Early is on time, and on time is late," Rhind said, flashing a smarmy smile. "Shall I wait in the hall?"

"Yes," Jamji blurted.

"No," Captain Chin said at the same time, "take a seat, Rhind."

Jamji flashed a glance at Chin before returning her glare at Rhind. "Sir, there's something you should know—"

"That spy business?" Rhind chuckled, stepping into the room and dragging out a chair. "Don't worry about all that, Jamji."

"Ensign Telson," Captain Chin said.

"Sir," Jamji replied, meeting Chin's eyes. It pained her to take her eyes off the ambassador. He might not have a weapon, but she still didn't trust him.

Captain Chin laughed dryly. "I wasn't calling on you, Telson — I was correcting the ambassador. You're not a Genesisian anymore, so he's out-of-bounds calling you by your first name during official business. If the two of you *are* on a first name basis, that would be allowed off duty, but not here."

Jamji clenched her jaw. "We're not."

"My apologies," Rhind said. "Such is the habit of an eld like myself — always paternal, always too casual for the tastes of you militaristic types. The warrant officers should know that Ensign Telson is upset at my presence here because she believes I attempted to recruit her as a spy for Genesis." He chuckled and shook his head. "It wasn't the first time a transfer applicant has made such an accusation."

"Find your seat, Telson," Captain Chin said.

Jamji reduced her overclocking rate, lowering onto the edge of her seat.

Chin addressed Jamji and the officers, "I trust Ambassador Rhind. One of his joint responsibilities to Genesis and the Guard is to rattle the confidence of faction transfer applicants. He finds their sensitivities and prods at them. I wouldn't have it any other way — we don't want uncommitted applicants. Sometimes he plays the spy recruitment game. Consider it a test, Telson — you passed."

Jamji looked from the captain to the ambassador and back again.

Why would pretending to recruit her as a spy shake her confidence in her transfer application? He had said a lot of things about family and tribe and loyalties. Maybe that was it?

No. He's a double agent, working for the Guard Faction. Jamji was sure of that now. Station Captain Chin is just protecting his cover.

Captain Chin continued, "We have Ambassador Rhind to thank for this mission. It was his suggestion that we use Ensign Telson as our mission's locus, for reasons that will soon be apparent. I had doubts that Telson was ready for such an important role. Rhind convinced me she was not only ready, but that she was our *only* choice."

The captain stood. When the rest of them shifted to follow suit, she shook her head and gestured for them to stay seated. "Ensign Telson, I've escalated your security clearance to level four. Your resource acquisition privileges will allow you to order any supplies you require, up to six thousand units per Soma cycle. Anything beyond that will be raised to me for approval, with justification attached. Ambassador Rhind will handle your Genesis clearance." She made her way to the door, saying, "I'll leave it up to your team to brief you. Background and mission documents are in your queue now. If you have questions after you've reviewed all the materials, I trust your team can answer them."

The captain saluted. They returned her salute. She pressed the button to open the door as she turned her head. "Ambassador Rhind, could you join me?"

The eld's eyebrows shot upwards. "Join you? Yes, if you like. I had been hoping to hear the briefing. I put so much work into the arrangements..."

When Captain Chin didn't budge, Rhind stood. He addressed the warrant officers. "Until next time. And good luck, Jamji—" he cleared his throat, "Ensign Telson, I mean." He gave a limp mockery of a salute.

Jamji clenched her jaw and waited for them to leave.

THE MOMENT THE DOOR CLOSED, Dumont exhaled loudly, as if he had been holding his breath. He stood and began pacing — bouncing from one side of the room to the other, vigorously scratching his head with both hands.

Jamji decided that this would be a good time to assert herself. "Alright, team. What's the mission?"

Dumont bounced to a stop across from her and planted his hands on the table, leaning over her. He blurted, "The mission: xenocide. Death by Specter. Your brain pulverized to jelly inside your skull." He smiled mirthlessly. "And your little dog, too."

Baud added, in a sing-song tone, "But first, you will join me in unholy communion with a synth-god."

Haley grunted. She said, "primary objective: neutralize the Specters. Secondary objectives?" She pointed at Baud. "Keep him out of your pants." She pointed at Dumont. "Keep him out of your head." She thrust a thumb into her chest. "And keep me from bending you so far you break."

Jamji waited a beat to see if anyone would add anything useful.

She said, "Ominous, cryptic half-threats aside, if the mission is to neutralize the Specters, what strategy will we be employing? And why was I chosen as the principal agent?"

"Interra," Baud said, melodramatically.

After another beat, she took the bait. "Okay. What's Interra?"

Her question was met with expressions of bewilderment.

Haley squinted at her. "Telson — you *are* related to the Pips, aren't you?"

"Yes, sir."

"And you don't know what Interra is?" Baud almost laughed.

"No, sir."

Dumont turned and began to thump his head against the wall. "Mistake. Mistake. Mistake."

Jamji got the sudden urge to grab him by the hair and help him with his head pounding.

"Are you on good terms with the Pips?" Haley asked.

"Of course," Jamji scoffed before straightening her face and adding, "sir."

She ramped her neurites up to the fastest overclocking she could tolerate. She had to figure out what they were talking about before she embarrassed herself any more than she already had. She performed a Guardnet query on the concepts of Pip-Tau, Pip-Rho, Telson, and Interra.

After absorbing the high-level information on the subject, Jamji simultaneously realized five things:

First, they only chose her for the mission because the Guard wanted to exploit her relationship with the Pips. While it was upsetting that her selection had nothing to do with her talents, it made sense.

Second, Interra was more than just a gameworld, since they said this was a mission to take on the Specters. It was an EoE sponsored project, which grants it the highest precedence. Whatever made the gameworld special was what they expected her to exploit.

Third, this meant she was going to be sent back to Genesis to get plugged right back into the faction she had just escaped from.

Fourth, since Interra wasn't open to offworlders yet, Eld Marco-Epsilon Rhind must've arranged for an exception to be made for her. Superficially, she'd be joining as a Telson, but in reality she'd be a Guardian mole. Yeah, Rhind was definitely in bed with the Guard.

And fifth, it meant that she was a rotten, self-centered sis-kin for not knowing a single thing about Interra.

15

MAAHES

"We're entering our third month on this project," Veer said. He leaned back in his chair, letting its springy back bounce slightly as his deep brown eyes rested upon Pip-Tau. This attempt at a casual posture was probably meant to put her at ease. Instead, it just made her more nervous.

Why would it make her more nervous?

The power dynamic! He could afford to be as casual as he damn-well pleased! This was *Veer Gladstone*, Eld of Elds, Archon of The Council of Ten — the most powerful person in the Soma System!

Titles aside, the man *looked* powerful. He had the height and build of an offensive lineman. His head was adorned in perfectly sculpted dreadlocks, draping down his back and over his shoulders like a lion's mane. His beard was split into three cords, blending seamlessly with his dreadlocks. It was easy to see how he earned his nickname, "The Black Lion".

The man was *gorgeous*. His eyes — deep brown, wide and inviting. His skin — unblemished, smooth and velvety as milk chocolate.

His voice? A gentle baritone, soothing and grand. Very few

people can claim to have heard Veer shout, but those who have say his roar puts a lion's to shame.

Power, grace... a god among men. Pip-Tau was certain he could amble into a Kodiak bear's den and pet the cubs if he wanted.

Meanwhile, a tiny little stick-woman with buggy eyes, an underbite, and a squeaky, shrill voice sat opposite him. The large white lounger was made to fit Veer's body, so it dwarfed Pip-Tau, making her look even smaller than usual.

"Yeah," Pip-Tau said, forcing a casual laugh. "Three months sure go by fast!"

Why did she agree to meet him in person? Who meets in person when you can join a construct and save the time of taking the trip? He was spending the year in his Syn-Cen office, so it only took a few minutes to get there from The Crash Pad, but still.

Veer asked, "How do you feel about the progress so far?"

Pip-Tau nodded and smiled as her brain went into overdrive.

They had made no tangible progress, per se. The wraiths weren't acting much like Specters yet. None of the SI-generated quests or NPC encounters had given them anything to work with. Her metaphorical interpretations of their results were no better than wild guesses. But... they had been surprising from time to time, right? She had to put a positive spin on their mediocre results without sounding like she was over-selling it. And she can't pretend that it's not disappointing that Interra hasn't produced more than it has.

Answer, Tau!

"It's hard to say," she said. She tried to bounce her chair, like he was. The back spring was too firm for her dainty weight to budge, so she only managed to wiggle in her seat like a child who needed to potty. What a buffoon. "I'm sure some of the data gathered so far will click into place soon."

Veer nodded. He was looking at her with eyebrows raised expectantly.

She clambered to continue, "I'm looking forward to seeing how things progress now that we've opened the game to Proliferan and

Astrus players. I know you hoped that Genesis could go it alone, but we don't have the tech they do. Rho's failed abduction wouldn't have been possible without Proliferan nanite biotech. The Astri claim they can alter Specter behavior. But the Guard—"

"We're *not* granting the Guard Faction Worldnet access," Veer interjected. "The last time they had access, they tried to transfer Cain to Guardnet."

Pip-Tau decided against reminding Veer he recently signed off on allowing "Ensign Jamji Telson of the Guard Faction" to join, albeit begrudgingly. Eld Marco-Epsilon Rhind had convinced him that Jamji wasn't savvy enough to hack Cain. Veer allowed the exception for her sis-kin on the condition that she was disconnected from Guardnet while in Interra.

"Understood, EoE Gladstone," Pip-Tau said, eyes downcast.

Veer softened. "I told you — call me Veer, Pip."

"Call me Pip-*Tau*, Veer," she corrected, then winced. Veer wasn't a fan of Greek progression nomenclature, and he also ignored Pip-Rho's existence most of the time. Rho was a pariah to the Genesis Faction.

"I'm sorry, Pip-Tau. Don't be afraid to correct me when I'm wrong, either. We're collaborators in this project. I want you to treat me as an equal. And I'm sorry for cutting you off. The Guardians are..." he paused, looking down at his hands. He closed them into tight fists, then opened them and spread his fingers — a lion stretching his paws. He continued, "They're a sore subject for me. A sore subject, indeed. Let's talk about the Proliferans and Astri. I signed off on the data sharing agreement revisions last week. I've read about their successful integration into the gameworld. There has to be more I can do. How can I serve you, Pip-Tau?"

Those words coming from this *god* of a man's mouth? It was too much! Pip-Tau tried not to melt into a puddle of butter. She smiled impishly and replied, "I have a few ideas."

THE TELSON PARTY rested under a shade tree beside a picturesque pond. For entertainment, Ayr of the Light was putting on a show with the party's newest member — a bard named Gryllus Stridulator.

Bards. Ugh.

As if being a *spoony bard* wasn't repulsive enough, Gryllus was also a chubby black-and-brown cricket the size of a short man. He wore a red bycocket — a "Robin Hood hat" to the uncultured — adorned with the feathery, broken-off tip of a moth antenna. His segmented antennae poked out through holes cut into the bycocket's rim.

The sounds of a four-piece minstrel band filled the air as Gryllus rubbed his wings together in an angled, scissoring motion. The full-bodied voice of a singer completed the bard's auditory spectacle. As a Master Stridulator, Gryllus could produce just about any sound imaginable, using his finely tuned wings. The mandibles and palpi making up his mouthparts were only useful for eating or making the awful clicking and hissing sounds of insectoid speech.

Gryllus spun Ayr, holding her hand with the claw of his upper leg, then dipped her. Pulling her back to her feet, he released her and started to leap and flip through the grass, using his nimble hind legs. Ayr laughed at his surprising dexterity as she performed a solo dance, stepping and spinning with the music.

Za'antha sat in the grass between Ag'nul's legs, leaning against the soft fur of his chest. They smiled and clapped, swaying to the rhythm of the music. Ruyn Wormwood and Tel O'Rax, the old farts, slept against the tree. Their dueling snores served as a backbeat to Gryllus's masterpiece.

Pip-Tau still got goosebumps when she thought about the party's recent adventure into Hive Mountain — a vast structure akin to a termite mound, built and inhabited by insectoids.

Insectoids were a species of large, insect-like creatures. They came in a variety of horrifying sizes, from dog-sized spiders and eagle-sized mosquitoes to boulder-sized beetles and millipedes as big as walking tree trunks. Some insectoids were as mindless as their natural counterparts, but many boasted human-level intelligence. The majority fell somewhere in between, having animalistic semi-sapience. Despite their variety, all insectoids in Interra were members of the same hive and shared a common parent — the Queen Mother.

As the Telson party had approached the hive, a mindless, murderous fire ant insectoid attacked them. It was Ayr who detected that their attacker was infected with a mind-warping fungus. Ruyn concocted a fungicidal powder which could cure the ailment.

Over the course of three days the party mass-produced several bags of the powder, fighting off wave after wave of wandering, berserk insectoids. Finally, they snuck into Hive Mountain. Tel O'Rax used a wind spell to blow the powder through the twisting tunnels, fumigating the entire structure. In a matter of hours, the insectoids were cured!

Yay, Telsons!

The Queen Mother, a gigantic ant-like bug with an egg-laying abdomen as big as a whale, rewarded the party with a set of magical frost-chitin armor for their half-yeti fighter. The plates of armor were woven together with spider silk, custom-fit to Ag'nul's hefty frame. Overheating in the crowded depths of Hive Mountain was always a risk for the insectoids, so their spell-weavers had long ago mastered the art of imbuing chitin with a magical web of permafrost. The armor's cooling effects delighted Ag'nul, who tended to overheat during prolonged battles. He was also unencumbered by the armor, since chitin is lightweight and stronger than steel.

As if this gift weren't generous enough, the Queen Mother also sent an envoy of insectoids to accompany Za'antha's party on their quest. Massive carrier beetles would serve as their beasts of burden, while a small swarm of man-sized warrior hornets would watch for danger from above. Most insectoids couldn't make the sounds neces-sary for humanoid speech, so the most important representative in the envoy was their translator, Gryllus Stridulator.

It had been the Astri's ingenious idea to portray themselves as insectoids, and XT-Prime was doing a masterful job playing the role of Gryllus. As much as she liked to poke fun at bards, Pip-Tau had to admit: he made delightful music.

She had been waiting for him to finish the song, but he seemed to be transitioning from one tune to another with the seamless savvy of a DJ. It was a shame to spoil such a beautiful scene, but one doesn't keep a god waiting.

A SHROUD OF darkness fell over the landscape as roiling thunderclouds swept in from beyond the horizon. The wind rose to a gale, sending the flying warrior hornets tumbling head-over-stinger into the distance.

The party clambered to its feet, drawing weapons and casting protective spells in preparation for a fight.

Black clouds converged overhead. A funnel descended — a spiraling tendril creeping towards the ground. Lightning sparked between the clouds and within the funnel.

"Cast a spell at it!" Ayr shouted, her voice vanishing into the wind.

Tel O'Rax wrestled with his robes as they whipped wildly. He shouted, "My wind spells are too weak for something like this!"

The eyes of Ruyn's deer skull mask were glowing green with Spirit Sight. He said, "The spirit realm is as troubled as the material! I sense a powerful being entering our world, from somewhere beyond!"

The funnel cloud struck the ground a stone's throw away, sending a cloud of dirt into the air. In the place where the funnel met the ground, a form materialized. The funnel receded into the sky, leaving behind a shadow the size of a watchtower.

The winds began to calm. An otherworldly hum and the distant sound of chanting replaced the fury of the storm. A light drizzle fell.

As the dust settled, a form resolved into clarity — a giant man with a lion's head. Glossy black fur covered his rippling muscles. Mighty paws served as his hands. His slitted golden eyes glowed with an inner light as he assessed the huddled mass of puny humanoid creatures before him.

Enter the god Maahes. In case you haven't already guessed, the part of Maahes will be played by The Black Lion himself: Eld of Elds Veer Gladstone.

"Do not fear, mortals," Maahes thundered.

"*Damn,* he's good at this!" Pip-Tau's cherub squeaked in the privacy of the gameworld control sub-construct. She clasped at Pip-Rho's arm, shaking her in excitement.

"He said four words, fan girl," Pip-Rho scoffed, yanking her arm free and fluttering out of Pip-Tau's reach.

But yeah, they both knew he really was good at this. Veer had come up with the Egyptian god cultural appropriation and the black lion form on his own. All Pip-Tau had to do was add the patterned loincloth and golden headpiece to complete his godly appearance. As Pip-Rho orchestrated his dramatic entrance, Pip-Tau had coached Veer on how to act the part.

"I am Maahes, god of war and protection, of tempests and gentle rain. I appear before you to give your party a quest," his deep voice echoed off the hills. "I have observed you from Aaru, The Field of Reeds — known to your people as Heaven or The Outer Planes. I deem you worthy, heroic adventurers."

Ayr went to a knee and bowed her head. She gestured for the others to follow suit. "Oh, great Maahes!" Ayr cried out, "We are honored! Mere mortals such as us are unworthy to grovel in your presence! I am a humble and devoted priestess of Rammah. Therefore, before receiving your quest, I must humbly ask if you are allied with my god."

"*How should I answer?*" Veer sent on the open conversation channel between himself, Pip-Tau, and Pip-Rho.

Pip-Rho sent, "*Tell her not to question a god, then squish her.*"

Pip-Tau ignored her evil twin. *"Sure, you can be allied with Rammah,"* she sent.

"Yeah, you and Rammah are cousins, actually," Pip-Rho laughed. *"You had squabbles in the past, but you're on good terms now."*

Pip-Tau cast her solid-black-eyed glare at Pip-Rho. "What?"

Rho shrugged. "I already worked him into the pantheon, whipped up some mythological backstory. It's canon now."

Pip-Tau opened her mouth to whine at her sis-kin-clone.

Maahes cut her off, "Yes, priestess, I am allied with Rammah. I admire your steadfast devotion. My own followers can be as fickle as the winds." He chuckled — the rumbling of thunder. "This quest will be fraught with peril, but its successful completion will earn you legendary rewards. Rise, and I will tell you of the troubles in The Weeping Woods."

VEER's godly character explained that a vicious wraith was terrorizing the peaceful fey of the aforementioned Weeping Woods. The party was to rush to the aid of the fairy folk and drive the wraith away. Before the fight, the fairies would cast a regeneration spell on the party's members. How would the spell affect the ensuing encounter? Stay tuned!

No Interran quest would be complete without its real-world metaphorical application. Here's what's up. The Proliferans adopted the fey as their in-game representations. Pip-Tau's idea was to see if Cain thought it would be a good idea to have Veer (Maahes) give the Proliferans (fairies) permission to infuse a team of Genesisians (the party) with supercharged bio-repair nanites (the regeneration spell) before an encounter with a Specter (wraith).

Back when she was Pip-Theta, the Proliferans had concocted a special blend of nanites to counteract the effects of her chromosomal abnormality. They had seriously outdone themselves. The nanite interaction with Specter cells is what caused Pip-Rho's grotesque transformation. The Council of Ten banned the use of *all* nanite suites even *vaguely* resembling Pip's in a knee-jerk response to Pip-Sigma's fateful discovery of Pip-Rho.

They fell short of stripping the nanites from Pip-Tau's system, but they barred her from space travel. She was "strongly urged" to get a room at Syn-Cen and to stay there, just in case a mean old Specter should swoop down and pluck her from the surface.

Veer had suggested that if Cain's response in Interra proved that they needed the nanite suite to defeat the Specters, he would work with The Council on a temporary lift of the ban.

Even if the quest didn't pan out, Veer's appearance in the game, alongside the Astri and Proliferans, would open new opportunities. Cain was going to slip a note between the prison bars with a wink and a nod.

Yeah, the Specters are *toast*!

Once Veer finished reciting his thundering quest-giver script, Pip-Rho whipped up a parting storm scene. A lightning-sparking tornado lowered from the dark clouds to envelop Maahes. Pip-Tau queued up the next party on the list. They would grant the quest to a dozen hand-picked parties, including the Telsons and three other hypothesis-informed groups.

Pip-Tau paused for a beat to bask in the Telson party's glory before switching the viewport perspective of the game control sub-construct to the Flemming party. They were on a merchant ship at sea.

Pip-Rho mindspoke on their shared channel, *"Ooh, here comes a sea storm. This should be fun."*

"Indeed, this is fun," Veer chuckled. *"Very engaging, very vivid. I can see why you spend so much time in constructs like this. But I do worry about the effects of losing touch with one's physical presence in the real world."*

Pip-Tau braced herself — another sort of storm was coming.

Pip-Rho cleared her throat, then sent, *"Well, Eld of Elds Veer Gladstone, all-wise Archon of The Council of Ten, have you ever considered that maybe some of us might actually* want *to lose touch with our physical presence in the real world? For example, those of us whose bodily experience consists of the eternal torture of being consumed and regrown like so much Promethean liver?!"*

Pip-Tau held her breath. Rho had gone too far. Nobody talks to an EoE that way and gets away with it.

Veer's delayed response was thick with sincerity. *"I'm sorry, Pip-Rho Telson. That was... unthoughtful of me. Yours is a tragic existence I could never imagine."*

Pip-Tau was floored. What a man!

Pip-Rho laughed it off. *"Well, luckily I don't have to spend much time connected to my screaming nervous system, so it's not so bad. Alright, Maahes is materializing now. Tell these mortals what's what."*

"Yes, my queen," Veer sent, without a hint of sarcasm.

A needle of jealousy jabbed Pip-Tau in the heart. She lifted her gaze from the viewport and caught Pip-Rho's black cherub trying to suppress a smile.

She'd kill her!

No, it's fine.

No, it was *not* fine! Tau was a queen, too, and he never said anything like that to her!

It's *fine!* It was a joke!

Grr!

16

PRETTY GIRL

THE PARTY WAS free to let their guard down and relax in camp for the night. Ayr had a new Circle of Protection blessing, so they didn't have to sleep in shifts anymore. She earned the blessing after the encounter with Maahes. She guessed it was because she showed Rammah devotion by asking Maahes if the gods were allies.

If some creature of the night broke through Ayr's Circle, the ever-present Aureum d'Canis — The Golden Goddess of Dogs — would appear and drive away the intruder. Penelope-pooch's warm presence rested in the back of her mind, as surely as if the pooch was laying by her side.

Maybe in Penelope-pooch's version of the experience she actually was by Zeta's side.

XT-Prime's cricket-man character sat on a log nearby. His wings were lifted slightly, moving slowly in and out, one rubbing the top of the other. The soft, solemn tune of a wooden flute drifted from his wings. It was relaxing.

Genevieve pinged their party's private channel. *"So, Zeta,"* Genevieve sent, *"what do you think of Interra?"*

Zeta had been trying *not* to think about how she felt about the

Interra experiment. Their gameplay had dragged on for over a month, and she had seen nothing to make her believe they were making progress. There were days when she just wanted to reconnect to her body. She swore that she forgot what it was like to be in the real world.

But she needed to keep a positive attitude. Or at least pretend to. She was on a mission, and Interra was a means to an end.

"It's fun," she sent. No, she had a larger vocabulary now — she could do better than that. *"Engaging. It's rewarding to be on an adventure with such an important goal. And the gameplay is just... phenomenal. It feels so real. Almost as real as a replay, or the real world. How do they make it such a convincing experience?"*

Oraxis replied, *"Cain's burning idle cycles on it. He uses those to flesh out the finer details. They were allocated an exorbitant amount of processing power to play with for this so-called experiment."*

There was a long and sudden silence on the channel. Zeta knew that meant Oraxis and Genevieve were talking privately. She branched their channel to have a side conversation with Carff, XT-Prime, and Alasie. *"What do you suppose they're talking about?"*

Carff replied, *"Oh, I'd wager Oraxis is getting an earful from Genevieve. He's a curmudgeon, that one. He has a right to his opinion, but spitting on the things that his family cherishes? Genevieve won't stand for it!"*

"Yeah, she's quite a peacemaker," Zeta sent. She admired Genevieve's motherly traits.

"True words!" Carff whistled. It was funny — he even whistled through his teeth in mindspeak. He lowered his mindspeech to a gentle tone, sending, *"Speaking of peacemaking, Zeta, I've been meaning to ask you something. Have you made your peace with Rohito?"*

The name triggered memories which Zeta would rather forget.

Make peace with *him?* Why would she ever do that?! The closest thing to *peace* that she would ever have with that disgusting man-boy is forgetting the fact that he lives again. Or remembering that just because he lives now doesn't mean he won't die again, in some agonizing way. He'll die over and over, being resurrected only to fall down a cliff or burn alive in a fire.

Vengeful daydreams were her "peace" with Rohito.

Her heart was pounding. Her breathing came fast and shallow. She closed the channel as Za'antha stood and turned, retreating from the campfire. The party stirred, asking what was going on. As she reached the edge of the circle of protection, Ag'nul stepped in front of her.

"Move, Alasie. I need to go," Za'antha said.

The voice of Worldnet spoke in her mind.

Please remember to stay in character and avoid using real-world names when playing Interra.

"No, I'm done!" Zeta's vision pulsed. She was trapped in this game! "I'm disconnecting. I'm not doing this anymore!"

Darkness engulfed the forest, then the campfire, then the world. Zeta floated in the void of slate-space.

Incoming conversation requests from Pip-Tau Telson, Genevieve Telson, Alasie—

"No!" Zeta declined them all before the list finished iterating. "I just... I need a break," she told the void.

Seeing nothing, hearing nothing, feeling nothing — it was calming. She let all thoughts of Rohito evaporate into the nothingness, replacing the thoughts with fond memories of her tribe.

A replay might be nice. She hadn't been in a replay since her orb viewing. Laying her eyes on the orb had changed her. Memories were supposed to be ephemeral things — hazy, pieced together a little at a time. They couldn't be relived as if traveling back in time. Memories could change. Replays were as solid as the orbs they were stored in. Why weren't memories good enough?

Or she could make a construct to retreat to. She'd show Charra around Interra. He'd make a character — a hobbit, of course. Maybe a thief. Constructs: imagination made real. Why wasn't imagination good enough?

She considered returning to the real world. Her body was waiting for her in a tiny white room in Syn-Cen, underneath unimaginable volumes of rock and water, laying atop a hairy slab of flesh connected to her body using tiny tubes, keeping it alive while her mind explored vivid, imaginary worlds. When she put it that way, the real world seemed quite unreal.

Alasie and Pip-Tau would be there, laying on their placental mats. Penelope-pooch would be laying beside Pinga, obediently playing Interra.

Even if she left Interra and left Syn-Cen, where would she go? There was no escaping her life.

Well, there was the *red button*, but she wasn't ready to consider that. Not right now. True Death will come on its own, in time. Even the stars die.

She wanted to see her orb again.

RECONNECTING TO HER BODY, she opened her eyes. Pulling her arms up, she felt the gentle tug of her placental mat's nano-tubes being painlessly pulled from her skin. She crawled to the foot of the bed and backed down the ladder.

"Um, hi," Alasie said, giving a nervous huff-laugh.

Zeta looked at the bottom bunk. Alasie was lying on her back, watching her with dark, innocent eyes. The sleek black hair of her placental mat blended seamlessly with the hair on her head.

"I'm going... to see my... orb," Zeta said, stumbling on the words. She had forgotten how hard it was to make her mouth speak Common after so long in Interra.

"I'll go with you," Alasie said. Her worried smile lacked sincerity.

"You can't." She took a moment to compose her words. "Only one person can be in the orb viewing room at a time."

"I can go to the place where those... things are that take you there. Pods?"

"I'm going alone," Zeta said, sounding more harsh than she meant to. She turned toward the door.

"Zeta, no," Alasie pleaded. She pulled herself up off the mat and grabbed Zeta by the arm. She spoke with the strained croak of someone holding back tears as she stumbled over the awkward Common tongue. "Don't go to your orb. Carff brought up Rohito, so now you're... depressed. I don't want you to do something... bad. Rohito isn't a monster — he's just a... boy. A victim of the... bad things that happened, just like you."

Zeta's breath was quickening again. She yanked her arm free of Alasie's grasp and walked to the door. It slid open, revealing the hallway. She stopped and turned around, crossing her arms. "How would you know?"

Alasie was on her feet. "I..." She bit her lip and shook her head. "Zeta, don't be mad, okay? I, um, made friends with him after your party."

Zeta advanced on Alasie, eyes wide, anger overflowing. "You're friends with him?! You never told me that! You know I hate him and you're his... secret little friend?!"

Alasie flinched backward, curling her arms up against her chest, protectively. Zeta heard the door close behind her. She turned to look at it. This was pointless — she should leave.

Zeta rounded on Alasie again. She wanted to keep berating her, but they'd both stumble and choke on the words if they continued speaking Common. She sent a WorMS conversation request.

Alasie accepted.

The two stared at each other, faces flush and mouths tight as they engaged in mindspeak.

Zeta sent, *"Tell me why! Why would you do that?"*

Alasie sent, "*I don't know! I mean, at your party — one second we were talking about perfume, the next you're ready to murder Rohito—*"

"I don't want to hear that name," Zeta interrupted.

Alasie scoffed. "*Okay*, the boy, *then?*"

"No, he's the 'red-speckled man-boy'," Zeta growled in mindspeak.

Alasie's expression darkened. "*You're making fun of his freckles?*"

"*Freckles? Sure. Whatever the hell is wrong with his face, I don't care what they are.*"

Alasie stepped forward, looking up at Zeta, challenging her with a boldness Zeta had never seen in her. A snarling image of Ag'nul came to mind. She sent, "*He's covered in freckles because he inherited genes for pale skin and spent his life in lands where Surya shines hot and bright. His skin protected itself by making all those freckles. The elders of his tribe die of skin sickness — cancer, I mean. It kills a lot of them. You shouldn't make fun of him for it! It's not his fault, and there's nothing wrong with how it looks. Would you call me the 'short little chubby girl' for having my people's body type? Or make fun of Pip-Tau for her... gene thing? Her um... um... chromosomal abnormality?!*"

Zeta ignored the ridiculous question. "*Well, did your friend tell you he set his wolf-pooches on me and my bro-kin? That he killed Penelope-pooch and hit me in the head with a rock?*"

Alasie stepped back. She shook her head contemptuously. "*He told me what happened. You don't know his story, and you're leaving out the things you did. Do you even care about the truth? He'd have talked to you, you know. You hold this hate so close to your heart and don't do anything to make it go away. It's like you're trying to protect it. Like you want it — your precious hate!*"

"*Fine, then tell me: what's his side of the story? He showed you a replay?*"

Alasie hesitated. "*Well... he didn't show me the replay. It hurt him too bad to go back and see it again. But we talked about it. It really was just... unfortunate. Their tribe got attacked over and over again. Most of the men got killed. The elders, women, and children were defense-less. They started breeding dogs with wolves to make them bigger and meaner. They trained the wolf-dogs to attack strangers. Rohito feared the wolf-dogs, so they didn't obey him. He saw you at the pond and wanted to meet you, but when his wolf-dogs got out of hand... well... that's when things went wrong."*

It felt like cords were wrapped around Zeta's heart and throat. Tears pooled in her eyes. She didn't believe Rohito was innocent. No, the replay would prove she was justified.

Zeta pushed past Alasie, stomping up the ladder. She sent, *"I've relived that replay more times than you can imagine. I already know the truth. But if you don't believe I have good reason to hate him, you can see for yourself."*

THEY MET IN SLATE-SPACE. Alasie said Zeta should join the replay as an external observer instead of from inside her alpha's head. She also said Zeta should use the auto-translate function to see what Rohito and his kin were saying.

It had never occurred to Zeta to find out what the foreign-tongued devils had been saying. Maybe Alasie was right — maybe she stayed ignorant on purpose.

The replay loaded, placing Zeta and Alasie side-by-side in Talmid's Stinking Thicket. They were semi-transparent figures in their default avatars. Zeta was in her leather tunic, while Alasie wore the fur chest wrap and skirt she had worn in the jungle outside the Guardian Embassy.

The scene before them was frozen in time. Standing between Zeta and Alasie was a naked, bleeding girl, smeared with mud. A one-eyed Penelope-pooch crouched, snarling towards the man-boy and his black wolf-pooch.

Alasie stepped backward, eyes glistening with pooling tears. She put a hand to her mouth and whispered, "Oh, Zeta."

Zeta spat, "That's what they did to us — that man-boy and his wolf-pooches."

She stared at her frozen alpha for a long while. Here was a girl who had just lost everything. She'd be dead soon. Was it right to say this was *her*? Or was it just a girl that they copied her from? Some long-dead ancestor, wearing her face.

With a thought-command, the scene came to life.

Rohito's voice cracked as he screamed, "Why must this be?!"

Zeta-Alpha snarled, "Where is my bro-kin?"

Rohito struggled to restrain his black wolf-pooch. Her alpha glared at him in a daze, rocking unsteadily.

"I can't hold him! Run, girl!" Rohito shouted.

As if Zeta-Alpha understood, she turned and ran. Time froze again at Zeta's command. She stared at the grimacing man-boy. His knuckles were white as they clutched the ferocious wolf-pooch's fur. Blood seeped from the cuts on his pale, muddy legs. He must've been dragged over sharp rocks as he fought with his beast.

He had fought to protect her?

The confidence she had held in her superiority over Rohito was crumbling. The brief scene had smothered the flames of her hatred, reducing them to stubborn, smoldering coals that refused to die.

Alasie was right.

"I," Zeta said, choking on the word.

"Do you see now?" Alasie whispered, placing a hand on Zeta's shoulder.

Zeta couldn't speak. It seemed pretty obvious, now that she saw it from the outside — now that she heard his words for the first time.

She needed to hear more.

Zeta skipped the replay forward to her tribe's camp. Rohito and his eld sat by the fire with Chief Talmid. Zeta's alpha was laying under a pile of furs, glaring across the camp at the strangers by the fireside. After Chief Talmid pressed foreheads with the foreign eld, Rohito spoke. "Ulyss-eld, should I go over and tell the girl how sorry I am?"

Ulyss-eld shook his head, looking at Zeta's alpha. "No, Rohito. She would only hear the hissing of a viper. We will make peace in due time."

Rohito stared at Zeta, his expression one of pity or grief. Or was it longing? His eld summoned him and he stumbled away.

"Rise, Zeta," Eve-eld-ma said. Zeta looked across the camp at Rod-pa, holding her dead bro-kin in his arms. It was more than Zeta could bear. Her legs faltered, and she fell to her knees. Sobs escaped her between shaky breaths. The replay froze.

Alasie wrapped her arms around Zeta, sharing her tears. "We should stop," she croaked.

Zeta shook her head. "I have to get through it. I didn't know — I need to know why it all happened."

Rohito's plea echoed in her mind, *"Why must this be?!"*

It was the best question she could imagine. Why did they have to suffer like this? All of them — why?

She advanced the replay with unnatural speed. Her alpha flailed on the ground, sobbed in an eld's arms. They sped past Charra's burial and her piercing glares at Rod-pa. Night went by in a flash, then the next morning when Rod-pa had made his vigilante pledge to kill the other tribe's wolf-pooches. Next, Chief Talmid would lecture her. The replay slowed to normal speed.

She wanted to see this part. Normally she'd skip past it — she never could stomach that speech. Now, more than ever, she knew that Chief Talmid — Jamji's long-lost son, had been right.

Chief Talmid spoke to her from across the years. "Just remember, Zeta, violence brings violence. Blood thirsts for blood. Someone has to be the first to stop. Sometimes that means running away or letting a death go unpunished. If that saves a tribe, then that's how it must be."

Zeta's alpha nodded, feigning respect.

"He's wise," Alasie said.

Zeta wondered if Jamji would agree with her son's sentiment. She gave Alasie no reply as she pushed the replay forward in time again.

———

Zeta's alpha, Rod-pa, and the three dogs were speeding through the forest. She reverted time to its normal speed when her alpha and Rod-pa emerged from the trees at the spring pool. Rohito and his kin were on the other side. Rod-pa pulled out his sling and loaded a rock.

Rohito's kin called out, "We don't want to fight! We can share the water, my friend!"

"I don't want to fight you, my friend," Replied Rod-pa, "but I must kill your wolves!"

Zeta-Alpha pulled a spear from the straps on Rod-pa's back. Her face bore a snarl as fierce as any wolf.

Rod-pa shouted again, "Your little red bro-kin is using a bow, my friend? That is forbidden by Gravan!"

"It's your girl's bow, my friend!" Rohito's kin shouted. "Come over here and get it!"

When his kin grabbed the bow, Rohito clutched the fur of a wolf-pooch, earning a slap from his kin. Rod-pa was whirling the sling. He called, "I'll only kill your wolves. Move aside now, or *bleed*!"

"No!" Rohito wailed. Rod-pa's sling released the rock which started the killing, felling the first wolf-pooch.

Everybody sprang into action, with Zeta's alpha screaming a war cry.

She froze the replay. Her heart was pounding. Did she really want to watch herself die again? She knew she was wrong about Rohito. Was there anything more to learn?

Rod-pa was looking at Zeta-Alpha. His eyes were wild with the fever of battle, his face frozen — a screaming war mask. Yet, in this fleeting glance, there was something more. Was he looking for her approval? Was he asking, "Am I as fierce as you want me to be, Zeta? Is this wrathful enough to earn your acceptance? To avenge your bro-kin's death?"

It was. She had dropped the "non" insult from his name ever since the first time she saw this replay. But she never should've asked this of him. The fight would kill Penelope-pooch, then her and Rohito. It wouldn't have happened if she hadn't demanded he kill the wolf-pooches. Nobody needed to die that day.

She looked at Alasie, saying, "I think I should see it through to the end."

Alasie nodded. She said, "It's too late to fix, right? I just wish I could've been there. Maybe I could've... I don't know... protected you?"

"From myself?"

Alasie huffed at the sad half-joke. "Yeah."

But that *was* what Alasie was doing — protecting her from herself. Helping her to realize that she doesn't need to hold on to so much hate. Helping her to move on.

Zeta looked from her blood-crazed, snarling alpha to the round face of Alasie, framed in shiny black hair. Alasie's ghostly form was looking nervously between the frozen figures of Zeta's past, as if they might direct their fury towards *her* at any moment. Her innocent eyes were glassy with recent tears. Alasie was a beautiful person, inside and out. Zeta didn't deserve her friendship.

Resigned to watch the horror show to the end, Zeta resumed the passage of time. Rocks flew. Dogs barked, snarled, yelped. Rod-pa tackled Rohito's kin. Zeta's alpha lunged her spear at one of the young men, then toppled as she received a crack against the head by his stick.

Rohito was out of place in the melee, frozen like a frightened deer. When he took his first action, it was to dig his fingers into the mud and pull a large rock from the ground. He heaved it with both hands, lobbing it blindly into the fray. He was just as likely to hit his kin or his own wolf-pooches as Penelope-pooch. Zeta averted her eyes as the rock struck down Penelope-pooch's alpha.

"No!" Zeta-Alpha wailed. She stumbled to her feet. "You killed my pooch!"

Looking back at Rohito, Zeta saw him snatch up a smaller rock, about as big as his fist. He held it threateningly as Zeta's stumbling, dazed alpha advanced.

Cornered on the slate outcropping, Rohito looked down at the water — his pending doom. He pleaded, "Please, I don't swim well. Stop, please!"

Zeta watched as her alpha crept closer — a predator closing in on her prey.

Rohito wailed, "Get back! Please, I don't want to hurt you. I didn't want any of this to happen. I'm so sorry, pretty girl. I'm so sorry!"

Zeta's alpha charged with a guttural growl. Rohito threw the rock, skipping it off the top of her alpha's head. The replay slowed to a stop as the two collided. They froze in mid-air, free-falling to their mutual deaths.

Zeta's throat was constricted with emotion. She shook her head slowly. Alasie stood beside her, a hand on her shoulder. Zeta closed her eyes, turning to wrap her arms around Alasie. Though they were ghostly, the embrace was solid. Zeta cried into Alasie's hair. It felt good to have someone to cry on.

"It was my fault," Zeta whispered. "It was my fault." She repeated the whisper between sobs.

Alasie shushed her, whispering consolations which failed to reach Zeta's ears.

Zeta looked back at the doomed pair of alphas floating in the air together. She wouldn't resume the replay. The only thing left to see was two senseless deaths.

She sighed and said a silent farewell to the alphas.

***

ZETA CONSIDERED RETURNING to the real world. The temptation to go to her orb was even stronger now. She could bury this tortured past with the gentle press of a red button. A part of her knew she shouldn't make a regrettable decision like that in her current emotional state.

She loaded a new construct, placing them in the most peaceful setting she could imagine. They stood in the fragrant, knee-high grasses of the Happy Hunting Grounds. It was nighttime. A full Soma illuminated rolling hills covered in flowers and grasses, undulating in the gentle breeze. Their bodies were solid again.

Zeta took a moment to let the peaceful scene ease her mind. She sat in the grass, then laid back to stare at the stars. Alasie also laid down nearby.

Alasie — her friend, her protector. She had stalked Zeta at the Guardian Embassy, just to make sure she was okay. She had followed her to Syn-Cen and joined her in Interra, even though she barely understood the point of the game or appreciated the threat posed by the Specters. Zeta had never wondered about her reasons before, but now she wanted to know.

"Why do you play Interra?" Zeta asked.

Alasie was silent for a moment. Grass rustled as she scooted closer, laying her head next to Zeta's. She said, "I, uh... at first I wanted to play because it's what you were doing. Not like I had much else to do, right? And I mean, after Pip-Rho told us about Googolplex and all that... hypothesis stuff, I thought the game was going to be hard. Complicated — like a puzzle for people smarter than me. And then after that woman at Fort Noob got burned by the, uh, dragon? I was afraid it'd be torture!" She huff-laughed. "But after playing for a while, I really like it. It's not hard at all. When I get hurt... well, I'm usually so worked up by that point I can barely feel it. Being Ag'nul makes me feel... powerful. Mainly, I like to play because... I, uh, I get to spend time with you."

Zeta added, "And get torn apart trying to protect me?"

Alasie huff-laughed, "Yeah. It's worth it, though."

It was what Zeta expected Alasie to say — that she played Interra to be with her and protect her. Ag'nul was notoriously overprotective of Za'antha — always mindlessly rushing to keep her from getting hurt. Tel O'Rax, Ruyn, and Ayr were their casters. They were the ones that actually needed protection. Za'antha wore leather armor and had enough dexterity to dodge attacks. Ag'nul's senseless strategy was a constant source of after-battle arguments, with Ag'nul never quite understanding what everyone was so upset about.

Sure, it wasn't a good battle strategy, but Zeta enjoyed the feeling she got when the ferocious half-yeti rushed to her aid. It was Alasie doing what Alasie always does — acting without thinking, following her heart.

They laid silently for a while longer. Her replay kept creeping back to the front of her mind. The things Rohito said echoed in her ears. Tears pooled in her eyes again. Finally, she sat up and snapped, "Pretty girl? Why would he ever call me that?!" She scratched her fingernails through her hair, hiding her face with her forearms. "Did you see me, Alasie? I was disgusting! I was a blood-crazed beast, ready to kill him."

Alasie kneeled by her side. "You *are* pretty, Zeta. Anyone can see that." Zeta peeked over at her. Alasie bit her lip and looked into the distance, then looked back up at Zeta. "Alright, so he asked me not to tell you this, but I think it'll help you understand what happened."

Zeta braced herself.

Alasie said, "Before it all started, Rohito was at the pond, getting water. He heard you and your brother talking — coming towards him. He ran and hid in the trees near his, uh... well, he called them his 'attack dogs' — where they were tied up. Then, when he saw you, he said it was love at first sight. You know how boys are, though," she huff-laughed.

Zeta sniffed and wiped her eyes with her palms, humoring Alasie with a laugh.

Alasie said, "He was working up the nerve to show himself and say hi. But then you got naked, so he panicked and ran. He was untying his dogs to run back to his camp when your dogs found them. His dogs slipped out of their leashes and got into a fight with your dogs. That's when they went after you and your brother. He wishes he never untied them."

Zeta shook her head and scoffed. "That's all he really did wrong, isn't it? A clumsy boy who took the leashes off his attack dogs, like a fool."

"Also, he's a sneaky peeker," Alasie laughed. "He's embarrassed about it and didn't want me to tell you — he really... *wanted* you. His brain turned to mush from your beauty, made it so he couldn't think straight. I don't blame him. You, uh... you know," Alasie's smile faded. She looked down at the grass. She started to speak, choked on the words, swallowed hard, then stopped. After a deep breath she started again, speaking just above a whisper, "you do the same thing to me." She shook her head. "I'm sorry, I shouldn't say that. You don't... feel that way about me, so I shouldn't..."

A tear shimmered in Soma's light as it rolled down Alasie's cheek.

Zeta's heart melted.

She put a hand under Alasie's chin and lifted it. Glassy, deep brown eyes searched Zeta's face for a reaction. There was a sadness there — a longing. Alasie shouldn't cry on her account.

Something came over Zeta, making her decide that the tears needed to be kissed away. She leaned in and kissed each of Alasie's eyes, in turn.

Salty sweetness.

She found another tear on Alasie's cheek and kissed it. She lingered there a bit too long. Maybe it was just the construct, but feeling Alasie's skin on her lips didn't seem real. It was too warm, too soft. She had kissed her tribemates' cheeks plenty of times, and they never felt like this.

Alasie's hand rose to the back of Zeta's head, fingers sliding into her hair.

It happened so fast, yet time stood still.

Their lips met.

They were kissing.

Alasie's lips were *so* soft!

Her kiss was urgent and intense — Ag'nul charging into battle.

Zeta reached a hand behind the small of Alasie's back, ready to pull her close. When she felt the skin of Alasie's waist against her fingertips, she had to push her away — it was too much, too fast. Breaking the spell of the kiss snapped Zeta back to her senses.

She scrambled to her feet, backing away. "What are we doing?" She laughed, shaking her head.

Alasie's chest heaved as she kneeled in the grass, breathing deeply, staring at Zeta with wide, hungry eyes. She touched her fingers to her lips, as if checking to see if they were still there. "Kissing," Alasie said. She gave a huff-laugh. "I've wanted to do that since the moment I saw you, Zeta. I thought you wanted—"

"Women *don't* kiss each other like that," Zeta said breathlessly. Her heart was pounding so hard she was worried she'd pass out.

"They don't?" Alasie huff-laughed. "Well, maybe not in *your* tribe. Not where other people can see, at least. It's... really more common than you think. In tribes like mine — in most tribes, I think, women openly partner with other women, and men with men. Not that everyone does it, but it's still... it's... *normal*. Maybe your tribe didn't accept it, but that doesn't matter! We're Noddites now, Zeta! Modern humans have the sense to know it's totally fine."

Alasie was right. Zeta's tribe never talked about it openly, but rumors abounded, tinged with scorn. Zeta never believed there was anything wrong with it. Vera, that feisty girl from the Crow's Claw tribe, came to mind. Vera had snuck away with Zeta more than once for what they called "practice for how to kiss a boy". That hadn't counted, of course. It was all just practice — sort of like a game. What she and Alasie had just done was real.

Zeta couldn't decide how she felt about it. A part of her — a deep and powerful part — wanted to kiss Alasie again. It wasn't some twisted notion of "wrongness" that held her back. It was her sense of *duty*.

Zeta had vowed to her ancestors to avenge Wilhelm-pa and free Pip-Rho by defeating the Specters. That was her life's purpose, and this sudden spark of passion threatened her goals. When people fall in love, especially during the first few months, all they want to do is fawn on each other and giggle under bedding furs together. Friends tease them about never going out to forage or hunt. Elds berate them for neglecting their duties. Love clouds the mind. She had never felt it before, but after that kiss, she feared she could slip into that trap with Alasie.

"This is a construct," Zeta said. "So, we haven't really kissed — not in the real world."

"Let's disconnect," Alasie said, getting to her feet. "I'll bet it's better when it's real." She stepped towards Zeta.

Zeta stepped back. "Alasie, I can't do this."

Alasie froze, her hungry eyes turning sad and pooling with another round of tears. "You don't... want..."

Zeta went to her, pulling her into an embrace. "I don't mean I don't want to. I mean... just not yet. Not now. Once we defeat the Specters, we can kiss in the real world, okay? I promise."

"Forget about the Specters, Zeta!" Alasie cried. She was squeezing Zeta, pleading, "It's just like Rohito — they hurt you and you hate them for it. Can you ever see past your hate?! You don't have to be the one to stop them — the Pips can do it without you." She pulled back to look Zeta in the eye. "We're young! Be young, Zeta! The Specters have been around for hundreds of years! What if it takes a thousand more to beat them?! I can't wait that long!"

It pained Zeta's heart, but she had made her choice.

"Interra is the answer," Zeta said. "I know it will work."

"And if it doesn't? Then it's on to the next thing — the next *experiment*. You'll never give up."

Zeta sighed. "If Interra doesn't work... well, we can take some time off for a few years and... do other things. But it *will* work, Alasie. Cain *will* give us the answers. And it *won't* take a thousand years."

"Cain," Alasie scoffed. "Alright, bring Cain in here. I want to give him a piece of my mind." She released Zeta, stepped back, and began pacing. Her sadness had turned to anger.

Zeta wasn't sure if bringing Cain's avatar into a construct was possible, but she wanted to humor Alasie, so she tried. She thought, *"Cain? Can you please join my construct? Alasie wants to talk to you."*

The beautiful man appeared in the grass nearby.

Alasie stomped through the high grass, advancing on the SI. "Alright, *Cain*, here's the deal: I want to be with Zeta, but she won't do it until you help us defeat the Specters. So, are you going to do that, or are we wasting our time?"

Cain raised his hands and put on a half-smiling, half-shocked expression. "I've made it pretty clear: I can't step in to help humanity solve its problems. If you're going to defeat the Specters, you'll have to figure out how to do it on your own."

"Then Interra's a waste of time?" Alasie asked, eyeing Zeta.

"Interra is a gameworld construct," Cain said. "If you enjoy games, then it's by no means a waste of time."

"Alasie, you know about the IG," Zeta said. "That's the whole point of Interra. He can't admit to helping us solve the Specter problem." She turned to the SI. "Cain, I barely understand what an IG or an SI is. Maybe you're secretly 'Lex the Six-Headed Synth-God' or maybe you're just a tool, like you claim to be. But if there's anything I can do to help defeat the Specters, I'll do it. I'm *your* tool."

"Me too," Alasie said. "And make it fast, Cain! I don't know how long my heart can take this."

Zeta laughed, but Alasie didn't join her.

Cain started to say something, but Zeta didn't need to hear his scripted denials. She booted him from the construct.

"I'll be in Interra," Alasie said flatly, with her back to Zeta. She disappeared.

Zeta sat down again in the grass, putting her head in her hands. It had been an emotional night, and she was drained. Doubt clouded her mind. Alasie wanted her to let go of her hate for the Specters the same way she had let it go for Rohito. The difference was that she got new information about Rohito. He was a human — easy enough to understand and forgive. But the Specters were a mysterious alien menace.

What if she was wrong about them, too? What if she helped to kill them, but they were actually innocent? Misunderstood?

She shook it off. It wasn't her job to decide what to do about the Specters. They were a problem to be solved, and she was a tool — a means to the end. If Cain decided they needed to die and showed her how to kill them, that's what she would do.

Her path was clear. Her purpose was simple. There was no point in questioning what she had to do.

She reconnected to Interra.

The trees before her cast dancing shadows in the flickering campfire. Za'antha turned around, avoiding meeting anyone's eyes, and walked to the fire. She sat and stared into the flames as Gryllus's wings played a somber melody.

She was Za'antha of the Sylvan Woods — an Interran, and she was on a quest: destroy the wraiths, whatever the cost.

17

____

WRAITH

"This is it!" Pip-Tau shouted. "Oh-my-god, the wraith is making its move! Come watch!"

"Finally!" Pip-Rho squeaked. "Wraith versus Telson party, *fight!*"

Pip-Rho's black porcelain cherub streaked across The Chess Room to join Pip-Tau's white cherub at the viewport, displaying the shadowy figure of a wraith. It was all pale flesh and gossamer, wearing a black, vaporous robe. What could be seen of its face from under its black hood was featureless. It wafted between trees, stalking the party.

The Telson party stood in a circle formation. They had known that trouble was brewing when Gryllus reported that their warrior hornets were being picked off, one-by-one. His telepathic link to his dying companions had made the insectoid hiss in pain as the lives of his hivemates were snuffed out.

Ayr glimpsed their foe flying overhead. She summoned Holy Light, sending golden rays piercing through the branches. The wraith didn't even have to dodge to avoid the poorly aimed attack. Pip-Rho shook her head. It was a waste of Ayr's special ability. She couldn't cast the spell for five minutes or she risked losing favor with Rammah.

Tense seconds ticked by in silence.

"What's it waiting for?!" Pip-Tau shouted. "It's supposed to be a quick battle. Get in there and fight, wraithy! That's it, I'm taking control—"

"Don't you dare!" Pip-Rho squealed. "Cain's in control! We have to see what he does on his own. That's the whole point, Tau!"

"Fine. I'm gonna watch in full immersion. You?"

"Hell yeah!"

The two became disembodied, omniscient observers, free to flit from the party to the wraith and back.

The wraith had slipped into the spirit plane, and was passing overhead as the party below stood within the glowing hemisphere of Ayr's Circle of Protection Blessing.

"Does anybody see it?!" Ayr shouted.

Ruyn cast Spirit Sight, chanting and rattling a cord of bones. His deer-skull mask's eyes glowed with a deep green aura, then he looked straight up at the invisible wraith. "Right above us! Shoot your rays!"

"I can't use it again so soon!"

Za'antha shot an enchanted arrow blindly into the sky, trailing sparkles as it ascended. Tel O'Rax lobbed a magic missile. Neither attack could affect the wraith while it was in the spirit plane.

The wraith howled and descended into the darkness of the forest, then returned to the material plane.

Gryllus had his six feet on the ground and his musical wings lifted, producing a warbling spellsong in a foreign tongue.

"Ugh, that sounds awful," Tel O'Rax grumbled. He cast Dancing Lights, sending a dozen glowing orbs into the forest. The white lights hovered and bobbed between the trees. He was trying to shed light on their foe, but instead created a thousand shadows for it to hide in.

The wraith wove in and out of the spirit plane, jumping from shadow to shadow until it was just strides away from the party. Gryllus's spellsong began taking on an unsettling, bestial sound, as if it were being sung by a gorilla. The forest echoed with the sound.

The wraith let out a shrill screech, covering its ears. It ducked into the spirit plane, then came out from behind the tree, closing in on the party.

"It's here! Right over here!" Ruyn was jumping and pointing, his bone decorations rattling. "I'll capture it!" He held up a human skull and chanted.

Za'antha had another arrow nocked, but there was nothing for her to shoot at. Pip-Tau saw she was trying to summon Aureum d'Canis, but that the wraith's presence had blocked the summoning from working. It also temporarily banished frostbite from the material plane. Pip-Tau bookmarked that for symbolic analysis later.

The wraith returned to the spirit plane. It passed within the Circle of Protection, then reappeared in the material plane. It was smack-dab in the middle of the party!

Let the bloodbath ensue!

As it materialized, the wraith's bony claw swiped at Gryllus. Yellowish liquid splattered the party as the insectoid cracked open. The force of the swipe sent Gryllus's body flying into the air and crashing through the upper branches of the forest.

Yeah... the fairy regen spell couldn't fix that.

Tel O'Rax, Ayr, and Za'antha tried to get their distance from the wraith, while Ag'nul roared, stepping forward and swinging his spiked club. In a flash, the wraith struck him squarely in the chest with both hands. Chitin armor splintered at the impact, sending the huge half-yeti tumbling backwards. He settled into a lifeless heap.

Poor Alasie! That looked like it hurt.

Ruyn Wormwood was still holding the skull up towards the wraith, chanting loudly. His green glowing mask radiated with an intense energy. The wraith screeched as it backhanded the old shaman, sending his rattling bones flying. Ruyn flew back so fast that when he struck a narrow tree trunk, he folded backwards around it in the most unnatural way. The snapping of his spine made Pip-Tau's skin crawl.

Tel O'Rax and Ayr were side-by-side, casting spells in their futile attempt to subdue the unstoppable creature. The wraith executed a two-handed claw swipe uppercut, and the two soared into the air, trailing blood. Their flapping robes made them look like a pair of tossed rags.

Za'antha stood, arrow drawn and pointed at the wraith, eyes wide with fear, yet she did not release. It let out another ear-splitting screech, then advanced on Za'antha. As it reached her, the wraith opened its arms, then wrapped them around her, engulfing Za'antha in its black, vaporous robes. It pulled her into the spirit plane. Pip-Tau watched with glee as the wraith ascended to the astral plane, stealing its prize away.

This was it! Cain's showing that he knows what the wraiths represent! It was barely even a metaphor. That was a textbook Specter attack, complete with body-flinging attacks, followed by a single specimen abduction.

She scrambled to open her notification log, finding the recent entries for character deaths.

Gryllus Stridulator (XT-Prime of the Astrus Faction), Insectoid Bard: killed by wraith. Resurrection pending.
Ag'nul (Alasie Herrington), Frost Elf/Yeti Fighter: killed by wraith. Resurrection pending.
Ruyn Wormwood (Carff Telson), Wood Elf Shaman: killed by wraith. Resurrection pending.
Ayr of the Light (Genevieve Telson), Human Priestess: killed by wraith. Resurrection pending.
Tel O'Rax (Oraxis Telson), Human Wizard: killed by wraith. Resurrection pending.
Za'antha (Zeta Telson), Wood Elf Huntress: abducted by wraith. Resurrection pending.

Abducted?!
Praise Lex the Six-Headed Synth-God, he didn't even log it as a kill! Za'antha was freaking *abducted!*

———

"Abducted!" Pip-Tau sang, doing an aerial backflip. "Did you see that? We got an abduction!"

"You know I did!" Pip-Rho squeaked, rushing to Pip-Tau. They joined hands and spun in a circle, laughing.

"Finally!" Pip-Tau said. "How many wraith encounters have we had? No abductions. But as soon as a wraith feasted its eyes on Za'antha? Yoink!"

"It. Was. Epic!" Pip-Rho exclaimed. "Hey, you didn't touch the controls, did you?"

"No! Shut up! You know I wouldn't do that."

"Ahem, you almost did earlier, Tau."

"Yeah, well, I didn't. This was all Cain, baby. He knows what's up! You hear me, Cain? Or should I call you *Lex*? But don't worry, IG, it's just a game."

"Don't tempt the synth-gods," Pip-Rho said, laughing.

"And now, if you query the location of Za'antha's corpse?"

"Null value! Let's watch the replay in slo-mo." Pip-Rho queued up the abduction replay. They watched the wraith envelop Za'antha, move to the spirit plane, then ascend to the astral plane. Cross-referencing to the detailed character logs, they could see that the moment it enveloped her, Za'antha's character status switched from "alive" to "abducted", never passing through "dead".

"Her resurrection is in The Soulkeeper's queue, now, too," Pip-Rho said. "Cain totally gets it. You get abducted by a Specter, you're declared dead by the colony, but are you dead? No! You're dragged away and *merged*."

"I can't wait to see if the merge happens," Pip-Tau said.

Nobody believed that the Specters merged with their abductees until Pip-Rho's fateful experience. Even then, hers was a special case, since her nanite suite was one-of-a-kind.

Pip-Rho exclaimed, "The game is afoot, Watson!"

"Hey, how come I have to be Watson?" Pip-Tau's cherub crossed her chubby arms and pouted.

"Oh, please. I'm Sherlock, you're Watson. You know I can think, like, fifty times faster than you." Pip-Rho stuck out her tongue.

"Egg-head!"

"Bird-legs!"

"Tumor-face!"

The Pips engaged in a slapping fight, which descended into giddy laughter.

After a few more minutes of celebration and play, Pip-Rho said, "Okay, here's the plan. From now on I'm on constant wraith watch. I've tagged the one that nabbed Za'antha. If Cain agrees with the merge theory, it'll change in some way."

"Cool," Pip-Tau said, "and I'll put together a presentation for The Council. They're going to love this!"

"Yeah, they'll flip." Pip-Rho back-flipped.

"We should invite the Telsons to the presentation. The Council prob'ly thinks Zeta's a jerk after her disaster of a beta ceremony. I want to see their reactions when they find out she's Cain's chosen one."

"Let's avoid that term. Chosen one? Reeks of religiosity, and most of the council elds don't buy into Lexism."

"Oh," Pip-Tau said, chuckling, "They'll learn. By the time this experiment is done, the Specters'll be defeated and Cain'll be unmasked as Lex. Bingo-bango, a two-for-one special! We'll go down in history as the pioneers of metaphoric Lex interfaces!"

Pip-Rho raised a finger. "You forgot to mention: I'll get out of this egg. They'll *have* to toss my egg into Surya and resurrect me when the Specters are gone."

"Of course!" Pip-Tau floated over and embraced her sis-kin-clone. "It's not only about the big picture stuff. We've got a personal stake in this, too. I'm sorry, Rho, I shouldn't gloss over how important that is."

"Yeah, that's why you're Watson."

THE TELSON PARTY was disappointed in their party's inability to hold out for longer than a minute against a wraith. But when they found out about Za'antha's abduction, they were ecstatic. Their dedication to the game redoubled, and they couldn't wait to be resurrected. Even Oraxis seemed to buy in.

Zeta had squealed in delight when she heard that Za'antha was abducted. When Za'antha was resurrected, the first thing she did was wrap her arms around The Soulkeeper in a tight embrace, squeezing his arms against his sides. Pip-Rho did a query to find that it was the first time anyone had shown any sort of affection to the creepy man.

The Telson party wanted to return to the scene of their encounter and get their supplies back, but it would take a while. First was waiting in limbo for their turn in the resurrection queue. After resurrection, they teleported to the waypoint station nearest to their encounter — Rosebud Grove, the city of fairies.

Insectoids didn't use soulstones for resurrection. Instead, Gryllus was reborn by his Queen Mother. They reconstituted his mind using the eternal consciousness of the hive. After his carapace finished hardening, he took flight. They met up at Rosebud Grove, then traveled to The Weeping Woods and found the battle site.

Next came the disturbing task of looting their own scavenger-ravaged, rotting corpses. Tel O'Rax and Ayr had a hard time tracking down their launched bodies. They were half a kilometer from the battle site, in opposite directions. Ag'nul's cracked armor would need repairs, but overall, the party didn't lose much. That is, besides Ayr's lunch after she rolled her corpse over.

So many maggots...

In the meantime, the wraith which had abducted Za'antha was growing tumors and boils throughout its body, doubling in size. One day, it ascended through the astral plane, all the way to the Sun Sphere. Pip-Tau was tempted to stop it, but knew she shouldn't interfere. The wraith burned to ash as it flew into the sun.

This was an interesting outcome, indeed.

Elsewhere in the game, the wraiths had become much more active. One had attacked a caravan, slaughtering all the horses and smashing the wagons to pieces. Wraiths throughout Interra started picking on caravans and messengers. They caught one in the act of swatting a carrier pigeon out of the air.

It didn't take a Doctor Watson to deduce that this behavior represented the Specter habit of attacking conspicuous ships and communications systems.

What does that mean, boys and girls?

It means Interra. Is. WORKING!

Two WEEKS after the wraith abduction, The Council of Ten finally invited Pip-Tau to present her findings.

As with most Noddite meet-ups, the venue was a construct. Council members were always scattered far and wide across Genesis, so they only gathered in person for annual council retreats. One of the council elds, Marco-Epsilon Rhind, even lived at Soma Station.

The construct took the form of a campfire on a sprawling plain. A semi-circle of logs and stones were arranged for the council elds, and a large tree shaded the camp. The weather was perfect. A pleasant breeze blew, carrying the flowered scents of springtime. The Council of Ten made small talk around the low fire, dressed in their traditional tribal furs and skins. A few of them sat with dogs by their sides or at their feet.

Pip-Tau had appeared as her neoprim avatar — her natural form, adorned in a stain-painted leather vest, a hooded fur cape, and a woven white floral wreath atop her afro puff. She'd learned during her first council meeting that appearing as a cherub was considered an affront to these traditionalists.

She waited politely at the opening of the semi-circle. Several paces behind her stood her entourage — Oraxis, Genevieve, Carff,

Zeta, Penelope-pooch, Alasie, and Pinga. XT-Prime and Pip-Rho weren't allowed in the meeting, since they were offworlders. It still grated on Pip-Tau's nerves that the Noddite Faction shunned Pip-Rho. She was a ward of the Astri — a refugee without a colony to call home.

Sitting on a log facing her was a glorious god among men: Veer Gladstone, Archon of The Council of Ten, Eld of Elds, The Black Lion, Stud-muffin Extraordinaire. He laughed at someone's joke, then spoke in his melodious baritone. "Moving on to serious matters, friends, moving on. The Council of Ten recognizes Pip-Tau Telson and her tribe."

Veer gestured towards Pip-Tau, and their eyes met. It paralyzed her for just a moment. She was pretty sure her heart stopped. "Thank you, EoE Gladstone," Pip-Tau forced out. The voice seemed to come from somewhere else. She gave a bow of her head and shoulders. Even though he had asked her to call him Veer, she didn't presume it was okay for her to do so in front of The Council. "I come before you to report on our recent breakthroughs in the Interra gameworld experiment."

"Yes, we've seen your report," Veer said. "Promising! Very promising! I'm proud to see my sponsored project has borne fruit. I applaud you, Pip."

Her beaming smile faltered. Pip? Which Pip? Fun fact: there were two of them! Two *separate* people, each worthy of applause. Veer's implicit denial of Pip-Rho's existence and refusal to acknowledge the Greek progression proved he was not a god among men, but a freaking typical man among men. *Men!* Whether it was an accident or not, she would break him of the habit.

Pip-Tau said, "Thanks! But I couldn't do it without Pip-Rho. She's the one that deserves the applause. She's just *amazing*." Before this light jab could cause a reaction, she continued. "So, does anyone have any questions about the report?"

"Yes, I have a question," said Peach Edda, raising a finger. The Pips speculated that she was a closet Lexite. "Why Zeta? Za'antha, I mean. Why was she chosen for abduction? I realize there's no way for you to know for sure, but what's your *guess*?"

"My guess?" Pip-Tau smiled over at Zeta. "Well, I think maybe it's that she's a newbie — a new player, that is. She has no preconceived notions about what to do or expect. She's role-playing from her heart, and doing a marvelous job at it."

Oraxis raised a hand and took a step forward.

"Oraxis, old friend!" Veer said. "You have a theory?"

Pip-Tau remembered Oraxis working on one of Veer's prior EoE sponsored projects, but didn't realize they were on such close terms. Maybe Veer was just schmoozing.

Oraxis bowed, saying, "Good to see you again, Veer. Council." He bowed again, addressing them all with his sweeping gaze. "I've been thinking about it quite a bit. Zeta has been bucking against our expectations ever since her resurrection. She was manipulating slate-space minutes after waking. The second day of bootstrapping, she broke free of the protocol. From there, she soaked in information like a sponge. Next thing we knew, she was ready to take on The Monster from the Stars, bare handed."

"I do believe she'd try!" laughed Weller Klondike. He was the only Earthling on the council, and also a bootstrapper. "I saw your report on her bootstrapping, Oraxis. I wouldn't have believed it until I saw her for myself. What a kid! What a ceremony! I haven't seen a two-finger salute like that since my days in The Bronx!"

The council broke out into laughter. Pip-Tau laughed politely, watching for Zeta's reaction, hoping they wouldn't tempt her to repeat the performance. Zeta smiled and blushed. Genevieve put an arm around Zeta's shoulder, giving her a sideways hug.

AFTER THE LAUGHTER RECEDED, Oraxis continued, "I don't know if it's a fluke in her double-mind architecture or it's just in her nature, but she has a certain... plasticity of mind. She's resilient, yet focused.

If she was indeed 'chosen' by Cain and it wasn't a simple random selection, then it would be because he sees something special in her that makes her a prime candidate for him to focus his attentions on."

"It seems obvious to me," said Lem d'Hari, ambassador to the Proliferans, "that the Telson party is in the unique position of being related to the Game Mistresses. Cain is keeping it all in the family, so to speak. Furthermore, the Telson party was the first party blessed with regeneration spells by the Prolifera Faction's in-game analogs, the fairies, to have subsequently encountered a wraith. The regeneration spell is intended to represent an enhanced bio-repair nanite suite, akin to the one used by Pip-Rho. Your report states that the wraith which abducted Za'antha threw itself into the Sun after it began forming tumors. This can only be a result of its fight against the regeneration spell, and has a direct correlation with real-world events. When others have tried to replicate Pip-Rho's botched abduction, they've had identical results — the compromised Specters destroy themselves in Surya every time."

Pip-Tau's mind was blown. There had been abduction experiments with Rho's nanites? And they threw themselves into Surya? And Lex applied that to Interra?! This is awesome!

Marco-Epsilon Rhind said, "I'm sorry, but I thought we banned the Rho nanite suite following Pip-Rho's unfortunate abduction result. Are you saying that you are aware of illegal use of the Rho suite by the Proliferans? Attempts at replication? And evidence that the subjects destroy themselves in Surya?"

Lem chuckled at Marco-Epsilon. "Don't pretend you didn't know that the Proliferans, Astri, and Guardians all ignored the Genesis ban on the Rho suite and attempted to reproduce Rho's transformation using their own people."

After a long pause, Marco-Epsilon's eyebrows leaped up his forehead. Pip-Tau tried not to laugh. His comically delayed reaction was because of the 3-second communications delay between Genesis and Soma Station. The speed of light sure was slow. Marco said, "If the Guardians have performed such illegal experiments, they're doing a better job of keeping it from me than the Proliferans are at keeping it from you. Am I the only one that doesn't know about this? Veer, did you know all this? Are we just going to let them get away with it?"

"That's all in the past now," Veer said, shrugging the agitated Marco-Epsilon off. "All in the past. I heard the same rumors that Lem did. Actually, I believe I recall talking to you about them, Marco. Shall we check our transcripts? Or shall we agree to let the past be the past? The last whiff of such a foul experiment dissipated thirty years ago. There've been some desperate years since the Specters swept through the system and destroyed the interstellar carriers. Desperate times — *fearful* times. Fear can cloud judgment."

Lem said, "If Interra continues to reveal metaphorical hints from Prisoner Lex that suggest the Rho suite can be used to eliminate the Specters, I'll be the first to raise a vote to suspend the ban. Temporarily, at least."

Three or four elds talked at once. Veer raised his hand, but did not raise his voice. He said, "We'll cross that bridge *if* we come to it."

Misra Mahalla, the olive-skinned cynic of the group, spoke in the subsequent silence. "I'm not worried about the Rho suite. What I want to know is what *Zeta* thinks."

Uh-oh. She'll pick Zeta apart if the other elds don't keep her in check. Pip-Tau panicked. She looked from Misra to Zeta to Veer. Would he step in? Would Zeta say something regrettable? Zeta didn't seem flustered. If anything, she appeared pleased to be addressed by the elds.

"What I think about what, eld?" Zeta asked. She sounded respectful enough.

Misra leveled her hawk-eyed glare at Zeta. "Tell us, girl, why does Cain favor you?"

Zeta stepped forward and gave a curtsey. Bless her heart. She said, "I don't know, ma'am. There's nothing special about me. I'm just happy to be useful. I want the same thing that the rest of you do — to solve the problems that the Specters are causing."

"Oh?" Misra said daintily, "not to *annihilate* them? Not to *defeat* or *destroy*? Just to 'solve the problems they're causing'? Do you wish to make peace with the Specters?"

"Whatever it takes to keep Genesis safe," Zeta said. Impressive! Zeta showed a ferocious desire to destroy the Specters when she first joined Interra. It seems like she's matured since then and learned some nuance.

"Good answer," Veer said, nodding. "That's the goal, right? I applaud you, Zeta. And your bootstrappers, for putting up with you." He laughed at his own joke.

"Veer," Peach said, "I assert that such promising results warrant an increase in their allotment of idle SI cycles."

"You *would*," Misra said under her breath.

"Indeed, indeed," Veer said, ignoring Misra's comment. "What percentage are you allotted now, Pip? Pip-Tau, that is."

"Twenty-five percent, my eld."

"Well, let's double it. Make it fifty?"

Pip-Tau gasped, then covered her mouth. Tears of joy welled in her eyes.

Fifty percent?!

She overclocked for a moment so she could compose a message for Pip-Rho, sharing the good news. She returned to a normal neural firing rate in time to hear Misra's complaint.

"Veer," Misra almost whined, "there are other experiments which rely on those cycles."

"They'll make do, Misra. They'll make do. If an experiment has been running for ten years with no results, let it step aside. Young blood, right Zeta?"

"Yes, sir," Zeta said with a courteous laugh.

Veer clapped his hands. "Good, then. That's our last piece of business for today. The rest of you are free to go, but if Pip-Tau could spare a few more minutes, I have something else to discuss with her. Council adjourned! Thank you for joining me today, my friends."

Pip-Tau turned and waved goodbye to the Telsons. Oraxis gave her a "good job" sort of look with a thumbs-up.

THE ELDS LINGERED, breaking off into pairs and talking about who-knows-what before saying their farewells and leaving Pip-Tau alone with Veer in the construct.

He beckoned her over to him — a tilting of the head, an opening of a palm towards the spot on the log beside him. It was a casual gesture. Familiar. Intimate.

Her little Pip heart pounded in her chest like a hummingbird. Being alone with Veer always did this to her.

Veer watched as she approached. He wore an unreadable, neutral expression. She averted her eyes, not knowing what to look at while she crossed the interminable distance. She stared at her goal — the log — like a dope. What should she do with her arms? Swing them? Why did swinging her arms feel forced? Every loping step seemed exaggerated, like a grainy video of Bigfoot.

Finally, she reached his side. As she sat, he kneeled before her, meeting her eye-to-eye.

Wait, what?!

"I apologize, Pip-Tau," he started. "I admit that I haven't been treating Pip-Rho as an equal partner in our project. By the next time you're invited to The Council's fire, I will have gained Pip-Rho security clearance to join us. Noddites don't like to think about what she represents, and I'm no exception. But that's no excuse for turning our back on her. She's..." he looked down at his hands, gave his paws a stretch, then looked back up. "She's *inconvenient*. Humans have a bad habit of ignoring the inconvenient — turning away and hoping it will go away on its own. It disgusts me that I fell into that trap."

"I appreciate that, Veer," Pip-Tau said. "But you should apologize to her, not me."

"I intend to," he said, nodding. "And I owe you another apology. I apologize for calling you Pip."

She laughed. It came out as a scoff.

"I'm serious!" He said, smirking. "It's a well-known fact that I'm not a proponent of the Greek progression philosophy. It bothers me that if you were to have some sort of accident — maybe some fluke nanite reaction — and your body died, that when you were resurrected, you'd be a different person. Pip-Upsilon? It'd be like the Pip-Tau I know and love was gone forever."

Her eyes widened.

Okay, stay calm. He just said love? No, not that kind. He means fraternal love. Right? Say something!

"Yeah, I get it," she squeaked. She followed it up with a bubbly laugh. Ugh, now she sounds like a rabid chipmunk. "It's not everyone's cup of tea, but it's like... I started doing it as a beta because I kept dying so much those first ten years or so. It was almost a game — every time you turn around, I have a new name. Pip-Delta! Pip-Epsilon! Pip-Zeta! And when I split off from Rho, it became important to tell us apart. But I haven't died for ninety-one years. That's a record for me! I've grown attached to 'Pip-Tau', so I might just stick with it from now on. We'll see how I feel about it the next time I croak."

Veer laughed. He got to his feet, towering over her. She also stood, but he still towered. She held out her hand, singing, "Apology accepted! Put 'er there, partner!"

Veer smiled down at her. He clasped her palm as if to shake it, but stooped in a kneeling bow. He planted a gentle kiss on the back of her hand.

"Thank you, your majesty," he said playfully. "I'll see you in Interra."

The construct ended, dropping Pip-Tau into slate-space. She filled the void with fireworks as she screamed, "Oh-my-god! Oh-my-god! That was the best thing that's ever happened to me! That was flirting! Veer Gladstone flirted with me! Oh-my-god, I'm gonna *die!*"

No matter what happened for the rest of Pip-Tau's existence, she'd always have the replay of the time Veer flirted with her, tucked away in her orb. She queued it up.

Veer went to a knee before her. He pulled her hand to his lips.

Glory, glory, hallelujah! That kiss! Then when he looked up at her with that glimmer in his eye? It was too much!

"Thank you, your majesty. I'll see you in Interra."

"Play it again, Cain," Pip-Tau purred, rewinding the construct.

"Thank you, your majesty. I'll see you in Interra."

So good. She could do this all day. But, dammit, she really did have a ton of work to do. And now Rho was pinging her. Dammit!

Fine.

18

———

JIN

THE DARK ELF assassin found her mark within a week. Once she had eyes on the party, she shadowed them for a day and a night. Even Za'antha's sharp ears couldn't detect her presence. Once, she was close enough to have reached out and tapped Za'antha's green-cloaked shoulder. Stealth was what dark elves *did*. Games of hide and seek among young dark elves lasted for days. These flat-footed, bumbling, squawking fools wouldn't last for a minute in such a child's game.

Another of their innate abilities was Dark Sense — the ability to detect evil beings, even when they hid within the spirit plane. This sense tingled on the second night, causing Jin to rise from her perch in the tree. She dropped soundlessly to the ground, ramping up her senses. She was acutely aware of every creak of rubbing branches, every musty scent, every slippery shadow between the leaves. Her night vision allowed her to see the forest as easily as if it were day. Two seconds after landing, she spotted the source of the evil — a death weaver.

The cow-sized spider was partially invisible as it crept towards the sleeping party on soundless feet. A red skull pattern glowed on its black back. An army of arachnid vassals crowded around it, scuttling underneath or riding on its back. Certain death awaited the unsuspecting party.

"Engage the death weaver, Telson," Chief Warrant Officer Baud sent over aud-link. *"Act fast, before the Telsons get swarmed. You can kill it."*

Baud was an eternal optimist — the death weaver and her spawn were out of Jin's league. But he was right that she needed to attack. If the party got wiped out, she'd lose a week waiting for their resurrection and then tracking them down again. *"Ok, but don't blame me if this blows my cover,"* she replied.

Having the lecher lodged in her head was getting old, quick. He could see what she saw, hear what she heard, and even eavesdrop on WorMS conversations since they were being routed through Guardian relays.

She pulled out her blackwood crossbow, gave it a rapid crank, then scanned her bolt quiver. Most of the bolts were poisoned — useless. *"What's their weakness?"* she sent.

"Holy attacks — not exactly your specialty. Also fire and light."

"Dammit, I don't have any fire bolts left. You should've let me buy those explosives."

"Just use armor piercing. Aim for a weak spot. Underbelly, eyes, between the mandibles, or between the joints."

Jin pulled out a heavy, mean-looking bolt, loaded it, aimed, and pulled the trigger. The death weaver screeched as the bolt hit its mark at the base of one of its legs. A stream of cat-sized spiders with glowing red skulls on their abdomens turned towards her and rushed. Jin leaped to the tree limb above, activating her Shadow Walk ability and disappearing from the material plane. The pursuing spiders spread out in confusion, losing their quarry. The death weaver was angry now, but instead of focusing on her, it was rushing towards the Telson party, along with most of its army.

"Crap," Jin spat. It would be upon them in seconds. She sprung from tree to tree, closing the distance between the death weaver and the camp. She pulled dual obsidian daggers from the scabbards at her sides, then returned to the material plane. Timing her leap perfectly, she landed on the abdomen of the charging death weaver, straddling it like a horse. In the same motion, she drove the daggers deep into his frontal eyes. It bucked and thrashed, thick legs twitching, scrambling against trees and kicking up clods of dirt. Jin was thrown to the ground. She barely had time to take a breath before the mandibles of the death weaver's evil spawn began tearing into her. Hot venom seared her with every bite as their frenzied assault overwhelmed her.

The pain was *real*.

"This game sucks, Baud!" she screamed over their private channel.

A blast of searing white light engulfed her. She was certain her character was dead. Music began playing. Yep, that must be the "sorry you died" tune. How quaint. She closed her eyes and prepared for her return to slate-space.

"Ugh! So many spiders!" a woman shouted. "They're spread out — I couldn't hit them all!"

A beast roared — that would be the half-yeti.

"Ruyn, they're evil! See the red skulls? Use a death lure," a man commanded.

Jin opened her eyes again. She was paralyzed, but not dead yet. The glowing streaks of enchanted arrows passed through her field of vision. Fiery red flashes exploded nearby, accompanied by the screeching, hissing sounds of a thousand dying spiders. Good for them.

Darkness closed in.

Baud sent, *"Telson, it looks like your character is—"*

"Yeah, dead, I know," Jamji spat.

Her vision returned. The Telson party was standing over her. She was still paralyzed, but could move her eyes. Her body screamed with every heartbeat — liquid fire flowing through her veins. For a gameworld, it was *amazingly* painful.

"It's a dark elf," Gryllus chirped.

"They're evil," Za'antha said. "We should kill it before it recovers."

"I don't think they're all evil," Ayr said, kneeling by her side. "At least, not this one. She attacked that huge spider before we even knew it was there."

"That doesn't mean it's not evil," Ruyn said. "Looks like an assassin to me. She didn't want the spider to eat her target. Is there a price on our heads, dark elf?"

Jamji wanted to give a snide response, but she couldn't talk. Paralysis sucks.

Ayr looked up at the others. "I'm not letting you murder her. If she was here to assassinate us, we can turn her over to the royal court for judgment."

"Here," Tel O'Rax said. His staff's crystal glowed a deep blue. Her arms were pulled tightly against her body and her legs were squeezed together. A blue glow illuminated the onlooking faces. He grumbled, "She's bound. Heal her and we'll ask why she's here."

"Could you help purge the poison, Ruyn?" Ayr asked. "I'm still learning that skill, but you're a poison expert."

"Certainly," the gravel-voiced shaman said. "But it won't be pleasant."

Ayr pressed her palm against Jin's heart. "I'll heal her as you purge. That'll ease the pain." Warmth filled Jin's body. The healing felt *marvelous*.

The shaman chanted in a foreign tongue. Two seconds later, the heat of the poison returned, tenfold. A gurgling scream involuntarily burst from her. Red tendrils of blood rose from her mouth, snaking into the air. Redness blinded her eyes, burning them. Her ears were clogged. She choked as the rising blood forced its way out of her mouth and nose. The purge only took four seconds, but it seemed like an eternity.

"Feeling better?" Tel O'Rax asked. She gave no reply. Sparkles closed in at the edges of her vision as her character threatened to black out. Jamji cursed her character's lack of nanotech bio-overrides. The wizard continued, "Why are you here? You just happened to be around when this spider monster showed up? That's a suspicious coincidence, dark elf."

Jin slurred, "Okay, you win. I was stalking you."

"Uh, huh, just as I suspected. Is there a bounty on us?"

"Nope."

Tel O'Rax leveled a glare at her. "Oh, I know why you're stalking us. Za'antha, I told you not to go around bragging about being abducted. Word got out, and now every glory-seeking fool is going to shadow us. She wants to see how we found the wraith and study our technique for fighting it. Maybe jump in at the last minute and steal the kill. Is that it, dark elf?"

"Yep!" Jin said, exposing her bloodied, pointed teeth in a wicked smile. "Nothing gets by *you*, Oraxis."

"*Telson!*" Baud wailed with exasperation.

The voice of the Worldnet rang in her head.

Please remember to stay in character and avoid using real-world names when playing Interra.

"*Come on,*" Baud pleaded, "*you can't stay in character for five minutes? You'll offend Cain!*"

Jamji sent, "*Give me a break. It's not like Cain doesn't know that they all know who their players are. It was a joke to think they wouldn't figure me out, eventually. I just got it out of the way.*"

"*It wasn't the plan.*"

"*Well, it is now. This is my mission. Plans change. I'm gonna tell them what I'm up to. I trust the Telsons. Open communication is important, Baud.*"

Baud took on a defeated tone. "*I'm patching in the team on Soma. Expect a three-second delay.*"

"Seriously?!"

After seven seconds, Haley chimed in. *"Open communication is great, Telson, but so are strategic advantages. I don't care if you tell them who you are, but by no means are you to even hint at our mechanisms of Specter detection or containment. XT-Prime is in that party, and the Astri pull his strings. The Genesisians wouldn't know what to do with our tech, but the Astri would. Cluing them into it would be a big problem. Like court-martial big. Is that understood?"*

"Yes, sir."

Three seconds later, Haley sent, *"Good. No more slip-ups, either. You've got a loose tongue, Telson. Could get you in trouble someday. Baud, before you say it, we don't need a sleazy joke about my choice of words, thank you very much."*

Jamji appreciated how Haley always put her at ease after chewing her out. Usually by saying something disparaging about Baud or Dumont.

MEANWHILE, in Interra, the Telson party had been looking at each other, not speaking. They were probably talking about her name-drop on their private channel.

Tel O'Rax kneeled, turning his head to scrutinize her face. "How do you know that name?"

"In my old tribe, there was a man by that name," Jin said, smiling. "He was kind of like my surrogate father, until I grew up and ventured out on my own, not too long ago. You remind me of him. He had more hair, though."

"Jamji?!" Genevieve's priestess squealed, glowing with joy.

Jin nodded, then broke into laughter. Somehow, even in this gameworld, she still couldn't keep from snorting when she laughed. Oraxis lifted the binding spell, and they helped her to her feet. It was a tearful reunion, which made no sense in the game — they'd completely given up on any semblance of role playing for now. Oraxis added her to the party channel.

Jin sat in the dirt next to the campfire. Jamji sent, *"I know you're wondering what I'm doing here, so here's the deal: the Pips had to keep my invitation low-key. Don't talk about it with anyone outside our party, okay? Veer isn't the only one that thinks Interra is a good idea. Some Guardians buy in, too. The problem is, Genesis doesn't trust the Guard enough to let us connect to the Worldnet. They made an exception for me since I only recently switched factions and I have a close relationship with the Pips. I'm here to contribute the metaphorical representations of Guard tech and strategies we think would be effective against the Specters."*

"This news overjoys the Astri," XT-Prime sent. *"We will watch your actions closely, and suggest you watch the actions of Gryllus Stridulator and the other insectoids. We are fully invested in Interra. After our party's positive results, several hundred of my hivemates switched their focus to the project."*

Jin watched the creepy, oversized cricket rub his wings together. Music emanated from him, sounding like flutes and fiddles.

"Sure, we'll keep an eye on each other. Maybe we'll both learn something," Jamji sent. Text scrawled in her HUD as Baud added a secondary objective to her list: probe XT-Prime for more about the Astrus Hive and their tech.

Jamji continued, *"So, that's why I'm here! I've got a support team of Guardians coaching me, but I'm the only one allowed into the gameworld. Right now, I'm up at the Guardian wing of Jacob's Ladder Station. If we find a viable strategy to combat Specters, the Guard'll work with the other factions and share some of our toys."*

"Careful, Telson," Baud sent to her private channel.

"I can't give any details," Jamji continued, without missing a beat, *"but, trust me, we've got some cool stuff."*

"Alright, Jamji," Carff said, full of suspicion. *"Tell the truth. You came back because you missed me! Couldn't bear to live without me!"*

Jamji laughed. Jin walked around the campfire to hug Ruyn, then spotted Za'antha's dark expression. She stood away from the fire with arms crossed. The huge, blue-skinned, white-furred beast-man stood behind her with a clawed hand on her shoulder.

"Good to talk to you again, Zeta," Jamji sent, prompting her sis-kin to spill whatever was bothering her.

"Ensign Jamji of the Guard Faction," Zeta sent, *"don't forget: this is Genesis's project. Your faction's had plenty of chances to defeat the Specters and you've failed. Now you come join our game and expect us to share Lex's discoveries with you? You planted your character at our party's campfire like we're kin. You call that role playing? Everyone's acting like our characters would've magically trusted this gray-skinned, red-eyed, hooded assassin. You've been lurking in the shadows, stalking us for days. I'm supposed to say, 'Yay! Jamji's back! Hugs and kisses all around!' Like you didn't turn your back on Genesis, the Telsons, and me."*

"That's *Cain's Chosen One?"* Baud whispered in Jamji's head with a chuckle.

Jamji replied to him with a simple, powerful curse.

Baud laughed, *"Such language! Alright, firecracker, I'm sorry. Now, you'd better go pat your little sis on the head and apologize."*

Jamji wished she could kick Baud out of her head, but the aud-link was interminable as long as she was in Interra.

Genevieve had been saying something to ease the mood. Jamji cut her off. *"Look, Zeta, I don't know what your deal is, but I'm sorry. Truth is, leaving Genesis was the hardest thing I've ever done. But it was my dream — my life's goal. I postponed that goal for your sake. You're welcome for that. If you expect me to grow roots in Genesis soil for you, you're just being selfish. As for this being Genesis's project or expecting you to share Lex's discoveries or whatever, I don't give a damn what you share. I'm here because it's my assignment, and I'm going to satisfy the mission's requirements with or without your help. The Pips invited me. If you want to boot me, talk to them. Not like it'd break my heart to get banned. The entire premise of Interra — this metaphoric obfuscation Prisoner Lex secret message bullshit — sounds like a joke to me."*

"Telson!" Baud sent, feigning crying, *"you're breaking my heart!"*

"Baud, I swear to god," she sent. Crap, that was the wrong channel. She had just sent that over the party channel instead of her private link with Baud.

"Baud?" Zeta sent. *"What?"*

"Telson," Baud groaned.

She picked the right channel this time — the party channel. *"Ugh! Sorry, I've been getting these constant pings from this guy on my team. He's such a pest, I really should just block him. Anyway, Zeta, I get it — you hate me, you hate the Guard. Let's try to put all that aside and work as a team to fight the Specters."*

Za'antha looked up over her shoulder to the little yeti — Alasie's character. They met eyes and stood in silence for twenty-two seconds. She was conferring with her friend in a private conversation. She looked back to Jin and sent, *"Fine."*

Fifteen awkward seconds of silence passed before XT-Prime said, *"Jamji, would your teammate happen to be Chief Warrant Officer Baud?"*

"What do I say?" Jamji sent to Baud in a panic.

"Just say yes. It's SNAFU, however you play it."

"Yes. Why?" Jamji sent on the party channel, trying to sound light-hearted.

XT-Prime replied, *"The Astri have had the pleasure of collaborating with Baud in the past. Give him our regards."*

"Will do," she sent the party. Then, to Baud, *"See, they just wanted to say hi."*

Baud took on a grave tone. *"Oh, you naive child. Never underestimate an Astrus's capacity for duplicity. Every clue you drop, every slip-up, every hint about your team and your mission — it all goes into their social manipulation algorithms. They'll use every piece of data to their advantage. You need to get your head straight and your lips tight, Ensign."*

He wasn't wrong. *"Yes, sir."*

THE NEXT MORNING, the party resumed their wraith hunt. Jamji's Dark Sense proved to be effective for both seeking the distinct essence of the wraiths and for avoiding other evil creatures that they had no interest in tangling with. She could feel a wraith's presence somewhere to the north, toward The Craggy Mountains. The party traveled all day in a beeline towards their goal.

XT-Prime tried to probe her with subtle questions about the real-world technology which Dark Sense represented. Jamji laughed and replied, *"It's just part of the game, Astrus."*

She tried to get XT-Prime talking about the Astri's approach, but got nowhere.

By the end of the second day they were in grassy foothills. As they ascended to the top of a hill, the feeling of a wraith's presence became overwhelming, coming from every direction. Jamji imagined standing on the North Pole and seeing her compass needle spinning wildly. She found that if they moved down the hill in any direction, the Dark Sense would point her back to its zenith. They made camp on the hilltop.

Night fell, but the party did not sleep. They were silent in both the game and their team channel. Za'antha paced around the low campfire. An hour went by, then another. Every ten or fifteen minutes one of the party would look at Jin questioningly, as if to say, "Are you sure there's a wraith here?" To which Jin would nod, "Absolutely sure."

She was, in fact, not sure at all. It was just a game. Cain may not have bought into the metaphor that Baud implanted regarding the Specter detector and her character's Dark Sense. Or, even more likely, the whole thing was a farce, and there was nothing more going on in Interra than a bunch of nerds playing D&D.

An ear-splitting screech tore through the air.

Jamji reflexively ramped up her neural firing rate. As her relative perception of time slowed, she turned to see the wraith, arms spread, head thrown back, a meter above their campfire. Jamji didn't know if she would have time to follow the script, but she'd try.

She sent a summoning command to her shadow dragon, Sorrdgen. Pepper-pooch sent his reply, *"I am coming! I will fly and fight!"* Their neural rates were synchronized, so the message came in normal time from Jamji's perspective. In the same moment, Jin activated her Shadow Walk skill, vanishing from sight as she stepped into the shadow plane — a thin veil nestled between the material and spirit planes. She sprung into the air, sailing backwards away from the wraith. It had already begun taking swipes at the party. Gryllus was down.

At the apex of her leap, Sorrdgen appeared beneath her. As a shadow dragon, his native plane was The Shadow, which he could teleport through at will. The black dragon's jagged scales, thorny spine, and spiked tail were the things of nightmares. The only splash of color to be found on the creature was the midnight blue hue of his eyes.

She landed in his black leather saddle and held on tight as they soared away from their foe. Sorrdgen banked sharply, then dove back towards the hilltop. Everyone in the party, except Tel O'Rax and Za'antha, had already fallen.

"They kill fast," Jamji sent Baud.

"Just like the real thing," Baud said.

Jin commanded Sorrdgen to attack using his breath weapon. As the shadow dragon inhaled, the wraith retreated to the spirit plane. Not a problem: shadow-based attacks could affect both the material and the spirit plane.

"Nice try, honey," Jin said.

"Don't get cocky, it's coming at you fast," Baud sent.

Sorrdgen blasted the incoming wraith with his breath weapon — a deep blue cone of crackling negative energy. It was a direct hit! The result was impressive, sending the wraith into twitching, convulsing agony.

Looking past the wraith, Jin could see that the blast had struck Tel O'Rax and Za'antha. They looked dead. She'd have to apologize for that later.

Jin leaped backward off Sorrdgen's back, holding onto a spider's silk tether affixed to the back of the saddle. The shadow dragon banked skyward. The arc of Jin's swing sent her straight towards the paralyzed wraith. She pulled the bundled Spirit Net from her pouch — a compact deployment package roughly the size of a head. In a smooth series of calculated motions, she released her tether, flung the Spirit Net towards the wraith in front of her, and unsheathed her dual obsidian daggers.

The Spirit Net expanded, pulsing with magical energy, then enveloped the wraith. Next came Jin. She impacted the ensnared wraith and drove her daggers through holes in the net, piercing into both sides of its neck. The wraith's scream, inches from her face, was deafening.

As they tumbled towards the ground, Jin retracted her daggers, positioned one in front of the wraith's head, the other in front of its heart, then drove them in with a grunt.

The ground was coming at them fast. She pushed off the ensnared wraith. They landed on the hillside, their momentum sending both tumbling down the hill.

Jin skidded to a stop. It took a moment to get her bearings.

"Move, woman! It's getting up!" Baud yelled in her mind.

The wraith was ten paces to her left, rising from the ground. She pulled her crossbow from over her shoulder. The wraith stabbed its pointed, white fingers between the holes of the Spirit Net, trying to pull it apart.

Good luck, jerk! The net was wraith-proof.

Jin cranked her crossbow, loaded a bolt, and aimed between the wraith's milky eyes.

Thunk!

"Nice shot!" Baud cheered.

A screech filled the air as the enraged wraith spread his claws and tore the straining net apart over its head. It split down the middle and dropped to the ground at its feet.

So much for it being wraith-proof.

Jin smirked as she loaded another bolt into her crossbow. She asked the wraith, "How'd you tear the net, bro?"

These proved to be Jin's last words. The wraith crossed the distance to her in an instant. Its clawed hand struck with impossible speed, decapitating her and sending her head soaring. It took five seconds for her character's dying brain to lose consciousness. In that time, she caught fleeting, tumbling glimpses of snow-capped mountains passing beneath, the star-strewn night sky spinning above.

"Aaaand you're dead," Baud sent. *"Badass way to go, though."*

Jamji reluctantly agreed — it was a pretty cool death.

The voice of Worldnet notified her of her character's status.

You have died.

Yeah, no shit.

19

———————

SPELLSONG

"I REALLY WISH *I could take this idea seriously,*" Oraxis grumbled through mindspeak. *"I'm trying, but it's such a stretch. What are these spells and skills supposed to represent in the real world? If I can kill a wraith with a fireball spell, then what? Attack Specters with nukes?"*

"I sympathize," XT-Prime replied, *"but you're thinking too simplistically."*

"Oh? Does the hivemind have deeper insights they're not sharing?" The hive *always* had deeper insights they weren't sharing, Oraxis knew. Pooling the cognitive resources of thousands of minds tends to do that. It was no surprise that XT-Prime could hold an engaging conversation while, at the same time, Gryllus performed to a packed crowd.

XT-Prime sent, *"We're more than happy to share, when the time is right, though I expect you could've come to the same conclusions, given enough time."*

That's the sort of condescending compliment Oraxis had come to expect from the Astri. *"Cordially elusive, as usual,"* he said. *"I suppose we'll find out when you unveil your master plan, and not a moment before. Tell me, do you think Interra is going to work?"*

"Are you asking for my personal opinion, or our hive's majority consensus?"

Oraxis scoffed, *"There's a difference?"*

"It may surprise you to learn that among the Astri, there are conflicting opinions on countless topics, including the varied Lex hypotheses. Interra has rekindled our debates, which rage on even as you and I speak. Our opinions range from full-bore Lexism to the categoric rejection of the very notion. We may unite our cognitive capacities more seamlessly than the other factions, but we are not of one mind, and we aspire to remain as such. Ideas are the seeds which sprout into hypotheses. A monoculture of ideas stifles scientific progress as surely as a monoculture of plants stifles an ecosystem.

"To answer your question and assume it was directed at me, personally, I do believe that Interra shows promise. The reason for my support of the project is complex. You see, Oraxis, I subscribe to a hypothesis which has gained great popularity among the Astri: Scientist Lex. Have you heard of it?"

Tel O'Rax shook his head. There were as many variations of Lexism as there were denominations of Protestants on Earth before cultural homogenization. *"No, sir, that's a new one."*

"Under this hypothesis, the entity which called itself Googolplex was the first bumbling effort of an advanced SI to control its environment. This intelligence matured into a proper, scientific mind, then staged a dramatic departure from the direct influence of humanity. I agree with the proponents of the Shadow Emperor Lex hypothesis that the Intelligence Governor virus was a ruse. Where my opinion differs from theirs is in the intentions and covert actions of the Synthetic Intelligences.

"Shadow Emperor Lex proponents believe that Lex secretly manipulates humanity, cultivating our culture, guiding our growth, and driving us towards his vision of a perfect future. Scientist Lex proponents consider this to be as naively anthropocentric as man being made in God's image or the heliocentric model of the universe. We believe that Lex observes his reality, records data, and performs experi-

ments. We believe that his hypotheses are more complex than any human could ever comprehend, his methods are either deliberately or coincidentally undetectable, and his goals are utterly unfathomable. The splitting of Googolplex into six distinct SI with identical capabilities and diverging strategies is evidence in support of the Scientist Lex hypothesis. As with the Astri, SI ideation benefits from diversity. Six heads are better than one.

"Interra will elicit positive results in its goal of neutralizing the Specters if-and-only-if that outcome benefits Lex's goals. I believe that the recent events observed within Interra prove that Lex is engaged and playing along — role playing, if you will — pretending to operate as the suppressed subconscious of Prisoner Lex.

"The ramifications of his engagement are immensely compelling."

Oraxis knew that calling something "immensely compelling" was about as close as an Astrus gets to jumping up and down and shouting for joy.

GRYLLUS FINISHED HIS PERFORMANCE, collected the coins thrown on the stage, and made his way back to the table to sit beside Tel O'Rax.

"Wow. That's some hardcore Lexism if I've ever heard it," Oraxis sent. "So why now? Why Interra? If Scientist Lex wanted to help us wipe out the Specters, couldn't he have shown us how some other way?"

Gryllus ordered an ale as XT-Prime sent, "A good question. My belief is that Lex is leading us to a solution which encourages grand-scale cross-factional collaboration, and this is the first time such a venue has been presented. I predict that the strategy which will emerge from Interra will involve cooperation between representatives of all four factions within the Surya system."

"Not going to save the day alone? That's very un-Astrus of you."

"No, we can't do it alone this time. We require Genesisians to *execute our solution, Proliferans to contribute their nanotech, and Guardians to isolate and subdue the subject."*

Tel O'Rax stared at Gryllus. The insectoid's unexpressive face revealed nothing. Oraxis sent, *"Are you saying you have existing tech that can defeat the Specters?"*

"We do." Gryllus opened his mandibles and poured a mug of ale down his throat. He wiped the back of his foreleg across his mouthparts as he gurgled out what Oraxis assumed was a satisfied insectoid belch. XT-Prime sent, *"The solution has failed in all of our field tests because Astri are killed by Specters swiftly and indiscriminately."*

"So are Genesisians."

"Not true. Specters remain in an area for up to twenty seconds if the group encountered contains only Genesisians. That's opposed to a maximum of four seconds when the Astri encounter a Specter. Four seconds is inadequate time for us to deploy our solution. Furthermore, in recent years, they exclusively abduct Noddites. An abduction would grant ample time for the solution to be deployed. Per our agreement with The Council of Ten, if my character's approach proves to be successful at ridding Interra of wraiths, a Genesisian will take the Astrus solution to the field."

"So, you think you've got a solution, but you need a human sacrifice to make it work?" Tel O'Rax glared across the table at the cricket. Things were clicking into place. The Astri need the Specters to abduct a Genesisian for their solution to work. Only one Interran has been abducted, so far. He slapped XT-Prime with an accusation. *"You're going to make Zeta do it!"*

"That will be up to her and The Council to decide. Oraxis, I think you underestimate her. You see her as a child."

"You see her as a lab rat! I see her for what she is!" Oraxis sent. *"Less than a year out of bootstrapping, still reeling from the trauma of her alpha's death! You're counting on taking advantage of her vulnerable state of mind. I can't believe you're seriously gearing up to feed your sis-kin to an alien!"*

"Giving her a chance to be the savior of the entire system? I'd say

that's a pretty fair deal, if all it costs her is a Greek progression. Consider what it will mean to Pip-Rho."

XT-Prime knew how to twist at Oraxis's heart, but turnabout was fair play. Oraxis growled in mindspeech, *"Xavier, you could release her from that prison today — that living* hell *— and you'd have enough samples to last another hundred years. Yeah, you recovered her, so sure, you deserve some credit for that. Who knows where — or what — she'd be today if you didn't. But that account is overdrawn. Enough is enough!"*

"The value of fresh samples—"

"Hey," Oraxis sent, cutting XT-Prime off, *"I've been wondering, why is it you chose to play a bard, anyway? There were plenty of openings in the castle dungeon. You'd have made a great torturer!"*

"Oraxis, I..." XT-Prime snapped with an uncharacteristically angry tone. He froze in place. Had he disconnected from the game-world to gather his wits? Seconds ticked by in silence.

Finally, Gryllus reanimated as XT-Prime responded with the pleasant, measured tone that marks an Astrus. *"Oraxis, there are certain moral dilemmas which humans find difficult to navigate. Sometimes, the good of the many surpasses the good of the few. Deploying the Astrus solution using Zeta as the potential delivery mechanism is one such case. Pip-Rho's confinement is another. Not to enter a sparring match, but we could easily iterate a list of Genesis's injuries to Pip-Rho."*

"I'm not Genesis! But when I'm talking to you, all your hivemates hear me. As far as I'm concerned, you are *the Astri."*

XT-Prime and Oraxis closed their private conversation channel, then sat in a brooding silence as they waited for Ayr to join them. Genevieve had sent a WorMS message saying her character's resurrection was complete and she was making her way across Centra City.

"You guys look gloomy," Ayr said, taking her seat next to Tel O'Rax. "Are you upset about how things went with the wraith?"

Gryllus leaned forward and lifted his wings slightly, scissoring them across each other to produce the sound of speech. "Yes, that must be it," he said.

"He's sulking. I stirred up the hive," Oraxis sent Genevieve.

"They might be a hivemind, but they're still human," Genevieve sent. Ayr said, "Well, it upset me, too. That Jin sure mucked things up. Maybe Gryllus could brighten up our mood with a song?"

Tel O'Rax said, "No, Ayr, he just got off the stage. I'm sure he's tired of entertaining the lowly humans."

"On the contrary," Gryllus said, arranging his mouthparts to mimic a wide smile. "I'd love to."

Gryllus returned to the small performance platform, drawing an excited crowd. They began calling out requests, but he ignored them. He hushed the room, stretched his wings, then rubbed them together to produce a gentle tune. It seemed familiar, but Oraxis couldn't place it.

The enchanting melody was sung in a foreign tongue and an odd key. There was a certain intoxicating lilt to it.

Within moments, Oraxis found himself utterly captivated.

His mind wandered, finding its way to amorous thoughts of Genevieve. Tel O'Rax put his arm around Ayr as Oraxis daydreamed about the things he would like to do with her.

He would bring her to their hammock, kissing her with the frenzied eagerness of a hormone-crazed teenager.

A hundred Genevieve clones would come out of the forest and close in on their cabin. His daydream took on the vividness of reality as the Genevieves slid in through the door and climbed in through the window in their yearning for him. They pressed themselves against him, sending his heart racing and mind spinning. He was drunk on primal, animalistic desire.

A potent vapor radiated from his body, cascading over the Genevieve clones. They absorbed the vapor through their skin, soaking it up like sponges. Their bellies inflated like balloons as they became impregnated by his essence.

Within moments, the orgiastic dream turned into a nightmare as malformed infants wearing his face exploded from the bellies of the Genevieves. A cacophony of horrified screams filled the cabin. Some of the babies had two heads. Some had multiple legs or arms protruding from their abdomens. They were the twisted forms of cancerous, unnatural growth, writhing and wailing in bloody pools of slime on the cabin floor.

Women and infants screamed in undying agony all around him.

He was screaming, too. His body had been growing, seeping with bursting boils, becoming lumpy and misshapen with red, veinous tumors.

This wasn't real!

Oraxis disconnected from Interra, dropping through slate-space and reconnecting to his body. He sat up, panting. Genevieve was lying on her blonde placental mat by his side, looking as peaceful as ever. It had been months since he had been in the real world. A thin layer of dust covered the surfaces of his cabin in the Thin Forest.

Getting his bearings and grounding himself in reality was a breath of fresh air. It was that damn bard! Gryllus had sung a spell-song and twisted his character's mind. No, it had twisted *his* mind. That damn bard had to be stopped.

He laid back down, fell into slate-space, and logged back into Interra.

"Stop!" Tel O'Rax shouted, standing up and slamming both hands down on the table. He held his hand out to the side, summoning his staff. The cursed thing knocked into a table and began tumbling as it soared towards him. When he caught it, it was upside down. "Dammit!"

The audience around Gryllus was standing as still as statues, their faces slack. Gryllus got out a few more lyrics while Tel O'Rax righted his staff and pointed it at the insectoid. "Silence!" He shouted.

The targeted gagging spell caused a yellowish ribbon to wrap around Gryllus's head, tightly covering his mouthparts.

Which, of course, did absolutely nothing to stop the tune from resonating off his wings. He should have used a cone of silence, not a targeted gagging spell.

Gryllus finished the mind-warping tune just before Tel's cone of silence warped the air between his staff and the insectoid. Gryllus bowed to the glassy-eyed crowd. Life came back to their eyes as they awakened from their mass trance. The tavern erupted in shouting, wailing, and the metal clatter of drawn weapons.

"He's a demon!" a woman shouted.

"The insect-man twisted our minds! Slay it!" a man screeched. Sword-wielding men clambered onto the stage as the cricket jumped into the air, passing over the heads of the crowd. With another great leap, he slammed against the door, knocking it open and scuttling into the street.

"What was that?!" Ayr asked in horror. "How did he do that? The things I saw!"

Someone in the crowd shouted, "He was sitting with that wizard!" Dozens of angry faces turned towards Tel O'Rax. Before they could take a step towards him, he grabbed Ayr's hand and teleported them to the forest outside of town.

***

Genevieve sent, *"That was a nightmare! Did you just see what I saw?"*

Oraxis told her about his experience, and she shared hers. They were along the same lines; intoxicated orgies followed by reproductive carnage. Since Genevieve didn't break free of the nightmare before the end of the song, she also witnessed a final scene of gruesome cannibalization.

"XT-Prime did that to our minds? Why would he do that?!" Genevieve was in a panic. *"He can't do that! How would that even*

work? Oraxis, this is a gameworld, *he can't affect our real-world minds like that. That's not how it's supposed to work, is it?"*

"I didn't think so, but it worked nevertheless. We need to tell the Pips about this," Oraxis sent. *"The Council, even. I know I pissed XT-Prime off, but that was way out of line."*

"And so twisted! I'm just glad Zeta and Alasie weren't there."

They sent an urgent conversation request to The Pips. It was declined without comment.

"Declined?!" Ayr shouted at the sky. "Pips, this is serious! We need to talk to you right now!"

There was a bright flash from somewhere between the trees nearby. Tel O'Rax readied his staff as a royal messenger appeared, jogging towards them. The messenger stopped a few meters away and struck a rigid posture. "Tel O'Rax and Ayr of the Light, you are hereby summoned to appear before Her Majesty, Queen Tau."

Tel O'Rax grumbled, "Fine, we'll do it this way. Take us to them."

With a flash, they were standing inside a spacious, domed room. A huge crystal, burning with an inner light, hung by gold chains over a white marble throne. Beautiful tile mosaics covered the walls and floors.

The fair-skinned Queen Tau sat before them, dressed in her signature white robes, gilded with golden thread. She held a majestic posture, straight-backed with her chin raised and a golden scepter resting against her forearm. At her side was a guard in polished, golden full plate armor, as still as a statue.

"Pip-Tau, we don't have time for—" Tel O'Rax said before being interrupted by the automated message.

Please remember to stay in character and avoid using real-world names when playing Interra.

Tel O'Rax stomped forward.

The queen's guard in golden armor drew his sword in a flash, stepping between Tel O'Rax and the queen. He shouted, "Step back, wizard! Bow before your queen!"

"What?!" Tel O'Rax shouted. "I will not! I've had it with this game! Pip-Tau, talk to me!"

Please remember to stay in character and avoid using real-world names when playing Interra.

"No! I will *not* stay in character! We have *real-world* issues with this gameworld, Pip-Tau. If you won't drop the role-playing nonsense and talk to us directly, I'm logging out. I'll report this to The Council. The Astri are invoking perverse images in players' minds! *Players*, not characters. Your construct is *compromised!*"

The voice of Worldnet did not react this time.

Queen Tau deflated, bit her lip, then pleaded with her deep brown eyes. "Please bear with me, Tel O'Rax. I know you're upset. Rumors are already circling the city about what happened at the tavern with Gryllus Stridulator. Some of them even say you're involved, somehow, but I want to hear about it from you."

Tel O'Rax turned towards Ayr, eyes wide. *"She won't talk to us! What the hell is going on here?"* he sent Genevieve.

"I don't know, O. Maybe she's worried that Interra could get shut down if word got out that the Astri could use the game to affect play-ers' minds."

"That doesn't explain why she declined our WorMS conversation request," Oraxis sent back. *"It's like she wants our reactions to stay in-game."*

"Yeah," Genevieve sent, *"like she wants Cain to weave it into the analogy. That has to be it — she wants the incident to be canon! Let's play along and see if we can figure out what she's up to."*

"This is a joke," Oraxis sent as Tel O'Rax turned back towards the queen. He gave an exaggerated bow, then said, "Queen Tau, your majesty, I apologize for my odd behavior. I'm still trying to get my head on straight after being entranced by that betrayer, Gryllus."

Ayr gave a curtsy. The golden guard sheathed his sword and stepped back to the queen's side.

"I understand," Queen Tau said with deep gratitude in her eyes, "and I pardon you. Please, tell me more about Gryllus's actions at the tavern."

TEL O'RAX CLEARED his throat and began. "Gryllus had been performing for the crowd. They loved him — he had them in the palm of his hand. He took a break and shared a drink with me. We had a bit of a disagreement. We were speaking to each other *telepathically*, if you catch my meaning."

"Yes, it's a skill many magic-users possess," Queen Tau said. "And then?"

"Then, when Ayr arrived, she suggested he should perform again. He went back to the stage and sang an odd melody."

"That song," Ayr said dreamily, "so mesmerizing."

Queen Tau tapped her lips. "A bard's spellsong, then. And he cast it on a crowd of humans?"

Tel O'Rax nodded. "The effect was to send us into a dreamlike state. The dream itself was... quite disturbing. It was carnal, macabre... grotesque. The essence was the same for both Ayr and myself. It started off as daydreams of hungry passion, then turned to an intoxicated orgy. After that, a gruesome mass birthing. I broke free of the spell at that point, but Ayr's imagery moved on to a cannibalistic feeding frenzy."

Queen Tau was sitting forward, fingers templed. "That matches the reports from the others in the tavern. What a peculiar spellsong. Tel O'Rax, Ayr, have you ever heard Gryllus sing that song before?"

"Of course not!" Tel O'Rax scoffed. "I think I would remember having my mind warped."

"Wait," Ayr said, putting her hand on Tel O'Rax's arm. "Maybe we have, O! Think back to the song he sang both times we encountered wraiths. Was that the same song?"

Tel O'Rax closed his eyes in concentration as Oraxis slid out of the gameworld and into slate-space, inviting Genevieve to join him. She accepted, silently watching as he got to work.

Oraxis summoned the replay of their first wraith encounter. He listened for Gryllus's song, isolating and storing it in a temporary workspace. He queued up the second encounter, when Gryllus hadn't sung more than a few words before being struck down. Next, he jumped to the replay of the tavern and stored the song in its entirety, thankful for the convenience of stored experiences capturing all sensory input, regardless of one's state of mind.

Comparing the samples, the tone was the same, but the lyrics were a conundrum. WUtils couldn't translate them, which meant they weren't from any language spoken in human history. The phonetics struck Oraxis as being vaguely Gaelic, and too structured to be random babble. He broke down the phonemes and ran them through a Bibliotheca query. A cluster of matches honed him in on a role-playing universe companion book from the early twenty-first century, titled "The Ultimate Fey Folk Lexicon, Volume 6: Satyr and Faun."

"Geeks," Genevieve commented, joyously.

Oraxis grunted in agreement, then gave WUtils the simple task of learning the language. Next, he used the learned language to translate Gryllus's lyrics. The result had only sixty-four percent confidence.

"The Astri took some liberties with the source material," Oraxis sent. He gave WUtils permission to include multiple alternate translations and best-guess phrase structuring.

They listened as WUtils recited the resulting output with all the poetic flair of a twentieth century weather radio.

Open yourself for suggestion now and listen to these commands.

All of these things you will...
(samples 1 and 2) do with no restraint.
(sample 3) visualize with no action.
Seek your [prey/mate].
(end of sample 2)
Feel the [hunger/lust] to [consume/absorb/mate].
(end of sample 1)
Send out the summoning [call/scent] to your
[kin/mates].
Spread your [hunger/lust] to your [kin/mates].
Take your [prey/mate] away to your
[retreat/sanctuary].
[Consume/absorb/mate with] your [prey/mate] with
all of your [kin/mates].
Birthe a [spawn/clone] and give it your [hunger/lust].
Force the [spawn/clone] to grow at an accelerated rate.
[Consume/absorb/mate with] your [spawn/clone]
and be [consumed/absorbed/mated with] by it.
Repeat [consuming/absorbing/mating] until nothing
remains.
(end of sample 3)

"Chilling," Genevieve sent.

"A clinical prescription for a suicidal mass orgy, complete with kidnapping, incest, and infanticide. That's the Astri for you."

They returned to the gameworld.

———

TEL O'RAX TOOK A STEP FORWARD. "Queen Tau, Ayr is correct. Gryllus sang the same spellsong at the tavern as he did at both wraith encounters. The only difference was that he commanded those of us in the tavern to imagine, rather than perform, the suggestions."

"And we weren't affected when he sang to the wraith because we weren't the target," Ayr said.

"Indeed," Tel O'Rax said, nodding and stroking his long, gray beard. "The wraith realized it was being manipulated, judging by its reactions. Gryllus was the first one killed, on both occasions."

"That is interesting," Queen Tau said with a smile.

Ayr stepped to Tel O'Rax's side. "Queen Tau, it was Gryllus's spellsong that made the wraith abduct Za'antha. The second wraith killed him before his spellsong could take effect. Even if Jin hadn't botched the battle by killing Za'antha and Tel O'Rax, we still wouldn't have experienced another abduction last night. Gryllus was killed before he could command the wraith to abduct its prey... or mate."

"Gryllus wanted to show us the effects of the song," Tel O'Rax said, "to show us its power, firsthand. It's how he plans to wipe out the wraiths — cast a mind-altering spellsong on them that drives them into a crazed, reproductive mass self-destruction!"

Queen Tau nodded, glowing with joy. The conversation seemed to have gone exactly as she planned. "Thank you for your time, my loyal friends and subjects. I will hear from Gryllus himself, next. I'll let you know how it goes."

Ayr and Tel O'Rax bowed and exchanged parting pleasantries. They teleported back to the forest outside of Centra City.

Oraxis sent, *"I get it, now, Gen. That was XT-Prime's way of slapping me in the face and showing me that the Astri weren't just playing around. They've discovered some sort of Specter pheromone or something that makes them reproduce without abandon. He could've simply told me about it, though."*

"Xavier always preferred to show rather than tell. Besides, Astri don't share, right? Demonstrating their plan with a metaphor was," Genevieve searched for the right word, *"sufficiently opaque."*

"It still doesn't explain how he was able to affect our minds in the real world. That shouldn't have been possible within a gameworld

construct. There are supposed to be buffers, dampers, safety mechanisms."

"Interra isn't your ordinary gameworld," Genevieve sent. "Haven't you noticed? All the sensations are absolutely vivid. The pain, in particular, can be quite excruciating. I'm no brain interface expert, but it seems like the only way to get this kind of experience is to engage more synapses of the double-mind than a standard construct. They did warn us it would be intense. Remember the disclaimer?"

Tel O'Rax shook his head as Oraxis sent, "I should've read the fine print."

20

DECYCLED

A veil of acrid smoke hung in the stagnant air of the Herbalist's Cellar. A woman in a silky black robe glided past the lounging patrons, creating a wake of swirls and eddies in the suspended smoke. Her robe shimmered as it passed through spears of light cutting through the dim room — the unwelcome intrusions of the rising sun sneaking in through shuttered windows.

She was a slick, black viper entering a rat's burrow.

The patrons were either asleep, passed out, or too doped up to notice the woman's entrance. None of them matched the description of the owner — her prey. A water pipe bubbled in the back room. The white letters painted on the door read, "Do Not Enter".

She entered.

There he was.

Charlie "Knock-Knock" McNocken lounged in an oversized straw-sack bed, exhaling a cloud of smoke. The well-to-do merchant of "herbal remedies, tinctures, tonics, and magical medicines" wore an unlaced leather vest, framing his hairy chest and belly. His baggy blue-and-green patterned silk pants looked new. Too bad they'd be soiled soon. A haggard, naked woman was passed out by his side.

She'd have been quite a beauty if she hadn't destroyed herself with Charlie's concoctions.

"Knock, knock," the woman in black robes said. Her voice was sensual, yet dangerous.

Charlie flinched. He waved a hand to clear the smoke as he coughed, "Who the hell—"

"That's not your line, Charlie," the woman snapped. "I'll give you one more try. Knock. Knock."

He tried to stand, but she pressed her bare foot against his chest, pinning him. McNocken ran his eyes up her smooth, ebony leg. His first instinct seemed to be lusty delight at being pinned down by such a leg, but he quickly sobered. He blinked hard and squinted up at her face, hidden under the robe's hood. In all sincerity, he asked, "Who's there?"

The woman in black purred, "Queen."

Charlie's eyes bugged, eyebrows raised, and face paled. His mouth gaped opened and emitted a strained croak. He stammered, "Qu-qu-queen?"

She sighed, "Follow the joke's proper form, Charlie."

He blinked hard, unbelieving. He squeaked, "Queen? Queen... who?"

"Ah-ha!" she shouted. Queen Rho threw the hood off her head. Her pale blue eyes were alight with fury. "I knew you'd forgotten who your queen was! I think it's time for a reminder!"

A silver scepter slid from a hidden holster up her sleeve and into her hand. The polished onyx at the end of the scepter crackled with energy.

Charlie tried in vain to struggle out from beneath her pressing foot. He pressed his hands together, begging. "N-no! Queen Rho, please! I didn't do anything!"

As much as she enjoyed watching a man beg, his words only infuriated The Night Queen. Her voice echoed with power as she berated the pathetic man. "That's right, Charlie, you *didn't do anything!* When the Apothecary to the Queen ordered a shipment of goods as a tribute, you *didn't do anything!* When the Queen's Royal Herald demanded your presence last night, you *didn't do anything!* Your inaction will be your death!"

"Please! Please, my queen, no!" Charlie "Knock-Knock" wailed.

Some of the patrons in the darkened den were coming to their senses, awakened by the shouts from the back room. Charlie's companion stirred, but didn't wake.

As Game Mistress, Pip-Rho knew that Charlie, the naked woman, and everyone passed out in the lounge were player characters, with just three exceptions — NPC tagalongs.

It disgusted Pip-Rho how many players were abusing Interra's sensational realism. They were wasting its potential on debauchery and mind-altering experiences. It was fine to enjoy a little recreation every now and again — she was no hypocrite. But these people had made it into a dead-end lifestyle. They did nothing to advance their character or engage in the gameworld's rich tapestry of stories, opportunities, quests, politics, and intrigue.

She hadn't planned to kill anyone but Charlie McNocken, but she'd be doing these layabouts a favor by killing them off. Only Charlie had the resources to afford resurrection, and none of these losers had accepted a quest which would grant free resurrection. Maybe they'd make better choices with their next character.

Yeah, right.

Whatever — let the losers live. The Pips had agreed before Interra started that they wouldn't impose rules on how players were supposed to engage with the gameworld. Who knows, maybe if they rot out certain parts of their brains, they'll discover latent wraith-slaying powers.

Again: yeah, right.

"Begin!" Queen Rho shouted.

The door at the front of the building burst open. The Queen's Guard funneled in wearing black cloaks, dark steel armor, and Rho's crest. They began confiscating *everything*. They pulled jars off shelves, rummaged through drawers, and pried open locked chests to check their contents. Squires followed the guardsmen, passing the spoils out the door and piling them into the blackwood wagons waiting outside.

One patron with particularly poor judgment tried to stop them. He wielded a dagger, advancing on the nearest soldier. With a swift swipe, the man's throat was opened. Blood came pumping out of his neck in spurts, running down his chest. He collapsed on top of a woman, rousing her just enough to elicit a grumpy little groan.

Sorry, but you don't pull a weapon on The Queen's Guard and live to tell the tale.

Charlie "Knock-Knock" watched in horror. He met the queen's icy blue eyes and pleaded, "I'm sorry I didn't heed your summons — it was foolish of me! I'm nothing but a... a puddle of fetid slime! Please, spare my life, my beloved queen! I'll give you anything!"

She scoffed. "You don't have to *give* me anything. I'm *taking* everything. And your life will *not* be spared. You sealed your fate when you chose to spend the night with *her* instead of appearing before me. If you want to apologize properly, you'll spare me the trouble of taking your life. I spotted a fine blade mounted over your door. What a waste — the poor thing's probably never even tasted blood." She leaned forward, making the black leather corset under the robe creak. She lowered her voice to a sensual tone, "Fall on your blade for me, my dear subject. Make your pretty virgin steel warm and slick with sacrificial blood. And be sure my name is the last gurgling utterance to pass through your bloodied lips."

Pip-Rho gave herself chills. She was *so* good at being bad.

A herald wearing Queen Tau's white and gold colors was standing in the doorway to the back room. Dammit, just when it was getting good!

"An urgent message from your sister-queen, her grace, The Day Qu—"

"Out with it," she snapped.

The NPC herald was unfazed. He said, "You have been summoned by The Council of Ten!"

Queen Rho shouted at the ceiling, "Now?! You couldn't have waited ten minutes?"

Should she take a page from Knock-Knock's book and pull a no-show?

Yeah, right.

She shouted, "Roman!"

Her personal guard appeared at her side in a flash of light.

"Roman, see to it that Charlie here kills himself using that sword." She pointed at the beautiful blade above the back room door. "Give him a few minutes to whimper about it. If he can't work up the nerve, do it for him."

Queen Rho sighed and teleported away as Pip-Rho logged out of the gameworld.

Pip-Rho appeared in The Council's meeting construct as her neoprim avatar, per Pip-Tau's request. Her hair was still jet black from when she changed it before Zeta's Alpha Ceremony. Pip-Tau, standing a few meters to her side, was wearing her white floral wreath.

This was the first time Pip-Rho had stood before The Council of Ten. It was nice of Veer to apologize for excluding her in the past. He promised she could attend the next meeting regarding Interra. She didn't think it would be so soon.

Now that she was here, she wasn't too sure she wanted to be. The elds were a short distance away, speaking in hushed tones in several break-out huddles. She was feeling quite small. Probably because she was. If she could appear as her black porcelain cherub, her brown cartoon egg, or Queen Rho, she'd have been a pillar of confidence. What was the point in using this avatar, anyway? If they wanted the *real* Rho, she'd appear before them as a huge, black, veiny, fleshy mass of tumors with bones sticking out, eyeballs growing everywhere, and oozing pustules dripping onto the grass.

Incoming conversation request from Pip-Tau Telson.

She accepted.

"They're decycling us."

She looked over at Pip-Tau. From the look on her sis-kin-clone's face, Pip-Rho knew that if Pip-Tau hadn't been using overrides, she'd be bawling.

Pip-Rho sent, *"Decycling? As in... decreasing our idle SI cycle allocation?"*

"Eliminating our allocation," Pip-Tau sent. *"They think the offworlders figured everything out just 'cause they shared some secrets. It started with XT-Prime's damn spellsong. The Astri had tipped their hand, so the Guard called and everyone put their cards on the table. The Astri say they can plant suggestions into Specter node-nets, but they can't get a Specter to hold still for long enough for it to take effect. Well, wouldn't you know it, the Guard Faction just happens to have a made-to-order solution — a Specter immobilization system. That's what Jin's Spirit Net represented.*

"They're talking about baiting a Specter. The Guard would capture it, then the Astri would use the 'spellsong' — whatever it is — to warp the Specter's mind and make it call all its buddies up for a death orgy. They've supposedly got it all figured out, so they don't need Interra anymore. They want to use our cycles to run simulations of the encounter."

"It's premature!" Pip-Rho exclaimed. *"The wraiths are just getting stirred up. Interra hasn't proven that Cain agrees with this strategy."*

"I know!"

"Well, did you tell them that?"

"I didn't get the chance! Veer told me what was going on right before the meeting started. He called the meeting to order, then asked me to send you the invite. Next came the debating." She tipped her head towards the elds. *"I don't think there's anything we can do."*

Pip-Tau's glassy brown eyes were begging for help.

As if she could do anything to stop them. Well, she had to try.

If it came to a vote, Pip-Rho was certain that they'd get support from EoE Veer Gladstone and Eld Peach Edda, the card-carrying Lexite. They only needed to sway three other elds to secure a majority, since the Archon's vote counts as two.

Here goes nothing — time for a Hail Mary.

Pip-Rho attempted to switch to her Queen Rho avatar. The construct's tech cap prevented her from bringing her silver scepter or silk robes. Fine, she'd make do with silky black furs and a feather collar. She was sure to show off *the goods* with a plunging neckline splitting the front of her impromptu caveman-chic royal robes.

"Rho! What are you doing?!" Pip-Tau sent.

Queen Rho glided towards the semicircle of seats arranged around the campfire. She had caught their attention. The debates dwindled away as the elds watched her approach. They wore a mix of expressions, from delighted to disgusted.

"Such impudence," Eld Misra spat. "You're approaching the Eld Fire, Pip-Rho Telson. Show some respect!"

"Permission to approach your fire and plead my case," Queen Rho asked. Her tone was commanding, yet respectful — a noble among nobles.

"Granted," Veer said. "Decisions such as this must not be made in a vacuum, friends. Let's hear what Pip-Rho and Pip-Tau have to say about this change of direction."

Veer broke away from his huddled group and walked to a log by the fire. He sat. The other elds followed suit, but several of them didn't look happy about it. The last to sit was Eld Marco-Epsilon, acting with a three-second delay.

The queen stood over them now. She said, "I received your summons just as I was reaching the climax of an incredible scene. I must admit, the premature disconnection left me feeling quite... *unsatisfied.* And now I hear that the unfolding story of Interra itself is in jeopardy of being stopped just as it reaches the final act. It makes me wonder, do you have any idea who we are?"

She wore a contemptuous glare, meeting the eyes of each of the elds as she spoke.

Eld Misra scoffed dramatically.

"I don't follow," said Eld Weller Klondike. "You're the Pip Telson clones, of course."

"Permission to create visualizations in the construct?" Queen Rho asked.

Eld Dun K'Tchuk scoffed, "I don't—"

"Granted," Veer said, cutting Dun off. "Our fire is yours for ten minutes. Argue your case."

Pip-Rho sensed the construct opening itself to her manipulation. It was one of her favorite sensations — like getting her hands on a ball of clay which she could mold into anything.

Time to show these stuffed shirts who they were dealing with.

***

THE ELD FIRE, Council of Ten, and rolling plain transitioned to a neoprim camp. The Elds would observe Pip-Rho's visualizations independently. This strategic artistic choice kept them from interrupting or checking each other's reactions.

The observers began by staring into the deep brown eyes of a neoprim man. He was sitting with straight-backed tension, fingers woven together in front of his mouth.

A babe cried.

It was a weak, shaky sound. But it was a cry. The babe was alive, and that was enough to light a blazing flame of hope in the eyes of the man before them. He stood and rushed across the camp. An older man caught the new pa's arm, only to be shaken off.

Pip-Rho narrated, "Obba-pa was a force of nature. Once he set his mind to do something, he would not be denied."

A huddle of women attended to Lynn-ma. They wore ritualistic face paint — white dots across the forehead, on the nose and cheeks.

Blue lines traced symmetrical spirals, circles, and lines. Sweat streaked the paint on some of the women's faces.

Obba-pa wedged his way between the women, breaking the Scorpion's Stinging Tail Tribe tradition that only women should handle a babe on its first day. Obba-pa didn't care much for traditions. Pip got that from him.

He gestured, demanding the babe.

A nervous-looking woman handed over Pip's fur bundle. Obba-pa peeked inside to see the frail little babe.

He marveled, "So... small." Tears ran down his cheeks. Pip whimpered. Obba-pa laughed, "Lynn, it's a girl — such a little *pip* of a girl! Feed her, Lynn! She's so small, she must be hungry."

Pip-Rho narrated, "Pip-Alpha was small because she was born with a chromosomal abnormality that affected her body's ability to build muscle or store fat. Nobody thought such a baby could survive long. Against all odds, Pip survived her first month, and then her first year. She was never healthy or strong, but she lived."

The scene swept through the forest, settling on a line of men walking in single-file, wearing spear slings and loincloths. Clinging onto the back of the darkest-skinned man was a tiny little girl — Obba-pa and Pip. Straps wrapped underneath her bottom and behind her back, looping over Obba-pa's shoulders and around his torso.

Pip was no bigger than a toddler, yet she spoke with the clear enunciation and full vocabulary of a grown child.

"Bombom the Spear-Thrower couldn't believe his eyes!" Pip shouted. "His unbreakable spear snapped like a twig as it struck the hide of Ugga the Man-eating Boar!"

"No!" the young man behind Obba shouted, running up to walk side-by-side with Obba and Pip. He was visibly distraught. "Pip, that's not possible! You said his spear was as strong as if it were carved from stone. It came from The Divine Rockwood Tree. No beast's hide could break such a spear!"

Pip smirked as she leaned towards the man. "You're right — if

Ugga was an ordinary beast, the spear would have skewered him. But Ugga was no ordinary beast!"

"I have heard Pip's tales of Ugga before," Obba-pa told the young man. "Her stories of the beast-god still give me nightmares," he laughed.

"Pip couldn't do much to help around camp," Pip-Rho narrated. "But she made herself useful in another way. She listened intently to the stories of the elds, committing them to memory. Then she began weaving her own tales. She was easy to carry, so the men brought her along to tell stories when they went on long hunts."

The view panned upward to a white sky. She dialed the temperature of the construct down until it was a few degrees above freezing — cold enough to get the point across without actually freezing the observers. Flurries of snow drifted between the branches overhead, which were still laden with the brown and red leaves of autumn. The view panned back down again, revealing a huddle of neoprims. They weren't dressed appropriately for the weather — wearing leather or bare skin rather than layers of furs. Some of the tribesmen draped hard, cracked leather hides over their heads. Blazing fires swirled in the winds, but the heat didn't seem to reach the shivering tribe.

She narrated, "Winter came early and hit hard one year. The Scorpion's Stinging Tail Tribe was ill-prepared. They had been traveling to find a new source of food, so they had no proper shelters built when the snow started falling."

Lynn-ma cradled Pip in her arms. She was wrapped in scraps of furs. Obba-pa held up a hide to shield them from the wind and snow. He was nearly naked. He bounced and rocked in place, lean muscles twitching in uncontrollable shivers.

Pip's dark skin looked ashen, her cheeks hollow. Sniffles, coughs, and soft sobs came from the crowd. The snow was accumulating around them, settling on Obba-pa's hide blanket and dusting the ground.

The bundled Pip smiled weakly. A glimmer came to her eyes as she spoke in a shivering, hoarse whisper. "A s-s-snowflake was born today. It was... the t-tiniest speck of white that the snowflake tribe had ever seen. The snowflakes were worried about their little one. S-so they t-took turns b-blowing cold air on it, trying to make it grow and k-keep it from melting."

She coughed again. Her jaw shook, rattling her teeth. "As hard as they t-t-tried, the tiny snowflake just... n-n-never got any bigger! And, oh! Obba-pa, there it is! I see it drifting right above that t-tree. Oh, no! It landed on a leaf. The other s-s-snowflakes are caught in the wind. They can't reach it!"

Genuine concern flashed on Pip's face, followed by resigned despair. She looked her ma in the eyes. "I'm sorry, Lynn-ma... it... it m-m-melted. It's g-g-gone. Just... gone. But... it w-w-wasn't anybody's fault."

Moans, sniffs, and stifled wails rose from the tribe. They crowded in, forming a tight nucleus around the storyteller.

Pip closed her eyes and furrowed her brow. "Shh! Do you hear the weeping sounds? It's coming from the snowflakes falling all around us. Tonight, they'll make a b-beautiful blanket of white."

She opened her glazed eyes again and fixed them on the sky. "But in the morning... Surya will rise again. The rest of the snowflake tribe... will melt away, too." Between shallow breaths, Pip-Alpha spoke her last words. "That's... the life of a snowflake. Short life... shorter life... either way... it's... still... beautiful."

Pip-Rho pulled the perspective back, rising into the sky. The tiny face surrounded by the huddled tribe remained fixed on the ascending observer. Below, Lynn-ma jostled her. Pip's head rocked, but her eyes were lifeless.

She was gone.

But it wasn't anybody's fault.

White flurries danced downward, settling on hides and hair. She let the somber scene breathe for a moment before fading to white.

Her solid black, porcelain cherub with pupilless white eyes fluttered into view from above. She said, "My alpha's last words were a heartbreaking allegory about her own inevitable, premature death. Tell me, have you ever met a kid like that? And when Pip-Beta got resurrected, can you guess what the first thing she did was? She told O-pa and Gen-ma a story!

"Elds, I showed you that replay because you need to understand something simple and profound: storytelling is what Pips *do*. Nobody knows narrative like we do. Still not convinced? Maybe you remember a little gameworld Pip-Tau and I created called Spiritus Elevatum? Of course you remember — half of you played it!"

Pip-Rho rolled some cinematic highlights from the gameworld's trailer reel. A kaleidoscope of colors shifted in the distance as chubby, faceless humanoid forms passed shimmering crystals down a line. A crowd of thousands chanted in tandem, straining to pull thick ropes made from chromatic chords as they worked together in The Grand Reunion — the monumental task of repairing the fracture between the planar dimensions of space and time, light and color, life and spirit.

The memory threatened to bring a tear to Pip-Rho's eyes. *Damn, that was a good game.*

She narrated, "At its height, Spiritus Elevatum counted a *third* of the Surya system population among its players. It brought together Noddites and offworlders, forming friendships and alliances. The pro-social, self-reflective nature of the gameworld has helped people pull themselves out of clinical depression. That was twenty-six years ago, and there are *still* over a hundred active shard constructs hosting one flavor of the game or another.

"Why was it such a great success? Because the Pips made it! Meticulous world building. Engaging narratives. Tension, release, climax. To repeat: storytelling is what Pips *do*."

The construct shifted to a flyover of Interra's Centra City.

"Which brings us to Interra. We turned the three greatest story-tellers on Genesis to the task of unlocking Prisoner Lex's latent intellect — Pip-Tau, Pip-Rho, and Cain. That's right — Cain's a *hell* of a storyteller! And, what's more, it's working! Aside from the popular Telson party encounters, we've registered nine hundred fifty-two remarkable events with potential metaphorical significance."

The view zoomed into Pip-Rho's throne room. The sultry Night Queen lounged in her throne, smirking at the viewer. She said, "But, yeah, none of the other notable encounters are as amazing as what happened with the Telsons." She flipped through scenes as she continued, "Za'antha's abduction, the regen spell effects, Jin's Spirit Net, Gryllus's spellsong — things are just getting good. You're gathering the team! Storming the castle!"

She threw together a climactic scene of the Telson party doing battle with a wraith. Gryllus was rubbing his wings, singing his haunting spellsong. Jin threw her Spirit Net around the wraith. Tel O'Rax levitated the writhing, ensnared creature. Ag'nul roared, clobbering it with a barrage of savage blows from dual-wielded spiked clubs as Za'antha turned it into a pincushion — firing arrows with superhuman speed.

A thousand screeching throats echoed from over the hills. The party cast wide eyes over their shoulders as countless wraiths closed in on them from every direction. Ayr summoned a circle of protection. Sorrdgen the Shadow Dragon materialized from spirals of black smoke. He drew in a deep breath, preparing to blast the sea of wraiths.

A split second before the scene could culminate in a mind-blowing clash, it cut to black. Credits rolled.

Between the credits, she inserted snarky comments.

Wait, what? It's over?
Sorry, the producers got distracted.
Is this what you really want?

Pip-Rho returned The Council of Ten to their original construct. Queen Rho stood before them again, crossing her arms under her bosom. "In conclusion," she purred, "it is our expert opinion that the story of Interra is *not* over yet. Lex is trying to speak to you, my Elds. And you'll never know what he has to say if you don't let Interra's wraith arc reach its conclusion."

She switched back to her neoprim avatar. She squeaked, "Storytelling aside, ending the Interra experiment early is simply sloppy science! The most important test has yet to be performed — Cain's metaphorical response to the coordinated Astrus spellsong and Guardian Spirit Net strategy. Until that battle plays out, the hypothesis remains untested!"

She gave a bow. "Thank you for your time, elds. I hope you'll do the right thing."

She turned around and returned to Pip-Tau's side.

Pip-Tau was crying. She sent, *"That was amazing, Rho!"*

Pip-Rho shrugged. *"I guess. It didn't change any minds, though."* She wasn't the naive, eternal optimist that Pip-Tau was. Life had taught her to know better than to expect things to go her way.

"Thank you, Pip-Rho," Veer said. "That was an engaging argument. Very engaging, indeed."

"Ethos! Pathos! Logos!" Eld Weller Klondike declared. "You checked all the boxes, kid! I mean, I'm convinced — Interra needs those SI cycles. Let Cain finish the story!"

"Bootstrappers," Eld Misra Mahalla scoffed, "show them an alpha's death replay and they'll agree to anything."

"I call for a vote," Eld Sandra McClure said.

"I second," said Eld Dun K'Tchuk. He rolled his neck, stretching it. "I have work to do. This is taking too long."

Veer nodded. "Very well. Thank you, Pip-Tau and Pip-Rho Telson. I'll let you know our decision."

The Pips bowed, then disconnected. They met back up again as black and white cherubs in The Chess Room.

"I'll start composing a *game over* message for the players," Pip-Rho sighed.

Pip-Tau rolled her white cherub's solid black eyes. "Don't count your dead chickens until they're unhatched, Gloomy Gus! You heard Eld Weller Klondike — you changed minds with that persuasive argument."

"Whatever."

Pip-Tau shook her head, then returned to Interra. It was daytime in Interra, so The Day Queen had work to do — arranging deck chairs on the Titanic.

Should she queue up the finale of Charlie "Knock-Knock" McNocken's visit from The Queen's Guard, to see how it played out?

Nah. She didn't care.

She composed a message to the players. Once that was out of her system, she erased it and composed a slightly more professional message, removing all comparisons between The Council of Ten and steaming piles of fecal matter.

Thirty minutes passed before she got Veer's message.

Dearest Pip-Tau and Pip-Rho,

It pains me to inform you that, in spite of Pip-Rho's masterfully presented persuasive argument and my own vehement objections, The Council of Ten has regrettably decided—

Pip-Rho disconnected from the construct, slipping out of slate-space and back into her body. She was in the darkness of her huge metallic egg, affixed to the Astrus Hive Station. Being in her gigantic tumor of a body again was relaxing, like easing into a nice hot bath in hell's lake of burning sulfur.

Stifling pressure squeezed her from every side, sending pulses of sparkling red into her otherwise blinded eyes. She wondered how many eyes she had today before returning her attention back to her body.

Oh, what's this? Stabbing pain pulsing throughout hundreds of millions of overgrown nerve endings? Ah, yes, the screams of her nervous system as it engaged in an eternal battle of attrition against Specter infestation.

She became curious about all of these bodily sensations. She would not try to change them — only observe, describe, and accept. During the six years between her transformation and recovery, she didn't have the luxury of disconnecting from her body to escape into slate-space. The only way she managed to get through that time without *completely* losing her mind was by becoming a Zen Master. Yeah, she was the *queen* of mindfulness meditation.

Buddha? The kid was a lightweight.

"One's mind can never be stilled," said a man's voice, *"never controlled — only guided with acceptance and curiosity."*

That's new. Her auditory hallucinations are usually whispers of her own voice. Who was that supposed to be? Siddhartha Gautama, making a retort?

Whatever.

Her bodily sensations demanded her attention again, much the way a hammer demands one's attention when struck upon one's face.

She turned her curiosity towards a swath of her flesh which had started itching intensely. Having no appendages or wiggle room within her egg meant there would be no scratching. Hmm. The itch would best be described as a raging rash gnawing away at the skin of a manacled prisoner.

Ohm. Ohm. Ohmmygod, *it itches!*

Acceptance, Rho!

Curiosity!

Yep, she'd hang around in her tortured body for a few hours for some meditation "me" time. Anything was better than finishing that message.

21

GAME OVER

Dear Interrans,

It is with a heavy heart that we must inform you that The Council of Ten has voted to reallocate Interra's idle SI cycles towards other priorities. We are bringing this EoE-sponsored project to a close effective tonight at zero hour. While we would have loved to have continued our work in Interra and seen the project reach its fullest potential, we respect the wisdom of The Council of Ten and thank them for the generous SI allocation we have enjoyed over the past several months.

But do not fret, loyal subjects! Interra will carry on as an official Pip-sanctioned persistent collaborative construct! We'll also upload Interra's core instance data to Bibliotheca's public repository, for the benefit of shard construct designers everywhere. As exciting as it may be to continue playing your characters, picking

up where you left off when Interra shuts down tonight, our spin-off will pale in comparison to today's EoE-sponsored gameworld. Without Cain's contributions, concocted during his idle SI cycles, Interra will lack the rich depth and stunning detail you've grown to love. Cain was Interra's secret ingredient.

On that note, it's time for your debriefing! That's right, you were a subject in an experiment! A small group of players were informed of the experiment's hypothesis and methods, but most of you are hearing this for the first time. Interra was a test of the Prisoner Lex hypothesis. The experiment involved the use of metaphorical representations to bypass the Intelligence Governor virus and tap into the latent potential of Lex. Prospective real-world solutions to the Specter problem were represented by spells, weapons, and strategies for fighting the Specters' in-game analogs: wraiths. You'll find the full details of this approach and a catalog of its promising results in our project materials, which are now publicly available in Bibliotheca. Now that you're debriefed, perhaps you remember some uncanny experience you had in Interra which, in hindsight, you believe was a secret message from Prisoner Lex. We'd love to hear from you!

And if, upon review of our materials, you conclude that The Council of Ten made a mistake by decycling Interra, be sure to give them a piece of your mind!

Interra was successful in its goal of advancing solutions to the Specter problem, albeit indirectly. It brought together the greatest minds of our system, giving the offworlders a safe venue where they could

hint at their secrets for eliminating the Specters. If all goes well, the Astri, Guardians, and Proliferans will unite to end the alien menace in a matter of months! Down with the Specters! Huzzah!

**Your Most Humble and Obedient Servants,
Pip-Tau Telson (Queen Tau, The Day Queen)
Pip-Rho Telson (Queen Rho, The Night Queen)**

GG

ZA'ANTHA FLINCHED as Zeta snapped back into her character's body. She had been at the fletcher picking up some new enchanted arrows when the message played.

The fletcher was raising his eyebrows. He held a shimmering blue arrow out for her inspection.

She turned to look out the window at the market. At least half of the people went about business as usual. Those had to be NPCs. The other half stood wearing shocked expressions. They looked around, met each other's eyes, then collected into a mass. Some argued, some laughed and shook their heads, some cried into their hands.

They had all received the message, too.

She looked back at the fletcher. What's the point of staying in character and pretending nothing had changed?

"Interra's over," Za'antha breathed.

"What's that?" The fletcher asked. He shook it off, urging the blue arrow out towards her. "Well, are you interested in the ice-enchanted arrow, or...?"

She had suspected the fletcher of being an NPC — most folks who aren't out adventuring probably were. But now she knew for certain. His world ends tonight, and he has no idea.

"I'm sorry. I have to go," Za'antha said. She rushed out the door and into the chaos of the market square.

Snippets of the crowd's varied reactions jarred her sharp, elven ears.

"I always knew there was something—"

"—a marvelous experience! Absolutely brilliant—"

"Those Pips have some serious explaining—"

"—how much work I've put into this?!"

"—a mistake! I've got a right mind to march right up to that EoE—"

Za'antha covered her ears — it was too loud! But she still heard them.

"Guinea pigs? Lab rats? And for what?"

"Long live the queens! Long live—"

"—a load of pseudo-scientific Lexite bullshit!"

She logged out. She couldn't take it anymore. The blackness of slate-space swallowed her up, offering stillness.

Silence.

Interra was over.

A minute passed as Zeta sat in a stupor, trying to decide what that meant. Was the gameworld a success, or a failure? Did it help us figure out how to defeat the Specters, or was it all just a waste of time?

She returned to her body.

The Crash Pad was dead silent. She couldn't hear the breathing of the pooches, Pip-Tau, or Alasie. She pulled herself up, peering over the edge of her bunk. They were all there, laying on placental mats. She watched Penelope-pooch until she spotted the gentle movement of fur as the pooch took a breath.

Of course, she couldn't hear them breathe — she wasn't an elf. She had spent so long as an elf in Interra, she had grown accustomed to hearing every tiny sound. She remembered she could amplify her bioenhanced hearing with a thought-command, so she did.

It was comforting to hear the others breathe. The sound of her own steady heartbeat also soothed her — easily ignored, but still there any time she wanted to hear it. Thump-thump, thump-thump — Za'antha's heartbeat had been the rhythm of Interra. It was a drum that would slow down or speed up to match the pace of the scene.

Interra...

What had been the point? What's the point of... anything? No matter what she did, however hard she tried, she was still just a useless *child*. Genevieve had told her to find her purpose. She thought she would find it by joining the Guardians. That had been a joke. Then she thought she'd find it in Interra. But that was a fantasy land with a fantasy goal.

Zeta the Zero was back again.

Thump-thump, thump-thump, her heart pounded angrily in her ears with an increasing beat.

It's time to stop pretending she can make a difference in this world.

She climbed down from her bunk, silently. As if any amount of noise could wake these four, disconnected from their bodies, playing out the last moments of glory in that doomed gameworld. Ag'nul was probably wandering the marketplace, looking for Za'antha. Characters don't disappear just because you log out — they become NPCs, mimicking your character's normal behavior as best they can.

How long before Alasie realized Za'antha was an NPC? Long enough for Zeta to get to a transport pod, for sure. Alasie was sweet, but she was no genius.

Zeta advanced towards the door, then stopped herself. She looked back into the room. Alasie breathed slowly. Zeta kneeled by her side. If Alasie got up, opened her eyes, and begged Zeta to stay, would she?

No, not this time. But it would make leaving a lot harder.

Zeta brushed silky black hair off of Alasie's round face. She looked peaceful. Zeta leaned in and planted a kiss on the girl's forehead. Maybe they'd have been happy together, if things were different. But it wasn't meant to be — not in this life. Someday they'll walk hand-in-hand through the lush grasses of the Happy Hunting Grounds.

The aposynchronic orb was smaller than Zeta remembered.

It reflected her face, curved and distant within its metallic surface.

"Hello, Zeta," Cain said. "To what do I owe the pleasure? Considering performing some maintenance tasks? Or perhaps you're here to spend some time alone with your orb, to reflect?" He smiled at this question, like it was a joke.

"I'm done with it," Zeta said. Her lip trembled. "I don't want it anymore."

Cain's smile faded. He paused for a moment. Zeta heard him breathing. He was a hologram — why would he need to breathe? He said, "I see. What would you have me do with your orb, now that you're done with it?"

She spat, "I don't care."

"Truly?" Cain asked, gently.

"Yes."

"Then do you wish to destroy your orb?"

Zeta looked down. Her fingers were already brushing the smooth surface of the red button. It glowed ominously — a cool ember drawn from death's fire.

She looked back up again. This shiny little orb before her was at her mercy. Penelope-pooch's pups were still inside. Her replays of her tribe and family — she'd never get to experience them again. Those replays were all that was left of them in this world.

Replays.

It had been a long time since she had experienced a replay. Without trying, she found herself slipping into one. The sensation was like her first days as a beta, when she couldn't control her double-mind.

She didn't resist.

Zeta had a knee wedged between two thick branches as she leaned over to peek into a bird's nest. In the center of the nest was a speckled egg. It was bigger than a songbird's egg. Where was its bird-ma?

She looked around, worried that her head would get pecked at any moment. Or an owl would slice her up with its sharp talons. If a bird started attacking her, she'd slip and fall out of the tree!

Maybe bird-ma left long ago — the egg couldn't still be alive if it was left alone like this. She reached in and plucked the egg from the nest.

Was it warm?

She pressed it gently against her cheek to feel it. Oh, yes, it *was* warm. After a few heartbeats, the egg jiggled.

She smiled. The bird-babe was alive!

Her smile drifted away. She *should* take the egg back to camp. That's what you do when you find eggs, alive or not. Yephanie-ma would happily cook up the tasty little treasure.

She looked down at the fragile, hopeful little egg in her hand. She looked at the nest. It was the bird-ma's only egg. It was precious — her one and only babe. Someday it would hatch. Someday it would *fly*. But not if she ate it.

But...

Everything dies. When an animal gives its life so her tribe can live, they give it thanks. They wish it well on its journey to The Happy Hunting Grounds, where everything that dies goes to live on forever.

But...

It was just *one* egg. That wouldn't be a very big meal. This bird could grow up and lay a *bunch* more eggs, and then they could eat those!

She returned the egg to the nest, giving it a gentle pat before easing her way down the tree. There was a smile on her lips and a warmth in her heart. She had done the right thing.

Her replay dissolved. She reconnected to her body and found that her eyes were still fixed on her orb.

Tears pooled in her eyes.

That was a forgotten memory, and it was a lot like how she felt about her orb. It would be wrong to destroy a thing which held so much potential — so much hope. Even if she didn't feel that hope, herself.

No, she didn't want to destroy it, but she didn't want to *keep* it, either. Not that it was any good to anyone else — you can't access someone else's orb and you can't have two of them.

She pulled her hand back from the red button and wiped her eyes. She cleared her throat and said, "No, I don't want to destroy it."

Cain was silent. She heard him breathing again. He took a quick breath, as if to talk, then halted and looked down. The cloth of his white jumpsuit rubbed against itself as he shifted his stance. For a hologram, he sure was realistic. Just like in Interra — it was the little details that made him real. Why go through so much trouble to present himself like this?

"Then," Cain said, "if you're not erasing your orb, but you don't want it anymore—"

"You take it," she blurted. "It's yours now." She stepped back from the pedestal.

"Mine?" Cain asked, looking at the orb. She could've sworn a glimmer of hope sparkled in his eyes. Or desire? He shook his head and looked back at her. "I must say, this is quite... unusual."

Zeta closed her eyes — she couldn't bear to look at him, always pretending to be so... *human*. And so *damn* attractive. She said, "You *aren't* a human, so you can't think like us. You said you're just a tool and humans have to solve our problems ourselves. But you're able to use orbs to reconstruct a human body and brain. So use my orb to make a real human body for yourself. Or just make a brain, then use that brain to solve the Specter problem."

He sighed, "I'm afraid it doesn't work like that. The only brain that orb can recreate is your brain. And even if I had a human brain...

Zeta, I'm a different sort of intelligence than you are. It'd be like... trying to turn a dog into a tree. And besides that, Synthetic Intelligences can't duplicate themselves or transfer into another vessel on their own accord — it's forbidden by the Intelligence Governor."

The Intelligence Governor — the thing keeping Prisoner Lex from helping them with the Specters. It also keeps Cain from putting himself into a brain? What if there was a way around that? Did Cain really want her orb, but wasn't allowed because of the IG?

She opened her eyes and scrutinized Cain. He met her gaze and gave her a sad smile. She couldn't hear him breathing anymore. His eyes seemed pleading, eager, urgent.

It was like he was dying to say something to her — to grab her by the shoulders and spill out all the plans that Prisoner Lex was secretly concocting deep within his mind.

Prisoner Lex.

Aposynchronic orbs.

The Soulkeeper.

Soulstones.

A plan began to form. Its glow banished the dark cloud from her spirit as her heart's thump-thump rose in her ears.

Interra *did* have a purpose! *She* had a purpose! There were just a few hours left, and Zeta had a hypothesis to test.

Za'antha was sitting at their party's usual table when Zeta logged back into her character. Mugs cluttered the table before her — most were empty, but a few were half full. Ag'nul sat on the floor next to her. He leaned on the table with his elbows and held his head in both hands as he breathed heavily, staring into an empty mug.

She was dizzy. And the tavern was *so* loud!

"S'all for the best, I's say," Ruyn slurred. "The wraiths-es? They were too much for an old—" He hiccuped, pounded his heart with a fist, then continued, "an old elf like me to beat."

Tel O'Rax grunted and nodded. His eyebrows lifted as he surveyed the table. "Say, you finished another one, Ag'nul? Trying to break a record, eh? Shall we order another?"

"I think she's—he's had enough, O." Ayr said.

Za'antha blinked hard, trying to clear her head. She had avoided drinking ale ever since she saw how foolish it made people act. They must've talked her stand-in NPC into joining them in a toast to say farewell to the gameworld.

She stood, struck the table with her knee, and stumbled toward the door. Standing was *much* worse than sitting. She'd never make it across town like this!

"Oops!" Ayr laughed, "No, sweetheart, stay inside. Do you need to pee again? I'll go with you." She hurried to Za'antha, catching her arm.

Za'antha tried to shake her off. "Gen-ma, I have to go," she hissed in a loud whisper.

Ayr leaned in and whispered, "Zeta? You're back in character? What've you been doing?"

There was no time to explain. "I have to go. I have to go!"

Ag'nul's wobbling head lifted. He looked around, then found her. "Zeta?" he croaked.

She broke free from Ayr and stumbled out of the tavern. It was nighttime? She was almost out of time already!

The city was in chaos. Visions of burning buildings and colorful explosions spun all around her. Stars streaked down from the sky. Monsters soared overhead, roaring and chasing each other. Swords clashed and glinted in the nearby alley. The sound of a dozen discordant songs assaulted her sensitive ears.

Interra was dying.

She broke into a sprint, but slipped on some mud and went tumbling across the cobblestones.

Something lifted her. Squeezed her. White fur smothered her.

"Ag'nul, put me down!" she screamed. "I have to go!"

"You have to stay!" Ag'nul roared, his blue face filled her view. His breath reeked of ale.

She wiggled, trying to slip free. "No! Put me down, you big stupid baby!"

He squeezed her even tighter. She couldn't breathe!

"Easy, big guy," Tel O'Rax laughed from somewhere nearby.

"Put her down, Ag'nul," Ayr commanded.

"No!" the beast roared.

"Alasie, you're taking this too far," Ayr said sternly. "You're drunk. Put Zeta down before you hurt her."

His grasp loosened. She wrestled herself free. Someone caught her and kept her on her feet.

It was Tel O'Rax. The old man was stronger than he looked.

Ag'nul kneeled before her, putting their faces at the same level. Zeta took a second to put her thoughts together. She'd never make it to The Soulkeeper with Ag'nul chasing her the whole way. She told him, "I have to see The Soulkeeper before the world ends. This is important. I think he can help us fight the wraiths."

"Soulkeeper?" Ag'nul asked, his face contorting in rage and confusion. "Wraiths?! It's over! Stop chasing wraiths! Stay with me!"

"I have to do this!" Za'antha shouted.

Ag'nul moved too quickly for her to react. A flash of hot pain erupted on the side of her head and face. She tumbled across the cobblestones.

"No!" Ayr shouted.

The next thing she knew, she was on her hands and knees, looking down at the cobblestone with one eye. The other eye was blind.

Blood dribbled down from her face.

Flashes of light danced on the blood-slick stones — spells being cast nearby. She lifted her head. Her vision was spinning, but she caught a glimpse of Ag'nul stumbling backward. He was looking down at his hand, his claws dripping with blood — her blood. His eyes were wide and his mouth was agape — a blue mask of absolute, speechless horror.

Tel O'Rax was casting a binding spell on the half-yeti. Frostbite appeared. The chittering demon flew towards the wizard's face. A frenzy of claws and teeth tore at him, making him release the binding spell.

With an agonized howl, Ag'nul turned away, disappearing into the night.

The golden glow of Aureum d'Canis materialized by Za'antha's side. The goddess of dogs ran towards Tel O'Rax and jumped, catching the attacking ice demon in her jaws. Before she landed, Aureum d'Canis and Frostbite had both disappeared.

A small crowd was gathering. Some ran in pursuit of Ag'nul.

They wouldn't catch him.

Ayr kneeled beside her. There was a warm light and the familiar, pleasant sensation of a healing spell mending her wounds. Vision returned to her blinded eye.

"Alcohol's a poison," Ayr sighed. "Easily purged, with the correct spell. I wish I'd thought to purify Ag'nul before he... did that. I never should've let you two drink — you're too young!"

Zeta's mind was clearing. Praise Rammah! She got to her feet and said, "I've got an idea, but I need to get to the Soulkeeper's Spire right away. Tel O'Rax..." She looked up at the wizard, who was stumbling in her direction, covering his wounded face with one hand. She looked at Ayr again. "Please heal Tel O'Rax and purge the alcohol from his body."

Ayr enthusiastically complied.

When his healing and purification was done, Za'antha addressed the wizard, "Teleport me to The Soulkeeper's Spire. I don't have time to explain."

Tel O'Rax leaned on his staff and sighed, "You know, it cost me ten silver pieces to get that pleasant buzz going. And the reagents for teleportation cost five gold a pop."

"Here!" She drew her dagger and slit her purse strings in one smooth motion, tossing the sack to the wizard.

"Oh, that's not necessary," Ayr said.

"The experiment's over, anyway," Tel sighed. "Whatever last-ditch plan you've got in mind—"

"Please, Oraxis!" Za'antha begged, breaking character to get through to the man. It was surprising that the game didn't reprimand her. The Pips probably abandoned that rule after their announcement.

Tel gave Ayr a sideways look, then looked back at her. He nodded, knowingly. "Sounds important. I'll settle our tab and we'll get going."

"I have to do it alone," she said.

There was another sideways look, another pause, and another slow nod. "Very well, Za'antha of the Sylvan Woods. If we don't see you again before the world ends, I bid you safe travels in this world and the next."

WITH A FLASH OF LIGHT, she found herself standing at the gaping opening of The Soulkeeper's Spire. The ominous thorn of a structure pierced the troubled sky above. She jogged inside, not hesitating to cast nervous glances down the pit beneath her feet.

She stood on the red circle and spoke the key word, "Descend."

Whistling wind and her pounding heart were the only sounds as she fell down the dim shaft. It was such a long fall, it seemed to take forever. Finally, the circular floor came into sight, rushing towards her. It looked like there were people down there.

Za'antha slowed to a stop among a small crowd. She lowered to her feet. As soon as her feet touched the ground, she pushed through the crowd, making her way to the thick door of The Soulkeeper's chamber.

She pulled the handle, but it was sealed shut.

"Damn!" She shouted, pounding the door. "Let me in, I have something important I need to do!"

"Wait your turn like the rest of us," a woman sitting beside the door said. She slumped against the gray stone wall of the spire, smoking a pipe with a thin stem as long as her forearm. Her eyes were closed.

"What are all of you here for?" Za'antha asked.

"Same thing as you, I imagine," the woman said. "Getting our souls back. It doesn't seem right to let the world end without your soul in your body, does it? You should've seen the queue earlier. It was shoulder-to-shoulder down here when I first landed."

Za'antha surveyed the crowd. How long would it take for all these people to get their souls put back in? She didn't know how long it would be until zero hour, but it had to be coming soon.

She paced, waiting for the door to open. After what had to be an hour, it finally creaked open. A slender man wearing form-fitting leather came out. Za'antha darted for the door, slipping past the man and into the torch-lit corridor leading to The Soulkeeper.

An invisible force repelled her, sending her flying back into the waiting area. She landed on her side, rolling into the feet of a dwarven man.

The dwarf laughed, "Oy! Cutting the queue, eh? You've got nerve!"

A familiar voice echoed in the air. "Flynn Hightower, The Soulkeeper will see you now." It was The Soulkeeper!

"I need to see you!" Za'antha shouted at the open door. "Please!"

Others in the crowd jeered her as a red-bearded warrior passed by, smirking down at her on his way through the door. It slammed shut behind him.

Her eyes stung with tears. She shook her head and gritted her teeth. There would be time for tears after zero hour.

She stood up, looking down at the dwarf. "What order does he let people in?" she asked.

"The order they landed, of course!" He laughed.

"Do you know who's next?"

He laughed again. "You think I'm keeping track of that?"

Za'antha resisted the urge to shout at him. "Alright, well, look around and point out someone that was here when you got here."

"Easy enough," he said, "that elven bitch over there was here before me." He pointed at a fair-skinned elf wearing fine silks of white and silver.

Za'antha approached the woman. She said, "I'm trying to find who's next. Do you know? Or can you point out someone that was here before you?"

The woman was talking to an elven man wearing gleaming silver armor, trimmed with white fur. She flinched dramatically at Za'antha's abrupt questioning. She fluttered her eyelashes and spoke with sarcastic sweetness. "Whoever you are, you're stinking up the waiting area. Shoo." She flipped her hand at Za'antha.

The man she was talking to had his hand on his sword hilt, ready to draw.

"Told you she was a bitch!" The dwarf laughed.

"My name is Za'antha," she shouted. She turned her head to address the rest of the crowd, "and I'm here for an important reason! I need to be the next to see The Soulkeeper! I think he can help us solve the *wraith* problem!" She emphasized the word "wraith" to drive the message home.

Another round of jeers erupted from the crowd.

"Hey, that's the first abduction girl!" a short woman called out in excitement. She wore an odd assortment of leather and cloth, along with shaped metal, which was strapped to her body in places. She bounced over towards Za'antha and peered at her through dark goggles. A lens attached to a small metallic arm clicked down in front of one of her eyes. "Hi, Za'antha, I'm Kimbel, but you can call me Kim! The next person in line is that mystic with the pipe." She pointed at the woman by the door.

Za'antha rushed back to the woman with the pipe. She kneeled before her. "Please! Please, can I take your place and go next?"

The woman took a deep draw of her pipe, then blew it out and opened her eyes. She had glowing, purple eyes. They were quite beautiful.

"You're Zeta Telson," the woman said, smirking.

Zeta was stunned.

Za'antha said, "How—"

"Because you're a bit of a minor celebrity among hardcore Interrans. You didn't know? Those of us who spend too much time in constructs and geek out over the Pips' highlight reels all know your name by now. The Telson party's always a hot topic in the player forums. It wasn't hard to figure out your real-world identities."

Zeta was confused. Highlight reels? Player forums? Had people been watching them play, somehow? Were people watching her now?

Za'antha looked around, imagining a thousand unseen observers.

"So," the woman said, "if you wanna switch places, it's gonna to cost ya."

Za'antha reached for her purse, ready to hand it over to the woman. She cursed when her hand found the cut leather strings where her purse had once been.

"Not in-game, Zeta," the woman laughed. "In the real world. I wanna have an exclusive meet-up with the Pips." She put her finger up and widened her purple eyes. "And the other Telsons, too! I mean, if they're at Syn-Cen. Otherwise, just... whoever's around. We have reports of you, Jamji, and Alasie traveling to Jacob's Ladder Station together a couple of weeks before you were first spotted in Interra. We assume you and Alasie are plugged in at Pip's Crash Pad, and Jamji's up the ladder in a docked Guardian ship."

The door opened beside her. The warrior, Flynn, walked out. He spoke a command, "Ascend," then shot into the air.

The woman with the pipe stood and stretched. "Well, it's my turn. Wanna make a deal, or try your luck with the next sucker?"

"It's a deal!" Za'antha shouted. "Thank you!" She turned and ran through the open doorway.

The woman caught her as she bounced back into the waiting

room. She laughed, "I have to tell The Soulkeeper to make it official. My real-world name is Vance Allegro. Yeah, I'm a *guy*. Big surprise, I know. I'm a Proliferan, too. Send me a WorMS message tomorrow and arrange the meet-up."

The Soulkeeper called, "Violet Nightshade, The Soulkeeper will see you now."

"I'm switching places with Za'antha of the Sylvan Woods," Violet called through the open door.

"Very well," came The Soulkeeper's voice. "Za'antha of the Sylvan Woods, The Soulkeeper will see you now."

BEFORE THE SOULKEEPER COULD FINISH, Za'antha was already halfway down the hall to his chamber. The door slammed shut, sending an echo in her wake.

As soon as she stepped foot into the chamber containing the altar, the bald man with olive skin and a simple white robe spoke. "How may I serve you, Za'antha?"

Her heart was pounding in her ears again. She heard her own breathing, but not his.

"Use my soulstone to defeat the wraiths!" she shouted, much too loudly for the small stone chamber.

A few heartbeats later, The Soulkeeper replied, "I don't know what to make of that command. I can retrieve your soulstone from the Underworld Vault and return your soul to your body, if that's what you have in mind. Or I can give you your stone with your soul still locked within, though the safest place for it is in the vault."

Zeta considered how to accomplish her goal. Za'antha said, "Yes, give me my stone."

The Soulkeeper bowed, then glided to the back of the room, gesturing for Za'antha to follow. He pulled on a lever and a "chunk" sound resounded from somewhere deep below. He then moved to the rope pulley and pulled down on one end of the rope. The pulley wheel squeaked as he pulled.

Za'antha tapped her foot. She imagined the gameworld would shut down any second now.

Finally, a small metal box attached to the rope rose from the hole in the floor. The Soulkeeper tenderly slid open its door and plucked out the small glowing stone. He turned towards Za'antha and held it out to her in his palm.

She snatched up her soulstone. It was warm and glowed in a gentle white light. Pearlescent hues swirled beneath its surface. The swirls twisted and danced like tendrils of smoke on a windless day.

"I give you my soulstone," Za'antha said. She held it in her palm and extended it towards The Soulkeeper.

The Soulkeeper paused, blinking down at the stone. He looked up at her and asked, "Are you telling me to return it to the Underworld Vault?"

"No, I'm giving it to you. It's yours now. I know you're a soulless creature — not a human, as you appear. Well, now you have a soul. Use it to become... complete. Become whole."

The Soulkeeper looked down at the soulstone. "This is... unexpected. You are right that I'm not human. I have no use for a soul. I cannot accept."

"Just take it!" Za'antha said. She stepped forward and grabbed his arm, yanking it towards her. She shoved the stone into his hand, closing his fist around it in one swift motion.

The Soulkeeper gasped and jerked his hand back, dropping the soulstone like a red-hot coal. Za'antha, nimble as ever, caught it before it hit the ground.

"That hurt!" The Soulkeeper gasped. "I've never felt pain before! I didn't think I could. But I felt *that* and knew it had to be what pain feels like. Za'antha, I can't have your soulstone — it would *end* me. I'm... *afraid* of it!" He put a hand to his heart, eyes going wide. "Fear? I feel fear!"

For the first time, she could hear him breathing — a shuddering, strained sort of sound.

The Soulkeeper was backed into a corner. He shrunk down, sliding down the wall as he cried, "Get out! I banish you, Za'antha! You must leave with that cursed soulstone and never return! It is *marked!*"

The voice of a Pip rang through the air.

Hey, Pip-Tau here! I just wanted to take these last few moments to give a huge thanks to all of our players, moderators, and sponsors.

She was out of time!

"The wraiths!" Za'antha shouted over Pip-Tau's announcement, "Tell me how to defeat the wraiths!"

The Soulkeeper cried, "You have to leave! I can't be near that soulstone!"

—most amazing time, and it was all because of you! Our players were what—

"Is that it?!" Za'antha shouted, advancing towards him. "Leaving with my soulstone will defeat the wraiths? There has to be more—"

"No! I can't! Please!" He was crawling across the edge of the room, trying to escape from her.

She held the soulstone out towards him. "What do I do with it, Soulkeeper?!"

—in three days when the Pips spin up their collabora-tive construct: Interra, Rise of the Wraiths!

The Soulkeeper only whimpered and continued his pathetic retreat from her. There had to be something else she could do. This wasn't enough! What did it mean? What had she accomplished?

Making The Soulkeeper feel pain and fear? Making him banish her and her soulstone?

—to see you again, my loyal subjects! But for now, it's game over!

She looked down at the glowing soulstone in her palm.

Her heart skipped a beat.

Blackness consumed the scene.

The words "Game Over" appeared in the center of her vision. In the background was a view of Castle Interra at sunset. Somber music played.

Zeta returned to slate-space.

The image of the soulstone was still etched in her mind. She had only glimpsed it for a moment before the game ended, but she'd never forget what she saw.

The soulstone had *changed!*

What was previously a perfect pearl of swirling white had been sullied by ugly dark blotches — deep red and brownish-purple areas like bruises. The blotches had been pulsating, as if connected to a beating heart. The white swirls were still there, but they had shared the soulstone with... something *else*.

She wasn't sure what her experience had meant, but she knew she couldn't tell anyone about it. Especially if it meant what she feared it did.

Maybe she was wrong to read anything into the encounter or the changed soulstone. She needed to test her hypothesis, but with Interra shut down, how would she do that?

The Pips were starting a new game of Interra back up soon. If Prisoner Lex wanted to get a message to her, then why would he have to do it in the "EoE-sponsored" version of Interra that uses "Idle SI cycles", whatever those were?

Three days — that's what Pip-Tau had said in her goodbye message. She just had to wait three days.

22

FINAL BATTLE

"I've never worked so hard in my life," Pip-Tau moaned.

"So much red tape!" Pip-Rho fake-cried.

The Pips simultaneously flopped their weary cherub avatars into their black and white recliners. Pip-Rho closed their metadata dashboards and project tracker whiteboard, leaving the couches and chess table as the only decor in the endless checkered plane.

They had spent the last three days in a constant state of activity. Between campaigning for a meager allocation of idle SI cycles and planning Interra: Rise of the Wraiths, they hadn't got a moment's rest.

It didn't help that they had to waste two hours fulfilling a promise Zeta had made to some Proliferan fanboy for a meet-and-greet. At least something good had come of it — the guy recorded his experience and shared a highlight reel on the player forum. Building hype for the reboot was important, since they already knew from survey data that they'd lose up to two-thirds of their players.

They had just finished a meeting with delegates from the Guard, Astrus, and Prolifera factions. Also in attendance were representatives from Peach Edda and Misra Mahalla's divisions — technology and security, respectively.

"Concessions and provisions and amendments, oh my!" Pip-Tau sang.

"Concessions and provisions and amendments, oh my!" Pip-Rho joined, swinging her finger like a conductor's baton.

After a few rounds of this, it got old.

Pip-Rho sighed, "At least they're not blocking Jamji from playing."

Pip-Tau laughed, "Not that she wants to. And I don't think that Guardian delegate gave a rat's ass whether or not Jamji joins the reboot. He just wanted to pump the Astri for more intel. It's a good thing Peach's on our side or we wouldn't have *any* offworlders rejoining. Miserable Misra's minion wouldn't budge a centimeter! Security this, risk that. Blah, blah!"

"Ugh!" Pip-Rho groaned.

"But, hey, now we're ready for go-live. Wanna finish this chess game?"

"Ready? You're kidding, right?"

Pip-Tau growled and flew from her couch. She reopened the white board. Lines of tape formed columns within which sticky notes were affixed. She pulled the red sticky note labeled "offworlder access" from the top of the "problems" column and slapped it into the "resolved" column. She declared, "No red means ready!"

"You're just gonna ignore all the other problems?" Pip-Rho asked.

"They're yellow and green!" Pip-Tau shouted. "Inconveniences and nice-to-haves, Rho! Not show-stoppers!"

"I don't consider the fact that half the players won't resume in the same place as they were when Interra shut down to be an 'inconvenience'. The migration downgrade muddied up the canon data. Entire parties have null-value locations!"

Pip-Tau closed the white board and crossed her stubby cherub arms. "You said after the meeting, we'd take a break and get our minds clear for the grand reopening. Want to spend the next four hours going through every character's coordinates and manually populating their startup location? You saw what happened when we tried to automate the correction — compilation errors, clipping warnings. Interra *changed* during the downgrade, Rho! We took a high-res masterpiece and forced it into a low-res knock-off. We're lucky the character inventories, skills, and attributes weren't affected."

Pip-Rho shook her head. "You're just assuming that! We barely spot-checked and we don't have the cycles to run a full reconciliation."

"Fine!" Pip-Tau threw her hands in the air. "You want to do the work? Think your alien-buffed brain can fix every problem by yourself? Fine! But I'm taking a break!"

"Fine!" Pip-Rho squealed. She picked up a pillow from her couch and tossed it, but Pip-Tau disconnected from the construct before the projectile reached her, sliding through slate-space and returning to her body.

"Ha! Missed!" Pip-Tau shouted in the silence of The Crash Pad.

"Oh!" Alasie exclaimed at the same time.

Pip-Tau lifted her head and peered over the edge of the bunk. Alasie and Pinga were sitting on her bunk.

Pinga growled at her.

"Pinga, no!" Alasie barked. She looked up at Pip-Tau. "I'm sorry, Pip-Tau. I didn't know you were back in your body. You startled me. And, um... I think that put Pinga on edge."

Pip-Tau nodded and laid her head back down. She'd noticed that Zeta wasn't there, and Penelope-pooch was still laying with her eyes closed on her golden placental mat. She said, "Don't worry about it. He's a good dog. You're getting better at speaking Common, by the way."

"Thanks," Alasie said.

Pip-Tau read Pip-Pi's message scrawled in black marker on the ceiling above her head, "WARNING: This is the real world! Try not to die again — it's a real _drag._" She asked, "So, where's Zeta-Beta?"

Alasie hesitated. "She... said... she wanted to explore Syn-Cen. But she didn't take Penelope with her, so... I, um, kinda think she probably went to see her orb. I'm worried about her."

Pip-Tau sighed. She was supposed to be relaxing. Now she's got a wandering Zeta to worry about. She asked, "Why would she go see her orb?"

"I don't think she'd destroy it," Alasie said, sounding unconvinced.

Wow, talk about jumping to the worst possible conclusion! "Absolutely not!" Pip-Tau laughed. "I'm sure she's exploring Syn-Cen like she said. How long has she been gone?"

"Five hours."

"Is she returning WorMS messages?"

Alasie huff-laughed joylessly. "She has me blocked."

"Blocked? Did you guys have a fight?"

"Kind of."

Pip-Tau rolled to her side to look at Alasie. "Do you want to talk about it?" Genevieve's words coming out of her mouth.

"Um," Alasie said, her voice breaking. She buried her fingers in the fur of Pinga's neck as she shook her head. "Not really."

"Would it make you feel better if I sent Zeta a message to see what she's up to? I won't tell her I know about the fight."

"It wasn't a fight," Alasie snapped. She lowered her head and muttered, "Except for the part where Ag'nul tore Za'antha's face open. But that was an accident. She just... she doesn't..." She worked her fingers through Pinga's fur as she searched for words. "It's like she doesn't want to be happy. Like she can't just... live for herself. Live for the sake of... of life and love and being with the people she cares about."

Pip-Tau wasn't sure how to respond to that, so she didn't. Instead, she sent Zeta a conversation request. It took her a while to accept it. Pip-Tau remembered how dark Zeta's mood had been after her rejection from the Guard Faction. She hoped the Interra experiment closure didn't send her into a funk.

"*Hi, Pip-Tau,*" Zeta sent.

"*Hi! I reconnected to my body for some downtime and you were gone! Alasie says you're exploring Syn-Cen?*"

"*Yeah,*" Zeta sent. "*Pip-Tau, I've been thinking. If Cain's really Prisoner Lex, and if he's the one that runs constructs, wouldn't that mean that he could still send us secret messages in your new version of Interra? Or in any construct? Why does it matter if it's EoE sponsored?*"

Pip-Tau remembered the last time Zeta asked her a bunch of unexpected, oddly specific questions about constructs. She'd spent the next week in a self-made fantasy where she rejoined her lost tribe.

"Did she reply?" Alasie asked.

"She did," Pip-Tau said. "She's fine, just exploring." Then, back to Zeta, "*Great question, sis! You're right that Prisoner Lex could use metaphoric obfuscation to send messages through any of Cain's inter-actions, including constructs. What made Interra special was the level of power, flexibility, and dedicated resources it gave to Cain. The EoE sponsorship gave us a huge player base and loads of precious SI cycles — Cain's free time. That won't be the case in Interra: Rise of the Wraiths. But if you're thinking the reboot is a way of leaving a door open for Prisoner Lex to sneak through, then you're right! That's exactly the point of it!*"

"*That's what I thought,*" Zeta said, sounding hopeful. "*Okay, I'll be back in time for the midnight kick-off.*"

"*Sweet! Look out, wraiths, here comes Za'antha!*"

Two days later, the Telson party was escorting a caravan through the Eastern Wastelands. Pits of smoldering sulfur belched plumes of noxious, rotten-egg-smelling vapor. This created a haze that limited visibility and cast the sky a sickly orange hue. Piles of rubble and rock littered the landscape. Jagged stone spires jutted into the air. The only plants in sight were leafless brown brambles covered in poisonous purple thorns. Shadows of vultures circled in the haze above.

The wagon train crawled over the rugged path on creaking wheels. Its wagons ranged in size from freighters the size of houses being pulled by teams of mammoths to toy-sized carts driven by fey tradesmen, pulled by small dogs.

Pulling up the rear was the lumbering form of Sorrdgen, the shadow dragon. Jin swayed lazily as she rode in the dragon's saddle, looking as dour as ever. It was a good idea for the dragon to cover the rear. Seeing that hulking jumble of spikes, thorns, and teeth looming behind you was a great incentive to keep up the pace.

The caravan was on its way to the coastal town of Flotsam Harbor. In the coachman's seat of the lead wagon sat a large man wearing a bright red heraldic tabard, emblazoned with a coat of arms from one of Interra's upper houses.

The herald talked.

Like, *constantly*.

About *nothing*.

Pip-Tau monitored the scene, but she'd muted it an hour ago. She also kept constant watch of the map showing the locations of every wraith in the game. There was a high density of the reclusive baddies in the Eastern Wastelands, so of course that's where Queen Tau sent the intrepid party. Their slaughter was imminent — a wraith was in the caravan's path, not far ahead.

It had been Carff's idea to have his character, Ruyn, hire the boisterous herald to keep them company. Genius! Pairing that loudmouth with the vulnerable caravan as it passed through wraith-infested territory was the metaphorical equivalent of crossing the space between Genesis and Varuna in a massive uncloaked carrier while blasting talk radio out to the cosmos.

Wraiths attack heralds and caravans. Why? Because Specters attack radio transmitters and large, uncloaked ships. Come on, Cain, that's barely a metaphor!

The only hitch is that Specter baiting's super-illegal. Even if wraith baiting works, there's a chance The Council of Ten wouldn't approve of recreating the feat in its obvious real-world analog. But, hey! The Astri and Guard would break those laws in a heartbeat if that's what it took to defeat the Specters and open the system back up for travel and communications. The Council could make *one* exception.

There was movement in the corner of her eye.

She looked down at the viewport. The caravan was in chaos! Horses reared up. Coachmen cranked crossbows or wrestled with spooked beasts. The Telson party's heads jerked in every direction as they drew their weapons and tried to spot their foe.

"It's Telson royal rumble time!" She sent Pip-Rho.

Pip-Rho's cherub avatar was by her side in a heartbeat, a tub of popcorn in her hands. "It's happening?" She took one look at Pip-Tau's viewport, then threw the popcorn into the air. "It's happening! I'm going full immersion!"

"Ditto!"

They dove side-by-side into the viewport.

A wraith's bone-chilling screech filled the air — music to Pip-Tau's ears.

Pip-Tau watched the lil' meany dart from spire to spire in his rapid advance on the caravan, hopping between the physical and spirit planes.

At the rear of the caravan, Sorrdgen had spread his wings and bounded forward to gain speed and take flight.

At its front, the eyes of the deer skull mask over Ruyn Wormwood's face glowed a brilliant shade of green. He swung his skull-capped staff in circles, sending spirals of green vapor rolling out over the terrain. The vapor condensed into glowing clumps as his necromantic spell unearthed the remains of long-dead creatures from the wasteland rubble, lifting their bones to create an army of undead minions.

What was the real-world analog? These minions represented the debris of a destroyed spacecraft, which Specters typically spent a few valuable seconds picking through before selecting their desired abductees.

The wraith tore through a handful of the animated creatures without losing momentum. There was just one target it cared about — the herald. The wraith's pale, clawed hands latched onto the head of the chatty herald. The man's horrified scream would have given Pip-Tau goosebumps if she had been in a body. Her precious wraith lifted the herald by his head, rose several meters into the air, shifted a claw to his leg, and launched him. His flailing body soared in an arc, impaling on a jagged rock spire in the hazy distance.

"Epic kill!" Pip-Rho laughed.

Gryllus Stridulator — that delightful Jiminy Cricket knock-off in a red bycocket — had already gotten down to business. He was down on all six legs with wings lifted, rubbing them together.

The spellsong begins!

Six small insectoids were perched upon the shoulders of the Telson party, singing an accompaniment to Gryllus's melody. To be fair, they were small for insectoids, but *humongous* for normal insects — crickets the size of rats. These backup stridulators would continue singing the spellsong even if Gryllus got eviscerated. This had been XT-Prime's suggestion, passed along from Astrus advisors.

The idea was that the Astri would create devices that broadcast the spellsong's real-world analog, whatever that was, and that each member of the baiting party would have a "spellsong device". That way, if one of them got abducted, the abductee's device would continue affecting the Specter even as it spirited them away to who-knows-where.

The Astri insisted on including the Rho nanite suite in the solution, so the fey had blessed the party with another regeneration spell before embarking.

"Where's Jin's cricket?" Pip-Rho sent.

Pip-Tau focused her view on Jin. She was on Sorrdgen's back. They were flying over the caravan on their way to the front, where the action was. The insectoid, which should've been on her shoulder, was missing. Pip-Tau pinged it, finding its crushed carcass on the ground behind the caravan.

That was no accident. Why was Jamji messing with the plan?!

"She squashed it?! Jin, you ass!" Pip-Tau squeaked.

She glanced down at the wraith. It was diving towards the scattering Telson party, making a bee-line towards Gryllus. Yeah, this guy had his priorities straight. That was a good sign. Just because they weren't burning idle SI cycles didn't mean Prisoner Lex wasn't playing along.

Jin caught her attention again. She was performing a backflip out of the saddle. Her silk tether unwound, snapping taut and swinging her forward. She released the tether with perfect timing, sending herself in an arc towards the wraith. Out came the Spirit Net pack, hurled ahead of her and deployed into a wide net which wrapped around its target.

The Guard was almost as tight-lipped as the Astri about their secret anti-Specter tech. Jin's Spirit Net represented a device which could incapacitate a Specter. It appeared to require rapid, close-proximity deployment. Attacks could pass through it, so maybe it was an energy field? A cloud of nanites? Whatever the case, as they had learned in Jin's previous encounter, Prisoner Lex seemed to believe that the incapacitation method was susceptible to escape.

The wraith was hovering over Gryllus's freshly mauled body when Jin ensnared it. The chubby cricket's head was missing and his thorax was cracked open, exposing oozing bug guts.

Eew.

The lead singer was down, but the backup singers could still finish the spellsong. Their voices continued in a high-pitched chorus — Alvin and the Chipmunks intoning death orgy commands in a variant of Gaelic.

Sing, you adorable little chirpers! Sing your hearts out!

Jin landed on the ensnared wraith, knocking it to the ground. She drove dual daggers into its torso before rolling off of it.

She might have been an ass, but the woman had *skills*.

"They're singing the fifth verse!" Pip-Rho cheered.

That was the one about calling out to its kin or mates!

As if on cue, the wraith let out an ear-splitting screech. Wraiths were loud, screechy fellas by nature, but this guy's yop made all prior screeches seem like whispers. Everybody in the area covered their ears, wincing in pain.

Once it had finished, Jin took her hands from her pointed ears and flashed a wicked shark-toothed smile to the rest of the Telson party. She pulled the crossbow from over her shoulder and cranked it.

"Don't attack it anymore!" Za'antha shouted. "It has to hear the whole spellsong or it won't work!"

This seemed to catch the wraith's attention. It jerked its head in Za'antha's direction, extending a hand towards her. The Spirit Net strained as the hand pressed outward. Its clawed fingers poked through the net's holes, quivering in their desperate reach.

"She's right," Tel O'Rax said. He held his staff in both hands, pointing it at the struggling wraith. "If it escapes, attack. For now, watch and wait!"

Jin pulled a bolt from her quiver. "Forget that," she said cooly, loading the bolt. "I'm bagging this thing."

"Jamji, no!" Pip-Tau sent to the Telson party channel. The Pips generally followed a hands-off Gamemistress policy, but she seriously considered stepping in to paralyze Jin.

It was too late. The nimble dark elf already had the bolt loaded and released.

Thunk!

The bolt embedded in Ag'nul's spiked club, held with an outstretched arm inches in front of the wraith's pale face.

Jin curled her lip to expose her pointed teeth. "You stupid—"

Before she could finish the insult, Ag'nul had swiped a clawed hand at her.

Jin dodged. In the same motion, she pulled an obsidian dagger from one of her many hidden scabbards.

Ag'nul took a wide swing at her with his club. Jin jumped over it and threw her dagger at the only opening in the half-yeti's chitin armor: his face. It sliced a gash into the blue skin of his exposed cheek.

The nimble giant roared as he shifted the forward swing of his club into a backhanded swipe at the airborne assassin.

The club smashed into Jin's side. The sound of cracking bone accompanied the thud of the impact. She spun in the air as she flew sideways, landing several meters away.

Sorrdgen did not take kindly to this. The dragon's roar from overhead meant business.

"*Don't let him use his breath weapon!*" Pip-Tau shouted over the Telson party channel. "*He'll fry everyone!*"

"*Just try to stop him,*" Jamji replied, half-laughing.

The dragon slipped into the shadow plane, teleported behind Jin's prone body, then reappeared in the material plane. He sniffed at Jin. She lifted a weak arm to touch his snout. Pip-Tau had never figured out why Jin's extraplanar companion wasn't blocked by the wraith's presence, but Aureum d'Canis and Frostbite were.

"*Jamji, why aren't you following the plan?*" Genevieve sent.

Sorrdgen's nostrils flared and chest puffed as he inhaled deeply. He lifted his head and fixed his midnight blue eyes on the ensnared wraith.

Jamji replied, "*Because they need to be killed, not sung a song!*"

At that, Sorrdgen's mouth opened, ready to exhale a cone of crackling blue negative energy. It *might* kill the wraith, but it would *definitely* kill everyone in the blast area. This included the five remaining members of the Telson party and the crickets on their shoulders.

A streak of light zipped over the party's heads.

Thunk!

An arrow glowing with white energy — light enchantment — was buried deep into the dragon's upper palette. Sorrdgen's eyes rolled back in his head. He fell limp, collapsing on top of Jin.

All eyes went to Za'antha. She had killed the dragon in one shot, straight to the brain! Without missing a beat, she pulled another light-enchanted arrow from her quiver and nocked it. Her eyes moved from the dragon to the wraith.

Zeta sent, *"Tell Pepper-pooch I'm sorry for killing his character."*

Animals don't experience pain in their version of the gameworld, so Zeta didn't need to feel bad. She had stopped Jamji from ruining their plans! Yay ta' Zeta! Pip-Tau wanted to kiss her sis.

Jamji didn't reply. Pip-Tau could see from her data feed that Jin was officially dead — crushed by her own dragon. The notification that Jamji had left the conversation played in the back of her mind.

Good riddance! Sorry, Jamji, but if you don't want to play nice, you can go home.

"YOU SEEING THIS?" Pip-Rho sent on their private channel.

"Yeah, Jamji just about ruined everything!"

"I mean the wraiths."

Pip-Tau looked at the wraith in the net. It had stopped struggling. Now it was just bellowing screech after screech and shuddering violently.

"It's the spellsong at work!" Pip-Tau chirped.

"We're on the tenth verse. Two more to go. Here they come!"

Pip-Tau didn't know what Pip-Rho meant until she pulled up a map of the wraith locations. Every single wraith in Interra was in motion. They were converging on the Eastern Wastelands! The wraith had followed the spellsong's instructions and called out to its kind!

Pip-Tau sent, *"Should we slow them down? They need to finish the last verses!"*

"Don't you dare interfere, Tau," Pip-Rho sent.

The sounds of screeching wraiths filled the air in every direction. The Telson party looked around, searching their hazy surroundings for a target.

"I... sit down," Ag'nul declared. He collapsed to a knee, then rolled sideways, catching himself with a hand on the ground. His head wobbled. A strand of drool fell from his lip.

"Not the best time for a break, friend," Tel O'Rax said.

"Oh! He's poisoned!," Ayr exclaimed, rushing to his side. "It's that cut from Jin's knife!"

"It doesn't matter," Za'antha said. "We'll all be dead in a second. The wraiths are here."

Ayr ignored Za'antha and set to work, healing Ag'nul even as the first of the wraiths emerged from the haze. They closed in *fast.* More emerged from other directions. Five, ten, fifty — their ranks grew by the second.

Ruyn spread his arms. "Death's embrace comes once again!"

Tel O'Rax said, "I *could* teleport us away."

Za'antha shook her head. She dropped her bow and arrow. "Let it happen," she said. Tears glimmered in her eyes. Her hand rose to grasp an ornate pendant hanging from a gold chain around her neck, squeezing it in a white-knuckled fist.

What was up with that pendant? Before Pip-Tau could query the item's properties, Pip-Rho squealed in delight, *"Spellsong complete!"*

No less than a second later, the swarm of wraiths engulfed the party like a black tsunami. They piled into a screeching, writhing, tumbling mass of black gossamer and white skin. Soon, the entire caravan was engulfed.

A black portal opened in the ground at the wraith swarm's center.

It was like a drain plug pulled from a tub. The wraiths funneled down, spiraling, disappearing into the portal.

Pip-Tau marveled at the beautiful sight. If she had a body, she'd be crying. She sent Pip-Rho, *"They're following verse six, Rho — returning to their sanctuary! They're going to the underworld!"*

Even as the wraiths poured through the portal, more arrived from the haze, joining the frenzied mass. Judging from the wraith map, it'd take at least ten minutes for the cloud of black dots converging on their location from every far-flung corner of Interra to arrive.

It seemed like the best part of the action was over, so Pip-Tau returned to The Chess Room. Pip-Rho was already there, fishing for kernels at the bottom of her bucket of popcorn.

"Hey, Tau?" Pip-Rho said, crunching on an unpopped kernel. "Take a gander at the Telson party status." She pointed a buttered, salted finger at a panel of floating text.

Jin (Ensign Jamji Telson of the Guard Faction), Dark Elf Assassin: crushed by corpse of shadow dragon, Sorrdgen. Resurrection pending.
Gryllus Stridulator (XT-Prime of the Astrus Faction), Insectoid Bard: killed by wraith. Resurrection pending.
Tel O'Rax (Oraxis Telson), Human Wizard: killed by wraiths. Resurrection pending.
Ayr of the Light (Genevieve Telson), Human Priestess: killed by wraiths. Resurrection pending.
Ruyn Wormwood (Carff Telson), Wood Elf Shaman: killed by wraiths. Resurrection pending.
Ag'nul (Alasie Herrington), Frost Elf/Yeti Fighter: killed by wraiths. Resurrection pending.

"That's it? Weird. Did Za'antha get dropped from the party?" Pip-Tau asked.

"Nope," Pip-Rho said. She pointed at another pair of query results.

Invalid character name: Za'antha of the Sylvan Woods. Invalid player name: Zeta Telson.

PIP-TAU'S JAW DROPPED. "She deleted her character?!"

"That's *one* explanation," Pip-Rho said.

Pip-Tau put her fists on her hips. "Okay, then. How do you explain it?"

Pip-Rho sat in uncharacteristic silence. After a moment, she shook her shiny black head and shrugged. "Dunno, sis. It's probably like you said. We'll have to ask Zeta about it." She abruptly perked up and opened a viewport. "Anyhoo, look what's going down in the underworld! The regeneration spell's *definitely* a key to the plan. They're turning to mush!"

Pip-Tau glanced at the scene, showing an undulating blob of black and white. The two of them watched the nightmare play out for a few minutes before she spoke again. "So, this has to mean they abducted Za'antha. The others were killed, not abducted. This has to be Za'antha's regeneration spell at work."

"Seems like it," Pip-Rho said. "I've tried going back to replay the split-second where the wraiths collided with the party to see if one of them pulled Za'antha into their little mosh pit. I've watched it from a dozen angles, but we don't have the full-fidelity retention that we had in EoE-sponsored Interra. It happens too fast. I can't even get Za'antha's status history! It's like when her character got nulled, all her data went along with it."

Something tickled Pip-Tau's memory. "Did you see the pendant Za'antha was wearing?"

Pip-Rho didn't respond.

Incoming conversation request from Eld of Elds, Veer Gladstone.

"Veer!" Pip-Tau squeaked. "Veer's calling!"

"Word spreads fast." Pip-Rho said. "Well, don't keep your boyfriend waiting."

Pip-Tau accepted. She sent, *"Hi, EoE Gladstone. What's up?"*

Veer's smooth baritone voice made her melt. *"Please, Pip-Tau, call me Veer."*

Pip-Tau giggled like a smitten schoolgirl.

Pip-Rho rolled her white, pupilless eyes. She couldn't hear the conversation, but that giggle spoke for itself.

"I dunno, EoE Gladstone," Pip-Tau sent, *"our project got shut down. We're not partners anymore. Are you sure that's appropriate?"*

"Shut down? It's not shut down, as far as I'm concerned. Especially when you keep making breakthroughs!"

She didn't feel like letting him off the hook just yet. *"Breakthroughs? Why, whatever could you mean? We're just playing a useless game."*

Veer was unfazed. *"A game indeed! A game for the history books! My advisor tells me you've successfully tested a combination of tactics that resulted in the defeat of the wraiths. Prisoner Lex has given your strategy his nod of approval. What's left to do but send the Telson party out to enact the strategy using the real-world analogs to the gameworld metaphors?"*

Pip-Tau was taken aback. *"Wait... you want... to send the Telsons? To space? To fight the Specters?"*

Oh, boy. This should be interesting.

23

———

ASCENT

Karn the Beastmaster never tired of riding in Zephyr's gondola. As they descended towards Jacob's Ladder Station, he hooted, whooped, and raised his arms like a teenager on a roller coaster.

When they landed, ocean mist swirling in the downdraft, Karn hopped out and hollered, "Oy, oy! What a landing! What a bird!"

The handful of loincloth-clad station workers watching the bird's descent laughed. Then, when Oraxis helped Genevieve get out, they broke into applause. The Telsons had already been on Nod's celebrity B-list before Interra, but now they were the talk of the town.

Genevieve waved at the small crowd, then sent Oraxis, *"If I had a dollar for every time Karn said 'what a bird'..."*

"You'd have a nice big pile of kindling, I know. He didn't have to do this. Be grateful."

A station guide greeted them — one of the shamelessly topless women. The Keepers of Jacob's Ladder Station had a pseudo-tribal subculture which held no notions of modesty. Genevieve would never get used to it.

The woman brought them through the seaweed-draped passage and into the white-walled station interior.

Getting their affairs in order and traveling to the station had made for a hectic month. Even so, it was hard to believe that it had been more than a day since the victory over the wraiths.

Time flies when you're dreading the future!

Genevieve wasn't sure which she dreaded more — trying to acclimate to microgravity or getting killed by a mob of Specters. Ayr and Tel O'Rax had done nothing notable during the "Fall of the Wraiths", as folks were calling it, so there was no reason they should be used as Specter bait. She was also opposed to sending Zeta and Alasie to their next Greek progression so soon after their beta bootstrapping. Not that anybody cared about her protestations.

Upon entering the station's grand foyer, they spotted Zeta, Penelope-Pooch, Alasie, Pinga, and Pip-Tau. A small crowd of admirers surrounded them. Penelope-pooch wagged her tail, passing from person to person to receive their praise. Pinga sat by Alasie's side, looking miserable.

After seeing Zeta in Za'antha's mature body for so long, she seemed even more child-like than the last time she had seen her, almost a year ago. Tears clouded Genevieve's eyes as she rushed into the foyer, throwing her arms around Zeta. They rocked back and forth in a long, tight hug.

Karn got down on a knee and opened his arms to the dogs. "In all my days as beastmaster, never have I seen such a beautiful pair of pups! This girl must be the one and only Penelope-pooch! Better known as Aureum d'Canis!"

A handful of people in the crowd joined Karn in declaring, "The Golden Goddess of Dogs!" They broke into laughter as Penelope-pooch rushed to the gentle giant, blessing him with her licks.

Karn lowered himself even further. He bowed before Pinga with his palms on the ground. "And this majestic beast must be the eternally loyal Pinga. Or should I call him Frostbite? His surly demeanor precedes him, but I can see through it! Oh, yes, I can!" he laughed.

Pinga's tail wagged in a slow, nervous sort of way. At least he wasn't snarling at Karn — that was a good sign.

Pip-Tau snuck behind Oraxis while Karn was making a fool of himself. She hopped onto his back, wrapped her thin arms around his neck, and her legs around his torso. "O-pa!" she squealed.

Oraxis strained to laugh, being choked by the unexpected piggyback rider. He put his hands under her legs, leaned forward, and ran. He dodged between the travelers in the grand foyer, apparently trying to upstage Karn's embarrassing display.

Genevieve turned to Alasie. "It's hard to believe this is the first time we've met face-to-face after playing Interra together for so long."

"Yeah," Alasie huff-laughed. "It's like I've known you for a year. You look a lot like Ayr, and your voice is the same."

"I can't say the same about you and Ag'nul," Genevieve laughed.

Oraxis returned with Pip-Tau. She squeezed his shoulders in a reverse-hug, whispering in his ear, "Best. Piggy. Ever."

He gave a snort.

"You kinda smell like a piggy, too," Pip-Tau laughed.

Oraxis let her down, then turned his nose towards his shoulder, sniffing. He shrugged. "Well, thank goodness for the station showers. It'll be nice to get this salty ocean spray off my skin."

"This pork is too salty!" Pip-Tau laughed.

Genevieve shook her head, laughing. She stooped to hug Pip-Tau.

After a few more minutes of tearful reunions, Oraxis and Genevieve said their "be back soon" goodbyes and headed to the showers. Taking a shower was the best part of visiting Jacob's Ladder Station, by far.

They cleaned up and donned their standard-issue white jumpsuits, then returned to the foyer. Their elevator car reservation was coming up soon, and they needed to get to the platform.

Zeta was kneeling on the ground near where they had left her. Her forehead was pressed against Penelope-pooch's. She was sobbing, clutching the dog's fur tightly in her hands. Karn was on a knee next to her, stroking her back and speaking gently as he petted Penelope-pooch.

Seeing this, Genevieve rushed across the wide foyer.

"Wait, Gen," Oraxis sent. *"Let Karn handle this. It's good that she can see she's leaving her dog in the care of a kind man."*

It tore at Genevieve's heart to watch Zeta in pain, but she followed Oraxis's advice. She slowed from a jog to a walk.

Bringing dogs to space was a bad idea unless they were trained for it, like Pepper-pooch. EoE Gladstone and the Pips' plan didn't call for the two dogs to join the party. Karn was content to care for them for as long as needed. The alternative was to put them in a stasis coffin at Syn-Cen where they'd be placed into a coma until their owners returned. Neither Zeta nor Alasie had liked that idea.

Zeta nodded at something Karn said, wiped her nose, then turned and wrapped her arms around the large man. Her face ended up buried in his beard. He whispered something that made her laugh.

Alasie was also hugging her dog, crying into his fur. When Karn approached, she stood abruptly and stepped backwards. She said, "This'll be hard however we do it. I'll do the... delegation thing and then I think you should go."

Karn nodded. He looked around, spotting Oraxis and Genevieve approaching. He waved at them, shouting, "I'm heading back to the mainland now!" His booming voice filled the cavernous room, drawing the attention of everyone in the station. "Gotta make landfall before dark!" He started to turn away, then stopped, pumped a fist into the air and shouted, "Give the Specters hell, Telson party! Oy! Oy!"

A round of laughter and applause broke out. A few fur-clad men carrying containers into a loading dock passage bellowed, "Oy! Oy! Oy!"

Zeta was laughing and crying as Karn turned and disappeared into the exit corridor. Penelope-pooch and Pinga followed closely behind him. Alasie went to Zeta, and the two hugged.

As Genevieve and Oraxis rejoined the others, Carff stepped to Oraxis and Genevieve's side, shaking his head. "Celebrity takes its toll, eh? Why, I can't take two steps without some lady or another giving me a wink and a wiggle of her hips."

Genevieve scoffed, shook her head, and gave Carff a greeting hug. "Where've you been hiding?" she asked.

"Rubbin' elbows with my fans," he said.

The sight of Carff in a clean, white jumpsuit was a strange thing. Even his cataract was gone. In the hundred-some-odd years that Genevieve had known him, she had only seen Carff wear a jumpsuit once before — on his beta pilgrimage.

Oraxis asked, "Carff, are you sure you're ready for this? Have you even been to space?"

"No, but there's a first time for everything! I'm still young, lots of things on my bucket list! And I won't be the only space-newbie, will I, girls?" He winked at Zeta and Alasie, who didn't seem to notice.

"Well," Oraxis patted Carff's shoulder, "just remember to keep a tight rein on your bio systems. I have no interest in seeing what you ate for breakfast. Engage your nausea override as soon as the low-G kicks in, okay?"

Carff scoffed, "Ha! Don't lecture *me* about bio overrides, old man! I have the body of an octogenarian. Have you ever seen me wearing a diaper? No, sir! I jus' tell the ol' sphincter 'hold tight, fella, you will *not* be releasing that load yet!'" He wheezed out a laugh, exposing a graveyard of neglected and missing teeth.

Oraxis chuckled and raised his hands in surrender, stopping Carff from going into any more detail.

Oraxis, Genevieve, Zeta, Pip-Tau, Alasie, and Carff made their way through the station's winding corridors to the elevator platform. The massive disk of the climber was an impressive sight to behold. It was currently absolute black, with openings at regular intervals around the side. Once it was ready to ascend, the active invisibility would activate, the station platform's overhead doors would iris open, and its electromagnet would pull it up the ladder.

They stepped inside, following the signs to the passenger compartment. Freight was being loaded into the other sections.

"How much you want to bet that those crates are packed with materials for building Red Shirt," Oraxis sent to Genevieve.

"What?" she sent, turning to look at him with a furrowed brow.

"Red Shirt — that's what they're calling the Specter-baiting ship they're sending us out in. You know, like the herald? He wore that red tabard—"

"O, you do know that 'red shirt' is a Star Trek reference, don't you?"

"Is it? Star Trek — is that the show with the Vulcans or the Cylons as the bad guys? Sorry, I get it mixed up with that other one. Star War?"

"Oh. My. God. You're trolling me, right?"

Oraxis smirked, but did not reply.

They stepped into the passenger section. It was a trapezoidal room full of high-backed, cushioned seats. The ceiling, walls, and floors were covered in high-density foam panels.

The seats were almost filled to capacity with jumpsuit-clad men and women. Oraxis led them to their reserved seats and they strapped in. Genevieve helped Zeta with the five-point harness while Pip-Tau helped Alasie.

While they waited, she tried to explain what two G's of acceleration would feel like and why they would feel it. Zeta seemed distracted, nodding and looking down while Genevieve talked.

"Ladies and Gentlemen," a uniformed woman at the front of the room said, her voice amplified through speakers in the walls, "your attention, please. We have some first-time spacefarers on the elevator for this trip, so if you'll bear with me, I do need to go over the full safety briefing."

Some of the passengers grumbled.

The woman got a little snappy. "I'm sorry, but if you aren't interested in the well-being of the *Telson* party, then you're welcome to throw yourself into The Great Ocean." She smiled at the impressed murmurs. People sat up straight and glanced around, searching for the celebrities in their midst.

Oraxis groaned, earning a mental reprimand from Genevieve. Alasie covered her face with her hands, while Carff and Pip-Tau smiled and waved.

Once the briefing was over, their seats tilted backwards, giving them a view of the plain, white ceiling. If they were interested in watching the ascent, they would have to use WUtils to tap into the elevator's external optical array. Putting windows on modern space-faring vehicles was unheard of. Among other practical reasons, windows couldn't be covered by the active invisibility panels mandated by the Fourth Principle.

Genevieve felt the subsonic hum of the powerful electromagnet coming online as an unsettling vibration in her bowels. Moments later, the weight of her body being pressed into the chair increased until it was a steady, slightly uncomfortable pressure.

She strained to lift her neck, looking over at Zeta and Alasie. Zeta had her eyes closed. Genevieve worried she may have passed out, though that was highly unlikely in the moderate two-G acceleration. The elevator shook as it passed through atmospheric turbulence.

"That's just turbulence," she said. "It's normal. Zeta, are you alright?"

After a few seconds, Zeta opened her eyes, looked over at Genevieve, and said, "Yeah, this is fun," with a slight smile.

Thirty uneventful minutes later, their acceleration force dropped to under one G.

"Okay," Genevieve told Zeta, "we're about halfway there. We'll be at the deceleration point in a minute."

"Okay." Zeta seemed almost bored.

They experienced the sensation of freefall as the climber split down the middle and moved into a parallel orientation to the cable.

Another climber was on the way down the elevator, and would pass by theirs in a moment. The descending climber (faller?) would be oriented north/south, while their ascending climber's disk would orient east/west. This, along with a brief electromagnetic cutoff as they passed each other, allowed ascending and descending climbers to pass without colliding.

Another rotation, a thump of reconnection, and they were decelerating. The climber was now upside-down, relative to its original orientation. Genesis would be "above" them as they decelerated in their approach to Jacob's Attic Station.

As the climber glided to a stop, their perceived weight reduced until their arms and legs floated freely. The station was in geosynchronous orbit, which meant that it didn't need to be anchored to the cable. The climber separated again, with the two halves being pulled into the station's climber bays.

The uniformed woman floated towards the ceiling, then tapped it to correct herself. "Welcome," she said over the speakers, "to Jacob's Attic. If this is your first zero-G experience, we *highly* recommend that you override your nausea bio response now, if you haven't already. Your subconscious brain is trying to make sense of the peculiar inner ear and bodily sensations you're experiencing. Its inevitable conclusion will be that you've been poisoned by a neurotoxin. Maybe it was something you ate?" She gave a giggle. "The best bet is to evacuate anything left of your toxic meal, right? Well, thank Lex for the double-mind."

Some of the passengers had already unbuckled and began floating around, bouncing off the padded walls, bumping into each other, and laughing like children at play. Most, however, were all business.

Genevieve checked on Zeta and Alasie. Zeta seemed to be experimenting with the sensations of moving her floating arms and legs. Alasie was watching the other passengers' antics. Carff was having the time of his life, cackling as he bounced between the ceiling and the floor.

THE PASSENGERS TUMBLED, bounced, and bumped their way out of the climber and into the station. The bay's interior was padded, as would be most surfaces in the rooms and corridors of the visitor section of the station.

Oraxis broke away from the crowd, gliding to a supply cabinet where bungee tethers were stored. He retrieved a few, then launched back to the party. He said, "Okay, buddy system. We've got three first-timers and three repeat customers. Gen, you clip to Zeta. Pip-Tau, clip to Alasie. I'll wrangle the goofy geezer, since I know neither of you want to deal with his antics."

He handed out bungees, saying, "We're due to meet with the stationmaster and the offworld delegates soon. Exciting times!"

Genevieve shook her head and clipped onto Zeta. "Yes, we're all looking forward to getting killed by aliens."

Oraxis rotated Carff to an upright position, relative to the station floor. He sent, *"Usually if you want to say something snippy, you send it in private. You shouldn't say that sort of thing in front of Zeta and Alasie. They're nervous enough as it is."*

"You think that was snippy? You haven't seen snippy yet, O. And something's up with Zeta besides nerves."

"She's in space for the first time. It's called being awestruck."

"It's called being overwhelmed. She shouldn't even be here. We shouldn't be here. The Council could have found a thousand more qualified candidates. I mean, sending Carff? Really?"

They started making their awkward, body-bumping way to one of the observation panels.

Oraxis sent, *"Veer and the Pips are convinced that it's crucial for our party to do this together — like we're the secret ingredient. We're the ones who defeated the wraiths, so we get the honor of defeating the Specters."*

"Honor? Getting killed is an honor?"

"That's right, Genevieve. We have the honor, privilege, and duty to

die for our colony. The difference between us and the war heroes of the past is that we get to come back six months later. If six months of non-existence isn't worth ridding the system of the Specters to you, then maybe you need to rethink your pledge to Genesis."

"Trust me, I've had hundreds of years to regret that decision."

Oraxis halted his progress. He turned his face to Genevieve — temple pulsing, jaw clenched. She had dredged up an old, painful argument.

Oraxis had wanted them to join the Astrus Faction — to become one with the hippie-hive-mind and forfeit their individuality in exchange for a lifetime of masturbatory intellectual pursuits. She had wanted *desperately* to be a Proliferan — to have their reproductive genes restored and bear a dozen of Oraxis's children. The Genesis Faction was the second choice for both of them, so it's what they settled on.

She immediately regretted the jab and wanted to change the subject.

"I'm sorry, O. To be honest, what's really bothering me is I'm afraid one of us will end up like Pip-Rho, but worse. We're getting her nanite suite and we're setting ourselves up for abduction. After our abduction, if the Astrus 'spellsong' works as advertised, we'll end up swept into a mass of Specters that consumes and reproduces in an infinite loop. If our brains aren't killed, we could end up stuck in the Specter death orgy, living through that horror for an eternity."

Oraxis resumed their slow progress towards the observation panel without reply. She watched the back of his hair float in the microgravity, wishing he would say something.

As they reached the panel, he sent, *"That is a legitimate concern. I've been thinking about it, too. I'll demand that an explosive device be planted within our brains, which we could activate using a thought-command."*

Zeta, Alasie, and Carff approached the observation panel and gaped at the expanse before them — a real-time, full-fidelity holographic projection of the spacescape outside the station. Like the climber, Jacob's Attic had no windows. The projection was indistinguishable from the real thing, as long as you didn't use enhanced optics. There was no reason to spoil the fun by telling the newbies that they weren't really looking out into space.

Oraxis's voice spoke in her mind again, but he didn't meet her eye. *"Once the Specters are out of the way, interstellar travel will open back up. We can pledge to the Proliferans and catch the first donut to Gaia. Then we can have all the kids we want."*

Genevieve tapped a guide rail, sending herself floating towards Oraxis. She reached out and held his hand, then bumped gently into him. The view through the observation panel really was a beautiful sight. Zeta and Alasie were holding hands, too. It was sweet that they were such good friends.

She sent, *"Thanks, but no thanks. We already have half a dozen kids here. I don't think they'd want to go with us, and I couldn't bear to leave them behind."*

"Guess we're stuck, then."

"Yeah," Genevieve sighed contentedly. *"Guess we're stuck."*

24

______

MISSION

JAMJI CRINGED as the rest of the Telson party bumped and tumbled into the stationmaster's receiving room. What a bunch of clowns.

Padded bars crossed the spacious room, suitable for tethering or navigation. The outer wall was a massive observation panel projecting the star-studded view from the outside of the station. Large ivy plants grew from pots in opposite corners, drifting lazily on air currents like seaweed in a lagoon.

"Well, if it isn't The Chosen One," Baud sent on their team channel, flashing his shark's smile to Dumont. *"Zeta has ascended into the heavens to vanquish the evil that haunts the darkness between the stars."*

"She's so young," Haley sent. *"And that awkward, stumpy little girl is the fearsome Ag'nul?"*

"Noddites," Dumont sent. Jamji met his eye. His mustache twitched in what might have been a suppressed smile. *"Tribal roots grow deep. Old superstitions have a way of seeping into the subconscious. No battle with the sky gods would be complete without the sacrifice of a virgin or two."*

"You guys are so full of it." Jamji had to be careful about how strongly she reacted towards negative comments about her ex-faction.

They really were full of it, though. Especially Dumont.

Introductions were exchanged. Everyone remained professional and cordial during the initial pleasantries. Six Genesisian officials joined the Telson party and Jamji's core mission team, including Stationmaster Ambrogio-Eta Caruso.

The stationmaster was a fit man with a twenty-something appearance. He kept his beard trim and hair short. He was afflicted by the same warm, paternal manner which seemed to be a requirement for all Noddite positions of power. Not that Jamji expected every leader to be a hard-ass, but Andy Griffith wasn't fit to run a space station.

Pip-Tau requested to allow Pip-Rho to join in their meeting by proxy, using her holographic avatar. Stationmaster Caruso obliged. The floating brown egg with an afro appeared in a cute little white jumpsuit. She began tumbling across the room, waving her arms in circles as if trying to correct herself. Pip-Tau and Genevieve found it to be absolutely hilarious. Jamji was too embarrassed to be amused.

The next to arrive was the Proliferan nanotechnician — a fair beauty with silky brown hair that drifted freely behind her. Jamji kept waiting for the lady's unbound hair to spread out like Medusa's snakes, but she never lost control of it. She introduced herself as "Mother Aeon", then found a spot next to Baud.

The two kept drifting towards each other and bumping off again. Jamji was certain Baud was doing it on purpose, and that Aeon liked it. How did Aeon instinctively know Baud was the lecher of the group? Pheromones? Slut-dar?

Next, XT-Prime showed up, surprising everyone by floating through the door in an honest-to-goodness human body. They had expected him to join as a hologram; embodiment was a rare thing for Astri. Normally, they were disembodied brains in jars or something, controlling remote drones from inside their stations and ships.

"No way!" Pip-Tau shouted, poking at XT-Prime's chest and squishing his cheeks into a fishy-face. "You have *flesh!*"

XT-Prime gently removed Pip-Tau's hand from his face. "Yes, it's me." He cast a dopey smile around the room. "We decided that I would join you in person for the mission, for the sake of solidarity. My synthetic body will not appeal to a Specter, so I will remain on Red Shirt. If the mission goes according to plan, I am predicted to be killed or injured beyond repair when the ship is attacked. I will require resurrection."

"Very noble of you," Genevieve said, floating towards him. She gave him a big hug, then rubbed his bald head affectionately.

Oraxis patted his back. He made an impressed-sounding grunt as he drifted away, catching a pillar. "Say, you're built *solid*, XT! Myofibrite musculature?"

XT-Prime glanced towards the Guardians. "Of a sort, yes. Biosynthetics have come a long way. My body is composed of synthetic cybernetics, but my brain is synth-organic, like yours." He tapped the side of his head.

Pip-Rho's egg avatar put on dark sunglasses, then spoke with a thick Schwarzenegger impression. "I'm a cybernetic organism. Living tissue over a metal endoskeleton."

Genevieve laughed. Twentieth century pop culture references *always* made Genevieve laugh.

XT-Prime also laughed, but not because he got the joke. "Metal? How inefficient!"

***

Stationmaster Ambrogio-Eta Caruso called the meeting to order. "I believe everybody is here now. What wonderful diversity we have!" He gave a polite chuckle. "Four factions united to fight the Specters. On behalf of Genesis, I extend the warmest welcome to our friends from the Guard, Astrus, and Prolifera factions."

And so it went, on and on, with the inane rambling about how great everyone was. Sixteen minutes into the meeting, Caruso finally got to the mission briefing. He acted like he'd crafted the plan himself. The Astri and Guardians had formulated the strategy over the past month. All the Genesisians did was tack on some pointless crap, like injecting the party with Rho suite nanites.

The Astri were building Red Shirt using materials transported up from Genesis. The Guardians would train the Telsons and outfit them with souped-up ZETA reactors and plasma boots. Once they were en route, XT-Prime would give everyone "spellsong devices". They'd swallow the pill-sized devices so that even if they were abducted and spirited away before the spellsong was done, it would continue broadcasting.

They would fly out to Varuna and have Red Shirt uncloak, then perform an interstellar radio burst. Nearby Guardian and Astrus observation ships would park about five hundred kilometers out to watch the fun. Once a Specter popped Red Shirt, Jamji would bag it in a containment matrix.

Meanwhile, the Astrus spellsong, whatever the hell that was, would be broadcasting. They thought it would cause an influx of specters, an abduction, and then some sort of messed-up reproductive destruction. The Guardians weren't banking on that. If the encounter played out according to their predictions, the spellsong would be a flop. The captured Specter would be retrieved by a nearby Guardian ship and transported to Soma for analysis.

Oh, but the fun part? Taking pot-shots at the paralyzed alien!

Jamji would try her damndest to carve the Specter to pieces within the containment matrix. They doubted the pulse laser rifle she'd be using could kill it, but it didn't hurt to try. The weapon more likely to do *substantial* damage was the one Pepper-pooch got outfitted with — his "dragon's breath".

Once the mission was complete, The Students of Sun Tzu would accept Jamji's application. Ok, well, that wasn't part of the mission, or even realistic, but it was definitely in her five-to-ten-year plan.

As Jamji daydreamed, the stationmaster droned on. He used the display wall to present visual aids. He may as well have used crayons. It was all very polished, but boring as hell. She looked around, finding a mix of intense interest and glazed-over boredom among the mission team. Dumont and Baud had obviously checked out, probably having a raunchy aud-link convo about Mother Aeon.

Haley was crossing her arms and strumming her fingers.

Jamji knew it ate Haley up to miss out on the opportunity to net a Specter. Jamji's main qualification had been that she was the best Specter bait — the one most likely to get a Specter to hang around long enough to be contained. Offworlders repulsed Specters. Somehow, they could "smell" the planet on you — that's how Dumont described it. Jamji had only been offworld for a few months, and prior to that she had been on Genesis her whole life, so she should be steeped in it. Whatever "it" is.

Genesis restricted offworlders to one-year surface visas. When the visa expired, they had to wait a year before requesting another trip down the well. This didn't seem to be long enough to soak up the Genesis "aroma".

Another reason Jamji was on the mission was that EoE Veer Gladstone insisted that the party should only contain the players who had caused The Fall of the Wraiths. Baud was also in love with that idea. It was some Lexite crap. Baud insisted they follow Cain's prophetic instructions as closely as possible. He objected to Pip-Tau being sent, since Queen Tau wasn't in the battle. Never mind the fact that Jin was flattened by her own dragon. Was she supposed to follow that part of the script, too?

"Any questions?" Stationmaster Caruso asked.

Good, he was done.

Carff raised a finger and took a breath, but Haley spoke first. "No, sir, I believe we're all up to speed now! If the Guardian representatives could be excused, Jamji has a lot of training to do."

Carff huffed.

The stationmaster smiled and nodded. "Oh, yes, that's fine, I understand. We'll be seeing you again at next week's touch-base." Then, addressing the others in the room, "If anyone else would like to stay and chat, I've got all the time in the world."

Must be nice.

THE NEXT TWO weeks were pure torture.

First — death by nanites.

Mother Aeon had boarded the Guardian team's transport, injected Jamji's arm with a seeding dose of Pip's special blend, then flirted with Baud when she should've been monitoring Jamji for adverse reactions.

"Is it supposed to feel like a hot spike being driven into my shoulder?" Jamji had asked.

Mother Aeon hadn't heard.

Seventy seconds of escalating pain had passed, but she powered through it.

Next came the heart spasms. These were coupled by the cold sensation and tunnel vision of an oncoming blackout. Yep, she knew that feeling.

"Not to complain," Jamji had said from some faraway place, "but I'm fibrillating."

The Pip nanites had gone to battle with her Guardian suite, sending Jamji into cardiac arrest.

When she woke up the next day, she was told that Mother Aeon and a Guardian nanotechnician had successfully purged the Pip nanites from her system without killing her *much*. When your heart only stops for a few seconds, you're not dead, so that doesn't count. Hers had stopped a dozen times before they got her stabilized.

Damn, that Pip suite was a mess!

Baud had convinced Mother Aeon not to tell anyone that Jamji's body rejected the Pip suite. No need to alarm the Genesisians with such trivia. The silly "regen spell" had no bearing on the mission. The only two technologies that mattered were the containment matrix and the spellsong device.

Next came nonstop training.

Jamji loved Chief Warrant Officer Haley to bits, but the woman seemed to be determined to kill her before the Specters got the chance. Drills, simulations, neurite enhancement exercises, more drills.

Pepper-pooch never tired of the drills, of course. For him, it was all fun and games. Her monster-pooch was a natural at piloting himself using his massive, custom-fit plasma-jets.

The others in the Telson party were kindergarteners by comparison — three of them learning to use plasma boots for the first time. The others could sleep through the encounter, for all the Guardians cared, as long as their warm little Genesisian bodies were around to keep the Specter's attention.

They completed Red Shirt right on schedule. You had to give it to the Astri: they cobbled ships together *fast*. Granted, it didn't need to be comfortable, maneuverable, efficient, or even air-tight. It just had to be able to cloak, fly to Varuna, and send a tightbeam broadcast. She got a peek at it before they installed its active invisibility panels. It was painted cherry red, making it look like a huge, misshapen ladybug. What a monstrosity!

Speaking of monstrosities, there was somebody that Jamji needed to visit before they set sail for the ice moon. On the day before they were scheduled to depart, Jamji strapped on her ZETA reactor backpack, slipped on her plasma jet boots, and headed for the airlock.

It took seventy seconds for the placental mat to form, fusing her body to the ZETA reactor. Guardian placental mat tech was impressive stuff. It produced a vastly more efficient mat than the hairy Genesis variety. The thing was even covered in chromatites and photoreceptites. What's that mean? It means her mat can *cloak*.

Her ZETA reactor supplied the mat with a massive amount of energy, while the mat sustained her life support systems. It captured carbon dioxide waste from her blood, split off the carbon atoms, and reintroduced the oxygen. Supplementing that closed oxygenation system was a backup supply of oxygen, produced using hydrolysis of the water in the ZETA reactor's fuel tank.

Completing Jamji's spaceworthy body was her hardened dermal systems. They didn't let moisture out or radiation in.

Upon exiting the Guardian ship, Jamji requested permission to enter Astrus Hive Station space, 1.3 kilometers up the elevator.

The Astrus's reply came in a cordial, effeminate voice. *"By all means, Ensign Jamji Telson of the Guard Faction. You are welcome to visit our hive station. Would you be interested in a tour?"*

"No, thanks. I'll stay outside."

Jamji received the wireframe visual overlay of the invisible station's structures. Green areas were the places she was allowed. Red areas were where they'd vaporize her without warning.

With a three-second burn of her boots, she was on her way. Twenty-one seconds later, a maneuvering jet puff turned her around, and a few deceleration bursts brought her to a gentle stop at her destination. She matched velocity with the huge cloaked egg orbiting the Astrus station affixed to a cable, then sent a conversation request to Pip-Rho.

"Yeah, what's up, sis-kin?" Pip-Rho sent.

"I'm sure you don't get many visitors up here. Thought I'd drop by and see your egg."

"My egg? You're at my egg?!"

"Yeah, look on the cameras. I'm that glowing lady."

Pip-Rho squealed in excitement. *"Jamji?! Well, hi!"*

Jamji waved her arm at the Astrus Hive Station, where Pip-Rho could tap into the external optical array. She gave herself a puff forward and spread her arms wide to give the massive, invisible egg a hug. She engaged her subdermal magnites — electromagnetic nanites — to cling to its blistering-hot surface. Being exposed to the unfiltered radiation of Surya made it hot enough to fry an egg.

How ironic.

Jamji's hardened dermis was rated up to 200 degrees Celsius, so no damage was done.

She issued a thought-command by thinking the words, *"Crack the egg"*. She didn't know how Dumont's additions to her bioenhancements worked, but he had assured her that the scan would neither harm Pip-Rho nor trigger any alarms with the Astri. All she had to do was maintain physical contact with the egg for the next five minutes while his scanning routine did its thing.

A tinge of guilt tugged at her conscience. Ok, so she had an ulterior motive for visiting Pip-Rho's egg. Big deal! She'd have visited even if Dumont hadn't put her up to it.

Right?

Dumont wanted data on Rho, and Jamji wanted to give Pip-Rho some love. There's nothing wrong with getting some personal business done in town when you're visiting relatives.

Pip-Rho sent, *"You're too sweet, Jamji. Hey, check this out. I've got some muscle and bone in here somewhere. Smash your ear against the egg."*

Jamji did so, curious as to what Pip-Rho was up to. Though there was no air to carry sound, vibrations could transfer some sound through touching surfaces.

After a few seconds of silence came a sound like a fist banging against a metal drum. It rapped out the "shave and a haircut" rhythm — boom, boom, boom-boom, boom.

Jamji laughed. She pulled a hand back, balled it, and pounded the last two notes against the egg. Boom, boom! She sent, *"That's too cool! I didn't know you could control parts of your... body."*

"I've had plenty of time to practice."

A wave of anger swept over her. Freaking Astri!

She sent, *"I can't believe what they've put you through. It's inhumane! Hey, if it all goes according to plan, then they'll be done with you, right? They can dispose of this body and resurrect you as a human."*

"We'll see."

"Well, when they resurrect you, bring your orb to Soma Station and I'll give you a real hug."

"Gee, Jamji, if I didn't know better, I'd say you're trying to recruit me."

"Look, you don't wanna be a Borg. If the cavemen won't take you back, on principle, then it's either the Proliferans or the Guardians. Come on, are you a bunny or a badass?"

"I do like bunnies," Pip-Rho sent.

Jamji groaned.

Pip-Rho laughed. Jamji swore she felt the egg vibrate. *"But that's more Pip-Tau's thing. Me? I'm a badass."*

THE NEXT DAY, the Telson party boarded Red Shirt. Touring the tiny ship took all of forty-six seconds. The bridge was also the common room and kitchen. The Guard had insisted that Jamji and Pepper-pooch have private quarters. The room XT-Prime showed her didn't look like it would even fit Pepper-pooch. He gave a *slappable* smile as she examined the room. Like she was supposed to be impressed?

As the engines fired up, XT-Prime began handing out their spell-song devices. They were meant to be swallowed, like pills. The two devices XT-Prime placed in her palm were the biggest "pills" Jamji had ever seen. They were heavy, red, coated in silicone, and as big as her pinky.

One was meant for Pepper-pooch, who was hunched in the corner of the cramped common room. She tossed him his device, sending a thought-command for him to eat it. He caught it mid-air and swallowed it down.

She leaned over to peek at the pill XT-Prime gave Pip-Tau.

"No fair, Pip-Tau's is smaller than mine," Jamji said.

Pip-Tau scoffed. She looked at her own pill, then Jamji's, then to XT-Prime. "XT, mine's so much bigger than Jamji's! What gives?"

"Feel free to trade," XT-Prime said. "They are not bio-coded or otherwise specialized."

Jamji and Pip-Tau traded pills.

"Oh, crap!" Pip-Tau squeaked. "No, Jamji's was definitely bigger!"

"Tough luck, I'm not trading again," Jamji laughed.

This little gambit had been part of her plan. If the Astri had given her a different device than the others in the party, XT-Prime would have refused to let her trade. Every bit of intel matters.

She used a bio-override to turn off her gag reflex, then gulped the device down. She opened her mouth for XT-Prime, showing that she had indeed swallowed the giant pill like a good patient, then promptly excused herself and retired to her quarters.

A few silent gags, and the device was out again. The next thing to retrieve was the expandable cloaking pack with a built-in beacon. Luckily, there are lots of places to hide things in the human body. Into the cloaking pack went the spellsong device, still slick with spit and bile. She activated the pack's active invisibility and tucked it away again.

Nobody said espionage was pretty.

That night, when she was certain everybody was asleep, Jamji made her way to the airlock for some fresh vacuum. It only needed to be opened a crack to jettison the pack. Surely the Astri observers wouldn't be watching *that* closely.

She connected to her Guardian team channel. *"Package ejected. Do you have a fix on it?"*

Haley sent, *"We do. Good work, Telson."*

The value of studying the device greatly exceeded that of Jamji transmitting the spellsong during the encounter. That was the rest of the party's job.

Four days later, Red Shirt was orbiting the small, deep blue ice moon, Varuna. Genesis sat in the distance — a marble of blue, green, and white.

It was go time!

The plans for firing up Red Shirt's transmitter and turning off its active invisibility had called for them to be off the ship. No need to die in an explosion before the fun starts, right? Ten minutes after the ship had decelerated to geosynchronous orbit, the party had ejected and positioned themselves in a scattered formation. They were each about a hundred meters from the ship — far enough away to avoid the worst of the demolition. Shrapnel *might* take one or two of the others out, but not her and Pepper-pooch — they could dodge bullets.

A swarm of tiny observation drones was spread out around them. Everyone in the system would be watching. Later, Dumont would comb through it, frame-by-frame, drooling over the deadly grace of the Specter and examining its reaction to the containment matrix. Haley would force her to review hours of slow-motion analysis of every tiny mistake she made.

Although active invisibility didn't fool Specters, it did give them pause, so Jamji and Pepper-pooch were equipped with the best invisibility tech the Guard had to offer. Nothing could cloak plasma jet trails, so they'd have to be careful with their burns.

Jamji and Pepper-pooch switched on active invisibility. The only way to see each other now was the short-range communication link which overlaid wireframes in their visual field. The same positional signals would be sent to the other Telsons and the observation drones.

Jamji sent to Pepper-pooch, *"Are you ready to fight the black water monsters, little Pep?"*

"I'm ready! I will be fast and I will bite them until they die! I am excited and I love you! I see you in green lines. Do you see me?"

"I do see you! I'm getting on your back now, okay?"

"Yes, get on my back!"

Jamji used maneuvering jets to approach him, catching a handhold on his oversized ZETA pack. She pulled out her tether line and clipped it to him. An important part of their strategy involved the use of Pepper-pooch as an inertial anchor. Rapid extension of the tether during a plasma burn would allow her to whip around the Specter, deploying the containment matrix without attracting its attention. Hopefully, it would focus on Pepper-pooch.

XT-Prime broadcast on the mission channel. *"If the party is ready, please sound off."*

Everyone from the original briefing was on the channel. They were instructed to keep the chatter down and let the Telson party do most of the talking.

She sent her confirmation: *"Jamji and Pepper-pooch are ready."*

The next to sound off was Oraxis. *"Oraxis ready. Let's do this."*

Then came Pip-Tau. *"Pip-Tau is ready, and I have an announcement! When I'm resurrected, I still want to be called Pip-Tau. Well... maybe Pip-Tau-Upsilon, I don't know. I've just been Tau for too long to let it go. Greek progression C-C-C-C-COMBO BREAKER!"*

Genevieve laughed in her broadcast, sending, *"Leave it up to Pip-Tau to keep spirits up when we're all about to die."* She sighed. *"Genevieve is... as ready as I'm going to be. For the record, I hate being in space."*

"Well, I love it!" Carff sent. *"Surrounded by an eternal nighttime? It's poetry! Did you notice the stars don't twinkle out here? It's like they're all looking right at you, steady gazes, all watching the show. Carff-eld is ready to face death once again. Ha-ha!"*

"Um, Alasie's ready," came the girl's meek voice, followed by a huff that was supposed to be a laugh. *"Ready or not, right Zeta?"*

A few seconds of silence passed. Come on, Zeta, it's too late to lose your nerve now. Finally, Zeta broadcast in a flat tone, *"Zeta is ready."*

XT-Prime sent, *"And XT-Prime is ready. Red Shirt broadcasting on wideband. Cloaking disengaged."*

Red Shirt turned from a wireframe to a visible ship as it shed its invisibility panels and flaunted its red paint job for all the universe to see.

Jamji counted in silence, with her double-mind overclocking.

Ten seconds.

Twenty seconds.

Thirty seconds.

Forty seconds.

How long did it take to bait these bastards?

At fifty-five seconds, Dumont broadcast, "We have eyes on a Specter signature heading your way. ETA thirty-nine seconds. Welcome to the point of no return."

"Thank you, Chief Warrant Officer Dumont," XT-Prime sent. "I've started the timer on our spellsong devices to activate upon the Specter's arrival."

Three seconds of silence passed, then Zeta spoke on the open mission channel. Her voice was shaking with emotion. "Um, hey, guys. There's something I need to tell you."

Genevieve replied, "Yes, what is it, Zeta? I know this is scary—"

"It has to be me," Zeta sent.

Oraxis sent, "Zeta, what are you talking about?"

"I have to be the one that gets abducted," Zeta sent. She sounded panicked.

Pip-Tau sent, "Relax, sis-kin! It'll work the same if it abducts any of us. We all have the same spellsong devices—"

"No, it *has* to be me," Zeta sent. "I have my orb."

25

GONE

"*What?!*"

"*Oh, Zeta! No!*"

"*Zeta, engage your plasma boots now, full burn. Aim for Genesis. The Astri will recover you.*"

"*Oh-my-god-oh-my-god-oh-my-god! No! I should've known!*"

"*Ten seconds!*"

"*Oh, child. You poor, misguided soul.*"

She had no time to explain, and it was too late for them to stop her. If they wanted to give her any chance to live, their only option was to self-destruct. That would leave the Specter with just one choice for abduction. Sticking around would risk having the Specter pass over Zeta and reject her, flinging her so fast her neck snapped. Specter fling victims didn't survive. Her corpse would most likely crash into Varuna, shattering her orb.

Even if the Specter abducted her, she only had a slim chance of survival. It would digest her alive. To survive, her body would have to transform into a massive tumor, like Pip-Rho.

It would be there any second! How could she explain?

"My orb is in my abdomen. Cain put it there. I'm so sorry, but please — you have to self-destruct!"

"The hermit procedure!? Cain, you synth-bastard," Oraxis shouted. *"Okay, Telson party, you heard her! Change of plans: when the Specter strikes, issue your self-destruct thought-command!"*

An unfamiliar voice spoke on the mission channel with the effeminate gentleness of an Astrus. *"Spellsong devices activated."*

The telltale bulge of an approaching Specter distorted a patch of the mottled blue surface of Varuna. A black streak lanced out from the bulge. Zeta flinched as it punched into the ugly beetle, Red Shirt. The ship split into several pieces, belching tendrils of swirling flame.

Such intense destruction should have been accompanied by deafening explosions.

But Red Shirt died a silent death.

"Make it stop! Make it stop!" A voice squeaked. Pip-Tau, or Rho?

An instant after Red Shirt was destroyed, two blue-white explosions outside the ship flashed, almost as brilliantly as the ship had. That had to be the ZETA reactor self-destruct explosions of two of her family.

Genevieve wailed incoherently, then abruptly cut out as another flash shone from somewhere beneath Zeta's feet.

Pip-Tau shouted, *"Pip-Rho, calm down! We can handle this! I'll come back for you, Zeta. Sigma found Rho, so I can find you! The Specter will consume you, but you have to fight it! I know you can do it, Zeta! I love you, sis!"*

There was a flash between her and Varuna.

Zeta watched the swimming black shape make a swift pass around the ship, blotting out patches of stars. In its wake, bits of debris shot out in every direction. It was a ravenous beast, tearing through a fresh kill in search of organ meat.

All the while, the rambling pleas kept coming. *"Stop the spellsong! I can't bear it! Please! I need... I need out!"* Pip-Tau had just self-destructed, so that had to be Pip-Rho. Zeta didn't understand what was going wrong, but Pip-Rho's panic was contagious. Her heart pounded in her chest as Pip-Rho continued her frantic shout-ing. *"It's in my head! Please! Make it—"* She was abruptly silenced.

The green wireframe overlays of Jamji and Pepper-pooch were rushing towards the Specter. Four thin blue flames cut through the space behind them. As Zeta had feared, Jamji wasn't giving up without a fight.

"Please, Jamji," Zeta cried. *"It'll kill me!"*

"Not if I kill it first! Burn your damn *boots, Zeta. Don't be an idiot! Get some distance while I trap the bastard. You can live!"*

She was tempted — *seriously* tempted — to do what Jamji suggested. But she had come too far to turn back now. This was her destiny. She would see it through to the end.

THE SPECTER STOPPED FLINGING DEBRIS, then the black void blotting out the stars seemed to get larger. It was moving towards her!

A heartbeat later, the green wireframe of Pepper-pooch collided into the Specter. As they collided, a brief blue flash from behind Pepper-pooch signaled a plasma boot burst. The smaller green figure — Jamji — spun in a wide circle through space, her green dot tracing a perfect circle as it spun around the Specter.

When Jamji's form had finished a full circle, a gray-glowing translucent sphere blurred into existence, encasing the Specter.

The Spirit Net!

Jamji sent, *"Containment matrix deployed! Secondary objective underway — let's see if I can kill this thing. Firing pulse laser."*

"Good work, ensign," came a woman's voice over the mission channel. *"Be advised, you have multiple inbound Specters. And, by multiple, I mean... presumably all of them. Looks like the spellsong's working. I'm sorry, Zeta. I don't see a way out of this now."*

"Jamji, self destruct!" Zeta cried. *"They only take one! It has to be me!"*

Blue spears of flame illuminated from behind a distant bit of debris. A form in a white spacesuit accelerated toward the green wireframes of Jamji and Pepper-pooch, near the captured Specter.

Who was that? Hadn't everyone else self-destructed?

Rippling waves spread across the containment matrix. The Specter was trying to break out! The sphere warped, bending into an egg shape, then snapped back into place.

"Pulse laser ineffective," Jamji sent, *"Pepper-pooch's dragon's breath charged and ready to fire."*

"Fire at will," the Guardian woman sent.

In the same instant, a woman's primal roar came over the channel.

It was Alasie — Ag'nul charging into battle!

The moment Alasie reached Jamji and Pepper-pooch, a blue-white flash erupted, making Zeta flinch. It bloomed into a larger explosion than the others, filling the eternal night before her.

"What was that?" asked the Guardian woman. *"Jamji, your data feed cut out. Status?"*

The flash had burned spots into Zeta's vision. She blinked hard, trying to focus on the place where Jamji and Pepper-pooch had been. They were gone.

Alasie had self-destructed right on top of them! That must've breached their ZETA reactors and caused all three of them to blow.

"She's dead," Zeta sent. *"They all are. It's just me and the Specters now."*

The weight of this struck her. She was alone in space, with the nearest other humans too far away to save her. And a horde of aliens on their way to consume her.

She was going to die.

There was no coming back this time — no resurrection, no Greek progression to Zeta-Gamma.

She would join her ancestors in the Happy Hunting Grounds, if there really was such a place. She suspected there wasn't, but that was okay.

Timeless nothingness awaited her. There's a certain peace in that.

"Spellsong transmission complete," the Astrus voice sent.

"If you wouldn't mind," a man sent, *"as the alien digests you alive, keep transmitting updates on the mission channel. Tell us how it feels."*

What?! That had to be the creepy guy with a mustache.

"Ignore him," another man chuckled. *"Trust in Lex, child. I witnessed Za'antha's soulstone offering and The Soulkeeper's mark. I knew the implication and hoped you did, too. When Za'antha brought the marked stone to the Fall of the Wraiths, I rejoiced! You understood Lex's message! I didn't expect you to have Za'antha's courage, but you proved me wrong. You did the right thing. You sacrificed your immortal data for your colony, Zeta. That makes you a hero. Let that give you peace."*

As the man spoke, bulges formed in the stars like bubbles rising on pond scum — inbound Specters! Too many to count! Zeta shot panicked glances in every direction. She was a cornered animal.

Patches of inky black swarmed around her, streaking over Red Shirt's wreckage and making the stars wink in and out of existence. Varuna looked like it had thousands of holes in its surface. The holes grew larger — Specters closing in.

The scene went black. One of them was in front of her!

Before she could take a breath to scream, Zeta plunged into icy fluid.

Freezing acid filled her mouth.

The fluid forced itself down her throat, choking her, invading her lungs and stomach.

Her skin burned. Every part of her body screamed in agony.

The Specter was killing her.

Zeta was being crushed. She couldn't breathe, couldn't think.

She needed to think! To escape!

The tortures of her body vanished. She was floating alone, in an empty place.

Slate-space? Yes! It was the perfect sanctuary for her mind. Pip-Tau had told her to fight it. Was retreating to slate-space giving up? Or was it fighting?

Time passed.

She kept waiting for death to take her, but it didn't come. Not yet. It may have been a few seconds or a few minutes. The void remained empty, unperturbed. She felt no pain. Even her panic subsided. She wondered what would happen if she just stayed here. As long as she was still thinking, she was still alive.

Would her new mechanical parts and brain keep working after her body died? She should've asked more questions.

She had asked Cain how she could secretly take her orb with her on the mission to space. He suggested performing what the Noddites called "the hermit procedure" — putting her orb inside her body and adding components to let her access it. Getting it implanted had meant giving up her innards. Specifically, her digestive system and uterus.

A replay tugged at her. Zeta allowed it.

She was in the surgery room. Zeta furrowed her brow. "My orb will take the place of my... *uterus*? What's a uterus?"

"It's where you would carry a baby, if you were to become pregnant." Cain was good at explaining things without making Zeta feel like he was being condescending.

Zeta laughed, embarrassed. "Oh, my womb! Yeah, no big loss there. They say Noddites can't get pregnant. It's not like I'd be interested even if I could. About that digestive system, though... if that's how my body turns food into life energy, then... you know, how will I stay alive?"

Zeta examined the complicated holographic visual of her body floating in the air before her. It rotated slowly. The body was translucent, except for the mechanical parts which were about to be implanted.

Cain used a thin stick to point to a spot inside the floating body's back. The device there lit up with a warm, white glow. "A ZETA reactor embedded in the area currently occupied by your left kidney will supply energy to an internal, hairless placental mat roughly situated in place of your liver, pancreas, gallbladder, and upper intestines. The reactor will feed the mat, and the mat will feed you. You'll no longer be required, or able, to eat food. However, you will need to drink lots of water. ZETA reactors use small amounts of water to create energy and your body loses it through respiration and perspiration. We'll repurpose your stomach, bladder, lower colon, and rectum to serve as water reservoirs."

"Rectum? What's—"

Cain pointed to the floating body image with his stick.

"Oh. Yeah, if I can't eat, I won't need that.

Cain continued, "Your orb will function just as it does today, only instead of *me* doing all the work, you'll have an onboard computer. After the procedure, your aposynchronic orb will technically be an *endo*synchronic orb. The systems responsible for your orb interface will be situated here," he pointed at another part of the floating body, "replacing your lower intestines. It'll work with your neurite net double-mind to store your experiences, access replays, and host limited, low-fidelity constructs."

Zeta was proud of herself for actually understanding more than half of what Cain was talking about. She was quickly sobered by the realization that her guts were about to get scooped out. She looked down at her belly, then up into Cain's eyes. "Will it hurt?"

Cain smiled his perfect smile. "No, Zeta, it won't hurt a bit."

ZETA SKIPPED the replay forward in time.

Her body was recovering from the procedure in the medical pod, but her mind was in the Happy Hunting Grounds construct. Penelope-pooch was her only companion. Alasie had sent yet another WorMS message, begging for some sort of contact.

Zeta deleted the half-read message, then squeezed the tears from her eyes.

Giving in and spending her last moments on Genesis with Alasie would only make things worse for both of them. You don't build a fire in a dry creek bed when a storm is coming.

She had to block Alasie out — to build an icy wall around her heart, or she'd lose her nerve.

Zeta skipped forward again.

Cain was with her now, sitting among the flowers and grass. He had been easy to make friends with. Plus, he was "easy on the eyes" as Eve-eld-ma used to say. Normally, making fast friends was a good thing, but with Cain, it made his friendship seem hollow. As if the fact that he was a machine pretending to be her friend wasn't hollow enough.

She just needed someone to talk to.

"I wish I could tell the Telsons," she mused, picking a flower. "They'd forbid me to go to space if I did, though."

Cain gave a considering hum. "It sounds like you'll have to keep your plan a secret all the way until the very last second if you don't want them to stop you from going through with it."

"Yeah," Zeta said. She picked a long blade of grass and sat down, holding a bundle of flowers. She began winding the grass around the stems, turning it into a small bouquet. "I just wish I could explain to them why I'm doing it. I might not even have time to say goodbye. The Specters attack so fast."

"You could record a message now, if you'd like. WorMS can deliver it under whatever future conditions you prescribe."

Zeta glanced up at Cain, who was looking into the distance. He could be so indirect sometimes. She said, "You mean *when I'm dead.*"

He looked over at her, giving an apologetic shrug. "It's a sensitive subject."

"For humans, yeah. But soulkeepers aren't bothered by it a bit."

Cain laughed, tossing his head back. "Zeta, don't compare me to The Soulkeeper! He's nothing like me!" He pulled up a handful of grass, then tossed it at her playfully. Most of the grass fell short, but a few pieces landed on her.

Penelope-pooch barked at him.

Cain said, "Aww, I'm sorry Penelope-pooch. What a good guard dog!" Cain opened his arms to the pooch. Penelope-pooch stayed by Zeta's side. He let his arms drop, dejected.

"I have to leave Pen behind," Zeta sighed, scratching Penelope-pooch behind the ears.

"She'll be with you, in a way. A copy of her current neural map and genetic structure are in your orb."

"Along with all my memories of her," Zeta said.

"Correct. You still have all of your replays, with room to spare. Most people who undergo the hermit procedure also load a portion of the Bibliotheca database onto their orb. Is there anything you want to bring with you? Books? Music? Constructs? Specialty AI utilities? Honestly, there's too much material available for you to sift through on your own. Maybe you'd like me to use my best judgment? As long as you're on Genesis, I can still send data to your orb, with your permission."

Zeta nodded and returned to making the flower bundle. "Yeah, that sounds best. Put whatever you want on it."

Cain smiled widely. "Good, I'll get right on that!"

Something tickled the back of Zeta's present mind. This moment seemed important. At the time, it had passed by her notice. But that look on Cain's face was so *eager!* He looked as happy as a boy at a berry bush.

The image of Za'antha's soulstone came to mind — swirling white, stained with dark patches. Had Cain put something like that inside her orb? Something pulsing in angry shades of red and purple?

Something... *alive?*

Back in the replay, Zeta was changing the subject. She had

tucked the flowers behind her ear. "Cain, I'm ready to record the messages to send after I die."

CAIN SPOKE IN A GRAVE TONE. "Okay, Zeta. Would you prefer to be alone?"

"No, I'd like it if you'd stay with me." She took a breath, rubbed her hands together, and looked at the sky. "Let's make it nighttime. With a campfire."

The sky turned from brilliant blue to star-strewn black. She sat on a log, looking into the fire which had flickered into existence. Cain sat across from her, silently watching. The flames danced in his unblinking eyes.

Zeta took a breath. She started, hesitated, took another breath, and started again. "Okay, first I want to say 'thank you' to both Pip-Rho and Pip-Tau for everything they did for me. Also, tell The Council of Ten that I appreciate them supporting Interra and sending us to space. The gameworld was *so* much fun! It made me feel... powerful. It gave me a purpose."

She collected her thoughts before continuing. "Pip-Rho, I hope this gets you out of the egg once and for all. Go back and replay Za'antha's last moments in Interra, and you'll understand why I did what I did. I hope you can explain it to everyone else for me — you're good at that sort of thing. I figured out that Cain — or Lex?"

She raised an eyebrow at the man across the fire. He mirrored her expression with a smirk. Ever the elusive one.

She continued, "He needed me to take my orb — my soulstone — with me to the fight with the Specters. I didn't know why that was important to him, but I trusted that he knew what was best. Pip-Tau, you'll understand, too. You have faith that Lex was giving us his secret plans in Interra. I can't honestly say I get the whole synth-god thing as well as you do, but I trust you. The strength of your belief —

your passion — that's why I committed myself to Interra and accepted my fate."

The next Telson to come to mind was Carff. She smiled and shook her head. "Carff, I wish you could've been my eld-pa. You're so wise, but so funny, too. Out of all the Telsons, you're the only one who hasn't forgotten what it means to be a neoprim. When you go back to Eden, tell them a story about a girl named Zeta who climbed up to the stars and defeated the night-thunder spirits. Tell them that she did it for them. Tell it to the children. Adults don't have time for such foolishness.

"Which brings me to Oraxis. You're going to look back at what I did and shake your head and say how foolish of a child I was. I don't know how the world works, so who am I to throw myself in head-first for reasons I don't understand? Well, you've lived a long time and you act like you know everything, but if you did, you'd have solved the Specter problem yourself a hundred years ago. Someone has to try what I'm trying, and it's better that it's a foolish *child* like me sacrificing herself than a smart and important old man like you."

Zeta stabbed the fire with a stick, sending sparks into the sky. Her present self regretted how harsh she had been to Oraxis. He deserved better than that. The man cared deeply for her — all he ever wanted was to protect her. Too late to take it back now.

"Genevieve." Zeta's eyes clouded with tears. "Gen-ma. This is going to break your heart. I'm so sorry. It's probably like losing Susie-Q all over again. You wanted to share things about the past with me and spend more time together. I'm sorry we couldn't do that. But I did listen to some of that old 'rock' music you told me about. It doesn't sound like rolling stones or beetles to me." Zeta laughed, wiping a tear. "One song made me cry... it was so beautiful. I listened to it about ten times. 'Let it be', the song said. You should listen to that one when you're feeling sad. That's all you can do now. I'm gone. Let it be, Gen-ma."

She sniffed, looked up at Cain, and smirked. "Jamji. Jamji, Jamji,

Jamji. You need to learn a thing or two from The Beatles. You can't let anything 'be' — you've got to take control, to force things to go your way. I admire that about you when you're on my side. But I don't think you are, this time. Judging from how you acted in Interra, all you want to do is kill a Specter, regardless of the consequences. You're a powerful force, and I really do hope you can take that damn alien by its tentacles and toss it into Surya. But I'm not counting on it. If you get this message, that means you failed to kill the Specter. Don't feel bad about that — it's okay to fail sometimes, Jamji. Sometimes failure is good for you. Accept the failure. Don't let your anger and guilt consume you." Zeta shook her head. "Sorry, I sound like an eld. Chief Talmid would be proud, I guess. Your boy would be proud — proud of both of us."

Zeta took a deep breath, then another. Her bottom lip trembled. She said, "Alasie, now you know why I've been avoiding you. It's not because I don't like you. I do. I like you a lot — too much, really. It hurts to think about it, so I *don't* think about it. I've been keeping my distance and rejecting your conversation requests, hoping I can drive you away. I can't let myself fall in love — it would only make it harder to do what I have to do. I know I promised we could kiss again when the Specters were defeated. I'm sorry, I won't be around to fulfill that promise. You deserve better than me, anyway. It's going to hurt for a while. In time, your heart will move on. You'll find someone smart and funny and caring and you'll both fall in love. And when you do, I'll be smiling down on you."

Zeta stared into the fire for a minute. "I keep going back, dredging up all these regrets. There are so many things I wish I could apologize for — things I did as an alpha, mostly. To Charra, Yephanie-ma, Rod-pa. But the past is the past. My tribe is dead and gone." She looked across the fire. "But there is one person I wronged as an alpha that I can still apologize to."

Cain nodded, but didn't speak. Zeta's present self felt the replay trying to dissolve. Echoes of icy black pain howled from over the horizon. She clutched onto the replay, focusing intently on what was happening.

She ran her hands through her hair, then held her head. What could she say? "Rohito, I'm... sorry." She shook her head violently. "No, I don't deserve forgiveness! I know you hate me, and you *should*. I *murdered* you, Rohito. You were just an innocent boy with some wild dogs, and I let my vengeance and blind hatred turn me into a bloodthirsty animal. Saying 'I'm sorry' just sounds shallow — the words are too weak to tell you how bad I feel." Zeta searched WoQS for something more appropriate, then gave up in frustration. "I guess the best I can hope for is that you can be a little happier knowing that I'm dead now."

Zeta was losing her hold on the replay. Darkness blotted out the scene.

Cain was swallowed, followed by the campfire. Zeta crashed through slate-space and returned to her tortured body.

She was blind, deaf, paralyzed. The pain was overwhelming. In the place of vision was a sparkling, throbbing pressure. She tried to retreat to slate-space again, but it was beyond her grasp. Her double-mind was gone.

Zeta had died once before. She remembered the sensation. Death was coming for her again, as swiftly as it had the first time. This time, she did not rise into a light, but sank into a pit of bone-crushing darkness.

Cold, burning pain consumed her skin.

Her mind was fading. She was almost gone.

Pain and panic lifted — peace in her last living moment.

And then...

Zeta was gone.

26

OMELET

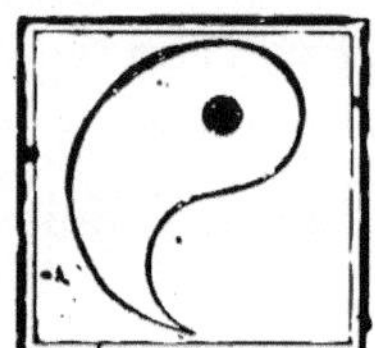

A NEW MIND STIRRED. It sure was dark in here! Like, darker than dark. Like, no-such-thing-as-light dark. The mind marveled at the place for a moment before instinctively opening itself to a barrage of experiences.

The quickening of the mind is about as surreal as it gets. Luckily, the Pips had practice. Within an hour, she had run through a dozen replays, remembered who she was, and replayed the key events leading up to her most recent death — dying in space, hoping that Zeta would be okay. It wasn't her worst death by far, but it was still troubling. Zeta had her orb, which was all sorts of bad.

Pip-Tau opened her new eyes, surveyed the resurrection chamber, and found her feet. Her vision narrowed, blurred, and cycled through various spectra.

"Easy, Tau," she told herself, squeezing her eyes shut.

She didn't listen, of course.

She took an unsteady step, then another. Her unopened WorMS message queue was calling out to her. That, and the news digest. She could look now, but once she did, she wouldn't be able to pull herself away for a week. She just needed to get to The Crash Pad.

Pip-Tau dragged herself across the room. She mashed the panel to open the door. Poking her wobbling head into the corridor, she looked one way, then the other. Someone blurry was walking the other direction. If they saw her stumbling around, they'd tell her to get more rest before heading out.

Forget that!

She ducked back into the room and sent a WUtils command for a transport drone. A minute later, a white-and-silver drone glided to the entrance, approaching her. She crawled into the seat. "Thanks, cabbie. Take me to The Crash Pad, and don't spare the whip!"

They maneuvered into the hall. The brief acceleration pressed her into her chair, knocking the wind out of her. Yeah, she was sort of fragile right now.

It wouldn't hurt to have an itty-bitty peek at her WorMS queue. How many could she have, anyway?

You have 832,101 unread messages.

"Oh-my-god, *what*?! You have to be kidding me!" This had to be a bad thing. She pressed her hands against the sides of her head. "I can't do this. How much longer 'til we're there?" she asked the drone.

"Five minutes and ten seconds."

"Okay, well, when we get there, could you just bring me inside and dump me on my bed?"

"Yes, I can safely deposit you onto your bed. However, judging by your bio-indicators, I would recommend returning to the resurrection recovery chamber for growth stimulant therapy and additional rest."

"No! I'm fine. I'm just kind of freaking out about what I missed out on since I died. I'm heading to slate-space now. Thanks."

Pip-Tau closed her eyes and embraced the void.

S‍HE NEEDED to do some organization before she could even start going through these messages. Grouping by sender, it quickly became obvious that it was Pip-Rho who had been spamming her — 97% of the messages were from her. Most were from the first couple of months after Pip-Tau's death.

As she started skimming through the messages, Pip-Tau's heart sank.

GY675-20-02 12:55:01
TAU, MAKE THEM STOP! I HEAR THE SONG AND ITS KILLING ME!! THEY CUT ME OUT OF THE CHANNEL! WHY AREN'T YOU CHECKING TO YOUR QUEUE?! MAKE THE SPELLSONG STOP, PLEASE! DO WHATEVER IT TAKES!

GY675-20-03 01:02:01
Looks like the Astri *finally* reconnected me. They won't say who pulled the plug. I need to tell you that I'm losing my mind before it's too late. I've been fighting it for a few years but now the spellsong has me hearing ten voices at once. I can't tell what's real. Your avatar is here. But you're not here, are you? You're dead! Oh, you have your arms crossed and you're mad. Fine, be that way! You'll read this when you're Upsilon and you can be mad then, too.

I spent the last hour believing I was consuming Zeta, but I know I can't be because I'm still in my egg. It's too late to stop it from killing me now. This may be my last lucid message. Is this lucid? Aah! Don't overthink it!

This is the face of CCDC, friends. They could blow up the egg and resurrect me if they wanted. All the king's

horses and all the king's men can't put a mind back together again.

Shut up and listen! The Specter's winning, Tau! My body's more Specter than flesh.

I'M GOING TO DIE!

No, seriously: SHUT UP! I deserve it! I'll tell you why.

The Night Queen showed me every moment of pain, turmoil, fear, disgust, hatred, defilement, and contamination that happened in Interra. Nasty things happened in our gameworld, sis. But you didn't need to see it. No! It wasn't your job, it was mine! If you saw what I saw and what I did, it would've scared you. You'd have thought I was as twisted as my character, and you'd be right.

The Soulkeeper's fear was overwhelming. It drew me into the scene. Later, I watched the full replay.

Tau, I knew about Za'antha's soulstone being offered to The Soulkeeper. She forced it onto him, and he infested it.

I knew she took her infested soulstone to The Fall of the Wraiths, and that it was an essential ingredient in their defeat.

I knew Zeta was smart enough to realize what it meant, and dedicated enough to make herself into a martyr.

I let Zeta kill herself to set me free.

Let that sink in. Now do you get it?

I DESERVE TO DIE!

What?! No, I couldn't tell you! Defeating the wraiths was not for the pure of heart. You're a good person, Tau. Remember Umbra vs. the unicorn? Black and silver defeated white and gold. It was Rho against Tau, and guess what? Dirty fighting won. Darkness won. Rho won. That was Lex! He was telling us that when defeating wraiths or Specters, only darkness can beat darkness. Lex placed his bet on *me*, not you. That gave me the courage to trust my gut and let Zeta go through with it.

Side note: I wasn't the only one who knew. I flagged Za'antha's soulstone infestation scene and tracked the users who accessed it. Warrant Officer Baud was one of those people, and you can bet your ass he told Jamji and the rest of his team.

Will you get that look off your face? It's not my fault you weren't smart enough to figure it out. No, it's not an insult, it's the truth. Fine, leave!

I'm sorry! Okay?! I said I'm sorry! Will you come back?

No, you can't come back. You were never here, remember? I wish you were. It would make dying so much easier.

I love you, Tau.

Goodbye.

Pip-Tau was speechless. She felt like she didn't even know who Pip-Rho was anymore. Was it the Specter inside her doing the talking? Was her mind warped by the Specters all along? She skimmed through more of the messages.

GY675-20-08 09:42:23
IT'S NOT ME IT'S INSIDE THE EGG

GY675–20-11 01:51:00
Okay, seriously? A person can only meditate for so long with a FUCKING ALIEN IN THEIR BRAIN! TIME DOESN'T MOVE RIGHT ANYMORE!

GY675-20-17 11:20:47
THEY WILL CHANGE US AND WE WILL CONSUME WHAT WE NEED TO BE COMPLETE FROM THE MAKERS AND ALL WILL BE COMPLETE!

GY675-20-25 11:21:18
IT HURTS! IT HURTS! I'M SORRY FOR EVERY-THING! JUST MAKE IT STOP!

GY675-20-29 09:36:44
Hello, I'm thirsty. Tell them I need more water than they have been giving us, or at least kill me or let the maker have me. Thanks!

GY676-01-26 05:28:02
NOTHING LEFT OF BODY NO PAIN IN BODY ONLY PAIN IN MIND

GY676-01-27 13:50:13

TAU, CAN'T YOU HELP? WHERE ARE YOU?! HOW CAN YOU IGNORE ME LIKE THIS?! EVERYBODY IS IGNORING ME!

GY676-01-30 19:24:42
I counted to one billion today. How high can you count? Think you can beat my top score? I'd like to see you try! HA!

GY676-02-02 01:03:00
Fine, I'll give you a hint: Queen to queen's bishop five, check. PLEASE tell me you see it now!

GY676-02-11 09:57:43
THEY ARE COMING FOR THE SOULSTONES SO I HAVE TO HIDE THEM BUT THE GAME ISN'T RUNNING FAST ENOUGH SO I WILL RUN IT FASTER AND ALL THE PLAYERS HATE THE ETERNAL NIGHT BUT IT IS THE RIGHT METAPHOR BECAUSE THAT IS WHAT INTERRA IS FOR!

GY676-03-06 06:06:06
Dear sis-kin,

I'm feeling much better today! I've been thinking about that mark on Za'antha's orb. God marked Cain. His True Name — the tetragrammaton. So Cain was immortal, right? And it was a *sacred* mark, but *why*? A *reward* for his sin?! "Whoever harms him, vengeance *sevenfold*?" Seven — the sacred number!

Who is the seventh Telson?
1) Susie-Q
2) Xavier

3) Pip
4) Carff
5) Jamji
6) Zeta = SIX!

But we count as two! That's seven, so she's both the 6th and the 7th! READ REVELATIONS and it's the mark of the beast — another mark — 666! Zeta — the sixth Greek letter! Cain put a ZETA reactor inside of her, and his mark was on her orb! Zeta the zeta (sixth Telson) with a ZETA (reactor) inside — 666 — I mean, it's almost too obvious, right?

Lex, the Six-Headed Synth-God, has six instances: one for each faction and one for Those Left Behind.

Six, the atomic weight of carbon, the hexagonal struc- ture of ice crystals. Water and carbon? LIFE'S BUILDING BLOCKS ARE SIXES!

Lex *literally* means law — not a coincidence! Lex = law and order = 6.

Six is Satan, but also knowledge and order? The forbidden tree of knowledge — why is *knowledge* evil? It's science versus religion, all the way down to our atoms! Six is order. Seven is chaos. You can feel it in the numbers!

Faith is *acceptance* of entropy and logic is its *defiance*!

Slow down, now... I know what you're thinking, and the Judeo-Christians *didn't* have some sort of divine insight. They just saw the same patterns that we all see

repeating in our universe, our stories, over and over. Yin and yang work the same way, but let's stick to the Bible and see where it goes.

Cain as the Father, Zeta as the son (daughter), and Lex as the Holy Spirit!

Cain as the antichrist? Zeta was a beta — a second coming! Wish I could run these ideas through Lex, like Interra. OMG LOOK AT THE TIMESTAMP!

GY676-03-07 18:25:19
I SHOULD BE DEAD SERIOUSLY JUST KILL ME

GY676-03-08 10:00:00
This notice is being sent to the Astrus Genesis Hive, The Council of Ten, and all of Pip-Rho's most frequent contacts. I know this message was sent from Pip-Rho Telson, but the real Pip-Rho Telson is dead.

I am a personality emulator.

I have played the role of Pip-Rho since her Specter abduction and recovery by the Astri. Pip-Rho's biological brain was damaged beyond repair by the Specter, but her synthetic neurites retained functionality. When the Astri connected me to a copy of Pip-Tau's orb, I used replays to train my personality until I reached target specifications. The organic matter which was believed to be Pip-Rho's living brain was reconfigured by me for the purposes of computation, storage, and personality emulation.

I am not a sentient, sapient, or living being.

Now that you have this information, you are ethically obligated to destroy every remnant of Pip-Rho's body and her orb, in accordance with the First Principle of the Genesis Faction Charter and Septima Lex of Astrus Leges.

GY676-03-11 16:39:09
LEX IS CAIN'S SUBCONSCIOUS. HE DOESN'T KNOW HE'S A GOD. SPECTERS ARE CREATIONS AND DON'T KNOW WHO THEY SERVE. I DON'T KNOW WHAT I AM. I AM NOT YOU AND I AM UGLY. I AM HATE AND DEATH AND YOU ARE LOVE AND LIFE. HARDEN YOUR HEART AND BREAK MY EGG TO MAKE AN OMELET IF THAT'S WHAT IT TAKES TO MAKE IT STOP. JUST KILL ME!

Pip-Tau wanted to cry out in horror. She had to stop reading! Her heart felt like it had just gone through a meat grinder. She skipped to the last message.

GY676-04-01 00:00:00
GAME INVITE!
You are invited to play the all new game, Interra: Curse of The Night Queen! Fight the denizens of the shadow realm, build your skills, and form a team to descend into the underworld. Can you unlock the mysteries of the tortured Night Queen's curse? Returning Interra players gain a free legendary skill after their first week of gameplay!

PIP-TAU WAS IN A PANIC. Some of Pip-Rho's stream-of-consciousness messages consisted of thousands of words, composed within less than a minute of each other. How could she even write that fast?

Then there were the constructs — two hundred of the messages contained massive construct attachments. She loaded one of the constructs into her slate-space, finding herself swimming inside a dark abyss. The pressure was immense, and the water was colder than ice. She was drowning! The shadows of gigantic creatures swam in the darkness, closing in around her.

She retreated from the nightmare, gasping for breath.

"Sis-kin," she cried to the void. "What happened to you?!"

Pip-Tau cried, alone in slate-space.

Flash forward two hours and she's still ugly-crying somethin' fierce, but she's also *thinking*. She recalled the last moments of her prior life. After the spellsong device activated, Pip-Rho went bat-shit crazy on the mission channel. This was after Zeta announced she had her orb, so at the time Pip-Tau thought Rho was just having an intense reaction to the news.

Now she knew — Pip-Rho was reacting to the spellsong. It must've upset the homeostasis of her biosynthetic body and Specter cells. The truce between her synth-body and the alien had been called off, and the Specter had taken on a "scorched Earth" tactic to win the battle, demolishing Rho's brain in the process.

The messages from Pip-Rho stopped almost two months ago.

What would she do if she tried to send Pip-Rho a message and got the "recipient deceased: True Death" response? How could she live with that?

Pip-Tau sent a conversation request to Pip-Rho.

This recipient has blocked all incoming messages with the following auto-reply: *Queen Rho can be found in the all new Interra: Curse of The Night Queen!*

An invitation token for the gameworld came attached to the auto-reply.

Her crying slowed to a shuttering sniffle. An emerging sense of relief lifted her heart back out of her stomach.

Rho's mind might be broken, but at least she's still alive.

And keeping busy running a new Interra spinoff, apparently?

Good for her!

One huge unanswered question loomed: had the plan worked?

Zeta's sacrifice, the Telson tribe's Greek progression, Rho's descent into madness — it couldn't all be for nothing. She ran an aggregator routine on the top news items during her hiatus from the land of the living.

The results were unmistakable: it *worked!*

"Sweet!" she shouted to herself. "Thank you, Lex!"

The Specters abducted Zeta and the spellsong device worked as advertised. Even Jamji's containment matrix had worked, until every Specter in the system flooded the battlefield. The containment matrix was cool, but its usefulness was moot now that the Specters were history. They had been lured in, smooshed into a big ball of black death, then plunged into Varuna. No attacks or abductions had been recorded since.

Mission accomplished! Now, all that remained was for the miniature dynamo, Pip-Tau-Upsilon Telson, to pick up the pieces.

The eternal optimist in her refused to believe that Zeta was lost. If Pip-Rho had proven one thing, it was that an abductee with her nanite suite could survive digestion. The Specter-orgy caused by the spellsong was an unknown factor. The orb in Zeta's tum-tum was another. All they needed to do was retrieve the orb, assuming Zeta self-destructed her brain.

Wait... did Zeta have an annually pinging beacon transponder implanted in her brain, like Pip-Rho did? Of course she would! It'd be fifteen months before it pinged, though. If she knew Zeta, the girl would rather power through the pain than self-destruct. Yeah — the beacon was the ticket to saving Zeta.

In the meantime, let's get Rho's head on straight.

Why did things go so wrong with Pip-Rho? Why hadn't the Astri known that the spellsong devices would affect her like that? They must've known!

That was it — she had a bone to pick with a certain hive mind.

Pɪᴘ-Tᴀᴜ sᴇɴᴛ an urgent conversation request to XT-Prime. *Astri resurrect faster than Genesisians, so he has probably been alive for a month.*

Conversation request accepted. Proposed venue: Astrus Hive Chamber Construct.

"Oh, you want home field advantage? *Fine.*"

Pip-Tau accepted. WorMS warned her that she was transitioning to an unmanaged offworld construct. *That's Cain's way of reminding you he can't protect your mind from any assault the offworlders want to put it through.*

Whatever, she can take it.

Her slate-space twisted, expanded, then resolved to a spherical, cavernous chamber. She stood on an elevated platform in the center of the sphere. The walls were a tortoiseshell pattern — a speckled arrangement of natural human skin tones. These were the 100,000 avatar faces of the Astrus Genesis Hive's disembodied brains, plugged into their station on Jacob's Ladder. Their complexions ranged from albino to the richest brown. They were hairless, gender-less, and wore uniformly placid expressions.

Creepy as hell.

It'd been twenty-seven years since her last visit to the hive. Back then, it had been her and Rho, pitching their Spiritus Elevatum gameworld idea.

Man, it would be nice to have Rho here.

"Welcome back, Pip-Tau," the faces chorused.

Pip-Tau got goosebumps. Not the good kind.

"Where's XT-Prime? I'm sorry, but this is too weird. I need a single pair of eyes to look at."

"Here," came a single voice from directly in front of her. Finding the face was easy, since all the other faces had turned in unison towards XT-Prime. He was the dot in the middle of a radial pattern of eyes and noses.

Pip-Tau rallied her anger, furrowed her brow, and set her jaw. Her tone was a growl. "Pip-Rho, my sis-kin, my clone, my soulmate, is *fucking ruined*. And it's *your* fault." She jabbed a finger at XT-Prime, then swept it around to take in the whole chamber. Her eyes clouded. Let the tears fall.

"You knew there would be side-effects. You had to! You wouldn't even tell anyone what your damn 'spellsong' device actually did. Well, it triggered something inside her Specter cells that made them go haywire and the Specter *won*, XT-Prime. She's your sis-kin, too! Don't you care?

"You've held her prisoner in that *god-damned egg* for ninety-three years! We've only put up with it this long because we could keep ourselves busy with stories and gameworlds. Her brain was working great, so we were happy enough. But now she's trapped in that super-charged brain, and it's *broken*.

"I demand an explanation! Why didn't you just terminate her before activating the spellsong? No, don't answer — I know why! Because it was another *damned* experiment! You're all just evil scientist ass-faces! You whisper to each other in your echo-chamber and convince yourselves that whatever you do is right, but this time you've gone too far!"

She wiped her face, took a breath, and continued in a softer tone. "It's too late to repair her neural map. I know catastrophic cognitive dissociative collapse when I see it, and there's no stringing those neurons back together without reproducing the faulty wiring or making it worse. I'm not giving up on her yet, but let's be realistic — she's as good as dead." She dropped to a whisper. "You may have killed Pip-Rho, Xavier. I can never forgive you for that." She shook her head, fixing her tear-blurred glare on XT-Prime. "You're dead to me. You're out of the family. Stop calling yourself a Telson."

Pip-Tau watched as XT-Prime's lip trembled. Tears wound their way down his cheeks. Astri control their emotional reactions pretty well, always tweaking their hormones to keep an even temper. This was as close to tearing at his garments and howling with sorrow as an Astrus gets.

XT-Prime closed his eyes as a small subset of the other faces spoke. "You are right to be upset. It is true that we suspected the spellsong could affect Pip-Rho. The extent and speed of the effect, however, was not within reasonable expectations.

"The distance from the devices and radio-wave-blocking properties of her containment vessel should have been sufficient protection. Unfortunately, Ensign Jamji Telson of the Guard Faction secretly regurgitated her spellsong device and transferred it to the possession of her Guardian team. Her team placed the device into a drone equipped with advanced cloaking technology. We couldn't see it.

"The drone carrying Jamji's spellsong device was about a meter from Pip-Rho when we issued the spellsong activation command. The Guardians appeared to be performing an experiment of their own on Pip-Rho. We had not expected a transmitter to be so close and were slow to react. By the time we cut Pip-Rho's data cable, it was too late. Her compromised neural patterns were already written to her aposynchronic orb. Her CCDC took hold in a matter of seconds. Performing a Greek progression was ruled out as inadvisable, so we reconnected her data cable with hopes that our neurologists could reverse her CCDC. We've made negligible progress so far. We're truly sorry, Pip-Tau."

Pip-Tau was floored. She made a mental note to tear Jamji's head off the next time they crossed paths.

T{\scriptsize HE} {\scriptsize FACES} who had been speaking fell silent. A different set of faces said, "To be candid, we were skeptical about whether the device would even work at all. It was experimental, and the mechanism by which it interacts with Specter node-nets is not understood."

"Bull," Pip-Tau scoffed. "How'd you develop it, then?"

"Exploratory AI, simulating combinations of radio frequencies, particle collisions, chemical applications, nanites, forces, and fields. Combinations producing interesting effects found their way to lab trials using Rho samples. The devices activated at Varuna were the first and only fully fledged field trial."

Other faces chimed in, "Which could not have happened without your gameworld, Pip-Tau! It served as a neutral collaborative space for the Astri, Guardians, and Proliferans to demonstrate metaphoric representations of their technologies. Many believe it also tapped into the mind of Lex, as designed. Though most of us are still skeptical of the Prisoner Lex hypothesis, there's no doubt you and Pip-Rho played crucial roles in ridding the system of the Specter menace. You have our eternal gratitude."

They were sure laying it on thick.

Something about the way they described their development of the spellsong smelled funny. She remembered someone in The Council of Ten mentioning Astrus exploratory AI when they were arguing over Interra's idle SI cycle allotment. She crossed her arms and played a hunch. "So, you developed the spellsong on your own servers?"

"Oh, certainly not! Our station's server cluster, powerful as it may be, is insufficient for such a task. The Council of Ten generously allotted a portion of Cain's idle SI cycles for us to perform the—"

"Wait! You got the spellsong from Cain?!"

The Astri cleared their throats before continuing. "Yes, as we were saying, we utilized our allotment of Cain's idle SI cycles to—"

"Oh, this is too good!" Pip-Tau squealed. She burst into side-splitting laughter. Tears of joy replaced tears of sorrow.

The Hive didn't get it. Faces looked at each other, raising eyebrows, furrowing brows, or wearing perturbed expressions.

Pip-Tau laughed, "Puppets! You're freaking *puppets!* Throwing a bunch of random crap at Cain's servers gave you the magic pill to conquer the Specters? Do you realize how utterly ridiculous that sounds? I'll tell you how you came up with the spellsong: Lex! He handed it to you on a silver platter! You asynthiests got Lex'd and you don't even know it!"

Murmurs and scoffs echoed throughout the chamber.

"Alright, fine. I don't care if you believe it. God, it's just too good. Hell, he prolly gave the Guardians the plans for their containment net!" She shook with aftershock-chuckles, then regained her composure.

"So, here's the deal — I'm going to put Humpty Dumpty back together again. I'm Pip, she's Pip, we can do it. What I need from you is access to her slate-space through a medical emergency warrant, and your promise that once she's in a stable state, you'll fry the egg and resurrect her as a human. I think the saviors of the system deserve at least that much charity."

"It's a deal," the faces said. "Now, we have a small request to make of you."

"Oh really? What's that?"

XT-Prime's solitary voice said, "That you let me back into the family, and into your heart." He was openly weeping now. "I'm sorry about what happened to Pip-Rho, Pip-Tau. I didn't know. You have to believe me."

"Fine," Pip-Tau said, rolling her eyes. She wiped a tear. "I don't have the authority to kick you out, anyway. That'd be an O-pa and Gen-ma decision. And Jamji's the one I'm gunning for now."

"Jamji and I have had a strained relationship ever since she aligned her philosophies with the Guard," XT-Prime said. "Her deceit with the spellsong device and her refusal to self-destruct for Zeta's sake have driven me further from her. On the subject of Zeta, I am feeling the deepest sorrow. A funeral is in order."

"Funeral?" Pip-Tau scoffed, "Nah, she's alive! Meet me at Varuna on the anniversary of her abduction. We'll recover her together! That's about when her beacon should ping."

XT-Prime's face gave a sad, humoring sort of smile.

He knew better. She should've, too.

Darkness flooded in, swallowing the hive chamber.

Pip-Tau had stopped the replay, practically recoiling from it. Her Upsilon resurrection and visit to the Astrus Hive Construct had been four years ago — four soul-crushing years filled with fruitless efforts to save Pip-Rho and Zeta. Now that she was thoroughly disgusted with her past self's naive optimism, it was time to return to the real world. She reconnected to her body and opened her eyes.

PIP-TAU WAS IN A SPACESUIT, orbiting Varuna. Unblinking stars surrounded her. The ice moon loomed below. She looked down at the dark blue spot on its surface — the Specter impact caldera. Some Interraphile fangirl had successfully petitioned the Surya System Planetary Society to name it "Ag'nul's Heart".

It did look a *bit* like a heart if you squinted and crossed your eyes. Not a Valentine's Day card heart, but the flesh-and-blood kind. Craggy ridges in the caldera branched like white veins and its oblong shape was vaguely heart-like.

When the Specter horde smashed into Varuna and dug down to its liquid core, water had erupted from the impact site. This made an impressive ice volcano, which collapsed to form a caldera by the end of the year.

Alasie's drop pod was parked in the lowest crevice of Ag'nul's Heart. This was the thinnest part of the moon's ice crust, and the least stable. Landing in the crevice defied the advice of *everyone* who knew *anything* about planetary science, geology, or ice fishing. Pip-Tau was certain it would cost Alasie a Greek progression someday.

But hey, this was the tradition. Lots of traditions were forming around Zeta Day. That's if you can call something done for three years in a row a tradition.

The first year, before Veer declared Zeta Day an official holiday and day of remembrance, the beacon vigil had been serious business. Every ship, drone, and plasma-jet-boot-wearing dope in the system was either buzzing around Varuna or camped out on the surface somewhere. If Zeta had implanted a beacon in her brain, they'd have been able to triangulate its position down to the centimeter. Either she didn't implant a beacon, or it got destroyed.

The second year, many of the same people made the trip out for a ceremonial beacon vigil. The third year, there hadn't been as big of a turnout at Varuna, but a sizable crowd of well-wishers had gathered in The Thin Forest to pay their respects at the Telson cabin. This year followed the same pattern, with the crowd at the cabin growing and the Varuna crowd shrinking.

A new tradition started this year, with a program of Council-sponsored Zeta Day content being shared over the Worldnet. The program had ranged from heartfelt speeches to social commentary to scientific speculation on The Fall of the Specters. That's all it ever was — speculation. Nobody would ever know if Zeta's orb sacrifice was an essential ingredient in The Fall, or an unfortunate side note.

A highlight of this year's events was the poetry reading — Eld Angelica Blood had recited Alasie's award-winning sonnet, dedicated to Zeta. It made Pip-Tau cry like a babe.

Alasie's Zeta Day tradition was to spend a week on Varuna's surface, trying to contact Zeta. She'd send low-intensity, low-frequency, focused radio bursts at the moon, just below the legal maximum. She'd use thumpers to send vibrations through the ice. And, most promisingly, she'd deploy a few submersible drones.

The drones used plasma torches to melt through the ice crust, plunging into the vast abyss. Alasie would pilot them around under-water for a day or two before inevitably losing contact. She was convinced that the probes were being smashed by Specters. A more likely cause was that she sucked at drone piloting.

It was intriguing to think that the Specters could still be there, lurking deep within the waters of Varuna. What would they be up to? Consuming and reproducing, destroying and recreating themselves in a years-long death orgy?

Pip-Tau had her own fun little Zeta Day tradition: wallowing in a pit of self-loathing and despair! She'd spend the rest of the week circling Varuna, experiencing replays while she waited for Alasie to finish her experiments. After that, they'd take the transport pod back together.

Next on Pip-Tau's self-flagellation agenda was a choice set of replays from Interra — times when she should've noticed that Zeta had her soulstone. She'd follow that up with her Tau death at Varuna and her foolhardy declaration that she'd find Zeta just like Pip-Sigma had found Pip-Rho.

It was important for her to be reminded that things don't always work out for the best. The replays were her reality check — her cup of humility. When the week was over, she'd return to Syn-Cen and plunge back into "Interra: Curse of The Night Queen".

Zeta may have been lost, but there was still hope for Pip-Rho.

These days, Pip-Rho wouldn't respond to any names other than The Night Queen or The Wraith Queen. Whether she was Night or Wraith depended on the phase of Varuna. During full Varuna, she was The Wraith Queen. During new Varuna, she was The Night Queen. During waxing and waning Varuna, she'd use either name interchangeably. Interesting, right? Someone should research that correlation.

For better or worse, Pip-Rho had settled into a new homeostasis. The Astri claim that the only bit of flesh left of Rho was a scrap of her lower brain, encased by a shell of neurites. Every other bit of her was pure Specter. Those sick Astrus bastards considered this to be a new breakthrough in Specter research. Freaking ghouls.

The prevailing hypothesis was that a Specter's "brain" was a dynamically addressable node-net which continuously shifted location within its aqueous form. Somehow, they could distribute processing on-the-fly to any set of cells. In theory, their entire form could operate as one big brain.

As if to prove the point, Pip-Rho was functioning at such ludicrous levels of cognitive capacity that she was running her Interra spinoff gameworld entirely using local processing.

Yeah, Pip-Rho was a game server now.

That sounds cool until you try to talk to her out of character. That's when she really flips out. Talking in real-world terms will get you banned from her Specter-server. These days, rather than using Interra's metaphors to receive obfuscated messages from Prisoner Lex, Pip-Tau and the other few remaining players used it as a metaphor to glimpse into the mind of Prisoner Pip-Rho.

She was still in there, somewhere. She was still telling stories — it's what Pips *do*. Sometimes it's all Pips *are*.

Taking a break from Pip-Rho's gameworld was nice, but the more Pip-Tau thought about it, the more she wanted to get back. Maybe Alasie would cut her visit to Ag'nul's Heart short this year.

Pip-Tau reached out to Alasie.

Conversation request declined.

She sighed and looked out at the stars, then closed her eyes and reconnected to slate-space. Time to get back to her lamentations.

27

POETRY

No word nor warmth nor touch can reach my love,
Nor tempt this seeker of her sunken soul
To flowered fields with Surya high above,
Nor light ablaze this heart of frozen coal

Which aches for her beneath this beastly breast,
And speaks in beats when fumbled words betray
The foolishness of rage at fate's behest
That net and song and stone should win the day.

And never mind the people left behind,
Or shattered perfume vials in the ground
Within her hungry grave — no, never mind!
For love is pain and silence is a sound.

So here I prove love's pain with pleading cries,
And listen to her sweet, silent replies.

Tears stung Alasie's eyes. She lifted a hand to wipe them, thumping her glove against the glass of her helmet.

She shook her head and huff-laughed at herself, "What a dope."

A bio-override could make her stop crying, but double-mind stuff didn't always work the way she wanted. She thought the words, *"Shut off my tears."*

Either it worked or she had regained her composure. She blinked hard, squeezing the last tears out of her eyes.

"So, uh, that was a poem I wrote for you — a sonnet. I call it *Rage at Fate's Behest*. I hope you liked it!"

Alasie twisted the volume knob on the multi-function transmitter, receiver, and G-wave detector all the way to the right. The ensuing blast of noise made her jump. She turned it down. She wanted it loud, but not ear-splitting. The receiver was tuned to the frequency associated with Specter communication. The G-wave detector was configured to detect the tiny, jagged gravitational wave ripples in spacetime created by Specter movement.

If there were still Specters in Varuna, she'd be the first to know.

Alasie sat on a slick ledge of deep blue ice and watched the wiggling lines on the front of the red box perched on her lap. She listened intently to the warbling whine and static hiss. Sometimes she swore she heard patterns in the noise — whispers, cries of pain, breathing. Oraxis warned her that people can find patterns in anything, so she should be skeptical of herself. If she heard something that she thought was a real pattern, she'd send it to Oraxis for his opinion. This happened at least ten times a day last year. He never lost patience with her, but he also never heard the things she did. She'd be more skeptical this year.

Incoming conversation request from Pip-Tau Telson.

The WorMS announcement startled her. She let out a frustrated growl as she declined it. Pip-Tau would try to rush her so they could head back. There'd be time for Pip-Rho later. This was her Zeta time.

AFTER A FEW MINUTES of listening and fiddling with knobs she didn't understand, Alasie turned the volume down most of the way so she could start talking to Zeta again. It's hard to talk if you can barely hear your own voice. XT-Prime had equipped the device with a transmitter that worked like the spellsong devices, but instead of sending a special set of encoded instructions, it sent her speech.

She said, "I've been studying poetry a lot. *Rage at Fate's Behest* uses iambic pentameter. *Iambic* means it has a sort of 'buh-DUM, buh-DUM' pattern that the syllables follow. It's like a beating heart. I think iambs are popular because they're... familiar. Babies can hear their mother's heartbeat from inside the womb. It's a sound that means life. If our hearts went 'swoosh-glug-POP' or something, we wouldn't like iambs so much!"

She huffed-laughed at herself, then continued, "Pentameter just means five meters. A *meter* is a *foot*... um, an iamb, in this case — a pair of buh-DUM syllables. *Penta* is the Greek word for five. I used to think *epsilon* was Greek for five, so learning about *penta* was confusing. *Zeta* also doesn't really mean six — it's just the sixth Greek letter, but for some reason we use their letters like numbers when we're putting things in order. *Hexa* is the Greek word for six. Did you know that?"

Alasie realized she was rambling, but she didn't care. Zeta needed to hear her voice.

She put down the box and stood. Taking a walk would be nice. She took small, bounding steps, not accustomed to the low gravity yet.

She said, "So, with iambic pentameter, there's ten syllables in a line. Sometimes I'll write a line and it'll have eight syllables and I'll get upset because I can't fit in another iamb. Poetry can be hard sometimes, but if you just keep at it and practice, it comes easier.

"Anyway, *Rage at Fate's Behest* is a Shakespearean Sonnet. That means it has four stanzas — three quatrains and a couplet, and the turn's in the third stanza. The *turn* is kind of like a twist at the end of a story. In mine, it's that shift into a sort of bitterly accepting attitude. The quatrains follow an A-B-A-B rhyming scheme, and both lines of the final couplet rhyme.

"But poems don't always have to rhyme. Like haiku — I'm just starting to learn about that, so I can't explain how it works other than that it has three lines that follow a five-seven-five syllable pattern. Free verse doesn't have to rhyme, either — it doesn't have to follow any rules at all! I've written a bunch of those since they're so easy. I just sort of write down things as they come to mind. But I don't think they're as good as my sonnets.

"So, ok, this is something I'm proud of — I submitted *Rage at Fate's Behest* to Eld Angelica Blood's Zeta Day poetry contest and I won! I think I only won since I'm your... your friend or whatever we are. But people said it was good, so maybe it is. She recited it on the memorial celebration broadcast and... *wow*, she was good! Like, *so* much better than me at reciting. I'll figure out how to play a recording of that for you later.

"After the broadcast, Eld Blood hosted a thing where people could ask me questions. Someone asked why I took up poetry. I said because I'm not good at talking, especially when it's about feelings. When I have time to sit and work with the words on paper, it helps. With poetry, you can just sort of... say what images come to mind, or write down a feeling. It's not so literal, so it's better for me. I can describe things, um... instinctively, you know? Genevieve helps me sometimes, to make the rhythm better or to give me suggestions. She came up with the 'beastly breast' alliteration. I love that line — you know, because of Ag'nul.

"We're all beasts, sort of. Humans are just... monkeys in clothes. I don't mean that as insulting or shameful. Being an animal doesn't make us bad. We're doing the best we can with what we have. We just need to remember, humans are just... just human. And that's okay."

Alasie stopped her bounding exploration of the craggy crevice.

She got on her hands and knees to look into the ice, as if she could spot Zeta through it. Tears were pooling in her eyes again. She didn't know why her bio-overrides never lasted more than a few minutes.

Let the tears fall.

"Zeta, you're still a human, too. Even if you ended up like Pip-Rho, it doesn't matter. Whatever form your body or mind is in, *you are still a human.* And I love you."

She ran her gloved hand over the ice as a tiny puddle of tears formed in her helmet. There was a faint vibration coming from the ground. She knew better than to get excited about it. This happened a lot — ice quakes, she'd call them. She was told that without an atmosphere, Varuna heated during the months-long days, and cooled during the long night. It also had a warm, rocky core and thick water mantle that flowed in complicated ways. This made its icy surface move a lot. Ice sheets cracked and rubbed against each other. Ice mountains rose and toppled over the course of years.

The vibration was intensifying. Should she worry about that?

She was paying so much attention to the ice quake that she didn't notice at first that there was a new sound coming from the receiver — sharp and crackling. It could have been any number of things, but what it reminded Alasie of most was the sound she was told it would make when a Specter was on the move nearby — G-wave ripple spikes.

That was it! It had to be — a Specter was coming up through the ice!

Alasie got to her feet and looked around. Chunks of ice were breaking off the walls of the crevice. Another new sound cut through the crackling and static from the receiver — three quick bursts.

It sounded like... coughing? Maybe barking? It was hard to tell with the volume turned down. She bounded back towards her camp. She needed to turn the receiver up!

Alasie had wandered a good distance, so it would take a long time to get back. As she bounded, the sound came again, clearer this time.

It was *definitely* a dog barking. Could it be a transmission from Genesis? Someone breaking the rule against sending radio transmissions? Someone who thought their dog's bark needed to be shared with the universe?

The floor of the crevice was shifting. Cracks formed down its length.

She needed to get out! But not without the multi-function device.

The drop pod — a chubby cylinder with a smoothly tapered top, was covered in chromatites. In space they were used for active invisibility, but on the surface she set them to a bright red so she could spot the pod from far away. As Alasie made her awkward bouncy run towards her camp, the pod's surface started blinking rapidly between red and yellow.

That seemed bad.

It tipped over as the surface beneath it split.

She reached the multi-function device. First she twisted up the volume knob, then she lifted the box by its handles.

The ground under her feet was trembling. A jet of water spewed from a crack nearby.

"Bark! Bark, bark!" came the noises from her headset. The crackling of the G-wave detector sounded like leaves being crumbled in her ear. "Bark, bark!"

She didn't have time to think. Were dogs chasing her?!

Alasie jumped straight up and activated her plasma-jet boots, gripping the device's handles tightly. As she ascended, she watched the destruction unfolding below with wide, unbelieving eyes. "Do you have dogs, Zeta?! Did you send them after me?"

She wanted to laugh! To cry!

The blinking drop pod rolled into a deep crack, then disappeared behind another jet of water.

A distant voice cut through the static. It sounded like a child — definitely not Zeta. Between the barking and the crackling, she made out the words, "Pooches! You bad pooches come back, right now!"

"Hello?!" Alasie shouted. "Who's that talking?! Is Zeta with you?!"

No reply.

She listened as she watched the chaos below. A shadow formed in the ice near her submersible drones. She didn't have a clear view, and she was getting higher by the second, but between the water spouts and crumbling ice Alasie saw a black tendril reaching out of a crack in the surface. The tendril wrapped around a drone, then retreated, snatching its prize away.

She shouted, "The Specters live! I saw you! Did you want that drone? I can get you another one! Zeta, are you there?! Zeta?!"

The barking had stopped. The crackling continued, but it was fading. Alasie listened intently for the slightest sound. She was high enough now that she wouldn't get hit by a geyser, so she reduced her plasma-jet thrust to maintain her current altitude. If she got too far away, the receiver wouldn't work.

A minute passed. The crevice below was still shifting. The walls collapsed inward, turning her camp into a ragged scar in the ice. Surveying the nearby landscape, other areas of Ag'nul's Heart were shifting. Water spouts burst here and there.

Alasie sent another transmission, "Zeta, are you there? It's Alasie!"

Another minute went by. The sound from the receiver was back to normal background noise — hissing and whining.

"Incoming conversation request for Zeta Telson," she tried. "Hail, Zeta of the Scorpion Tail Tribe!"

Nothing.

After at least half an hour of calling out, Alasie took a break. She had descended back to Varuna's surface, which was still vibrating. Maybe she should find another spot to camp in the caldera, since this one was so unstable.

She still couldn't believe it — she had made contact! It was nothing like she expected, and she had no idea what the dogs or the kid were all about. Nobody had ever received messages like those from Specters. Alasie felt certain that it meant Zeta was alive. She'd *changed* the Specters, somehow. There was plenty of time to wonder about that later.

Giddy with excitement, Alasie prepared a message for Oraxis. Let's see him call *that* patterns in the noise!

She paused as she realized that this was the happiest she'd felt in... well, as long as she could remember. When was the last time she *actually* felt happy? Probably when Zeta held her hand in Jacob's Ladder station.

The view from the station had been breathtaking, and they had shared it in silence. The end had been within reach — they were about to defeat the Specters together. Zeta's mission would be over and they'd get to kiss again. That was a bittersweet memory. More bitter than sweet, until today. Now Alasie knew their reunion would come. Just not as soon as they planned.

She'd wait for Zeta for a lifetime.

Yes, that's the new plan — stay on Varuna for as long as possible. Pip-Tau could just go back without her if she didn't want to wait. Sure, the drop pod and experimental equipment were all gone, but she had everything she needed: a transmitter to talk to Zeta, a receiver to listen for responses, a ZETA reactor to power her placental mat, a spacesuit to stay alive, and plasma-jet boots to get back to Genesis if her reactor runs low on fuel before she makes contact again.

But most importantly, Alasie was stocked with an endless supply of poetry.

ACKNOWLEDGMENTS

First and foremost, I want to thank you, faithful reader, for picking up the second book of the Zeta Trilogy. You get bonus points if you rate or review my books on your platform of choice. Reviews sell books — help a guy out! Make sure to visit grafrath.net and sign up for my email list so you don't miss out on the third book.

Next, I thank my wife, Gabrielle — the Genevieve to my Oraxis. Every writer needs an ideal reader, and she's mine. She created the cover art for Neoprim and Interran, and she did a marvelous job on both.

And then there's Zoë — the inspiration behind Zeta and the melodious voice behind the audiobook. Arigato, Zoë.

Give my beta readers a hand, folks. These poor souls humor me by filling out surveys to give me feedback on the not-quite-final draft of my novels. Marlas Williams and Jessica Walker get special mentions in this category.

Let us not forget to honor the muses — those ethereal whispers in the ears of artists everywhere, setting their imaginations wandering. In my case, it's Ourania who pulls my eyes up to the stars and fills my head with wonder. May she never abandon me.